SAM COLT MADE 'EM EQUAL

"Hey, Hoss," Boo said, "I think we got company."

I turned my head and looked across the cemetery grounds. There were four—no, five—of them, fanning out as they crept among the crypts, using tombstones and monuments for cover.

A couple of years ago I was as normal as the next guy. That was before an untidy blood tran⸺ion with the Lord of the Undead netted me ⸺f that recombinant virus that change⸺ ⸺to night-sippers. And while it's t⸺ ⸺d faster than the vast maj⸺ ⸺o match for anyone wh⸺ ⸺to the other side of the ⸺e, I'd last about thirty seconds ⸺ed vampire if everything else was equ⸺

And if I couldn't out⸺ ⸺ch less outfight one vampire, what were my chances with five of them?

I reached up inside my shirt and unsnapped the leather restraining strap over the trigger. There's an old saying that "God made all men but Sam Colt made 'em equal." Well, even superhuman reflexes and a Glock-20 with silver fragmentation loads didn't make me the equal of five fanged assassins.

"How many is this, now?" Boo asked.

"Third attempt this year," I said, "and we're barely through January."

**Baen Books
by
Wm. Mark Simmons**

*One Foot in the Grave
Dead on My Feet
Habeas Corpses
Dead Easy* (forthcoming)

HABEAS CORPSES

Wm. Mark Simmons

HABEAS CORPSES

This is a work of fiction. All the characters and events portrayed in this book are fictional, and any resemblance to real people or incidents is purely coincidental.

A Baen Book

Baen Publishing Enterprises
P.O. Box 1403
Riverdale, NY 10471
www.baen.com

ISBN 10: 1-4165-2125-9
ISBN 13: 978-1-4165-2125-9

Cover art by Clyde Caldwell

First Baen paperback printing, May 2007

Distributed by Simon & Schuster
1230 Avenue of the Americas
New York, NY 10020

Library of Congress Cataloging-in-Publication Data: 2005022404

Printed in the United States of America

10 9 8 7 6 5 4 3 2 1

Special thanks this time around to The Wrecking Crew:
    Lee (Helen Wheels) Matindale
    Brad & Sue (Tag Team) Sinor
    Dennis (The Menace) Smirl (who was also
        instumental in recovering portions of my
        earlier drafts when my laptop went Chernobyl)

Golden Plume with Clusters to:
    Lynn (Mama Yard Dog) Stranathan
    Rhonda (Help, Help Me Rhonda) Eudaly
        for editorial service above and beyond . . .

Finally special thanks to:
    Marla (The Dog Ate Your Homework?) Ainspan
    And the Rest of the Folks at Baen
        for their patience on my long recovery
        on the medical and technological fronts.

We die with the dying:
See, they depart, and we go with them.
We are born with the dead:
See, they return, and bring us with them.

—T.S. Eliot
The Four Quartets

It's alive! Alive!

—Colin Clive as Dr. Henry Frankenstein,
Frankenstein

She's alive! Alive!

—Colin Clive as Dr. Henry Frankenstein,
Bride of Frankenstein

Who's going to believe a talking head?
Get a job in a sideshow!

—Jeffrey Combs as Herbert West,
Reanimator

This is a work of fiction.
As always, any resemblance to people living,
dead, undead, or some stage in—between,
is purely coincidental.

Chapter One

AT FIRST GLANCE Deirdre looked human.

Of course, Deirdre always got more than just a glance—even back when she was human.

Once upon a time she had been a stunning beauty with pale skin, blue eyes, and auburn hair. That was before she died last year.

In death she was transformed by the twinned viruses the undead carry in their blood and saliva. As a vampire she had gone from "stunning" to "unearthly" on the beauty meter. Her auburn hair turned the color of arterial blood; her sapphire eyes replaced by haunted rubies and her skin a whiter shade of pale and as luminous as the moon.

The fangs, of course, went without saying.

But she had undergone another extreme makeover in drinking my mutated blood a few months ago. Now her sharp, pointy teeth were all but gone. More obviously, her skin was approaching the mocha and cream shade that came from a daily regimen of sunbathing—something you rarely see in a redhead and never in a vampire. Which was the point, I suppose, as Deirdre was no longer technically undead.

My unique hemoglobin didn't make her human, again you understand. The crimson eyes were an obvious clue that she was no longer the girl next door. That and the fact that she could still bench-press a small truck. But while I couldn't give her back everything that she had lost in her original transformation, she seemed content: being "*un-undead*" suited her just fine.

If only Deirdre's situation suited Lupé, as well.

My significant other understood, of course, that I needed a security chief and bodyguard who was conversant with the unique nature of my enemies, could stop a bullet without flinching, and could—well—bench-press a small truck. She also understood the unique obligations involved as (technically speaking) I was the one who had brought Deirdre "over" and (literally speaking) I was the one who had brought her "back." Lupé knew something about blood-bonds and curses and debts-that-do-not-die even when we do the mortal coil shuffle.

Still, Deirdre was major eye candy. Worse, she had made it clear that, when it came to swapping body fluids, we needn't limit ourselves (as we had on the two previous occasions) to blood alone.

It required frequent reminders to all and sundry that my heart belonged to Lupé.

Deirdre, it seemed, had someone else's heart right now.

She was holding it in the palm of her hand.

And it was convulsing as if it were still alive.

"Where did you get that?" I asked, sensing light gathering at the dark edges of my vision.

She held the squirming cardiac muscle toward me, oily red fluids drooling between her fingers and sheeting down her arm. "Don't you recognize it?" She smiled demurely. "It's yours."

I looked down at the gaping dark hole in my chest . . .

And awoke in a tangle of sweat-soaked sheets.

The upside to having daymares on a regular basis is that you stop going through that whole disorientation phase and learn to wake up real quick. The downside was that they were lasting well past sunset and I still woke up feeling exhausted.

I groaned out of bed, hoping I hadn't murmured Deirdre's name while Lupé was in earshot. Even when she's in human form, Lupé doesn't have to be *in* the room to be within earshot.

In the bathroom I found a note taped to the medicine cabinet mirror.

Gone for groceries and DVDs.
Movie night tonight . . .
                    L~

I reached through the shower curtains and wrenched the cold water handle. Tonight was the Big Night: I had a lot to do and I couldn't waste time trying to put a Freudian spin on today's bad dream.

Even if there was a good chance I *would* get my heart ripped out before the sun came back up.

☙ ☙ ☙

T.S. Eliot's "Little Gidding" begins with: "Midwinter spring is its own season / Sempiternal though sodden towards sundown, / Suspended in time, between pole and tropic . . ."

The dead of winter in Louisiana is something like that: short sleeves one day, a sweater the next. Tonight, the weather hadn't made up its mind. I buckled my shoulder holster over a sleeveless tee and shrugged into a flannel shirt but left it unbuttoned so I could reach the Glock-20 loaded with silver frag-ammo under my left armpit. Opening the screen door, I stepped down and walked barefoot through the January chrysalis of my new back yard. The brown, withered grass sighed beneath my feet, not quite dead, not quite alive.

Like me, in a sense.

Except that, come true spring—mid to late February— the lawn would burst forth with new life while I would be . . . well . . . what?

All flesh is grass but, where most folks end up succumbing to the Lawnmower of Life, some of us cheat the mulching process and come back as ghastly perennials. Considering the last eighteen months of my so-called half-life, there was probably a fertilizer analogy I could come up with . . . but I didn't want to go there.

I stepped on a mushroom and felt it dissolve between my toes. Forget the green stuff; a pale, nocturnal parasite was probably a better analogy for my condition. That's me: a real "fun guy."

Buh-dump-bum.

By now you'd think there would be a clear-cut diagnosis

of my actual condition. But, no: I was left with two start-ing presumptions.

One, that I actually died in the automobile accident that killed my family and was "reborn" in the hospital morgue . . .

Or, two, that I was only presumed dead while "Virus A" from Bassarab's blood put me in a healing trance. Lacking the combinant factors of "Virus B" that resided in the old vampire's saliva, the infection started converting my body into something new—neither fully human nor technically undead.

Add to either scenario the subsequent contaminants and blood-borne pathogens from my encounters with Kadeth Bey's tanis leaf extract and the demon-laced blood of Elizabeth Báthory—well, the "either/or" factor became rather hazy. And while the distinctions seemed important to some, I had to wonder: in the end did it really matter? My wife and daughter were still dead and the Las Vegas Demesne was booking odds on me attaining the same sta-tus within the month.

But this wasn't the night to think about depressing things like vampire vendettas and daymares concerning misplaced hearts, it was an evening made for romance! A sliver of moon hung over the graveyard like a leprous grow-light in Death's terrarium. The wind had freshened, bringing the odor of distant rain and nearby rot. I could see a storm was finally brewing and that meant tonight *had* to be "The Night."

If Lupé and J.D. ever got back from Blockbusters, that is.

I reached into my pocket, fished past my grandmother's

ring, and retrieved a small vial of Mentholatum. I rimmed my nostrils with ointment before continuing to the far end of my property.

One minute I was alone, the next I was outnumbered three to one.

You might think that the ability to see into the infrared spectrum would give me all sorts of advantages. But infravision is worth diddly-squat when the creatures coming at you have no body heat. The dead were a dozen yards away before I finally saw them.

Three corpses shambled toward me; their clumsy, unbalanced rhythms reminiscent of a trio of winos in fully soused search-mode for the nearest liquor store. The one in the middle looked freshly dead while his wingmen had been in the ground a great deal longer. They stumbled to a stop against the waist-high stone wall that separated the cemetery from my backyard.

Unfortunately this wasn't a dream: the stench of dust, dirt, mold, and chemically retarded decomposition continued its forward momentum, slamming past the menthol barrier and up into my nostrils like a slow-motion train wreck. I sneezed and set a brown paper bag on the ground.

"Yo, Cséjthe," the big one on the left said. It sounded more like he was sneezing, in turn. The proper pronunciation of my last name, "Chay-tay," requires a tad more articulation than most decomposing tongues and palettes can muster.

I stood about a foot back from the stonework on my side and tried to breathe shallowly. "Boo," I greeted, "Cam."

Boo grinned; Cam nodded. Boo was scary when he grinned. Cam was scarier because he couldn't. In "The Mending Wall" Robert Frost wrote that "good fences make good neighbors." I wonder if Bob knew how well that analogy extended to graveyards.

In point of fact, however, it wasn't the cemetery wall that kept the dead off my property. My real privacy fence was the line of consecrated salt along the base of the crumbling concrete partitions that bordered my property on three sides. Don't get me wrong. I get along pretty well with a lot of the deceased-but-not-quite-departed. But some of them just aren't real clear on the issue of boundaries. Hey, if they're out of the ground—major clue!

Until Mama Samm came and put a hoodoo barrier around my property I had endured a nightly parade of rotting corpses to my back door. Some wanted help in matters of unfinished business, others were just lonely. Still, there had to be some limits. Now I just replaced the salt every month or so. More often when it rained.

"This here's The Professor," Boo said, indicating the cadaver between them. Cam sort of nodded. A suicide, Cameron had propped a double-barreled shotgun under his jaw and tripped both triggers as his last living act. While the mortician's art has come a long way the funeral was still a closed casket affair. Cam isn't geared for post mortem small talk.

The Professor didn't look anything like Russell Johnson so I politely refrained from asking after Gilligan or Mary Ann. He did, however, look as if he was in a state of shock. It's really hard to tell with the freshly dead; they all have that look of mild surprise or severe disappointment.

"You're not real," he said.

I've been told that I have "issues" but that wasn't what he meant.

"Well, of course he ain't the real Baron Samedi," Boo said. "Don't matter, though. He's still our—whatchamacallem—buddy-man."

I sighed. "Ombudsman. Except I ain't. Aren't. I'm not," I corrected. It didn't matter that I wasn't the Vodoun Loa of the Dead: half of the corpses in the cemetery still believed it, the other half didn't care. There's something in my tainted blood that draws them to me like moths to the flame.

"Aww, he's just modest," Boo continued. Cam just nodded.

"He's not real," The Professor insisted. "You're not real!"

"Huh?" said Boo.

"I am asleep. This is a dream!"

"A dream?" I looked around. "Looks more like a night-mare to me."

"Hey!" said Boo.

A moldy green hand rose up and gripped the top of the crumbling wall. "And many of them that sleep in the dust of the earth shall awake," intoned a new voice. In life it might have been deep and resonant, in death it sounded wheezy and clotted, as if the speaker were missing a lung and had something stuck in his throat. Something like roots and leaves and cemetery earth. " . . . some to ever-lasting life, and some to shame and everlasting contempt. The prophet Daniel, chapter twelve, verse the second," the new corpse finished, dragging itself more or less erect to lean against the stone barrier.

"Well, hell, Preacher," Boo exclaimed in a wounded voice, "which ones are we?"

I think the new arrival was attempting an expression of contempt—something hard to pull off when you don't have the complete palette of skin and muscles to work with.

"He's got a point, Jerome," I said to the cadaver whose Pentecostal proclivities had earned him the nickname "Preacher." "Ole Boo, here, has never given evidence of having any shame whatsoever."

Cam wheezed as though he was laughing. The Professor squeezed his eyes shut and looked as if he was wishing himself back into his bed.

"Atheists," Jerome scolded.

"Now hold on there, Preacher," Boo puffed, "that ain't entirely true. By strict definition I'm an agnostic and Cameron, here, was Unitarian. I'm bettin' that The Professor is one of them secular humanists. Right, Doc?"

"Organized religion is nothing but codified mythology mixed with superstition," The Professor said, still careful to keep his eyes squinched shut.

"A rational mind," I observed, "dedicated to logic and the scientific precepts."

"Yes," he said, easing one eye open.

"Boy, are you in deep doo-doo!"

"How about you, boss?" Boo asked.

I considered the rows of aged and crumbling head-stones. "I don't know anymore."

"If you so-called agnostics would read the Bible—"

"'O that thou wouldst hide me in the grave,'" I interrupted, "'that thou wouldst keep me secret, until thy wrath be past, that thou wouldst appoint me a set time, and remember me.' The Book of Job, chapter fourteen, verse the thirteenth."

They all stared at me as if I had grown an extra head.

Reaching down, I pulled an old book out of the sack. "eBay's gotten pricier of late, Jerome, but I got you the Kübler-Ross." I handed it to born-again dead man.

"*Josephus?*" he queried, taking the old tome with trembling hands. "I know there's a copy in the West Monroe library."

"I'm not kyping library books for you, Jerome."

"I'll give it back when I'm done."

I shook my head. "You don't take care of them. It's not your fault, considering your present address, but I think it's best if we get you your own copies."

"What you need books for, Preacher?" Boo shifted his grasp on The Professor's arm as he tried to pull away. "Can't you just pray to God for your answers—you bein' so righteous and all?"

"Now, boys," I soothed, "we're all just doing the best we can to figure out how it all works."

"And some of us," Boo added, "are trying to figure out why we're not already in heaven instead of slumming with the sinners on the slag heap of the dead."

Jerome turned on his heel and stalked off in a huff. Well, actually, it was more of a shamble-off-in-a-huff kind of thing.

"Hey," the big corpse called after him, "have you tried hopping? Maybe y'all gotta jump-start that Rapture effect! Beam me up, Jesus!"

"That's not very nice," I said.

"Aw, he's always askin' for it." But he did look a little ashamed. "And what am I gonna do? Piss off God? Oooo, He might strike me dead! No, wait . . . He might banish my soul to wander the earth after I die! No wait . . ."

"Alright, you've made your point." I rummaged through the sack and pulled out a packet of oddly shaped dice. One die had eight sides, another ten, and yet another twenty. "Advanced Dungeons & Dragons game dice," I read off the package and handed it to Cam. "You play D & D?" It was a rhetorical question—in practical terms, anything you asked Cam was a rhetorical question.

"E & E," Boo answered for him.

"What?"

"Ectoplasm & Exorcists," he elaborated. "Plays with the Gorsky twins over in the northeast plots."

I just looked at him.

"You know . . . you're kibitzing at a séance and suddenly a fifteenth-level exorcist bursts into the room and begins reading from the *Roman Ritual*. What do you do?"

I shrugged. "Make a saving throw?" I reached into the sack and pulled out another book. "Here, Boo; Norman Mailer's *The Naked and the Dead*." As I handed it to him, he relaxed his grip on The Professor, who wrenched himself free and ran back into the mists of the cemetery.

"Oops. Guess we'd better go fetch our newbie before he finds a way off the grounds and really stirs up a ruckus!" As he turned to go, he ruffled the pages of his new present. "Hey, no pictures!"

"It's a war story, Bubba, not necrophilial porn."

He shrugged, took a step, and then stopped. "Hey, Hoss, I think we got company."

I turned my head and looked across the cemetery grounds. There were four—no, five—of them, fanning out as they crept among the crypts, using tombstones and monuments for cover. A couple of them were as cold as Boo and Cam but the others flickered like a banked fire— not warm enough to be alive but not cold enough to be completely dead.

Undead, to be more specific. Outtatown Revenants, come to do some wet-work at *la Casa de Cséjthe*.

No wonder I had bad dreams. A couple of years ago I was as normal as the next guy. That was before an untidy blood transfusion with the Lord of the Undead netted me one-half of that recombinant virus that changes day-trippers into night-sippers. And while it's true that I'm stronger and faster than the vast majority of humankind, I'm no match for anyone who's completely crossed over to the other side of the blood divide. One-on-one, I'd last about thirty seconds against a full-fledged vampire if everything else was equal. And if I couldn't outrun much less outfight one vampire, what were my chances with five of them?

I reached up inside my shirt and unsnapped the leather restraining strap over the trigger. There's an old saying that "God made all men but Sam Colt made 'em equal." Well, even superhuman reflexes and a Glock-20 with silver fragmentation loads didn't make me the equal of five fanged assassins. Still, I hadn't used my gun in self-defense yet and I was betting that I wouldn't be doing so tonight. I left the Glock in the holster for the moment.

It was a safe bet: the house odds were in my favor. The ground began to boil around the intruders' feet. Two of them lost their footing and fell to the ground. Correction: fell *into* the ground and disappeared without a trace. Another one fell to his knees. Three cadavers popped up around him, looking like ghastly manikins cut off at the waist. They grabbed the surprised vampire and dragged him down into the unsettled earth. The beginnings of a scream were cut off as dirt clods filled his fanged mouth.

That left two nosferatu on their feet. Dozens of arms were now thrust up out of the ground, moldy hands grasping undead ankles, shins, knees, thighs, a couple grabbing belts. One toppled and disappeared. The other gamely struggled on, ripping an arm loose from a corpse and using it to club at the others.

"How many is this, now?" Boo asked.

"Third attempt this year," I said, "and we're barely through January."

The reason I had survived three attacks was due, in no small measure, to our relocation to the new neighborhood. After our old house was badly damaged during last year's assault by demonically sponsored paramilitary forces, we found ourselves in the market for something with a little more seclusion and a lot more security. The property boundaries of my new domicile practically screamed the old Realtors' adage "Location, location, location!"

The front yard ended as a bluff overlooking the Ouachita River. Since most vampires won't willingly cross running water, the bad guys just figured it was easier to come at me across open ground on the other three sides. Well, "open ground" is a bit of a misnomer: an old cemetery borders my property line where the river doesn't.

And, so far, none of my bloodsucking assassins had made it past the necro-hood watch. Eventually the "people" sending them were going to get wise.

But not tonight. The last vampire disappeared beneath a dog pile of decomposing bodies and sank into the loamy earth.

"Five," Boo grunted. "They never sent this many before."

I leaned against the wall. "Kurt wants me to come back to New York. He thinks I could nip this in the bud by facing down the families there that want to challenge me for the throne."

"Throne? You people have a throne?"

"Figure of speech," I said. "I hope. And what do you mean 'you people'? I am not a vampire. Not fully, anyway. Not yet. And Lupé is a werewolf—you don't want to suggest otherwise while she's around. And Deirdre—well, we don't really know what Deirdre is anymore."

He grinned. "And you're not the voodoo Loa of the Dead."

I looked away. I hate it when they grin. "I've met Baron Samedi. He's still miffed that some of his subjects prefer my company to his."

"Guess we ain't the boyz in his hood. Ah, I see Cam's corralled our reluctant zombie."

I turned and saw The Professor being herded back toward us by Boo's faceless buddy. "What are you going to do with him?"

"Walk him around until first cock's crow. The first emergence is always traumatic for the newbies. And you can never tell who's gonna be hit the hardest—the religious types who expect to wake up in heaven or the atheists who don't expect to wake up at all."

He started toward the other two and I turned back toward the house with a troubled heart. The worst part of dealing with the living dead was not the smell or the gruesome reminders of one's own mortality.

It was the troubling question of why they were still here.

Back in the house I could hear the clanking of heavy weights down in the basement signifying Deirdre's presence. Lupé and J.D. were still unaccounted for.

That wasn't surprising as the trip into town takes a little longer from the new digs. For instance: the garage is on the other side of the river. First, you have to go down to the retaining wall at the edge of the front lawn, duck through the curtain of weeping willows, pass through the gate, go down about three-dozen stairs to the docks below, cast off and take the boat across the Ouachita River to a private landing on the opposite bank. Then you climb about three dozen more stairs to a private garage, disengage two alarm systems, neutralize Mama Samm's voodoo hexes, and drive one of the cars into town.

Lather, rinse, repeat for the return trip.

Yes, it's a hassle and deliveries *are* a bitch, but the whole crossing running water taboo for vampires combined with a graveyard serving as an anti-undead minefield had raised my life expectancy by another three to four months.

The house was a hundred-and-fifty-year-old, two-story manse with a columned front porch. A carriage house in the back had been converted into guest quarters by the previous occupant. That's where the security staff was housed and the boys were going to be in a lot of trouble if Deirdre or Lupé found out about the particulars of tonight's near incursion.

Of course, I would be in even more trouble if they learned that I had stepped outside unescorted so I wasn't about to tattle. Besides, I knew the hired help was extremely uncomfortable when it came to "The Neighbors"—I was still human enough to empathize a bit on that issue.

Kurt was right. I was going to have to go to New York and settle this somehow. The property boundaries had been very effective so far but eventually they were going to come at me in a different way. Perhaps skydiving nosferatu (nosferti? nosfertae?). If I was going to make any changes to the demesne system during my predictably brief tenure as Doman, I should probably start with their politics.

New York embraced the Klingon model of political advancement through assassination. Even if I hadn't been the primary target for lethal political ambitions, it would have vexed me. Powerful, ancient, bloodsucking creatures of the night should have a better means of governance than a science fiction trope.

Back in my study a fire crackled merrily in the small Victorian-style fireplace as I popped the magazine on the Glock and locked both in my desk drawer. I was getting better about not setting foot outside without being armed but I'd be damned if I was going to eat, sleep, and visit the john while carrying. If the day (or night) came that any hostile vampires actually made it as far as the house, they still had to be invited in. In that respect, at least, a man's home remained his castle.

I wandered around the room, considering the hundreds of shelved book spines that turned two of the four walls into colorful crazy quilts done in literary motif. I fingered a brand-new translation of *The Egyptian Book of the Dead* next to a cracked and crumbling edition of *The Peruvian Book of the Dead*. On the other side was a paperback copy of the Jerry Garcia book of *The Dead*.

I was still working the glitches out of my home-grown cataloging system.

The library was divided into two separate sections, the medical and the metaphysical. A 300-gallon marine aquarium served as a de facto divider, its cold-blooded inhabitants gliding back and forth, occasionally stopping to contemplate the incomprehensible world that unfolded just beyond their own saltwater existence. I stopped to sprinkle some freeze-dried brine shrimp over the bubbling surface and their questions were forgotten in a roiled feeding frenzy. The scorpion fish, a *Pterois volitans*, was circling the melee, venomous spines a-quiver, as if considering the feeders as potential feedees so I dropped a couple of prawns in to keep the mayhem down to an acceptable level.

The resultant chaos in the aquarium was reflective of my approach to sorting the half of my library dealing with the subjects of death and the hereafter. It remained a work in progress as I vacillated between catagorizing by author, religion, or general theory. Shelving genetics, viral science, and blood-borne pathogens is child's play by comparison.

The biggest problem is that most of everything believed or written about the afterlife or heaven or hell is based on hearsay or wishful thinking and very little in the way of eye-witness accounts. While there are those supposed "life after life" testimonials, who's to say it's not just a dream or hallucination—the by-product of a brain starved for oxygen during that abbreviated time-out called "clinical death"? I'd prefer to hear from somebody who took the extended tour, not just the poke-your-head-in-and-glance-around-then-hurry-back-home-to-the-ICU anecdote.

Returning to *Little Gidding*, Eliot wrote: " . . . the communication of the dead is tongued with fire beyond the language of the living." But in my experience, if the long-dead dream of heaven, they don't seem to remember anything if they come back. Ditto for vampires. In fact, just thinking about the whole concept seems to wig them out. They say there are no atheists in foxholes but reopened graves are an entirely different matter. The Bible doesn't record Lazarus' thoughts on his three days in the tomb experience. But legend holds that, during those long years in which he was granted a second sojourn among the living, the brother of Mary and Martha never smiled again.

So a note to all televangelists: resurrection may not be all that it's cracked up to be.

Still, you have to believe in something, I thought as I looked up at the great sword that hung above the fireplace mantel. I do, anyway. I'd rather believe in something and, in the end, discover there was nothing—than believe in nothing and, when the end comes, discover that there was Something, after all. You may not agree but we all have some kind of judgment day, some day, and some time, some where.

I'd already had a couple, myself.

I walked over and pulled the enormous blade from its twisted oaken sheath. The blue-green metal refracted the room's track lighting in coruscating rainbows. So far I'd resisted the temptation to send the magnificent blade off for serious testing. The metal might be some unknown meteorite alloy: it was stronger and harder but lighter than steel. I had seen the edge slice through fossilized dinosaur bones like they were so much papier-mâché. Under a magnifying glass, however, the edge remained impossibly sharp, showing neither nick nor notch.

What could a lab tell me, anyway? That the test results were anomalous?

And what could I tell them when they came back with questions of their own? That it had been left behind by an angel—possibly an archangel?

For now, it continued to hang over the fireplace like a mildly curving question mark, another mismatched piece for the jigsaw puzzle of Faith.

I wondered if "Brother" Michael was ever coming back for his sword.

Maybe all of that was a dream, too; the by-product of a once human brain being slowly turned inside-out by the necrotic virus I'd inherited from Vlad Drakul Bassarab.

As if to punctuate that thought, my computer chimed and a digitized voice announced: *"You've got mail! Let's count de messages! Vun! Two! Tree messages! Ah! Ah! Ah!"*

Deirdre, in one of her many fits of boredom, had upgraded my messaging system with .wav files of "The Count" from *Sesame Street*. Having a heavily-accented Muppet announce the arrival of email was kind of cute— the first couple of days. Forget haunted houses and graveyards; the scariest things inhabit the Internet.

I replaced the sword in its gnarled, wooden sheath and sat down to check my computer's inbox. Too bad she hadn't upgraded my spam filter. The first two messages turned out to be pleas from surviving relatives of assassinated African cabinet ministers who wished the temporary use of my bank account in order to launder millions of dollars from private government accounts. At least the virus hadn't sufficiently emulsified my brain for me to fall for scams like this. Sadly, there were people without hemophagic viruses ravaging their cerebral cortexes, who would.

The third message in my inbox was more problematical. As I scrolled down the virtual page, a pattern of Egyptian hieroglyphs appeared.

Familiar-looking hieroglyphs.

Followed by an even more familiar translation:

Oh! Amon Ra, Oh . . .
God of gods . . .
Death is but the doorway to new life.
We live today. We shall live again . . .
In many forms shall we return . . .
O mighty one . . .

The screen flickered.

It more than flickered; it ran through all 1,024 variations of the monitor's color settings in about twenty seconds.

I blinked and looked up from the monitor. And saw a stranger sitting across the room.

Except it wasn't my room.

A moment before I was sitting in my crowded little study. Now the room was cavernous. Panels of dark, gleaming wood replaced the bookshelves. The fireplace had grown into a giant, stonework affair that suggested the fiery furnace of Shadrach, Meshach, and Abednego: you could walk around inside without bumping your head.

An elderly man sat upon an antique chaise lounge across from me. His legs were elevated and hidden beneath a colorful stratum of quilts and comforters. He wore a maroon velvet smoking jacket with white edelweiss embroidered upon the lapels and a blue cravat or scarf that all but obscured his shirt. His white hair was sparse and his moustache wispy enough to be almost invisible. His head was round and vaguely he put me in mind of a *Peanuts* cartoon character—Charlie Brown some sixty years hence and waiting for a visit from his grandchildren. Snoopy's master grown sharp and crafty with age. . . .

"Mr. Cséjthe," the stranger began. I would have thought his speech without accent was it not for his pronunciation of the hard consonants in my name. " . . . please forgive this unorthodox intrusion but I simply must speak with you. Allow me to introduce myself. I am Dr. Pipt."

"What's up, Doc?" I growled, though I suspected that this was going to be a one-way conversation.

"As you may have already surmised, I am not actually here," the apparition explained.

As if to underscore the point a clown fish from my aquarium wriggled up to the old man as if in search of a handout. Finding none, it turned and disappeared.

"I have embedded this message in the code strings and algorithms of the computer message so that I might have a better chance of making my case," Pipt elaborated.

In other words, a pop-up mpeg that played inside your head. This was damned impressive!

He brought a slender hand from beneath the coverlets and smoothed a stray wisp of hair behind his ear. "I am a scientist who has spent his whole life unlocking the secrets of the human condition. I pioneered genetics research years before the discovery of the double helix ignited scientific curiosity in the rest of the world. I have devoted my entire life to one, great and overriding goal!"

As he paused to lean toward me, I considered how "have" sounded more like "haff" as it fell from his wrinkled lips.

"And do you know what that goal is?"

I went for the most obvious choice: "Creating microburst hypnotropic flash-spam on a global scale?"

"Immortality, Mr. Cséjthe!" he exclaimed.

Oh, too bad . . .

Tell me that you've invented the next big marketing technology of the twenty-first century and you've got my attention. But "Immortality"? Why not throw "World Domination" in and cackle like a demented madman?

Demented madman—now there was a nice redundancy . . .

"Yes," he continued, "I know it seems quite the hoary cliché. But clichés are based upon universal truths and immortality has been the dream and desire of the human race since ancient times! The idea—the *Ideal*—is so old that it is the basis of myths and stories from every proto-culture, every race and clime of recorded history. Science and technology may create this or invent that, but the motivation for every social, technological, and medical advance is rooted in the goal of extending life! Reducing the wear and tear on the human body so that it can last longer! And—" He paused and seemed to gather himself. "But I rattle on like an old skeleton. My time is limited and I must make my point quickly and succinctly."

He straightened his spine, striking an almost regal pose. "How old do you suppose that I am?"

That's the problem with advanced age. Genetics and/or quality of life—diet, exercise, stress—could tweak the physical signs either way. There were fifty-year-olds who looked seventy and seventy-year-olds who could pass for sixty. Since Cyrus the Computer Virus was making the pitch for his immortality research, I could guess that he was probably older than he looked.

"I was born on March sixteenth . . ." He paused for dramatic effect. " . . . in the year 1911!"

The second pause for dramatic effect was far more effective. If I could believe what he was saying.

"But longevity is not the same as immortality," he continued with a gesture that took in his blanketed lower extremities. "I have made my most significant break-throughs too late to keep me in this vessel much longer. I shall continue . . . but my next transition is not one I would choose if I could find an alternative . . ."

"And heeeeere's the pitch . . ." I murmured.

"You, Mr. Cséjthe, are that alternative."

Bingo.

"You have something to offer that would cost you very little and would benefit me very much." His deeply set brown eyes widened and seemed unusually alive in his less than lively body. "And, through me, the human race!"

Ding-a-ling-a-ling-a-ling: the alarm bells always go off when folk with vague and mysterious agendas invoke the human race. Call me paranoid but my experience with telemarketers was bad and my track record with paranormal power mongers even worse. Put 'em together . . .

And, speaking of bells, somewhere off in the distance, I heard my front doorbell chime.

"In return, I believe I can offer you two very precious gifts," Pipt continued, ignoring the sound of the chimes in my hallway. "I would like to meet with you to discuss these matters." He shrugged. "Alas, I do not believe you would make the journey on hearsay so I propose to send an emissary to meet with you and discuss our mutual interests."

He gestured and a dwarf dressed in lederhosen came into view, carrying a wooden box.

"I'll get it!" Deirdre called from the other room. The front door, I supposed, not the box.

The box was nearly square and about sixteen inches to a side in all three dimensions. Brass hinges gleamed brightly against the dark, lacquered wood and Pipt took possession of it as if delicate glassware were stored inside.

"I have just a few moments left. This messaging technology is still in its infancy and is somewhat limited. Plus, I must apologize in advance for the aftereffects. I do hope you are not susceptible to migraines—the headaches usually last only a few hours." He turned the box in his hands and braced it against his chest. "But I could not simply tell you—I had to *show* you." He fumbled at a catch and swung the side of the box out and open so that its contents and interior were visible. "Here is how you shall know my emissary and that the gifts I promise will be true!"

It was a head.

A human head.

Theresa Kellerman's long, dark tresses had been trimmed to shoulder length—a slightly miscast phrase as she no longer had any shoulders.

Her eyes blinked.

Her mouth opened as if to speak.

But she had no lungs and her voice box had been damaged if not lost when the machete had taken her head off in the voodoo *hounfort* last year.

"You son-of-a-bitch!" I said as Pipt, the dwarf, and the still-living head of Theresa Kellerman flickered and disappeared.

A full-blown migraine on steroids rushed in to fill the void in my own head.

Deirdre appeared in the study's doorway. "Somebody sent you a valentine," she said.

"What?" I blinked. *Ow.* Blinking hurt.

"I got to the door too late to catch the messenger. But they left something for you, special delivery."

I tried to focus. *Ow!* Focusing hurt!

Deirdre was walking toward me. Closing the distance helped. But not the motion. I tried focusing again when she stopped right in front of me.

She was holding something. A jar.
A three-quart glass jar.
Filled with a clear liquid substance.
And a heart.
The heart was still beating!
And this time I wasn't dreaming.

Chapter Two

"VALENTINE'S DAY IS still a couple of weeks away," Deirdre was saying, "but I guess someone wanted to express their sentiments early."

I knelt down and studied the immediate area of the front porch. No footprints, no fibers, not even a ring of moisture or disturbed dust to show where the jar had been set before the doorbell was rung. We lived too far out in the boonies for any hope of a *CSI: West Monroe* so I got back up and looked out into the darkness—something I could do better than anyone with a starlight scope.

Whoever the messenger was, he had to cross the river or the cemetery to leave it here.

And depart again by either of those two routes.

I still didn't believe in ghosts but either of those alternatives seemed even more unlikely.

"So, what do you think?" Deirdre asked.

I was thinking about my little daymare of just an hour ago but I wasn't about to tell Deirdre that she was showing up in my dreams—even if they had a nightmarish bent. "I'm thinking," I said, "of how, back in a more romantic era, the poets and troubadours articulated their passion with phrases like 'I offer you my heart' or 'I lay my heart at your feet.'"

"You think a wandering minstrel did this?"

"No." I thought about giving her The Look but I didn't want her to think I was so easily baited. "And while I've never reconciled myself to today's music distilling those sentiments into something along the lines of 'Yo, bitch' . . ." I contemplated the gory gift in the glass container, " . . . I think I'd prefer a little gangsta' rap over Victorian prose turned to bloody-minded literalness."

"Still, whoever left it was at least considerate enough to put it in a glass jar with a nice, tight lid. Otherwise it would have been very messy."

I gave her The Look after all.

She gave it right back. "I'm not being prissy, it means something! Anyone can cut out a heart and dump the mess on your porch if that's all there is to the message. This is something more sophisticated. The fact that it's in a jar and still pumping away is part of the message."

Oh.

"So," I asked as the fist-sized organ churned and turned in the clear suspension medium, "you didn't get any kind of a look at the messenger service?"

Deirdre shook her head. "Rang the bell and ran away."

"We shouldn't be handling this. The glass should be dusted for fingerprints."

She snorted. "Like whoever is capable of this would be

dumb enough to leave latents. You'd do better to run DNA from the tissue through the BioWeb database."

"BioWeb is gone."

"The facilities *here* are gone," she corrected. "Kurt said there are redundant network facilities in New York."

"Hmmm. Inconvenient, seeing as most people leave their hearts in San Francisco." It was the growing migraine; I was finding it increasingly difficult to think clearly. "This is assuming that it is a 'people' heart. Could be an animal's."

She shook her head and her red hair caressed my shoulder. "Human."

"You sound very sure."

"I am."

"That's rather disturbing." I held it up to gain the advantage of the porch light. "Could be a fake—some kind of latex model with a motor and battery to make it move like that." The heart stirred the semiclear liquid around it like the rinse cycle of a Maytag washer.

"Nope. It's real."

I gave her the eye. "I don't know which bothers me more . . . that you can tell the difference between a human and an animal heart? Or that you can tell that it's real with just a glance in the dark?"

She smiled. "I think you are more disturbed by the fact that I'm not squealing like a seven-year-old girl, doing the jitterbug, and hyperventilating to the edge of unconsciousness."

"Maybe. Maybe I'm more disturbed by the fact that *I'm* not. I certainly would have a year or so ago."

"You've changed."

"Yeah. Getting killed has that effect, I'm told." I was trying for wry but it came out sounding a little pissy.

"You're not dead," she said with a slight edge to her voice, "you're alive."

"Am I?"

"You're not undead."

"Yet."

She sighed. "You know, some people are 'the glass is half full' kind of folk and others tend toward 'the glass is half empty' sort . . ." She waited.

I obliged reluctantly: "And which am I?"

"You're more along the lines of the glass is chipped and dirty and the water is probably laced with toxic waste."

I held up the jar. "Looks to me like the glass is half-filled with a still-beating human heart." I turned back and stared out into the darkness beyond the porch light. "Jesus, I'm tired. It's been a hell of a year—and I mean that in the most literal, theological context." I raised my voice. "You know, I'm really getting tired of all this monster mafia crap! Somebody wants to send me a message? Write a letter, pick up the phone, send an email!" *Well, maybe not an email.* "Or be mensch enough to stay on the porch after you ring the damn bell and deliver your message in person!" I ended up bellowing into the faceless night.

The crickets were suitably cowed: they stopped their nocturnal screaming for a full twenty seconds.

Deirdre cleared her throat. "Well . . . that was nice . . ."

"Oh, shut up."

"No, I mean it. You've been like a zombie, yourself, these past few weeks. It's nice to see a little emotion for a change."

"Little" emotion was right. It seemed like the only emotion I could muster this past year was anger. And even that was on the wane, of late. Ever since my wife and daughter died, I had felt my humanity trickling out of me like the fine spill of sand in a dusty hourglass. Each month I grew emptier and more benumbed as the virus took its toll. As it rolled through my body, reprogramming my RNA and mutating my cells, it felt as if a myriad of tiny switches were being thrown, one by one, in a shutdown sequence for my soul.

Looking at the still-beating heart in the jar I knew I was supposed to feel . . . something. Fear? Horror? Wonder? I could barely work up a serious case of annoyance.

Not the best of emotional states for what I had planned tonight.

Deirdre swore at my back and clamped her hand on my arm. "What the hell am *I* thinking?!" She yanked me back inside the house so fast I nearly dropped the jar.

Spinning me around, she kicked the door shut and shook a finger in my face. "That was stupid! People are trying to kill you!"

"Well, I wouldn't exactly call them 'people.'"

"Well, as your Chief of Security, I'm declaring a state of Orange Alert! From this point on you let *me* answer the door!"

I touched her shoulder. "And do what? Take a bullet that was meant for me?" She wore shorts and a white tank tee, damp with sweat from the weight room in the basement. My fingers tingled where they touched the faint scars over her trapezius muscle where I had bitten her nine months and a lifetime ago. "You are no longer a vampire."

"Better me than you," she argued. "I may no longer be wampyr but I'm still less human than you!"

That was contestable but I let it slide. "I have a call to make," I said, turning and walking away.

"Hello?"

Even though he was more than half a continent away and filtered by countless telephone relays and switchers, there was a palpable presence in the room even before he spoke—Master vampires were like that.

"Stefan?" My asking was a polite formality. There was no question that Stefan Pagelovitch, the Doman for the Seattle enclave of the undead was on the other end of the line. "It's Chris."

"What can I do for you, my friend?"

How about modulating the subharmonics in your voice so that my head doesn't explode? Pipt hadn't been kidding about the headache. I cleared my throat. "Are you missing something?"

"Missing something?" I could feel his frown through the receiver.

"Yeah. A head."

"A . . . 'head'?"

Mine was throbbing painfully and, rather than play Twenty Questions, I cut to the chase. "Theresa Kellerman's head. Remember? I gave it to you for safekeeping. I've been expecting a report from Doctors Mooncloud and Burton."

"If you wanted a report, you should have given them a little more time."

"A little more time?"

"Look, Christopher; I am no doctor, no scientist. But

even I can see that a severed head—one that continues to live without a heart, without lungs, without mechanical life support—*that* takes time to study."

"Were they working on keeping any other organs alive and functional independent of the body?"

I felt his frown deepen. "What do you mean?"

I looked over at the telltale heart, now atop the fireplace mantel and just below the hanging, curved sheath of the ancient great sword. Like something from a grotesque Timex commercial—Gahan Wilson meets John Cameron Swayze—it continued to beat: *Takes a licking and keeps on ticking* . . .

"Christopher?"

As I struggled to rephrase my question, some part of my hind brain was observing that the sword should be rehung slightly to the left and the jar moved another eight inches to the right to achieve a more decorous balance of the—er—décor.

"Christopher, are you there?"

I shook my head. "Sorry, I was just channeling Martha Stewart."

"What?"

"Or maybe Attila the Hun doing *Fang shui*."

"What are you talking about?" The edge to his voice brought me back to the subject at hand.

"I'm talking about related experimentation," I said. "Were they attempting to grow or clone organs—say a heart, for example—to extend the—"

"Clone or grow organs? In what? A Petri dish?" He snorted derisively. "Cséjthe, have you ever read *Dracula* by Bram Stoker?"

"Uh, yes."

"And have you read *Frankenstein* by Mary Wollstonecraft Shelley?"

"As a matter of fact I have."

"And are you aware of why *Frankenstein* is the better of the two novels?"

"I wasn't aware of any such compar—"

"It is because one amounts to little more than tabloid journalism, playing fast and loose with certain details of history while the other is an ingenious work of *fiction*, springing from a fertile imagination, unfettered by such constraints as the laws of chemistry or physics."

"Um . . ."

"Do I need to explain which is which?"

"Not real—"

"Petri dish, indeed! The good doctors had just finished constructing an artificial breathing device when you took it away from them. That's artificial in the mechanical sense. As in pump and bellows. The next step was to graft a donor voice box onto the trachea. If you had waited, we might have found out if it was capable of speech."

"She's a *her*, not an *it*," I corrected. "And what do you mean 'I' took it away? Took *her* away."

"Your emissaries came and fetched Ms. Kellerman's head back to the East Coast. Said that you had more confidence in the facilities in New York. Nice touch, by the way, sending twins."

"Dammit, Stefan, I think I can trust Taj. And Gerald seems the decent sort. But I don't know or trust anyone besides Kurt back east. I don't care how impressive the equipment is, I didn't want Theresa treated like some kind of specimen!"

The shrug of his shoulders traveled down the wire. "Then you should have left her here."

"*I* didn't take her away! The people who came for her weren't *my* people!" *Whisper*, I told myself; *yelling only makes the headache worse*.

"So she's been . . . what? Head-napped?"

"Ha," I said, "ha."

"Who would want to get . . . a head?"

"Calls himself Dr. Pipt," I said, ignoring the bait. Why was yanking my chain such a popular sport these days? I proceeded to recount my evening's email experience, omitting the epilogue concerning my funny valentine.

"Perhaps you should add a human filter to your online interface," he suggested after digesting my story. "Anything so sophisticated as to encode an audio-visual experience and play it back in your brain could have other side effects."

"Like monster headaches?"

"Like post-hypnotic suggestions. False memory implants. You might have some mental time bomb ticking away until some preprogrammed event or time sets it off."

"*Time* bomb? I've already got a dozen hand grenades going off inside my skull!" I rubbed my forehead trying to massage some of the shrapnel out of my hairline.

"This could well be a political move on the part of your enemies."

"Ya think? Problem is it seems a little too subtle and too sophisticated for the East Village People. So far everything they've thrown at me has been teeth and talons."

"Christopher," he said in that voice that reminded me that he had a couple of centuries of maturity and sophistication on me, "your enemies are not confined to the New York clans."

I sighed. *"Now* what did I do?"

"Christopher, you may believe that your sudden displacement of Erzsébet Báthory has only stirred up enmity on the East Coast—"

"Gee, only the East Coast."

"—but the shock waves of your ascension have had a great impact on the other side of the continent, as well. I have had my hands full."

"Meaning what?"

"Everything is political, my naïve friend. New York is convulsed with infighting over who will transfer their loyalties to you and who will challenge for succession before your ashes hit the ground." He paused and let that delightful image sink in. "But other enclaves, long fearing the power and politics of the East Coast, now see opportunities during this period of uncertainty. Many feel the time to strike is while Gotham is crippled by weak and uncertain leadership."

"Ouch."

"I thought you were a big fan of the truth."

"Think of me as an 'oscillating' fan. But since we're on the subject of truth, ever consider taking a run at me, yourself?"

"Christopher, you do not have the ruthlessness required to rule the wampyri. You have made one brief visit to New York to meet with the heads of the various clans—and then retreated back to Louisiana where you have no power base, no demesne of your own. You are not fully transformed, not completely undead. You have no real clan or family. The only respect you have, at this point, is that you have survived seven assassination attempts—"

"Seven? I only count five. How do you figure seven?"

"—destroyed the demons Kadeth Bey and Lilith, known as Elizabeth Báthory, and were sired by Vladimir Drakul Bassarab the Fifth, known as Dracula."

"Not sired, exactly. More like a stepfather," I said. "Godparent, actually—light on the 'God' part."

"Every Doman I have spoken with sees you as a major threat to the demesne system. It was better when you were considered rogue. As the weakest claimant to leadership of the largest and most powerful enclave in the undead underground, you are destabilizing the order of things. Civil war is threatening to break out in a half dozen demesnes. My own people are divided over your status and what they should do about it."

"Gee, Stefan, when did you abdicate in favor of making Seattle a democracy?"

"I haven't," he said dryly, "but you make it very difficult to remain a benevolent dictator. And no, I have no ambitions to vie for the New York throne, myself. I would only consider making a 'run' at you if you threatened me and mine."

"Well, that's a re—"

"Which may yet be the case if matters on the East Coast are not resolved soon."

There wasn't much to say after that. Pagelovitch

promised to investigate matters at his end. He also said something about beefing up my security for friendship's sake. Now that was mildly unsettling—the "friendship" remark that is, not the security issue.

The front door rattled as I hung up the phone. "You're late," I said as Lupé made a blind entrance behind a couple of sacks of groceries.

"Talk to Siskel and Ebert," she growled as she swept toward the kitchen.

"Can I help you with that?" I asked, trying to keep up. "And it's Ebert and Roeper: Siskel died."

"Like that makes any kind of difference around here," J.D. groused, trying to close the door behind him with one foot while balancing two more sacks of groceries and a plastic Blockbusters bag in his arms. "My bad. I was tryin' to separate the darbs from the clams. I mean I wanted to make sure I didn't bunko the rest of youse on the picks. But then your barn burner here decided to hook up some business on the side and ankled out . . ."

I looked at Lupé. "I went shopping," she explained.

"She was gone a whole 'nother hour!"

J.D. was barely sixteen when someone with a set of brass knuckles patted him off to lullaby land during a gang war in Chicago. He "woke up" three nights later in a back alley under a decomposing heap of refuse and garbage. He never discovered who drained his body of blood, leaving him to rot like a regular corpse or combust like ignorant kindling upon his first encounter with the killing rays of the sun. Somehow, without benefit of Sire or sponsor, he survived. Impressive enough. More impressive that he had awakened undead in 1937 and survived into the next millennium as a rogue, dwelling outside the organized vampire demesnes.

The undead enclaves tolerated no loose cannons. Their attitude was: "Either you're with us and obey the rules or you're a potential X-File that needs to be canceled." When it came to The Kid, there were times when I could empathize with the latter philosophy.

"I don't know why I hurried," Lupé said, setting the bags down on the kitchen counter with a heavy thump. "When I came back he was still trying to make up his mind."

I caught up with her and caught her around the waist. "Ah, the vagaries of youth," I exclaimed, and kissed her. She kissed me back and then pushed me away. "Youth? He's older than the two of us put together!"

"True, but not half as pretty."

She grinned, her teeth bright against the backdrop of dusky skin and pomegranate lips. My beloved was French Canadian but looked Latin American. Dark hair and eyes, a face that was structured more for sensuality than classic beauty; I affectionately called her my big-nosed girl. "Go start the first movie or we'll be up past dawn."

I slid my fingers inside the fall of her smoky dark hair and cupped her face. "How about a little intermission snack between features?"

"I'll make some popcorn."

"That's not what I mean."

"I *know* what you mean." She turned her head and kissed the palm of my right hand. "But if you want some downtime before bedtime we need to get the shows started. There's company outside, too, you know."

"Already up and running," Deirdre announced from the back porch.

"When did that happen?"

"Made two trips out to the wall while you were on the phone with Seattle." She came into the kitchen and began toting cans to the larder as Lupé pulled them from the grocery bags.

"What are they watching?" Lupé asked.

"*Planet of the Apes.*"

"Heston or Marky-Mark?"

"The original. It's on tape. The remake is on DVD."

I nodded. The DVD player stayed inside. It had taken just about forever to teach some of The Neighbors how to use "play" and "rewind" on the VCR.

The Kid wailed from the den: "C'mon youse guys!"

Lupé gave me a little shove. "Go. We'll be there in a sec."

I fingered the ring in my pocket and considered negotiating for another kiss first. Decided she was right: sooner begun, sooner done, and I could get down to the business of popping the question. "Okay, but I need to borrow Deirdre for a sec."

"Sure. Just make sure it's a quickie. Tempus fugit." Only the way she pronounced her Latin, it came out sounding suspiciously rude and naughty.

"I need your help in backtracking an email," I told Deirdre as we made a side trip to the computer in the study.

"Anonymous?" she asked, moving behind me as I sat and tapped the spacebar.

The seti@home screensaver vanished, revealing the digital desktop. "That and more." I moved the cursor to the taskbar and restored the email client to full screen status.

Which was blank.

"Wow," she said, "that's really anonymous!"

The inbox was empty. I opened the deleted files folder and scanned a list of messages from the past week, culminating with my two African strike-it-rich offers.

Nothing from a Dr. Pipt. Nothing remotely close to the approximate date and time of my missing missive.

I minimized the email program, returned to the desktop, and opened the general trash bin for deleted files. Nothing, nada, zip.

"I've heard of self-deleting emails," Deirdre offered. "Timed to self-destruct after being opened or after a certain amount of time has passed."

"Oh, this was much more than that," I said. "Any chance of still finding traces of it in my system?"

"I can give it a shot," she said, nudging me out of the chair so that she could have a turn at the keyboard. "I'm not really familiar with that particular technology, though. What can you tell me about it? If I have enough info, I might be able to 'ping' your sender."

I thought about that as J.D. bellowed from the den. If Deirdre did manage to ping Pipt, what if he decided to "pong" back?

"Tell you what, just beef up my security," I said, reaching down to hit the escape key. "Virus protection, firewall, the works. Let's back up the hard drive. And don't open any new emails without calling me."

She nodded and began to clatter away at the keyboard. "Just give me a yell when the movie starts."

"Sure."

I started to walk away and stopped to again contemplate my new acquisition. It sat on the mantelpiece like a jar of preserves—a jar of throbbing, organic preserves.

My mutated blood had brought Theresa Kellerman back from the dead and, later, enabled her head to survive separation from her body. Could this be her heart? Had someone found a way to salvage her body beneath the tons of earth and concrete in the basement of the collapsed BioWeb complex?

I bowed my own aching head and rubbed my eyelids. Even though she had tried to kill me I couldn't help but feel remorse for her current plight. Was she aware? Had her brain retained some semblance of intelligence? Did she feel pain? Was she suffering unspeakable torment? It was my blood that had denied her the solace of death; perhaps I had some obligation in matters of her wellbeing and final disposition.

Living, dying, procreating, or passing along untold seeds of mischief and misery—funny how even in matters of the occult, everything seems to come back to the difficulty of keeping our various bodily fluids in their proper places.

"You okay?" Deirdre asked from behind me.

"Migraine," I said, trying to shake off the aftershocks of nausea while trying to hold my head as still as possible.

"Want me to rub it?"

Yeah. Sure. I was hoping to set the right mood for a proposal tonight and all that I needed to make the evening complete was for Lupé to walk into the study and find Deirdre caressing my fevered brow.

Poor Theresa Kellerman would have company because *somebody* would lose their head for sure.

"What would really help is for J.D. to *stop bellowing*!" I bellowed back as The Kid bellowed again. I waved her off and lumbered into the den.

J.D. took his new name in 1955, the day after a twenty-four-year-old actor had his own collision with immortality at the intersection of Routes 46 and 41 just outside Cholame, California. Sometimes, when he was tripping, he thought he *was* James Dean, immortal icon of the Fifties, rebel without a cause, come back to kick Raymond Massey's ass in *East of Eden*. He wasn't stupid—well, not in that way, at least—but he had acquired a twisted taste for the veins of potheads and heroin addicts.

He met me just inside the doorway to show off his haul from the video store. "The original *Frankenstein* trilogy," he was saying, "newly repackaged on DVD!"

"Interesting choice . . ." I skimmed the titles on the packaging. "But 'original'?" I asked, trying not to let my right eyebrow go too high.

He nodded. "Black and white. Vintage. Universal. Karloff. Reet, sweet, and neat."

"Two out of three, Junior."

His eternally teenaged face squinched down into combat mode. "Whaddaya mean?" He fanned the plastic containers. "*Frankenstein, Bride of Frankenstein, Son of Frankenstein.*"

I reached out and snagged the third rental, turning it around. "'*Young' Frankenstein*," I said, holding it up for his perusal.

"Young—?" He grabbed it back and studied the fine print. "Black and white . . ."

"Nineteen seventy-four," I said, "Gene Wilder, Marty Feldman, Cloris Leachman as Frau Blücher, Peter Boyle as the Creature. Mel Brooks directed." I smiled, trying to make nice. "A classic in its own right. But not *'Son'* of *Frankenstein. Not* Karloff. *Not* original trilogy."

"I thought . . ."

From the look on his face it was clear what he thought.

The Kid was becoming a regular cinephile under my expert tutelage. At least as far as horror movies were concerned. The previous week he had impressed me with a detailed comparison of the 1971 flick, *The Incredible Two-Headed Transplant* with its successor the following year, *The Thing With Two Heads*. My take on the double-header schlockfest was that one starred Bruce Dern just before his acting career took off while the other showcased ex-footballer Rosy Grier and Oscar-winner Ray Milland on their way to Hollywood oblivion. J.D., however, pointed out the pithy social satire that informed the second movie and opined that the Blaxploitation craze had never been better lampooned.

Still, he could be clueless at times. I had once asked him who the cinematic bogeyman of choice was: Jason or Freddy?

"Michael Myers," he replied with a shudder.

I'd started to agree. Never mind the sequels, the original *Halloween* had it all: killer theme music, Jamie Lee Curtis in peril, and, most frightening of all, an unstoppable force of Darkness wearing a Captain Kirk mask.

Then The Kid went on to say that the *Austin Powers* movies were the most disturbing things he had ever seen.

I patted him on the shoulder now. "Don't worry, Kid; if

you haven't seen *Young Frankenstein*, you're in for a treat."

"Hey," he said, still immersed in the fine print, "Teri Garr! She's in this? Is it like a romantic comedy?"

"Well . . ." I tried to remember.

"Man, Teri Garr! She could eat crackers in my coffin anytime!"

"Uh . . ." There are all kinds of ways the undead can be unsettling without slobbering on your neck. "There is," I said carefully, "a scene where she—um—has a little roll in the hay."

"Hey, hey, hey, Daddy-o; I can dig it!"

"Farm out," I said.

And then the lights went out.

"Fuse!" everyone chorused. It was a logical deduction based on a dozen previous episodes.

"Well, duh . . ." Deirdre's voice drifted in from the study where a blue glow still emanated from the flat-panel monitor. The computer and the aquarium were plugged into UPS devices giving them a little grace period before their power supplies went down as well.

"I'm guessing more than one, dear," Lupé called from the kitchen. "Looks like the whole house is out. Better hurry, the natives are getting restless!" Indeed, growling sounds were beginning to manifest from the backyard.

"You go settle them down," I told The Kid as I headed for the basement door. "Tell them if they break the TV or the VCR they'll be making do with sock puppets until next Christmas!"

The fanged runt scampered off with a little too much enthusiasm. He could be fearless in a fight, willing to face demons or vampires or even hordes of cranky corpses. But he had this phobia about electricity and I would have an easier time getting him to eat garlic over requiring him to change a fuse.

"Need help?" Deirdre called.

"I think I can manage." Heavy on the sarcasm there. "You just stay on task."

"I am."

Yeah? What task is that? Slipping enough innuendo into enough opportunities to wreck Lupé's trust and self-esteem? The woman was incorrigible! And I wasn't going to incorrige her any further. Maybe after tonight she would get the message, loud and clear.

Maybe they both would.

I clomped down the basement stairs, grabbing the flashlight from the peg at the quarter-turn landing. It was easy to find in the pitch dark: it wasn't like we hadn't been through this before. A half-dozen times. A backup emergency generator was supposed to have been installed and operational by now, not just for creature comforts but for the security system, as well. Things kept happening. The first one didn't arrive. The second one was broken. The third was missing a couple of key parts. The replacement parts weren't the right parts or didn't arrive at all. Deirdre had to hire people to go and fetch the necessary parts and equipment in person as it became clear that someone (or something) was tampering with the third-party delivery services. Then our people went missing. Or came back with certain of their parts missing. Deirdre had finally gone, herself, and we now (presumably) had everything necessary for an emergency backup generator system.

Except the people to install it properly.

That wouldn't happen until sometime in late March or early April—unless something happened to clear the local contractors' calendars. Another blown fuse or two and I was afraid that Deirdre or J.D. would slip out one night and do just that. Especially since my stern admonitions "not to" were becoming less stern of late.

The flashlight was dead.

Too bad there wasn't a wild storm outside; it would have all the hallmarks of a gothic thriller.

And then, all of a sudden, I broke out in an icy sweat. Gooseflesh pimpled my arms as I left the stairs and reoriented myself. I could feel the hairs on the back of my neck start to rise as I plunged through the darkness on a trajectory toward the fuse box on the far wall. No . . .

Dear Lord, please . . .

What if the fuses were all blown and there weren't enough replacements?

And on the heels of that thought came a sudden shock to my toes. "Shit!"

"What is it?" Deirdre called down from the open door above.

"Someone," I said slowly, carefully, nursing my bruised toes, "didn't put their *dumb*bells away when they were done working out!"

"I put them away."

"I beg to differ."

"I like it when you beg."

"Don't taunt him, dear . . ." It sounded like Lupé was suddenly standing behind Deirdre. " . . . that's my job."

With the reestablishment of territorial boundaries the upstairs door was closed.

Now it was really nice and dark.

And quiet.

Deirdre liked to crank up her boom box while she was working out so I had spent the past month stapling insulation, nailing sheetrock, and hanging a thicker, tighter cellar door so I could study to the strains of Wolfgang Mozart while she strained to the sound of Iron Maiden.

I carefully gimped my way across the floor, mindful that dumbbells came in pairs and that I had toes that were still unbroken. At least with the door closed I could cuss at the top of my lungs if I stumbled over any additional workout gear.

Where was I? Oh yeah: the icy fear was just starting to sink in that once I got to the fuse box I would find *all* of the fuses blown and I was pretty sure we didn't have enough spares to get everything back up and running.

Dead flashlight and shortage of replacement fuses: could it get any worse?

I bruised my shins on Deirdre's tanning bed.

I'd asked her once why she needed a man-made cocoon lined with UV lights when Louisiana provided plenty of natural sun exposure ten months out of the year. Aside from some mumbo jumbo about the difference between UV-A and UV-B wavelengths, I think she pretty much dodged the question. What's wrong with a blanket or a lawn chair? I mean, it's not like The Neighbors or I would be popping out in the middle of the day to gawk . . .

I climbed up on top of the closed lid of the bed to get to the fuse box and realized another complication: how could I tell which fuses to replace with what in the dark? A blown fuse does not make the same "tinkling" sound as a blown light bulb. And as for matching the correct amperages—I slapped the metal box in frustration but pulled my punch: the crapparatus was so old that it wouldn't take much to turn it into so much scrap.

As I prepared to climb back down, I caught the side of the box to balance myself and felt the circuit handle in the down or off position. That was odd—not that it mattered now, of course.

Unless . . .

I pushed the handle back up.

A lone thirty-watt bulb stuttered to life back toward the bottom of the steps. Distant cheers from the first floor and the backyard confirmed that I had solved the power problem.

"You don't look so tough," said an unfamiliar voice from behind me. "I bet you'll scream like a little girl before I'm done."

Chapter Three

I SPUN AND DROPPED off the tanning table, landing in a Karate Kid combat pose. Mr. Miyagi would've been proud.

"Correction," the voice said. "I should've said 'scream and *dance* like a little girl . . .'" The voice belonged to a sinewy caricature of a human being. He wore peg-legged jeans over cowboy boots and a denim jacket with the sleeves torn off to form a raggedy vest. He was whippet-thin, all muscle and sinew and made Iggy Pop look like the Michelin Man. His head was shaved; the only hair aside from his eyebrows was a razor-trimmed moustache and goatee framing his fang-filled mouth. He wasn't just a vampire, which was badass enough, but he was cultivating the whole "other vampires think I'm a badass" vibe. I would be out of my league tangling with his baby sister.

I *could* scream and I *could* dance but I would be dead before anyone upstairs would have a clue that the enemy was under the doorstep.

"How did you get in here?" I wasn't just affecting a cool disinterest; I was coldly pissed off. Somebody *had* to invite him in; vampires couldn't cross a private threshold uninvited. The implications of that were as disturbing as his actual presence.

He smiled. It was like opening a tin of frozen sardines. "The owner invited me in."

"*I'm* the owner, baldy, and I'm *dis*-inviting you right now!"

He shook his head in an almost lazy fashion. "I speak of the original owner. You may have a way with some of the dead like those hapless fools next door, but not all of the corpses you will encounter will turn out to be such fawning sycophants."

Fawning syncophants? Great. I have met my archnemesis and his name is Lexicon Luthor. "So, the original owner . . ."

"A Madame LeClaire. Buried under the weeping willow by the front gate in 1869. She misses her headstone."

"Didn't know she was there. No headstone when I bought the place."

"Should have done the research. I did. Found out she was unhappy with the present tenants. Guess she doesn't approve of the *Three's Company* living arrangements. Very traditional, Madame LeClaire is."

"A nineteenth-century ghost told you all this?"

He shrugged. "I hired a medium."

Crap! An eloquent biker-vampire-assassin who did research. In-depth research. When the predators are stronger and faster than you are, you hope to gain a little edge by being smarter. This one, however, could not only outrun and outfight me but probably would kick my ass at the undead science fair, as well. "You've gone to a great deal of trouble."

"The contract on you is worth a great deal of money," he said. Like he had to justify the extra trouble and expense of tracking me down to kill me. "Not to mention the street cred."

Yeah, he looked like the type who valued street cred over practical considerations. I wondered if he appreciated where an overinflated reputation had gotten me.

"You realize, of course," I said slowly, "that what we have here is a Mexican standoff."

"Really?" He grinned. "I don't see it that way at all."

"I know that I'm no match for you," I continued, "but, as you so colorfully phrased it, I *can* scream like a little girl before you kill me. And you are definitely no match for the people upstairs or the security team on the property. If you don't stand down, we both die." *Of course I would have to scream real loud now that I had soundproofed the cellar.*

"Stand down," he mused. "I like that. So military. Probably something to do with your service records. I did a lot of research before I came here and that's the one part of my file on you that's incomplete. Why are some of your military records under a Pentagon seal?"

"Come back next week and I'll tell you."

He shook his head. "The money or the mystery—decisions, decisions." He pulled a wireless detonator out of his pocket. "I think I'll take the money." He flipped a switch and a flash lit up the basement windows followed by a loud "bang!"

He tossed the detonator aside. "That got their attention.

The next one will get them moving. In three. Two. One." A second "bang," farther away this time and the accompanying flash was dimmer.

"Now," he announced, "while your security team is running about outside, seeking the source of the mysterious explosions . . ." Another, more distant "bang" sounded. " . . . we can conclude our business without untimely interruptions." He reached down and pulled a combat knife out of his left boot. I patted the empty shoulder holster under my shirt as he held it up. Yeah, I wouldn't need to carry a gun inside my own house: I didn't need to go to bed or to the john or to the dinner table armed. Apparently trips to the cellar were a different matter.

The vampire brandished the weapon, turning it back and forth so we could both admire how the silvered blade gleamed under the General Electric Soft White.

"Oh, thank God," I said, "a knife. And here I was afraid you were going to taunt me to death."

He nodded. "A smartass. I heard that about you."

I nodded back: "Jack . . ."

"That's not my name."

"How would I know? Because that's what I've heard about you."

He grinned now. "Maybe I was wrong. Maybe you won't squeal like a little girl after all."

"Bet I can get you to do a pretty fair impression of Mariah Carey, though."

Maybe I could keep him talking until the others came looking for me.

He stopped grinning. A look of slow surprise filtered across his scary visage. "You're trying to piss me off?"

"Jeepers, Jack, now why would I want to do that?"

"Probe for any weaknesses, goad me into making a mistake. And my name is not Jack."

"I figured that's what you've been doing with me. And what am I supposed to call you? Mister Cuddles?"

"Call me Razor." He was back to sneering.

"You're kidding."

"Do I look like I'm kidding?"

"You look confused." I tried to look like I was relaxing while preparing to dodge at the first sign of forward momentum on his part.

"Confused?"

"If you were standing there, brandishing an actual razor, by God, I would be more inclined to take you seriously. At least in terms of attempted packaging. But you're waving a knife, not a razor. Therefore your moniker, your alias, nom de plume should match your weapon of choice. You should be 'Shiv' or 'Shank' or 'Blade'—no, Marvel Comics would probably sue your ass. So, what sort of nickname is going to suit? I know! For the few remaining minutes that you remain corporeal, I shall call you 'Pigsticker!'"

He growled. "That would make you the 'pig.'"

"Or we could use your manhood as a metaphor and christen you 'Penknife.'"

He took a menacing step forward. "The money is great. The rep I'm gonna get out of this is priceless. But killing you slow is going to be the sweetest part of the deal."

"I win," I said. "I made you madder, first."

He leapt.

He missed.

If I'd been human I would have been skewered. As it was, he grazed me as I spun out of his way.

His momentum carried him smack up against Deidre's tanning bed, jostling the Bakelite clamshell frame.

I followed through on my spin and kicked toward him. My right foot missed him by a good six inches and my toes slid into the opening between the lid and the bed surface. A quick scissors kick dislodged my foot and caused the lid to fly up into the full open position.

"Ha!" gloated Pigsticker. "You missed!" I guess he was feeling a little sheepish about doing the same a half-second earlier.

"You think so?" I followed through with my left foot which was lined up with his solar plexus. I would have nailed him this time except he leaned back. The edge of the bed tripped him further and he fell onto the bed in a half-sitting position.

"And again," he mocked.

I think he expected me to turn and run for the stairs. He certainly didn't expect me to throw myself on the knife that he was thrusting toward me. By the time he decided I must be crazy enough to jump him after all, he had lost the better part of his advantage.

Two things saved me. I wasn't actually leaping on top of him; I was throwing myself against the lid and pulling it back down. And I turned as he jabbed at me with the blade. His awkward position, coupled with the descending cover, made the thrust less effectual. The tip entered my shirt beneath my left arm, hitting two thick layers of leather minus the customary handgun: he stabbed me in the holster.

I turned back, further loosening the knife in his grasp while redirecting the point to angle past my body, and reached over his wrist with my left hand. "I've changed my mind," I hissed as I pushed down the cover with my right arm. "'Razor' suits you, after all. *Disposable* Razor, that is."

He squirmed, trying to escape the awkward confinement. Although he was stronger, I had a momentary advantage of leverage. But only momentary: one-armed, I was starting to lose the battle to keep the lid down. The fingers of my left hand fumbled under the cover at the end of the bed.

"Oh, and one last thing," I said as I felt the toggle switch. "Neither of those kicks missed. They accomplished exactly what they were supposed to!" I pressed the switch.

Nothing happened.

Except that Not-So-Disposable Razor flung the lid up and sat up like a Jack-in-the-Box of Doom!

I shrieked like a little girl. And kicked him like Michelle Yeoh. As he fell back I slammed the lid back down and reached under the end. This time I found the timer next to the toggle and twisted the dial. The ultraviolet tubes flickered to life inside the bed and now Razor began to shriek—not like a little girl but like a 300-pound castrato. His legs kicked and I was knocked back across the room and into the weight bench. The bruises were worth it. Although the UV radiation was harder on a full-fledged vampire, I still risked a nasty burn by standing too close.

I circled the room toward the stairs, keeping my distance

as what was left of my would-be assassin thrashed and smoked and burned in the purple-blue glare of the special fluorescents. When I started up the steps I saw that he had taken extra precautions while I had first stumbled around in the dark. A chair and a brace of two-by-fours were wedged up against the door and under the door-knob: it couldn't be opened from the other side.

Easy enough from this side though, I figured—until I tripped on the fourth step up and fell on my face. That smarted—but not so much as the third step and then the second and the first and finally the floor as I was dragged back down into the cellar. Razor had a chary grip on my ankle and was looking rather crispy. Maybe I should call him Ashley from now on.

"I kill you!" he wheezed.

No more witty banter. No more smug exposition or questions of how and when. He'd dropped the knife in fleeing the fluorescent inferno but needed the blood even more: his fangs were fully extended in his hideously seared countenance. He'd drink me dry, regardless of reward or street cred.

I kicked up at him and broke his grip on my leg in a smoky explosion of ash. Rolling away, I leapt up and scurried under the stairs. Somewhere in the jumble of boxes stored beneath the ascending risers was a set of lawn darts—not the most ideal of weapons but one made do with what was at hand.

Except they weren't.

At hand, that is.

By the time Count Charcoala grabbed my leg and start-ed yanking me back out I'd only succeeded in uncovering a badminton set. I flung the net at him and then whacked him with a racquet. He was no longer operating at one hundred percent but I didn't seem to be inflicting any real damage, either. I grabbed at another box to slow my momentum but it just gave way, falling over and spilling a series of implements with a wooden clatter.

Croquet equipment.

With wooden goal stakes!

I grabbed for the nearest one but he kicked it out of reach. Then he kicked one of the wooden balls at my head. It barely missed, grazing my ear. I grabbed blindly, trying to pick up something that would serve offensively or defensively. My fingers closed around a piece of bent wire, about the thickness of the type used to make coat hangers. Deep Fry went one better by scooping up a wooden mallet. Yelling "It's Hammer Time!" he rushed me.

He had the better line. What was I going to say? "No rest for the wicket?" Still, I took the blow in the shoulder where the leather strap from the holster rig helped absorb the shock while he took both pronged ends in the chest, straddling the sternum and double punctuating his heart like a sidewise colon.

It wasn't a wooden stake but just about as effectual. Ashes to ashes and dust to dust.

I climbed wearily to my feet and tested for broken bones. None apparent but I was going to purple up like a Grand Canyon sunset on the tomorrow. Back when I was still fully human, the bruises would have lasted several weeks. Now? Maybe a couple of days.

Maybe.

Tonight?

I looked around the cellar at the minor mayhem left in the wake of the fight. The timer on the tanning bed ran out just as I noted that it was going to require some major detailing and rehab work. As for the rest . . .

I started up the stairs. It could wait until tomorrow. Tonight was movie night. I was going to relax and have a good time.

Even if it killed me.

Mr. Disposable Razor aka the French Fry Guy had planted flash-bangs, not bombs, on the property. Since their purpose was to distract and lure the others away while murder most foul was committed, their destructive potential was quite minimal.

After a quick recap of my story and making sure that I wasn't at Death's door, the ladies descended into the basement to check on the real damage. Deirdre's security team was out, combing the grounds and walking the perimeters in case anything else had slipped through. I was pretty sure that the rest of the night would be relatively quiet but then I had gone into the cellar unarmed so what did I know?

After a couple of moments The Kid closed the door on the sounds of Lupé sweeping up and Deirdre mourning her Solar-Tropic 9000 Ultra Bronzing Environment with duo-control tanning options. He sat down across from me and leaned close. "You okay, chief?"

"Ducky. My home turf is turning into Vampapolooza and my only recourse is to go to New York and face down the fang gang all at once so they won't keep dropping in on me a few at a time. Other than that—"

"Sure, sure, lissen: I need a palaver," he said in hushed tones. "I need some advice on the frail side."

It took a second to run that through the time-warp translator. *Frail: chick, squeeze, babe. Female.* It helped if one watched a lot of the old Warner Brothers gangster movies from the forties. "Two questions, Junior," I growled, "who is it and why me?" I had a new bodyache to go with my previous headache and I wasn't in the mood for any additional complexities to the evening.

"Well . . ." His gaze swept the room like a *film noir* lookout planning a bank heist. "You've got experience."

"Experience?" I knew the educational system didn't have sex ed when J.D. was dipping schoolgirls' pigtails in inkwells but the little undead runt had been around long enough to do two lifetimes of the other kind of dipping.

"I mean, dating a Warm."

"A what?" I didn't recall this particular bit of noirish lingo.

"A 'Breather,'" he elaborated. "You've been married. Had a family. And, since the transformation, you've been involved outside your species."

I grabbed his arm a little more roughly than I intended. The subject of my family was still a sore spot and it didn't take much to push the buttons on my mood elevator. "What the hell are you talking about?"

"Calm down, Hon," breathed a familiar voice in my ear.

I looked around even though I knew I wouldn't see my late wife. She rarely made a visual appearance anymore. It was as if something was causing her ectoplasm to do a slow fade. "He needs some fatherly advice," Jenny-the-friendly-ghost-ex continued, "not Daddy Dearest."

"I need some advice," The Kid echoed, unaware that our tête-à-tête had just turned into a three-way. "Date-wise."

"Date-wise?"

He nodded and lowered his voice. "Don't go all dark on me, Cecil; I'm askin' for the straight dope."

"He's serious, Chris," Jen chimed in. "Be nice. This is hard for him."

"It would help," I said, "if I knew what we were talking about."

The Kid opened his mouth, hesitated, and closed it again.

"I think it involves the birds and the bees," she kibitzed.

"What?!"

"I didn't say nothin'," he said.

I cocked an eyebrow. "You got a question about the birds and the bees? Or, in your case, the bats and the wasps?" I felt a ghostly finger thump my ear but I couldn't help the attitude: this was a little like your grandfather asking for advice on bedroom techniques.

"It ain't about sex," he huffed. "Leastways, not yet."

"What's not about sex?" Lupé asked, reappearing sooner than anticipated. She was toting the broom still dark with dust and ashes and I prayed Jenny wouldn't be tempted to snark. Even though she was dead and had already pronounced Lupé good for me, former wives can get funny about their replacements and Jenny still had her moments.

The Kid blushed—sort of. Being a vampire, however, he blushed in reverse. Excess blood in an undead body is drawn away from the skin during periods of physical or emotional stress or strain: a blush looks more like a blanch. And The Kid was now as white as a sheet.

"We're talking about man-stuff, dear," I said, trying to rescue J.D. from further humiliation. I wasn't being especially kind. Humiliating The Kid was my own province and I didn't like to share.

Deirdre was right behind. "What's the sitch?"

J.D. looked from Lupé to Deirdre and his eyes took on the appearance of a cornered animal's.

"James and Christopher are having a conversation about 'man-stuff'," Lupé explained.

"Man-stuff?" The redhead pondered for all of three seconds. "That means they're talking about sex."

The Kid glared at me.

I held my hands up. "I didn't say that."

Lupé smiled. "But you did, dear. All women know 'man-stuff' is merely a euphemism for 'sex.'"

"Not true," I tried. "Man-stuff can be about cars and sports and lawn care and stuff."

She stood her ground: "It's about sex when men don't want women to listen in."

"The question is," Deirdre chimed in, "why don't you want us to listen in?"

"I was just looking for a little advice," The Kid said with obvious reluctance.

"Then why is he asking *you* about sex?" my wife's ghost murmured in my ear.

"Hey, I know about sex," I whispered back.

Apparently not quietly enough. Everyone turned to look at me. "Is Jenny here?" Deirdre asked.

"For *Akela's* sake!" Lupé swore. "Don't encourage him!"

There were two mindsets when the topic of my dead wife arose. One was that her ghost really did "haunt" me from time to time. The other was that I hallucinated Jennifer out of some Freudian, psychosexual guilt complex, kicked up a notch by the necrotic virus that was mutating my brain chemistry. Deirdre bought into the former theory, Lupé was a firm adherent of the latter.

I wasn't always sure what I believed.

J.D. got me off the hook with: "I just wanted some advice on how to get dizzy with a dame."

They both turned to stare at him.

"You know," he said, further obfuscating the explanation; "advice on bumpin' the gums, pitchin' woo . . ."

Lupé fought a smile. "Woo?"

Deirdre waggled her eyebrows. "Woo woo!"

"Aw, now see? That's why I wanted to keep this on the Q.T. I knew youse would put the screws on!"

The girls tried on sober expressions. They almost fit.

"I think she's human," my ghostly ex murmured.

"Human?"

The Kid turned and glared at me.

I raised my hands. "Jenny's opinion, not mine."

His shoulders slumped. "Yeah," he finally admitted. "She's still alive."

Deirdre perked up. "A vampire and a human? Dating? You want advice!"

Lupé nodded thoughtfully.

"I mean," The Kid added, "it's not like there's anything in *Cosmo* or Dear Abby or nothin'."

"There's Buffy," my sig said.

"Huh?" The Kid and I both responded.

"The Vampire Slayer," Lupé explained without really explaining.

"Are we talking Spike or Angel?" Deirdre asked.

"Angel, of course."

The redhead shook her head. "Nah. 'Spike moves' is what J.D. would be wanting."

Lupé seemed taken aback. "What? Are you a sixth season 'shipper? That was sick and disgusting!"

The Kid looked at me. "What are they talking about?"

I shrugged. "I dunno. But sick and disgusting sounds right up your alley."

"Hey!"

"Maybe The Executioner is more to J.D.'s liking," Jenny whispered.

"The Executioner?" I asked.

"Who?" The Kid asked.

"Anita Blake," Deirdre answered.

"Oh, please," Lupé sniffed. "She's worse than Buffy, season six."

"I suppose you're a Giles groupie."

"What's that supposed to mean?"

J.D. and I looked at each other. We both took a step back.

"Hey! Buffy may be The Slayer but Anita's The Executioner!"

"Buffy Summers would kick Anita Blake's ass!"

The Kid and I both fled to the den.

Eventually there was violence.

Growling, screaming, anger, pain, and death. Strangulation, drowning, and presumed immolation as the windmill blazed and the Frankenstein monster disappeared behind a curtain of flame.

As the final credits rolled, Lupé leaned against me and murmured, "They're heeeeere . . ."

I looked over at Deirdre, ensconced in a disheveled beanbag chair. She was tossing single kernels of popcorn high into the air and catching them with her mouth.

She was very good at it.

J.D. lay with his back on the hardwood floor and his legs sprawled across the seat of the rocking chair. He sipped from a bottle of Tabasco sauce as he perused the liner notes on the next DVD.

I looked back at Lupé with my oh-so-familiar *I don't get it* expression.

"We've got company," she offered.

"Company?"

She nodded her head toward the window behind us. "Someone left the gate open."

I turned and looked.

Residential Evil. Or maybe The Killing Fields under glass.

A half-dozen fidgety corpses had their faces pressed to the great pane of the den's picture window.

Ghastly. And smeary! It was going to take a whole lot of ammonia and elbow grease to get the glass clean again.

"So, like, *The Bride of Frankenstein*—" The Kid was saying, "—is this one more of a chick flick?"

"Depends on the chick," I said, getting up off the sofa. "Some critics think *BOF* is the greatest horror movie ever made. Forget state-of-the-art effects, there are delicious subtexts on multiple levels."

He nodded. "Ya can't beat the classics, Daddy-o."

"Maybe next week you should rent *Dracula*."

He shook his head. "Nah. I want documentaries, I'll watch PBS. Movie night's for escapism."

Okay.

I stretched. "Go ahead and start the next movie, I've got to go put some things away."

Deirdre started to challenge me. "I don't think that's such a good idea."

"The security staff is out and about and on high alert," I argued. "I'll be carrying and the Neighborhood Watch is all around. I'm not spending the rest of my life indoors like some hothouse flower!"

"I'll tag along," Lupé volunteered, "while he plays sheepherder of the damned."

Deirdre grumbled, I retrieved my Glock from the desk, and Lupé followed, grabbing a sack of consecrated salt as we headed for the back of the house.

I checked the extension cord as we went out the back door. Everything looked secure; the plug was still in the outlet. I saw a knot of corpses gathered in the flickering glow of the spare television down by the cemetery wall. Walking around to the side of the house, I moved toward the clump of cadavers who were bunched up outside the big window. "Boys? What seems to be the problem here?"

They turned at my voice and managed to look a little sheepish. Only a little, mind you: when one thinks of sheep, one envisions them with skin and body parts intact.

"TV broken," one of them mumbled.

I put my hands on my hips and gave him the Serious Parent look. "Now, Roger, the TV is on—I can see it from here. And everyone else is down by the wall, watching intently, so it can't be broken. The only reason to be up here, peeking in the window is to see what we're watching. Are you all Frankenstein fans?"

"Noooo," hissed another voice. "Ally McBeallll!"

That one caught me off guard. "You're *Ally McBeal* fans?"

A loud chorus of "No!"s and more than a few growls cleared the issue up immediately.

"I see. Okay. Well. Let's go back and I'll tell the girls that it's your turn after their show is over."

They shuffled their feet but no one moved forward. "FX all ni' marat'on," someone lisped.

Oh.

How was I supposed to rule a major enclave of vampires when I couldn't arbitrate the viewing habits of the dead in my own backyard?

"You know, I read about this in *TV Guide*," Lupé said. "The zombie episode is supposed to be on pretty soon."

The growling died down. The deceased and dissenting looked thoughtful. "Wort' a looh, Uh spose," one said through decaying lips.

"Golla be beher than Frankenstein," opined another who had lost his some time back.

"Too boring?" I asked, backing toward the cemetery.

They began to follow. "Too icky . . . gross . . . disgusting . . . scary . . ." were the various responses.

Norman summed it up: "Digging up dead bodies to cut up and use for spare parts—I almost spewed my maggots!"

"Um," I said, "yeah."

"*Ali MahBeel*'s gola be beher'n tha!"

"Ya know, if you squinch your eye sockets jus' right, she even looks a little dead . . . emaciated . . . you know . . . cadaverlike . . ."

We got them back through the gate and Lupé resealed the gaps in the salt lines. "I didn't know *Ally McBeal* had a zombie show," I murmured, as she finished up.

"I doubt that it does," she whispered back. "But a couple of episodes should be enough to either get them hooked or fleeing back into their graves."

I stepped back and stared at her. "No wonder I love you: beauty and brains!"

The closest corpse turned and flailed against the wall. "Brains! Want brains! Must have brains!"

"Shut up, Kenneth."

"Why do they do that?" Lupé asked as we walked back toward the house.

"Do what?"

"Want brains."

Zombies . . . George Romero called them blue collar monsters. I wondered what sort of stand-up routine Jeff Foxworthy would develop if he moved next door. *You might be a Revenant if . . .*

I shrugged. "They sort of remind me of the Scarecrow from *The Wizard of Oz*."

"But they don't want to *have* brains, they want to *eat* them."

"Only the ones that are really far gone. Kenneth was just joking, dear."

Her lips twitched but she didn't quite manage a smile.

"Look, I suspect it's kind of like the planaria . . ."

"The building where they project the stars and planet on the ceiling?"

I sighed. Maybe this was the wrong night after all. *The Bride of Frankenstein* was doubtless underway by now. The Kid would dispatch search parties if we didn't show up in the next few minutes. But I held Lupé's arm and steered her in a half circle, away from the back porch. "Walk with me," I said.

The slivered moon had disappeared behind a solid soup of clouds and the light from the television sets had diminished so we held hands and picked our way carefully in the dark as we moved toward the front of the house. Stopping outside the window to my study, I pointed at the giant aquarium that glowed like a pale emerald in the dim room. "See that purple sluglike critter crawling over the rocks in the corner?"

She slugged my arm in turn. "Sluglike critter? It's a sea slug, you chew toy! A nudibranch. I'm not a moron."

"Well, you're not a moron," I said, rubbing my arm, "because it does look like a nudibranch and most people wouldn't know a nudibranch from a nudist colony. But that thing is a member of the flatworm family, not a mollusk. More specifically it's a *Pseudoceros ferrugineus*."

"And you are telling me this because . . . ?"

"A number of years ago some behavioral scientists discovered that they could train their cousins, the planaria or flatworm, to avoid light sources by associating their exposure with electric shocks."

"Gee, kinda makes Pavlov seem like a real dog lover by comparison."

"Just wait. They then discovered that they could cut a flatworm in half and it would become two individual planaria. Well, they already knew that. But what they discovered was that both flatworms retained the same avoidance conditioning."

"Lovely."

"So, they said, if memory is not specifically confined to the planarian brain, let's see what happens if we grind up a trained worm and feed it to an untrained worm."

"Yuck," she said. "Who wrote the research grant? Dr. Hannibal Lecter?"

"The point is the untrained worms that ate the ground-up remains of the planaria that had been preconditioned, were conditioned at a far more accelerated rate than the untrained flatworms that were fed the placebo invertebrates. Something of the memories of one creature had been passed on to another through ingestion or digestion.

"And you're suggesting that some zombies are like these flatworms? They want . . . want . . ."

"Well," I said, steering her away from the window and on toward the front of the house, "if their minds and memories are nearly gone, I guess they'd be looking for some replacement parts. You know the old saying 'You are what you eat'?"

"That's it!" she said. "No more popcorn for me, tonight!"

Great. The rumble in the cellar had already dampened the mood, this conversation wasn't helping, and I still hadn't gotten around to telling her about the evening's earlier developments. She needed to know about my "funny valentine" and Dr. Pipt's psycho-spam and Theresa Kellerman's noggin-napping.

But I had even more important things to discuss and, in these particular matters, timing was everything.

"You've been a really good sport about all this," I began.

"About all what?"

I gestured at the dim glow of the TV through the picture window as we passed by. "Having company over on a regular basis. A bunch of dead busybodies in our backyard. The Kid . . ."

"Deirdre," she added.

I cleared my throat. "Uh, yes . . . Deirdre . . ."

"Chris," she said, her head down, her voice soft, her grip a little firmer than before, "I was an enforcer for Stefan Pagelovitch before I met you. This is a trip to Neverland—Michael Jackson excluded—compared to my time at the Seattle demesne. The dead—well—they're like unruly children sometimes—brain issues aside—but they trigger my maternal instincts the same way they appeal to your father complex."

"Father complex?"

"J.D. now, he's a bit of a challenge but he needs a Doman with patience and someone who will encourage his best instincts instead of aggravating his worst. He needs you."

"Uh . . . and you."

She sighed. "Yes. I know. But Deirdre . . ."

We stumbled around into the front yard and I led her up to the porch steps. We sat for a minute before she continued. "Deirdre would be a lot happier if I was out of the picture."

"She likes you," I argued. "You're her best friend."

"I'm the only other woman she gets to socialize with. I'm the only other woman who could possibly understand what she is going through. And I'm not sure I'm even qualified to say that."

"Her situation is complicated," I said.

"Her relationship with you certainly is."

I sighed. "All my relationships are complicated." I reached into my pocket and pulled out the ring before she could turn the conversation back to Deirdre. "That's why I would like to simplify ours." I sank down on one knee. "Will you marry me?"

Chapter Four

LUPÉ WENT very still.

Her eyes went to the ring in my hand, the tiny diamond barely visible in the dim fall of light through a break in the window curtains.

"It's my grandmother's ring. There's a storm brewing and I figure we can go shopping for your own ring tomorrow, but I didn't want to propose empty-handed and so—" Her eyes hadn't left the ring and, belatedly, I realized she was focusing on it to avoid looking at me. "If you need more time to think about it?"

She finally lifted her big, brown eyes and stared at me. A single tear slid down her cheek and her nostrils flared once. Twice.

"I think I love you . . ." she whispered finally.

I think I love you? I propose and the first words out of her mouth are the title of a bad David Cassidy song? This did not bode well.

" . . . and sometimes I think you love me . . ." she continued.

"*Some*times? You *think* I love you?"

"I mean love in the way that a man and a woman must love each other to make a life together last," she said quietly. "But I am not a woman like other women and you are not a man like other men."

"Chantal Saperstein said 'All marriages are mixed marriages.'"

"Our . . . situation . . . is complicated. As you said, all of our relationships are complicated. Your wife—"

"Ex-wife."

"You're not divorced."

"She's dead," I said flatly. "Till death do us part, remember?"

"Yet, she's still around."

"You don't believe that."

"It doesn't matter that I don't believe it if you do!" She shook her head. "But that's not the bigger issue . . ."

Bigger issue? Deirdre aside, I didn't think it got much bigger than the issue of Jenny—paranormal phenomenon *or* psychological defense mechanism.

"You are a Doman, now," she continued. "As such, you must build your power base and forge alliances by taking consorts. I know I am incapable of sharing you with another woman. And, as Doman of New York, you will need to take many consorts if you are to rule and survive."

"Consorts," I said. "Kurt didn't say anything about consorts."

"Every time he calls, he talks about forging alliances."

"Alliances, yes. I *get* 'alliances.' Nobody ever said anything about 'consorts.'"

"You've read *Dracula* by Bram Stoker?"

"Um, yes."

"So you should be familiar with the concept."

I recalled some passages concerning a trio of female vampires. "Um, the three—what did Stoker call them? Sisters? Brides? Of Dracula?"

She nodded. "They were consorts."

"So he had three."

"That Stoker knew of. And that was in Walachia. In New York he eventually had close to a hundred."

I whistled. "And that was before Viagra."

She almost smiled. "Even if I could be persuaded to share you, your consorts would not. Not with me. The wampyr and the lupin are not equals." She reached out and touched my face. "Remember how Dracula was ready to kill us when I shared my blood with you?"

I nodded and kissed her palm. "The Big Taboo. But others have done it, lycanthropes and wampyri. It's how one acquires the powers of a Doman. Wherever there is an enclave, at least one vampire has tasted lycanthrope blood. So even if it is a big secret around Coffin City, taboos can be broken."

She shook her head. "Taking the blood of my kind doesn't put *us* on equal footing. If you elevate me to consort status, you assault the nature of the thousand-year-old ties between my people and yours."

"They're not *my* people." I tapped my chest. "Human—or, at least, semi-human, remember? And I'm not elevating you to consort status; I'm asking you to be my wife!"

She smiled sadly. "They would kill me for my impertinence and kill you to make an example."

I shrugged. "They're already trying to kill me. Might as well give them a good reason." I took her hand and tried to slip the ring on her third finger. "Or give me a better reason to try to stay alive." Grandma was petite; I had to settle for placing it on Lupé's pinkie.

She stared at her hand as if it had suddenly acquired a malignant growth. "You are bound and determined to shake the Kingdom of the Night to its very foundations."

"That's my motto: shake, rattle, and roll. What's the good of someone heading the leadership of the largest vampire enclave in the world if you're not going to effect positive change?"

"You could abdicate and live a while longer."

We looked at each other. She knew better. It was like trying to retire from the Mafia. Dracula had tried to walk away and the new Doman had hunted him for decades. The ancient traditions of power and position upheld in the best Darwinian fashion: The king is dead; long live the king!

No, my best protection was holding on to power for as long as possible.

Which wouldn't be much longer if I didn't go back to New York and settle some things.

And might be much shorter if I did.

"Let's go back inside," she said.

Colin Clive as Henry (not Victor) Frankenstein was back in the lab against his better judgment, working with the next mad-scientist-in-waiting, a Leopold Stokowski clone named Dr. Pretorius.

"What kept you?" Deirdre asked as we tried to find a

comfortable spot without blocking the scene of Dr. P's collection of little people under a series of glass bell jars.

"We were busy—" I began.

"—getting engaged," Lupé finished, moving her left hand so that the diamond in the antique ring caught the best of the dim phosphorescence from the television screen.

The room was suddenly still. Dr. Pretorius broke the silence as he informed Dr. Frankenstein that "science, like love, has its little surprises."

J.D. overcame his surprise first: "Oh, man! That's the bomb, wolf lady! Congrats!"

Then Deirdre launched herself out of the beanbag with surprising speed. "Let me see!" she squealed with enthusiasm. It was the best response I might have hoped for— even if her excitement seemed a notch too high to be unforced.

"You are going to have to get it resized," she said as she took Lupé's hand in hers to admire the ring.

"It's a loaner. Chris is taking me shopping for the real thing tomorrow."

"Tomorrow? That's a little short notice for me to plan security. How about—oh. I see. The storm." Deirdre nodded as she considered the weather's relevancy. Since my condition precludes going out between sunrise and sunset—at least not without risking spontaneous combustion—shopping was generally limited to the Internet or the Home Shopping Channel.

Some guys might be clueless but I knew two things for sure. You don't pick out wedding rings without your affianced. And you don't do it online or over the phone.

Apparently I did not need to connect the dots for Deirdre. "I'll speak with Archie and Marvin," she said. And looked at me: "What time?"

I shrugged. "Let's make it midmorning. If anyone's watching the house, they won't be expecting me to stir forth until late in the day."

"That doesn't give you much time for sleep," The Kid pointed out.

"Aw," I said, "how can I sleep on one of the most important days of my life?"

"Afterlife," Jenny's ghost whispered.

I pointedly ignored her.

"But this isn't science!" Frankenstein bewailed, "It's more like black magic!"

"You think I'm mad," Pretorius answered. "Perhaps I am . . ." Further dialog was muffled by the rumble of distant thunder.

"Besides, we don't know how long the front will last. Make hay while the sun doesn't shine, I say."

The Kid hit pause and *The Bride of Frankenstein* stopped its timeless story, literally freezing into a timeless moment. "Then you'd better flop before you drop, Big Daddy. We'll watch The Courtship of Eddy's Munster another night."

Deirdre pulled out her cell phone, all business. "I've got security arrangements to make. Shall we plan for a departure around ten-hundred hours?"

I looked at Lupé.

Lupé looked at me. Nodded. "Let's go to bed," she said.

I looked toward the window. "We'll have to get the other TV in before it rains."

J.D. shooed us toward the stairs. "I'll handle it. No point in cuttin' 'em off too soon. 'Sides, I think the Ally McBeal zombie episode is on next."

I was brushing my teeth and noticing how long and sharp they were getting when I caught sight of someone standing behind me. I turned from the bathroom mirror and looked at my dead wife who was looking very substantial for a ghost.

More than substantial, she was pregnant!

"Sorry I can't come to the wedding, Chris, but, as you can see, I'm in 'the family way.'"

I stared at her bulging belly. "What?" I tried to ask but couldn't articulate the question. "How? Who?"

"There is no father, darling. Unless it's you. I mean, you were always like a father to Kirsten."

My dead daughter was suddenly there beside Jen, her seven-year-old tummy swollen to third-trimester proportions. "Look, Daddy; Mommy and I are going to have the same birthday!"

My wife nodded. "You can be father to us both."

Kirsten grinned. "Nicky says we're gonna be sisters!"

Jennifer shook her head with a smile. "No, dear, I believe Dr. Dick said that we are going to *have* sisters."

"I—I don't understand."

Jen turned to me and her smile turned wistful. "I can't be with you for a while. Having a body changes things. And I suspect you will have to do all the remembering for both of us—all three of us—until we are old enough to remember with you."

She started to fade.

"What about my brother, Mommy?" Kirsten grasped her hand and started to fade, too. "Will Daddy save him, too? Will he save all of us?"

"Daddy can't save everyone. No one can. Let's just hope he can save himself . . ."

They were gone.

Once again a great dark hole opened up inside my chest where my heart used to be.

I fell into its deep blackness.

The darkness was ripped apart by a great flash of light.

I sat up in bed as the thunder crashed and boomed and shook the house.

I got up and made my way to the bathroom by the intermittent strobes of lightning licking around the edges of the windows' blackout shades and heavy curtains. Despite their brevity, each flash was brighter than a second's worth of sunlight. I wondered if I might not be more likely to combust on a dark and stormy night than on a bright and sunny day.

By the time I reached the bathroom, my sleep-numbed eyes were somewhat acclimatized by the billion-watt arcs of light outside: the overhead bulb inside barely dazzled.

I looked in the mirror at my dim reflection. Concentrating, I tried to strengthen the image in the glass. According to folklore, a vampire casts neither shadow nor reflection because he doesn't possess a soul. According to Dr. Mooncloud there are a number of mutations engendered in the brain by the necrophagic virus and one of the side effects is the telepathic ability to consciously erase one's appearance from other people's minds. Unconsciously, this extends to reflections in mirrors and even affects my own perception of self in same.

Since you can't trust what you see—or don't see—I opened my mouth and felt around.

No.

No fangs.

My teeth remained dull and straight and even. The parts of me that were turning into a monster remained hidden.

I could go back to bed hoping that the next dream would be more pleasant and less confusing.

I flipped off the light and padded back into the bedroom, pausing in the doorway as the next big flash of lightning revealed that the bed was doubly empty. Well, was it a wonder that neither of us could sleep through the night when we had pretty much slept through the preceding day?

I had finally told Lupé about the heart in the study. I didn't mention Dr. Pipt or his visionary email. She was in an odd mood to begin with and the subject of bloody valentines didn't help. Our love-making was curiously perfunctory for an engagement celebration and we both lay awake for at least another hour before sleep came.

I walked through the house now on the pretext of checking doors and windows against the storm. Everyone else was in bed. The back door was unlocked and Lupé was gone.

I went back upstairs and crawled between the sheets. It was a long time before I could fall back to sleep.

Longer than that before Lupé returned.

☠ ☠ ☠

It was a dark and stormy day.

More perfect than I might have hoped for. Purple and green thunderheads rolled across the sky like massive dreadnoughts from an alien dimension. Even the continuous rumble of thunder sounded like the growling of cosmic engines. Occasional flashbulbs of lightning lit the clouds from within but it seemed safe to venture out, now. Even the rain had moved on, drawing shadowy curtains in the distant northeast.

It was 10:12 in the a.m. but dark enough to seem like twelve hours later as we walked into Thibodaux Jewelers. Archie and Marvin had security detail but, for once, I made them wait in the car.

It was a small stand-alone structure with single, front and back entrances. Both were easily watched from the Hummer, parked back from the side of the building. Deirdre wasn't happy about the breach of security protocol: she was still squawking at Marv over his cell phone as Lupé and I got out of the back seat. We walked around to the front entrance. Once again I was out in the open and unarmed but this time I had an excuse—you try walking into a jewelry store with a weapon, concealed or otherwise.

And besides, if you're not safe in a jewelry store where can you be?

I smiled for the first of three security cameras as the tinted glass door closed behind us, shutting out the artificial night outside and ushering us into artificial day.

According to Lupé, Deirdre wasn't really so *un*happy about us taking one vehicle instead of two and she wasn't all that upset about being stuck at the house instead of accompanying us in the field. Lupè believed that the real issue for Deirdre was *what* we were shopping, not *how* we were going about it.

For some reason, Lupé wasn't happy either.

Though you certainly couldn't tell it from the expression on her face as she was greeted by the manager. She looked like a kid in a candy store. Rock candy, that is. Big, sparkly rocks with expensive price tags.

I slipped into automatic pilot mode, shadowing my beloved as the manager conducted her on a "lifestyles of the rich and debt-ridden" tour of the upper-end merchandise. Oh well, what did I care? I had plenty of money thanks to Vlad Drakul. And, as the lately elevated Doman of New York, there were certain appearances that needed to be kept up. My only job this morning was to show up, make the appropriate cooing noises, and write the check when the dust settled.

I was halfway through the process when the shop door opened and two more customers entered the store.

Who knows what evil lurks in the hearts of men? These guys might.

They were dressed like Lamont Cranston's alter ego: dark trench coats with turned-up collars, wide-brimmed slouch hats pulled low over their faces, mufflers pulled up to their noses, gloves, firearms. The mufflers were a bit much, even for January: the weather outside was cool and damp, not cold and sleeting. The hats, however, saved the ensembles, making that whole '30s retro look mesh smooth and grooved, like the gears of a Jaguar XKR ZF-6. If they had opted for a pair of .45s, they could have been the penultimate poster boys for Pulp Frisson—The Kid would have thought he'd died and gone to heaven.

Unfortunately the Uzis upstaged the overall look, making the clothes more of a fashion faux pas.

Instinctively I closed the distance between Lupé and myself, moving to shield her from the intruders. The sales clerk looked up and raised a tray of rings for my inspection. "If you've got an alarm button under the counter," I told him softly, "you might want to push it now."

A single shot rang out and the security camera near the upper corner of the ceiling exploded in a spurt of sparks and a burp of smoke.

"If an alarm goes off," announced a gravelly voice, "someone dies."

One of the cloaked gunmen herded us to the far side of the showroom while the other fetched two more employees from the back rooms. It was professionally done. They secured the premises before turning their attention to the display cases of jewelry. One covered the five of us while the other shook trays of rings into a large satchel. No questions about opening a time-consuming safe in the back office, this was a speedy snatch-and-grab operation designed to get in and out in a minimal amount of time. Good news for us: in a few minutes they'd be on their way, we could hang around long enough to give our statements to the police and, if the cloud cover held for another hour or so, we could continue our little jungle-gem safari at the next jewelers down the road.

Lupé looked at me and mouthed something. What? Was she suggesting that we rush them? Wondering what had become of our security backup? I was wondering myself. The sound of the gunshot should have brought the boys running. Perhaps it was just as well it didn't.

Two humans with handguns against automatic weapons was a recipe for disaster.

Even unarmed, Lupé and I had a better chance. We were stronger, faster, and harder to kill with conventional weapons. For a moment I seriously considered making a grab for the nearest bandit.

But the moment passed quickly. Even if the odds were in our favor, there were innocent bystanders in the room who could easily be hurt or killed.

Or, more likely, serve as witnesses to the fact that we weren't quite human.

Nope, the logical course of action was to step back, let them do their thing, and then let the police do their thing. After which, we'd be free to do our thing.

Logic took a dive as the silent crook finished emptying the last of the display cases and his gravelly-voiced partner announced that they had decided to take a hostage with them for insurance. Funny, I hadn't heard them discuss the issue—maybe they were telepaths.

He pointed his Uzi at me. "You," he said, "you're coming with us."

I half-lowered my arms before his muzzle-enhanced sign language persuaded me to raise them again. "Robbery," I observed, "bad enough. Kidnapping? Far more serious crime. You might want to rethink—"

Lupé interrupted. "I'd make a better hostage."

"What?" There was an echo to my response as the goons with the guns chimed in.

"I'm a woman," she elaborated. "More emotional value as a hostage. The police are less likely to put my life at risk." She gestured without actually lowering her arms.

"I'm smaller, weaker, more easily controlled. It makes more sense to take me."

"What?" I said again. "No." I knew that she felt safe in going with them. Once they were away from witnesses, they'd get the chance to see how weak and easily controlled a werewolf was as a hostage.

But I wasn't about to let that happen. "She's lying," I argued. "She has a black belt in karate and a photographic memory. I'm the better hostage." At least I wouldn't get overconfident while in close proximity to a pair of Uzis.

"He's lying," she countered. "He's depressed and suicidal. He'll force you to shoot him so he can go out looking like a hero."

I glared at her. "She's lying!"

She glared back. "He's lying!"

"Shut up!"

"You shut up!"

"Both of you shut up!" gravel voice shouted. "We're taking Cséjthe."

We both shut up and stared at him. *How did he know my name?*

It was beginning to dawn on us that the robbery might not be the main plan but only a bit of misdirection for something else—something like a kidnapping or assassination. And, with the dawn, the front door opened and two black women entered the store.

They were a study in contrasts. The first woman was immense. She wore a tent of gold lamé overlaid with a pattern of flowers done in iridescent greens and blues. A matching turban wobbled atop her head which was framed by a pair of gold, tinkling wind chimes that dou-

bled as earrings. The outfit was so garish that I didn't recognize Mama Samm D'Arbonne until she spoke.

And almost not then.

"I'm just not comfortable walking around in public with
all this cash in my purse, Pearl," she said in a voice that
was louder than necessary for a personal conversation. "If
these gennelmens would just take my check, I wouldn't
have had to go to all this trouble of withdrawing the five
thousand dollars from my account and carrying it around
in public!" She patted a huge satchel of alligator patterned
leather that hung from her left shoulder. I think it was
supposed to be a purse.

"Pearl's" purse was much smaller—as was the woman,
herself. The white clutch purse complemented her white
top and green tailored skirt and matching jacket. "You
should just keep your mouth shut, Luella!" she answered.
Luella? "Nobody needs to know that you've got five thousand dollars in your handbag exceptin' you keep blabbin'
about it! Leastways we're here, now. No one's gonna reach
in and grab it now!"

I glanced at Lupé who looked back. "Pearl's" real name
was Olive Purdue, my former secretary and now partner
in my part-time detective agency, After Dark
Investigations. She worked the day shift, now, and should
have been in the office a half hour ago. Why she was here
and doing this "Pearl and Luella" act with Mama Samm
eluded me for the moment. Maybe I was back home in
bed and still dreaming.

Mama Samm seemed to notice us for the first time.
Her eyes grew wide and she screeched: "Oh my Jesus!
There's mens with guns! They're gonna rob me!"

As wide as her eyes were my eyes were probably wider: it was as if the serene and unflappable psychic's persona had been scooped out of her mammoth body and she was possessed by some evil spirit from the Amos 'n' Andy circle of Hell.

"Hush up, Luella!" Olive said. "I think they're here to rob the jewelry store. They're not interested in what's in your purse."

"Of course they're interested in what's in my purse, girlfriend! I got five grand in my purse! You think they gonna let me walk back outta here with all that money?"

"Not if you keep yakkin' 'bout it! So *shut up*, Luella!"

"Yes," said gravel voice, "shut up the both of you!"

The other cloaked robber, who had remained silent till now, leaned in and murmured something to his partner.

He shrugged. "Cash is cash," gravel voice answered. "You don't have to fence it. Besides, we're not bein' paid enough for this job anyway. Go ahead."

The silent partner strode over to "Luella" and yanked the bag out of her grasp. She tried to retrieve it but "Pearl" held her back. That was the most surreal part of this little impromptu sketch: the sight of Olive Purdue restraining a woman more than three times her body mass.

"Luella" started shrieking as the bandit stripped off a glove and plunged his hand into the cavernous depths of the leather shoulder bag.

"Shut! Up!" gravel voice demanded, waving his Uzi in a threatening manner.

Mama Samm shut up but the shrieking continued because the silent partner was no longer silent.

As he dropped the bag he appeared to sprout tentacles from the end of his arm. His hat flew off as he began to dance and whirl about. Now that I could get a good look at his face, it was obvious why he hadn't spoken before: robber number two was Archie, the other half of our security detail. His hand was obscured by a quartet of water moccasins who had sunk their fangs into his wrist, palm, and thumb.

Olive fumbled her clutch purse open and produced a .22 pistol. Mama Samm pulled two enormous hat pins from her turban and brandished them like meat skewers. "Drop the weapon!" they both shouted.

Gravel Voice was caught off guard but not ready to surrender. Perhaps he thought the Uzi negated our advantage in numbers. As he swung the barrel around to point at Olive, Lupé and I both launched ourselves with preternatural speed.

She hit him low and I hit him high. The Uzi went off as we all went down, throwing a spray of bullets around the room like a demented water sprinkler.

Somebody punched an alarm button.

We rolled once, twice, and a second and third burst was muffled by the press of our combined bodies. Either one of us would have taken him down and stopped it right then and there. Unfortunately there were three people in the mix making our efforts confused and uncoordinated.

And it was taking way too long. A white-hot poker stabbed me in the thigh as I rolled and then jabbed me again in the left buttock. Lupé cried out and I knew that our time was up. I grabbed his throat with my left hand

and squeezed. Correction: I suddenly *closed* my left hand.
Gravel Voice was human so he didn't discorporate and go
all dusty.

But he was still very dead.

I rolled off and tried to rest on my right side; the
wounds in my left leg and—ahem—hip made any other
position untenable for the moment. Lupé just huddled in
a ball.

"Honey?" I reached out to touch her and groaned with
the effort. She didn't move. Just a little quiver and an
abbreviated whine told me that she was still alive.

"Need some help here!" I yelled.

One of the store employees announced he was calling
911 as Mama Samm knelt between us. "Baby, are you
okay?"

"Fine as frog hair," I grunted. "See to Lupé!"

As Mama Samm turned to my fiancée I looked over at
Archie, who was down on his knees, now. Olive stood just
out of his reach, pointing her gun at his head but I don't
think he even noticed. The venomous water snakes were
still clamped to his hand and wrist and the flesh of his arm
was already starting to turn dark and swell.

Mama Samm spoke. "Miss Olive, you think you can
hold the fort a few minutes?"

"This bad boy ain't going nowhere!" she said with unaccustomed vehemence. "You okay, boss?"

"We're partners now, Olive. I'm not your boss."

"*You're* okay," I heard her mutter.

"Well, I'm gonna need some help getting Miss Lupé
out to the car," the huge fortune-teller announced. "And
we got to get moving."

"Shouldn't we wait for the ambulance?" I asked, trying to turn over and get to my hands and knees.

Mama Samm shook her head. "Uh-uh. I wouldn't send a *dog* to any hospitals 'round here."

There was nothing wrong with any of the nearby hospitals but I caught the nod of her turbaned head. I followed the motion to gaze at the nape of Lupé's neck: dark hair was starting to sprout along her spinal column. Pain and shock was triggering a lycanthropic transformation. We couldn't take her to any human hospital.

"I know someone," Mama Samm was saying. "Why don't you ask these fine gentlemen to help me get Lupé out to my car?"

I looked over at the frightened faces of the store's staff. "Them?"

"Well, honey," she said, "you sure as hell in no condition to carry her. Or yourself, I'm thinking. Besides, I think you need to be talking to them about what they'll be remembering afore we leave."

She had a point. When the cops arrived, they'd want to know where we went. The last thing we needed was an APB for two gunshot victims fleeing the scene of a crime.

"What about Olive?"

"It's okay, baby. She knows."

I felt dizzy. "She knows?"

Mama Samm nodded. "You need allies. She can't help you or protect herself if she remained in the dark."

"So you told her?"

"A couple of months back. She had her suspicions."

"And she knows everything?"

"Not everything. She doesn't know about Jamal."

"Shit." That was the one thing I'd rather that someone *else* would tell her.

I eased myself around and looked at the trio of white-faced humans behind the glass counter. "You three—

"—come here and *look into my eyes* . . ."

Chapter Five

WE LAY IN THE BACK of a 1956 Chevrolet Beauville 210 station wagon while Mama Samm drove—no pun intended—like a bat out of hell.

The adrenaline had worn off somewhere around the city limits. Pain was making a serious attempt to get my attention while shock kept wrapping a fuzzy blanket of disinterest around my mind. Somewhere in between, I felt bad about getting blood all over Mama Samm's car. Despite being a half century old, its two-tone, blue-and-white paint job gleamed like new and the face chrome and bumpers reflected the streetlights like funhouse mirrors. The interior, however, was going to need some serious detailing once we were patched up.

I wasn't supposed to worry about Lupé. Anything that didn't immediately kill her should have been a minor annoyance: her lycanthropy would regenerate any wound short of a stopped heart or missing head.

But I was growing more concerned as we sped away in

the storm's backwash and headed south toward thinning cloud cover. My wounds had stopped bleeding almost before I finished crawling across the tailgate to flop. Lupé was still unconscious, however, and her side wouldn't stop leaking blood. I raised her shirt and checked her wound for the tenth time in as many minutes. At least it was a clean "through and through," the bullet apparently entering just inside the iliac crest of her pelvis and exiting just above her hip. Lucky her, I still had two slugs in me: the fun would begin when they had to be dug back out.

"What were you and Olive doing at the jewelry store?" I called to the front seat. A little conversation beyond "Are we there, yet?" was a welcome distraction.

"Saving your ass," Mama Samm answered with a cackle. "But, from the looks of your pants, it done got shot anyway." She craned her head around. "How's Miss Lupé?"

"You're the fortune-teller," I snapped, "you tell me."

"I tried calling your house but you had already left. Couldn't get through to Miss Deirdre, she was on the other phone. Just had time to call Olive and load my purse."

"You're telling me *what*; you're not telling me *how*."

The original 235 inline six with its three-on-the-tree and automatic overdrive kept the ride smooth as silk while we were on the highway but now we were on a side road and headed in-country. The wagon's jewel-like suspension couldn't compensate for bad roads once we went rural.

"I had a dream last night . . ." she began.

I shivered—whether from fending off shock or the reminder of last night's dream encounter with Jenny and Kirsten, I couldn't say.

". . . I saw you at the jeweler's. You and Miss Lupé were trying on rings. A strange man came up and gave you both a pair of real nice ones. When you put yours on, the diamond turned dirty looking. I looked real close and saw it wasn't no diamond after all. It was a bloodstone!" She stopped as if that explained everything.

"So you called Olive instead of alerting the police?"

"You think the po-lice gonna put any stock in the dreams of an old, black fortune-teller?" I couldn't argue the point seeing as I wasn't much on sharing my own dreams these days.

"'Sides, when the papers tell how Miss Olive foiled a jewelry store holdup—her little .22 pistol against two automatic weapons—your detective business gonna make more money than you know what to do with!"

"I already have more money than I know what to do with. And I'm not really keen on a lot of publicity—" My cell phone warbled. "—even if the witnesses have no memories of our part in what happened." I pulled it out and flipped it open.

She chuckled. "You sure are getting good at that mind hypnotizing stuff."

I was. Getting the jewelry store staff to cooperate was easy. Getting them to forget our presence and part in all of this wasn't much harder. I've wondered how many unknowing victims have provided a midnight aperitif to a vampire only to have the memory erased upon their parting. I hadn't applied my own powers of mental domination to such effect—yet. I could tell, however, that I would be more than capable when my transformation to monster was complete.

"You might do well to remember that," I growled at her.

The levity was suddenly gone from her voice. As was the uncultured patois that she affected for the crackers. "And you might do well to remember to whom you are speaking before you go talking trash."

"Uh," I swallowed, "yes, ma'am." I activated the phone.

"Chris?" It was Deirdre.

"Yeah."

"Olive called. Are you all right?" There was a hint of panic and a taste of something more in her voice.

"Been better. But we're alive and Mama Samm is taking us somewhere to get all fixed up."

"How bad is it? Should I put in a call to Dr. Burton?"

I looked over at Lupé. Tufts of sable hair were erupting on her face and her nose seemed longer, broader, darker. She whimpered softly. "Yeah. Not a bad idea. Make the call." I remembered the jar on the mantel at home and Pipt's email with Theresa Kellerman's head serving as his sig file. "In fact, talk to Mooncloud, too. Tell 'em that one of them should make the trip out. Listen, this is not a good time—I'll call you back after we get to where we're going."

"Where *are* you going?"

I turned my head back toward the front seat. "Where are we going?"

"To see the Gator-man," was Mama Samm's cryptic reply.

"We're off to see the Gator-man," I repeated. "Don't ask me, I really don't know. I just know that we can't go to a hospital with Lupé getting all furry."

"I understand. What I don't understand is what happened. Olive said there was a robbery . . ."

"No. It was supposed to look like a robbery. It was either a hit or an abduction. They knew my name and seemed set on taking me with them."

"What do you mean?"

"Deirdre . . . Archie was one of the two guys."

I heard the catch in her voice. "And the other one?" she asked after a moment.

"Didn't recognize him. He seemed to be in charge. Archie followed his lead, deferred to him."

"It wasn't Marvin?"

I shook my head and hazily remembered that she couldn't see me as I had the video turned off. "No. I saw Marv on the way out. He was still sitting in the Hummer and he looked dead."

The car swerved but caught a bad pothole with its left rear tire and Lupé shrieked. The high keening sound cut me to the quick but at least she was awake now. "Chris?"

I eased back down next to her and gave her a little squeeze. "It's okay, baby. I'm here." I turned back to the phone. "Gotta go."

"Right." Her tone suggested that the remaining security personnel were in for a rough time of it. "Don't go all Jack Bauer on me, Chris; keep me in the loop."

"What happened?" Lupé asked groggily as I clicked off.

"You got shot, honey. You took a bullet in the side."

"It hurts."

"I know, baby. We're gonna get you fixed up real soon." I turned my head and yelled up to Mama Samm in the front seat. "How much longer?"

"Almost there . . ."

"You said that a half hour ago."

"I'm getting there as fast as I dare. A fast bumpy ride's bound to be worse than a slightly longer, smooth one. How you doing, Miss Lupé?"

She coughed and groaned. "Oh, it hurts!"

"I know, honey child. Try and be strong like Mister Chris there. He shot twice as much as you."

Lupé gripped my arm. "Oh, Chris! Are you all right?"

I gave her my best mock scowl. "If I wasn't, would she be doing her Aunt Jemima voice for us?"

For that comment she laid it on all the thicker. "He is grievously wounded. They done shot him in the *ass*!"

I grimaced and Lupé matched my expression as she started to laugh. "*Ah!* Ah. Oh God, oh Jesus, oh Mary and Joseph . . ."

I tried to reassure her. "I don't think it's that serious."

Her grip on my arm tightened painfully. "It *is* serious!"

"I'm sure it feels like it but I've seen worse and—"

"You don't understand," she growled. Her face began to stretch and elongate. "This isn't the first time that I've been shot. I've taken bullets before! Worse than this!" She began to pant. "It never hurt like this though!" Her voice grew harsh as her vocal chords reconfigured with her changing anatomy. "I think I'm dying!" She began to choke and I watched helplessly as she convulsed in a growing pool of her own blood. It was time to think of the unthinkable.

"Lupé, I'm going to give you some of my blood."

"No . . ."

"It will heal you. If you're dying, it can save you."

"No! It might change me . . ." She coughed again but seemed to master the spasms that wracked her body a moment before.

I almost pointed out how ridiculous it was for a shapeshifter to worry about something changing them. "Change you how?"

Her grin was tight and forced, almost like a death rictus. "That's just the problem. We don't know now, do we?"

"It helped Deirdre."

"Deirdre . . ." A slight growl thrummed in her throat. "She was a vampire. Now we don't know *what* she is. I'm a werewolf. We're different."

"*Were*-different?" I echoed, trying to coax a smile out of her.

She ignored the bait. "You shared your blood with her before you tasted demon's blood. We don't know how much more that has changed you since."

"It may not have changed me at all."

She gave me a look I could not interpret. "It changed you." She reached out and gave my hand a little squeeze. "Ouch." She released my fingers as if they had grown hot.

More importantly, it might change her. Since my blood had defanged Deirdre, Lupé seemed concerned that her lycanthropy might be compromised. What did that mean? Did my beloved really want to remain a monster? Enough to chance death to do so?

There was a break in the clouds as we came to a dirt road. I was unable to brace Lupé as we bounced between cavernous ruts: I was trying to dodge stray beams of sunlight that were piercing the windows on her side of the cargo area.

"Talk to me," she demanded, as the wagon bucked over twisted cypress roots and the smell of fetid water puffed through the moss-draped trees. "I need a little distraction right now!"

"You talk to me," I countered testily. Her color was better when she was riled. "Where did you go last night?"

"Out," she gasped. "For a run." She didn't mean jogging. "How could I sleep before the most important day of my life?" she asked.

I couldn't tell if she was sincere or mocking me.

"I thought the actual wedding ranked higher on the events list than the ritual 'shopping for the rings.'"

She shook her head and reached for my hand again. "The *asking* is the only thing that matters. You can bring the justice of the peace over to the house and we can say whatever words you want and have whatever rituals and symbols that please you." She flinched and dropped my hand. "It is the *asking* that matters."

"Okay. But none of this justice of the peace/small, private ceremony in the backyard crap. We're getting married in a church. With plenty of witnesses."

She shook her head. "I think I would prefer something private . . . intimate . . ."

"You want intimate or safe? If we're in a church, it grants us claims of Sanctuary and keeps the nasties away."

"Even if that were a hundred percent true—which it's not," she argued, "there's no point in tempting fate."

"Actually, there is." I had given this some thought. "If I am to be the Doman of New York, I cannot appear to be weak. I can't skulk around and hide away in the name of security. I have to go out and face my enemies and show the undecided that I'm not afraid of the opposition—whether it's political or homicidal."

"And look how well that turned out for an anonymous little shopping expedition," Mama Samm interjected from the front seat.

"It's important that we have as many witnesses as possible," I continued, ignoring her. "If I'm going to do any good in breaking this particular taboo, I have to do it right in their faces. A vampire marrying a werewolf! It can't be a matter of rumor or hearsay. It's important that I rub their faces in it!"

I expected a debate over defining myself as a vampire. I wasn't expecting the tide of anger that washed across her face. "What am I to you? Some sort of campaign stunt? A bureaucratic pawn?"

"Aw, you know that's not—"

"You're *politicizing* our wedding! *My* wedding! How *dare* you—"

"Baby," I pleaded, "I just want everyone to know that you're going to be my wife, not my consort."

"Hold on!" Mama Samm bellowed. "We're going off-road!"

I grabbed Lupé and held her against me, trying to cushion her with my body as we began bouncing over uneven ground. She shrieked and stiffened in my arms. Blessedly she fell unconscious for the last ten minutes of our bone-jarring journey.

"Don't tell me we're going to find a doctor here."

It looked like someone had tried to back an old

Airstream trailer into an ancient clapboard garage, angled it wrong, and ended up pushing both out onto a boat dock before the driver gave up and walked away. Circa 1964. Someone had then attempted to build on a couple of rooms and add windows. Maybe Bob Vila—if he had been extremely drunk.

"Better than a doctor," Mama Samm promised. "A *traiteur*."

I'd heard the word used before. It was Cajun for "treater" and meant a backwoods cross between a medicine man and a homeopath.

A little, round man emerged from the shack as big, round Mama Samm emerged from the car. His tanned and weathered face split into a dazzling smile, his pearly teeth as white as his wavy hair and bristle-brush moustache. "Sammathea! What brings you out to see the Gatorman on the heels of such a big blow, eh?"

"Trouble, *mon ami*," she answered, her accent adopting a Cajun flavor as effortlessly as it had the Bryn Mawr tone just fifteen minutes earlier. "I got two in the back that be needing doctoring."

He followed her around to the tailgate and lost his smile as he looked from me to Lupé. "That one don' seem so bad," he said. "Strange—but not bad. But ma petite lupin, she in a very bad way, her! Let's bring her inside."

The tailgate was lowered and I crawled out. Surprisingly, I could stand. More surprisingly, I could carry her into the shack unassisted. Lupé moaned and squirmed as I hefted her. "You be hurting her, you," the little Cajun said as I hurried out onto the dock.

"I'll slow down."

"Non. It is you," he said over his shoulder as he hurried ahead to open the door.

The interior was a neat, clean, organized contrast to the train-wreck appearance of the exterior. I followed the little man, who hurried ahead to the kitchen. By the time I arrived he had hurriedly wiped down a Formica-topped table and put down towels as a makeshift surgery. Mama Samm appeared as I laid Lupé down on the towels. "I have your bag," she told the Cajun, hefting an old leather satchel onto the counter by the sink.

"More towels in the drawers," he told her. "If you will sterilize the instruments . . ."

I interrupted. "What can I do?"

"You can sit down."

"Uh, well, actually . . . I can't."

His moustache twitched. "Hmmm. Well, try to find a comfortable position and give me some room here, you."

I ended up hunched over the stove while I watched him probe Lupé's wound. Twice he exited the kitchen, returning with small bundles of dried herbs and ancient glass bottles containing amber liquids in a variety of shades and viscosity. He irrigated the entry and exit points with multiple potions and she seemed to breathe easier. Still, his brow furrowed and he finally selected a long, thin knife from the tray of freshly sterilized implements.

"I am afraid I must retrench the bullet's path," he told us. "I can give her something for the pain but I may need you both to hold her still."

Whatever he gave her worked but she still stirred and moaned in her sleep as he probed her side with the long blade. More than once I asked him if he knew what he was doing. He answered only once, saying: "I done this before, me." My other questions were met with grunts of vague acknowledgment.

Reopening the wound should have intensified the bleeding but, curiously, the blade—which he frequently rinsed with a milky liquid—seemed to be cauterizing the flesh without heat. When he was done, he packed the openings with an herbal poultice and bandaged her tightly about the middle. "Carry her to the bedroom, you," he said, "then come back and get up on the table."

"I can wait."

"No you can't," he insisted. "It may be too late, already."

I lugged Lupé into the back room of the shack and laid her out on the neatly made bed. She struggled in her sleep and cried out before I could make her comfortable. Reluctantly, I left her there and returned for my appointment with the knife.

I reclined on my side while he probed the wound in my thigh. It should have hurt a lot. He used a sterilized buck knife to reopen the wound and then moved it around, deeper and deeper, probing for the bullet. Thankfully I remained numb from groin to knee but I found myself starting to sweat as he got closer to the femur.

He stopped before touching the bone. "It's gone," he said. "Roll over on your stomach."

"What do you mean 'it's gone'? There's no exit wound! Where could it have gone?"

"Roll over, you," he insisted. "Hurry!"

I rolled but I wasn't done with the subject. I opened my mouth to speak but found myself speechless as he jabbed the knife into my gluteus maximus. He exhibited none of the care or gentleness that he had shown before. The blade dug deep and he worked with a feverish speed that abrogated any thoughts of tender concern.

"Sammathea!" he cried. "Champagne!"

"Great," I muttered, "what are we toasting?"

"Second cabinet, third shelf," he added as Mama Samm tried to maneuver around us. "I need a lavage." In short order a bottle of unchilled champagne was poured over my butt while a surgical probe and a pair of tweezers dug deeper toward the seat of my problem.

Mama Samm's cell phone rang.

"Talk to me, girl," she said, picking up. "Mmhm. Good. Good. What did they say? That's good. Does Miss Deirdre know what to say? Okay. Sure. You tell her that Mr. Chris is gonna be okay and Miss Lupé is startin' to look better. Not until after the sun goes down . . ."

"Ah! I have him!" he announced at length. The tweezers were held before my face, holding a small bloody pellet of metal.

"We suspected as much when she wouldn't stop bleeding," Mama Samm said.

"That's not a bullet," I said. "That's a frickin' beebee." I may not have actually used the word "frickin'" as I was weary and angry and frightened for Lupé and coasting along the borders of shock. "An Uzi fires a nine-millimeter slug."

"This is all that is left," the old Cajun answered.

"I'll tell him," Mama Samm continued. "This takes the play to a whole new level. You need any help at your end? If you do, you talk to that Detective Murray and tell him

Mama Samm said for him to run interference. Okay. What? Well, tell her that Mister Chris will be calling her soon. I gots to go. Later."

"It's only a fragment," I insisted. "There's got to be more than that."

"Nothing big enough to pull out with tweezers," he said.

"It's not lead," Mama Samm chimed in as she folded her phone closed. "Olive say the police pried a slug out of the wall at the store. These bad boys, they be shootin' with *silver* bullets."

Lupé was very lucky. A head or heart shot—in fact any "killing shot" for a normal human being—would have been just as deadly to a lycanthrope where silver was involved. She had been doubly blessed in that the bullet had passed through her. Still, the wound had resisted healing until it was properly cleaned and the tainted tissue excised. A werewolf could sicken and die from a mere flesh wound if the bullet remained in the body long enough. Her poisoning was mild and her color already better by late afternoon. I pulled a chair up to her bedside and sat with her until her eyes fluttered open.

"How you feeling, babe?"

"Like Socrates after the hemlock." Her smile was wan but her warm, dark eyes were clearing. "How about you?"

"I'm embarrassed to say that I feel pretty damn good. Apparently vampires aren't allergic to silver."

Her brow furrowed. "Actually, they are." Her slight frown grew into a wide smile. "Which means that, whatever you are becoming, you are becoming something *else*."

I sat there, stunned. "Really? That's great . . . I think . . ."

She gazed up at me, her brow starting to wrinkle again. "You 'think'?"

"Well, it's good news—sure. But remember how everyone was hot to put me under the microscope when I first started changing? After we came up with an answer of sorts, things started to cool down . . ."

"You have," she said dryly, "a curious perspective on what 'cooling down' actually means."

"Look, I know this sounds a little like the glass is half empty in the face of good news—and maybe I am being a little jaundiced when this would appear to give me a little more of an edge—"

"Jaundiced. Now there's a nice turn of phrase."

"—as I head up to New York to face down the opposition. But if everyone starts thinking of me as a lab specimen instead of the new Doman of New York, there won't be a hole deep enough for me to hide in."

"Poor baby," she cooed. "You know, a private home ceremony with a justice of the peace would make things less complicated."

"What?"

"I'm just saying that, given this latest complication, it makes even more sense to go for a simple ceremony over some kind of social statement that's like to get both of us killed."

"Ah, the wedding," I grunted. "Look, you!" I grabbed her hands and squeezed them tightly as she tried to pull away. "I *love* you and I'm not ashamed to stand up and declare it before the rest of the world! Or underworld, for that matter!"

"Ow. Let go!"

"What about you? Are you ashamed of me?"

"Let *go* of me! You're hurting me!"

"I'm not letting go until you tell me what's really bugging you." The more she tried to escape my grasp the tighter I held her hands. "Is it a public ceremony that you object to? Or maybe you just don't want to marry me at all?"

"Ow! *Ow!* Chris, *please!*"

"Tell me."

"My family!"

"Your family?" Her brother Luis, the only family member I had ever met, was dead. "What about your family?"

"They are opposed!" she gasped. "They are very angry about us!"

I released her hands and she shook and then cradled them as if I had done her some injury. "I see. So . . . what are they going to do? Make a scene? Disown you?"

She shook her head and there were tears in her eyes.

"Hey . . . maybe it's time to take me home to meet your parents. I could—"

"They will kill you!"

That shut me up.

"And me," she added softly. "I have told them that I serve you as adjutant. They suspect but cannot prove that we are intimate. As long as there is no evidence . . ." Her voice trailed off and she looked away.

"They'll let sleeping dogs lie?"

Her head snapped back and she glared up at me. "We serve the wampyr—but we do not do so willingly! We submit to their rule and authority in a carefully defined relationship and there are carefully drawn boundaries for all of us! Remember how Dracula threatened you when he thought you might taste lupin blood? Well, The Pack would tear us both apart—and I am not indulging in hyperbole here—if they discover that we have become lovers!"

I didn't know what to say. "That's ridiculous," I finally sputtered.

She gave me the same look Jenny used to use on me. *Maybe a ceremony was overrated: it was like we were already married.*

"Okay, okay," I said, "there's been a lot of ridiculous stuff this past year, why should werewolf mating rituals be any more logical. But lots of people already know we're—we're—"

"Lovers?" She shook her head. "We don't have that many close acquaintances. Who really knows about us outside of our own household? Stefan, Kurt, Dr. Mooncloud. Vampires and humans, no lycanthropes. The wampyr have a different attitude toward sexual subjugation than The Pack. And they make allowances for your unique status. You are one of them and you have authority as Doman, now. They will keep secrets for you."

"But if I drag you into a public place for a public ceremony," I mused, "all bets are off and your family will go all wolf pack on us."

"Yes, Chris," she reached out and touched my hand. Withdrew hers again. "When I say family, I mean clan and pack. The lupin will rise up as a whole to destroy us."

"Well." I stood up. "At least I can see one advantage if I was crazy enough to keep insisting on a public ceremony."

"What's that?"

"We won't have all those thank you notes to write." I bent down and pressed my lips to her brow.

She screamed like a frightened child.

I jumped back and stared down in horror as blisters began to bubble across her forehead where I had kissed her.

"It's not just that your body has dissolved the silver in the bullets and deposited the molecules in your epidermal surfaces," Dr. Mooncloud was saying as she made a preliminary diagnosis from a thousand miles away. "There must be something in your unique metabolism, your body chemistry that is intensifying the effect. Perhaps converting it into some kind of modified silver nitrate."

"What are you saying?" I hate cell phones: technology's never-ending quest to miniaturize everything had reduced this year's models into flimsy little trinkets that seemed too far from the mouth if held to the ear. "That I'm transmuting those forty-seven A-g electrons into some kind of preternatural kryptonite?"

"I'll need to do a complete lab workup on you both," she said, sounding far more intrigued than sympathetic. "It's possible that her own wounds have made her hypersensitive to silver in general. More so than before she was shot."

"Doc, I gotta know how long this is going to last!"

"I'll have a better idea once I can examine you both in person. Gerald is packing equipment even as we speak."

"At least tell me that it's not permanent!"

"Chris, I just don't know. Is Suki there, yet?"

"What? No. Why would she be h—?"

"Pagelovitch said you were having security problems. Sounds like an understatement to me."

I felt the floor move beneath my feet. No one else seemed to be looking for the exits so I had to assume it was me.

"Chris, honey; you be all right, you?" Mama Samm seemed to be reaching toward me in slow motion.

"I—I don't feel so good," I said. Blood loss? Stress? Delayed shock? I was light-headed of a sudden.

"Excuse," said the Gator-man as he took Mama Samm's cell phone from my clumsy hand.

"You come here and sit down," the fortune-teller said as she patted the divan cushion beside her. "You about the color of dirty silver."

Perhaps it was a delayed reaction to the silver buildup in my own tissues. Perhaps I was the one who was poisoned, now. Dimly I heard the old Cajun speaking into the phone.

"The bullet miss all the organs, Doctor," he was saying, "but the poison in her system give her some kind of shock. I don't know if she going to lose the baby or no . . ."

A moment before, the divan seemed a mile away across the room. Now the cushions were rushing up at my face like an express train running on full throttle.

We collided as I entered a long, dark tunnel.

The road from Cancun to Chichen Itza was a turnpike. The toll booths were manned by armed soldiers giving the impression that they had emerged from the dense jungle on either side and were posing as civil servants until the tourists moved down the road to the next checkpoint. It was more comforting than menacing: the presence of military vehicles and modern firearms made us feel that civilization had finally gotten a toehold and we might actually reach our destination before the jungle closed in again.

It was our honeymoon—mine and Jenny's. Kirsten wasn't born yet; her fate and Jenny's were yet to be writ at the intersection of 103 and US 69 outside of Weir, Kansas, some nine years in the future.

We spent the late morning touring Chichen Viejo, the original city, with the House of the Deer, the Caracol, the Temple of the Reliefs, the Church, Akabdzib, the Nunnery, and the Plaza of the Nuns. Through the growing heat of the day we worked our way into the northern site, Chichen Nuevo, its opulent grandeur reflecting the later Toltec influence.

As we climbed the steps of the great pyramid, called the Castillo by some, the Temple of Kukulcan by others, Jenny turned to me and began a discourse on the mathematical genius of the Mayans. There were ninety-one steps to each side, she pointed out, making a total of three hundred and sixty-five—if you counted the top platform—equaling the number of days in the year. Halfway up, I felt as though I had already climbed all of them. There was more moisture on my epidermis than could be accounted for by my half-empty water bottle.

Jenny appeared cool and dry as she described the mathematics that went into its architecture so that, twice a year, at the spring and autumn equinoxes, the shadows would form a large serpent which would wind its way down the northern staircase.

I interrupted her as she enthused over the fact that this event had been going on for over twelve hundred years. "This is a dream," I asked, "isn't it?"

She stopped and looked at me as if seeing me for the very first time.

"You don't want to relive one of the happiest times in our lives?" Her smile was dazzling but her eyes were haunted.

"There were a lot of happy times, my love. Especially after Kirsten was born." I looked out over the grand vista that included the Ball Court Complex, the Platform of Venus, and the Plaza of the Columns. "But I assume that I've been brought back here for a reason. What am I supposed to see?"

"Can't a dream just be a dream?"

I shook my head. "Not mine. Not anymore."

She took my hand. "Come with me."

We drifted back down the stairs like ghosts in a dream. "Where are we going?" I asked as we almost—but didn't quite—touch down on the *sacbé* leading northwards.

"To the Well of Souls," she said. A cloud passed before the sun and I noticed that we were alone, now. The site was deserted; the tourists vanished like ghosts, themselves.

There were two cenotes, great water-filled sinkholes, on the Chichen Itza site. The Well of Sacrifice lay ahead of us, more than a hundred and ninety feet in diameter with a seventy-some-odd foot drop to the murky waters below. Behind us, the Cenote Xtoloc was smaller in size and lacked the lurid reputation of the larger well: it was the city's water supply, not the sacrificial pit where young girls were once sacrificed to Chac, Mayan Rain God and Cosmic Monster.

But Jenny's hand pulled me to the east and we drifted out of the ruins and into the jungle.

We floated through a sea of green. Time passed. Dreamtime minutes can be hours. Or hours, minutes. We stopped a short dreamtime later at a rough clearing where lush vegetation and ancient trees limned an opening barely fifty feet across. Any ruins accompanying it were well concealed by the jungle that crowded around the cenote's perimeter.

"Why are we here?" I asked slowly, the saliva in my mouth turning to molasses.

She took my hand and led me to the edge of the great hole and we stepped off into darkness.

The Ancient Americans believed that the Land of the Dead was accessed through these vertical portages into the earth. While some began their journey through the nine levels of the Mayan Underworld by leaping into the vast watery depths below, steps had been chiseled into the living limestone so that the priests might descend and then return to the sun-drenched lands above.

We picked our way down a curving staircase of narrow rock plaques, placing our feet carefully as the light dimmed and the stone surfaces became slick with moisture. The cenote opened out beneath the collapsed portion of the ceiling, a great subterranean vault spreading hundreds of feet to the south and the east. A series of fissures and tunnels in the northern and western walls channeled off into deeper, danker darknesses.

Where the cavern roof remained, scores of red limestone stalactites stabbed downward like rusty sacrificial knives. Here and there, great twisted ropes of wood dropped like an inverted forest from the great trees above: thirsty roots in search of secret waters. A dark lake spread below us. It glowed blue-green at its heart where beams of sunlight penetrated its mysterious surface from the opening above.

Down and down we went, passing petroglyphs of gods and skulls and monsters, pictographs of ancient sacrifices, and shards of broken pottery that predated Columbus. A path at the bottom led to an outcrop of rock that jutted up and over the water like the first half of a bridge that was never completed. Jenny led me up the slippery stone path until we stood near the lake's glowing heart.

"Look," she said.

A great crimson stalactite hung just inches above the water, looking like a single bloody fang. At its very tip a single droplet of mineral-charged water trembled, stretched, and finally leapt to its own oblivion in the murky waters.

"It's coming for you."

I turned to her. "What?"

"Don't look at me. Look down. Look deep."

I looked down. The opening above throttled the sunlight into a closely focused beam. A few feet beneath the glowing liquid turquoise was a dark, gray-green zone shading to black that had been dark from the dawn of time. "What am I looking for?"

"Camazotz."

I felt a giggle forming. "Camelot?"

"Cama*zotz*," she said sternly, "also called Zotz or

Zotzilaha Chimalman. Bat demon, god of darkness and caves, and tutelary deity of the Tzotzil Maya."

"Why am I looking for a Mayan bat-demon in an underground swimming pool when I should be having a pleasant dream about our honeymoon?"

"Because I am leaving you now to be reborn," she answered as the water at the edge of the light began to stir. "And he is on his way to find you."

Down below, in the bottomless depths of the dark zone, two pinpoints began to glow. Red specks became dots became marbles as the water began to churn. Crimson marbles became great fiery eyes that grew as the thing at the bottom of the lake came closer to the surface. Behind those eyes was a need and hunger beyond human measurement.

And those lamps of hell were focused on me.

I woke up screaming.

Chapter Six

BY THE TIME the arguments were over it was dark outside.

We didn't discuss her pregnancy, much less why she had hidden it from me—we both pretended that the topic hadn't been broached yet.

It was decided that Lupé would stay with the Gatorman for a regimen of rest and a profusion of infusions for a few days. My own fainting spell had passed. The dream or nightmare (or vision) had even energized me some.

At least I knew that I didn't want to close my eyes again any time soon.

Staying with Lupé, however, was out of the question.

The accommodations were such that two was well past "company" and three was something approaching standing room only. I was not only in the way; I couldn't even sit by the bed and hold her hand.

Even worse, I thought I saw relief flood Lupé's eyes as I took my leave.

As I handed my cell phone to the old Cajun at the front

door I noticed a series of ridges that marked the outside of his forearms like serrated rows of calluses. *The heartbreak of psoriasis? Or was "Gator-man" something more than a poacher's nickname?* I gave instructions that I was to be called at any time of the day or night if she so much as hiccupped. Then I reluctantly climbed into the station wagon and allowed Mama Samm to drive me home.

I tried to memorize the route on the way back but it was dark and I was still a little woozy. The smell of blood from the back didn't help. I was getting hungry again and not for a Quarter Pounder with Cheese.

Mama Samm kept up a steady stream of questions about my dreams of late, but I was distracted and surly. And I found myself focusing on the way her pulse visibly throbbed along the side of her throat. When the topic turned to who might be inclined to send me a message and say it with hearts instead of flowers, I tuned completely out. I dropped my chin to my chest and half-feigned sleep.

My mind was a roiling stew of emotions. Questions about Lupé's recovery, about her feelings for me, about her devotion to her furry heritage. And about her secret pregnancy.

The woman I was going to marry was carrying my child. A son. (What about my brother, Mommy . . .)

And she had not told me.

Couldn't she trust me?

Could I trust her?

Deirdre and J.D. met us at the garage on the far side of the river and helped me down to the dock and into the boat. I didn't need that much help but I couldn't be too careful around deep water, now. It seemed my swimming skills had all gone to hell since inheriting one-half of the supervirus *Vampirus horriblis*. There was a weighty reason that caused vampires to balk at crossing running water.

"How are we fixed for food?" I asked as they prepared to cast off.

"You kiddin'?" The Kid asked. "Didn't you get a gander at all the bags me and Lupé toted in last night?"

"What about blood?"

"Blood?"

"Yeah, blood, FangBob SquarePants. I had a couple of packets at the back of the fridge. Are they still there?"

"Were those your packets?" His feigned surprise was all the answer I needed.

"Yes and yes: *my* blood bank and *my* stash for when the Hunger comes back." I tossed my keys to him. "Make another trip. You know the code for the alarm; I'll edit the surveillance video tomorrow."

He took off with a long look over his shoulder. Some people lose their appetites when they're sick. Me? It usually means I'm overdue for a meal. Right now I felt about three days overdue. And probably looked it, judging from the look my Chief of Security was now giving me.

Deirdre wasn't inclined to wait while J.D. drove to the blood bank. She took me across the river, docked the boat, and followed behind my unsteady stumble up the stairs to the top of the bluff. Once inside the house, I headed for the kitchen while Deirdre picked up the phone and directed Clay—our sole surviving security guy—to take the boat back across the river and wait for Junior.

I checked the refrigerator and then set a pan of water on the stove. My instincts were good: The Kid had finished off my emergency stash. Normally this wouldn't be a problem. I could still tolerate solid food and stayed away from hemoglobin for weeks at a time.

Eventually, though, I always gave in.

Back in my college days I had tried out a theory that I could train my body to go without sleep by setting my alarm to go off five minutes earlier each morning. As you might suspect, I made do with less but never made do without. Sooner or later I always crashed and burned.

Trying to reprogram my partially transformed flesh to give up the red stuff was just about as effective as my youthful attempts to give up sleep. Except the crashing and burning was a lot uglier when the Hunger finally overrode the last dregs of my willpower.

I hoped J.D. wouldn't take too long.

There was no point in standing around and watching the water come to a boil. I turned the gas knob on the burner so that the ring of blue flame was more suggestion than actual fact and then limped upstairs to change clothes.

A quick rinse in the shower was all I had patience for, peeling off the bandages and examining the grayish skin marking bullet wounds that already looked two weeks healed. I toweled off and dressed without rebandaging: what would be the point? A gray pullover and pair of gray Dockers to match my mood. I slipped on a pair of Doc Martens and glanced in the mirror as I headed back toward the stairs. *Gude eevning, I am Count GAPula. I vant to suck* . . . Ah hell, I just suck and let's leave it at that.

I descended the stairs and wandered into the library, my mood still descending as I waited for my food to arrive.

The heart continued to beat in its low-tech aquarium.

My email folder contained nothing but ordinary spam.

I went to the shelves and pulled a dog-eared copy of *Popul Vuh*, the creation myths of the Quiché Maya. As I pulled the book toward me I noticed that my hands were only slightly trembling. I decided to sit down before I fell down.

By translation *Popul Vuh* means "Book of Written Leaves." I wondered if Walt Whitman cribbed the title for his own magnum opus a couple of millennia after the fact. I had thumbed through it only once since my honeymoon a decade ago—last year, in fact. That was when I had figured out that I desperately needed wisdom on that twilight territory between life and death. Since Amazon.com had yet to list *The Afterlife for Dummies*, I was reduced to scavenging texts containing theological theorizing or tomes with treatises on cultural myths and legends.

In either I found little but fable, poetry, and allegory. Maybe that was a good thing: according to most ancient cultures the "afterlife" was a pretty scary place. Modern religion cleaned a lot of this up but left the stink of disinfectant on their generic version of the afterlife. I found little to persuade or reassure me outside of a little sect that called itself the Community of Christ. Since I doubted this Camazotz was a congregant, I flipped through the *Popul Vuh* looking for a catchier catechism.

A big chunk of the creation myth of the highland Mayan culture involved the underground realm of Xibalbá, a charming underworld whose name translated as

"Place of Fear." There was this whole Akira Kurosawa plotline where hero twins Hun-Hunapú and Vukub-Hunapú were lured to the ninth level of Hell to play Mayan b-ball against a bunch of demons. The game was fixed (big duh!) and the twins were slaughtered by the underworld kings Hun-Camé and Vukub-Camé via a horde of their grotesque subjects.

Not to worry: everything turned out okay because the twins were avenged by Hun-Hunapú's sons Hunapú and Xbalanqué.

The enlightening thing about this little intergenerational revenge fable was that ole Hun didn't have any sons before he went to Hell and got killed. The boys, it seems, were posthumously conceived on Xquiq, a passing demon princess. Nice to know that sex doesn't end with death. . . .

Of course, it's whom you have the opportunity with that determines whether that's a good thing—or a very bad thing.

At least the boys inherited some advantages from their mother. When one of them was decapitated by Camazotz and his head was used as the ball in a hellish ballgame, he obtained a substitute head and the boys went on to take the field against all comers.

So, maybe all demons aren't bad, just as all humans aren't good. Perhaps this Xquiq was the prototypical demoness-with-a-heart-of-gold. She probably didn't have to be that much of a looker to catch the eye of a young dead hero in love.

Just consider the competition.

Each of the nine levels of Xibalbá had its own pantheon of demons and death-gods. There was Ah Puk, the death-god who usually showed up on temple walls in the form of a seated skeleton wielding a sacrificial knife. His one saving grace was that his name was easier to spell than Mictlantecuhtli, the Aztec death-god. Then there was Ixtab, the goddess of suicides, often depicted as a putrefying corpse dangling from a noose. And Kawil, Lord of Blood, who thought knives were for sissies and required those performing his blood offerings to do so by passing a spiked cord through their tongues or genitals. By comparison to these guys, even the bat-demon Camazotz, Lord of Caves and Darkness, was a charmer.

Still, I wasn't looking forward to making batboy's acquaintance—assuming you could put any faith in the prophetic powers of dreams. I certainly didn't. But then, a year or so ago, I didn't believe in vampires or were-wolves, either.

The question was, what *did* I believe in, these days?

As I flipped through the pages a makeshift bookmark fell out and into my lap. It was a strip of plastic wrapped cardstock. Pressed between the clear plastic and the off-white backing was an orange and black butterfly with brief white markings: a Monarch butterfly. The Aztecs believed that the spirits of dead children returned to the earth in its fairy-like form. I kept the bookmark to remind me that not all Mesoamerican tenets of faith fell into Clive Barker territory.

As I replaced the bookmark, a new sense of horror and despair overtook me. I sagged in my chair and let the book drop from my uncertain fingers.

"What is it? What's wrong?" Deirdre asked a little while later.

I looked up and finally focused on where she was standing in the doorway. "I just realized something," I said slowly.

"That you nearly died?" Count on Deirdre to be direct.

"No. That someone actually did die today."

"Several people died today. If they hadn't, you would have."

"I'm thinking about Marvin."

"What about him?" Her eyes narrowed. "He was your bodyguard. He was doing his job. And not doing it very well since it got him killed. He should have taken a bullet throwing himself in front of you, not sitting out in the parking lot like a clueless twit! So, if you're feeling guil—"

"I'm not feeling guilty."

"Good. Well. It's okay to feel sad. He was still a good guy and—"

"I don't feel sad."

She looked at me as if my head might start spinning at any moment. "What *do* you feel?"

"Nothing. I feel *nothing*. A man died in my employ and I haven't given him a second thought all day."

She walked toward me and, as I watched her hips draw an endless series of infinity symbols, I remembered a time when her physicality took my breath away, how her proximity gave rise to primitive responses.

"You've been shot. Your . . . fiancée has been shot. You've gone through a lot since you walked into Thibodaux's this morning. Is it any wonder you haven't had time to think about him?" She stopped a few feet away. "What? What are you looking at? Have I grown an extra head?"

I shook my head and looked down at the floor. "Maybe I've been too busy to think about him until now. But now I sit and have the time. And I still don't feel anything. I don't feel bad about him. I don't feel bad for his family. The only thing I *do* feel bad about is that I *don't* feel bad about his death!"

"He was a soldier, in a war—"

"Yeah," I said, "he was a soldier in my wee little army. Out to help me claim the Throne of Darkness so that I might rule the East Coast undead as a benevolent dictator and make the nights safer for humankind."

"Don't tell me you were expecting a bloodless coup?"

"Bloodless? No. But I wasn't expecting a heartless one, either."

"You love Lupé," she said. "Marv was just an employee."

"And what about you?" I asked, looking up.

"Me?" She appeared startled. "What about me?"

"Are you just another foot soldier in this war? What am I supposed to feel if you die, too?"

The question seemed to annoy her. "You tell me."

"You are a very beautiful woman—you know that."

She stared at me, her gaze weighing upon me with a palpable heaviness. "Didn't we have this conversation some time back?"

"A lifetime ago."

She nodded slowly. "It was another lifetime. I was still human and grieving for Damien."

"And Lupé was more monster than woman to me, then."

"Your point?"

I knew the point but I was having trouble finding the words. "The fact that I love Lupé hasn't changed the fact that my pulse quickens whenever you walk into the room. You are still the most beautiful woman I have ever known."

She stood very still, her breathing seemed to cease.

"I could desire you . . . while still desiring Lupé more."

"Torn between two lovers," she said, "feeling like a fool."

"Please. I'm trying to make a point."

"That looks aren't everything?"

"There's nothing in which you lack. Love is a chemist's nightmare."

She held up her hand. "Please. You don't have to pat me on the head and tell me that I'm as good as the next girl."

"Woman," I amended.

"Then treat me like one," she snapped. "I'm an adult, not an adolescent!"

"Okay then." I sat back in my chair and locked my gaze on hers. "I don't feel anything for you."

"You've made that point."

"No, I haven't. I—I've always felt *some*thing for you." I forced my eyes to stay on hers. "Even when it was nothing more than animal lust when I first met you."

"Really? Tell me more!"

"Shut up and pay attention. I'm telling you that I haven't always been sure of what I felt but I know that I've always felt something. Until now."

She stared back, wanting to ask the question.

"I don't know why," I answered. "I just know that when I go to the emotional cupboard now, the shelves are bare.

I don't feel friendship. I don't feel love. I don't feel loyalty or desire."

"Well, Mother Hubbard, how about animal lust?" she asked, her fingers straying to the front of her blouse.

My answer was lost as the house lights flashed and the doorbell began to chime.

"Upstairs!" she snapped as I came out of my chair.

I didn't argue. I ran up the stairs toward the second floor and headed for my bedroom.

The security system included pressure sensors imbedded in the boat dock and the stairs up the side of the bluff: someone or something had just set them off. It was too soon for J.D. to be returning from the blood bank and he would have keyed in the code to neutralize the alarm from the dock. I skidded to a stop and grabbed the Glock out of the shoulder holster hanging on the bedpost. I checked the magazine and slide-cocked it before turning back to the head of the stairs. The alarm stopped as I set my foot down on the top step.

"That you?" I called quietly.

"I killed the alarm, yes!" Deirdre stage-whispered back in the sudden silence. She crossed below me, now wearing her own shoulder rig and loading a shotgun with silver and phosphorus-laced shells. "Now stay where you are! Don't come down until I give you the all-clear!"

The porch light came on signifying someone had tripped the pressure sensors on the last three steps at the top of the bluff. I didn't trust motion detectors: infrared was unreliable when it came to undead bodies in motion.

Deirdre pumped a shell into the chamber and I put my foot down to the next stair. It creaked.

"Get back up there!" she hissed.

"You've got no backup," I whispered. "I'm not letting you face whatever's out there alone!"

"You get back upstairs and lock yourself in right now!"

"Or what?" I said, coming down another step.

"Or pray whatever's out there kills me because if it doesn't, I'm gonna seriously kick your ass after we're done!"

Defiantly, I put my foot down on the next stair tread. This time the creaking sound came from the front porch. Deirdre turned back to the front door, knelt, and raised her shotgun. I sat back on the stairs, leaned against the banister, and extended the Glock, bracing my right wrist with my left hand.

The doorbell chimed again, this time without the lights flashing.

"Who's there?" Deirdre called.

The reply was unintelligible from where I sat, muffled by the door. Deirdre jumped up and moved to the entryway. Now she was blocking my line of fire: I stood and tried to descend the stairs without squeaking like the Tin Man in *The Wizard of Oz*. The door slowly swung back revealing a five-foot silhouette on the doormat.

I stared hard, trying to peer into the human-shaped darkness, hoping to make out a face. Instead I clicked over into the infrared band. The body on the other side of the threshold was cold.

"Vampire!" I yelled, just as Deirdre did the big no-no.
She invited it in.

In it came.

I eased down the remaining stairs, tracking it over the notched sight of the Glock.

The creature looked strangely familiar. Hair as black as starlings' wings swept around her head to fall over her left shoulder. Her almond-shaped eyes were the color of mossed jade but her pupils were crimson, splitting those deep green orbs like a cat's. She wore a red silk pantsuit that looked more like Hugh Hefner's pajamas than public attire. Her crimson lips smiled, parting just enough to show the tip of a single sly fang.

"Hello, Christopher," she said coolly. "Is that a gun in your hand or are you happy to see me?"

Part of my mind was critiquing the mangled punch line so it took another second to recognize her. "Suki?"

She bowed Asian style. "At your service."

She had been my first babysitter when I arrived at Stefan Pagelovitch's demesne, long on questions and short on answers. For the most part I had amused her then. That was before I got her spine snapped in two and left her in the mental ward of a Kansas hospital.

"Stefan likes you. He says you remind him of when he was young and stupid. He felt that you were in need of additional security personnel." She looked around. "Speaking of which, where are your bodyguards?"

"Standing right here," Deirdre answered.

Suki sat on the sofa; I sat across from her on the edge of the love seat. Deirdre continued to stand despite repeated invitations to take a load off.

Suki looked at her appraisingly. "Hmm. Yes. I heard that you're supposed to be human, now. Nice gun."

"I may be less than vampire but I am more than human."

"I meant no disrespect. It is just a matter of power matching power." Suki turned back to me. "How many have you turned to your service?"

I looked at her. "Excuse me—what?"

"How many vampire servitors have you created to protect you?" I guess I was taking too long to answer: she turned to look at Deirdre and her eyes widened. "None? How many bodyguards do you have?"

Deirdre looked at me.

"No," Suki said, "the dead don't count. Neither does Lupé. Especially for the foreseeable future."

"Stop it," Deirdre said through clenched teeth.

"One?" Suki seemed as disconcerted as my Chief of Security. "Just one human left? And you sent him with the vampire to pick up food on the other side of the river?"

"Get. Out. Of. My. Head!" Deirdre grunted.

I reached out and put a hand on the Asian vampire's arm. "What are you doing?"

"Threat assessment."

"You want to assess some threats?" Deirdre snarled. "Read my mind now, bitch!"

"Ladies . . ." I tried.

"Look, I'm sorry if I'm not taking the time for niceties," Suki continued, "but I don't answer to either of you. My Doman has sent me here to do a job and I may just have a few moments more before I have to make a split-second decision about Chris's safety."

"And what if I just decide to dis-invite you across the threshold?" Deirdre asked.

"You won't do that."

"And why not?"

"Because I have brought you the head of Theresa Kellerman."

"What?"

Footsteps sounded on the front porch. The door opened and three men squeezed through the doorway. You wouldn't think "squeezed" was the operative descriptor as they entered one at a time but they were each that big. And scary-looking. Somewhere there were a lot of beautiful people because these guys had used up an entire gene pool's allotment of ugly chromosomes.

"This is Kyle, Lance, and Beau," Suki said. "Your new security team."

Deirdre gave them the eye. "How will I know that they'll carry out my orders?"

Two of them gave her the eye back. One of them gave me the eye.

"They won't," Suki answered. "They're my human servitors so they'll carry out my orders. You can coordinate your security arrangements through me."

"I think you mean that I will coordinate the security arrangements and you will pass along my orders to your subordinates."

Suki smiled at her. "Of course. That's what I meant to say."

"Um," I said, "back up a moment, here. You were saying something about Theresa Kellerman's head."

"And I'd like to know," Deirdre chimed in, "how you got across the river."

"I brought them," said an unfamiliar voice from the porch.

The front door swung open a little wider and Theresa Kellerman's head floated into the house.

It turned out to be an illusion: Theresa's "disembodied" head now had a body. A body that was almost invisible in the darkness of the doorway wrapped, as it was, from the neck down in black leather straps. Her outfit looked like Versace Goth Mummy couture. Her long, wavy dark hair had been bobbed and gelled giving her the appearance of something sleek and wet and waiting to return to the water.

Her voice was different—different body, different voice box. It was lower, giving her an air of gravitas in contrast to her girlish tone of three months before. Her eyes should have been the same but they were not. These eyes, though the same deep blue, had gazed upon alien landscapes, terror incognita, and seemed to glow with a spooky, inner light.

But she smiled as she shared the sofa and explained how Suki and her entourage had arrived just in time to catch a ride across the river on her boat.

"You have a boat?" Deirdre asked. As if Theresa having a boat was a bigger surprise than her turning up with a new body from the neck down.

"It's a rental. I have to have it back by morning."

"You've been busy," I told her. "The last time I saw you, you were occupying a box on an old man's lap."

"That was a couple of weeks ago. It takes time to encode the email. And we both wanted me to be able to follow up without a significant time lag."

I leaned forward, my elbows on my knees. "Which

makes a question of asking the next question. Do I ask about this Dr. Pipt first? Or start with what your 'follow up' is about? Or should I lead with the most obvious?"

"My body," she said. It wasn't a question for her.

"It isn't yours. You're taller now."

"A lot taller than two weeks ago."

"Ha," I said. "Ha." Somewhere way off in a distant corner of my brain, I made a mental note to tell The Kid to rent *Boxing Helena* on his next outing to Blockbusters.

"Dr. . . . Pipt . . . is a genius. He knows more about organ transplantation, genetics—"

"Disembodied, still-beating hearts?" Deirdre chimed in.

Theresa nodded. "He wanted to make sure that you understood the scope of his capabilities."

"So," Suki finally spoke up from the other end of the sofa, "this Pipt is not only a surgeon and geneticist, he's a necromancer, as well?"

Theresa shook her head. "Science, not magic."

"Nanotechnology."

Everyone turned to look at Deirdre.

"Well, that's what's keeping it going, isn't it?"

Theresa gave her an appraising look. "Yes. How did you know?"

She shrugged. "An educated guess. Human heart. Still beating. No sign of necrosis. The only scientific explanation? The tissue must be swarming with thousands of tiny nanobots, stimulating the sinoatrial node, feeding and repairing individual cells—"

"Millions, actually." Theresa seemed a little annoyed that the heart trick was so easily deconstructed. "Some of the nanomachines are replicators."

Suki stared at them both as if they had suddenly begun speaking in Farsi.

"Nanotechnology," I explained, "is a science utilizing microscopic machines."

"Just as the white and red blood cells in your body perform different tasks—feeding and oxygenating your tissues and organs, carrying off wastes, fighting off infections—nanobots perform a variety of tasks!" Theresa enthused. No one could enthuse like Theresa. I remembered how she had once enthused about the prospects of torturing her former boyfriend to death. "Each one is simple, rudimentary, microscopic. But, in vast numbers, they can repair damage from the cellular level on up, enhance biological performance, even tinker with genetic material at the RNA and DNA levels."

While she regaled us with descriptions of Dr. Pipt's laboratories and his recent breakthroughs in bioengineering, a half-dozen suitcases and a couple of trunks were carried in by Suki's human servitors.

"Um," I said as Theresa took a rare pause to catch her breath, "dawn is just a few hours away and we should probably arrange accommodations for our guests."

"I can't stay," Theresa said.

"We need to arrange quarters for Suki and . . ."

"Kyle, Lance, and Beau," Suki said hurriedly. I caught her look: she knew I was going to say: "Larry, Moe, and Curly."

I turned to Deirdre. "Go help them settle in."

She walked over to me, saying, "I'm your Chief of Security. I can't leave you alone with strangers."

"They're not exactly strangers."

She leaned over and whispered: "Theresa tried to kill you before she lost her head. And the last time you saw Suki, you left her in a hospital mental ward."

"Actually, I'm very grateful for that," Suki said. "He saved my life."

"How's the back?" I asked as Deirdre flushed to match her hair.

"Fine," the vampiress answered. "It only twinges if I go without feeding for a long time. But then, I never go without feeding for very long."

"I want you to stay out of my head," Deirdre fumed.

"I wasn't in your head, dear."

"It's true," Theresa said. "Your voice really does carry—even when you whisper."

Deirdre looked at me.

I showed her the Glock. "We'll be fine."

She straightened up. "I'll show them where to unpack."

"Show Suki, too."

The Asian vampiress looked at me. "One of us should stay with you at all times."

I thought better of saying, "The shower is going to get awfully crowded," but it was already out of my mouth before I did. I avoided looking at Deirdre.

"I'll be right back," Suki said pointedly as she got to her feet. "I wouldn't want to miss any juicy details."

As Pagelovitch's enforcer and her entourage trailed after Deirdre on a caravan to the carriage house, I turned back to Theresa. "So. You can't stay?"

She shook her head and unclipped a black leather pouch from her black leather belt. "I must leave within the hour."

"Well, as flattering as it might seem, I doubt that you went to all the trouble to rent a boat and drop by in the middle of the night just to say howdy and catch up on old times."

"Yes. I wish I had more time. I could spend the next week apologizing to you for my behavior before we . . . um . . . parted." She got up and came over to sit next to me on the love seat.

Immediately I was enveloped in a cloud of perfume, so thick and cloying that I almost gagged. It would have overwhelmed anyone with a normal sense of smell. The barrage on my enhanced olfactory receptors was out of the comfort zone and moving into painful territory.

"Okay," I said as tears began to gather at the corners of my eyes, "but what do you really want?"

She looked away. "I . . . that is . . ."

"Just spit it out, kiddo; you've got to tell me sooner or later."

She stared down at her lap. The zipper on the leather pouch was halfway parted and something sharp and silver gleamed within.

"I need your blood," she whispered.

Chapter Seven

"THERE'S AN OLD SPANISH proverb that says: 'an ounce of blood is worth a pound of friendship.'"

"And an old Italian proverb," Theresa retorted, "says: 'blood alone moves the wheels of history.'"

I shook my head. "You don't strengthen your case by quoting Benito Mussolini."

"But think of all the good he could do with it!"

"Mussolini?"

"Dr. Pipt!" She got up and wandered around the couch. "The man is a genius! The advances he's made in genetics, cloning, nanobiotics—"

"It is a very impressive resume," I said, "but it also underlines the inherent dangers of turning over something that could be so potently misused and exploited. I don't know this Dr. Pipt well enough to trust him with my genetic material."

"He's a good man!"

"I can understand your enthusiasm; he gave you a body.

137

But I've got to wonder: whose body? And how did he obtain it? All I know about this guy is, he's stolen your—er—head from the people I had entrusted it to—"

"For the right reasons!"

"If it's so obvious that he was doing the right thing, why didn't he ask? If he's such a humanitarian, why isn't he sharing his medical breakthroughs with the rest of the world? And I confess to certain qualms about handing over tissue to a man who gets his jollies leaving disembodied hearts on other people's doorsteps."

"Well, if you would come with me, I could introduce him to you. You could get to know him. Decide for yourself."

I got up from the love seat. "I would love to meet this guy-whose-name-sounds-oh-so-familiar-but-I-just-can't-seem-to-place-it. But not right now. I've got major business brewing in New York this week. And I'm getting married—"

"*Married?*"

"You seem surprised."

She waved her hand dismissively, all nonchalance now. "Just that there's an old adage: 'Why buy the cow if you can get the milk for free?'"

I felt my eyes narrow. "I'm not sure I like an analogy that compares my fiancée to a cow."

"Or, for that matter," she said, ignoring my response, "why settle for milk when you can have cream?"

"Cream?"

"*Whipped* cream . . ." She licked her lips.

I was torn between the urge to scowl and to outright laugh in her face. "Look, the point—which we are rapidly digressing from—is that I am very busy right now. Under the circumstances, I'd prefer to get this Pipt's address and go visit him on my own terms, once things are all quiet on the eastern front."

She turned and her face twisted into a parody of a smile. "I can't wait that long."

"*Who* can't wait?"

"He's getting really old. His life may be measured in months or even weeks. None of us expect him to see next Christmas. He needs your blood!"

I stared at her. Theresa Kellerman had evinced the qualities of a true sociopath on our last encounter but she wasn't that good a liar. And she knew it.

"All right," she said after a moment and tugged at her sleeve as she walked back toward me. She stripped the glove from her left arm, exposing her hand and wrist. She held it before my face and wiggled her fingers. "This is why *I* can't wait."

Her skin was mottled and discolored, the fingers bruised and swollen. Then I caught a whiff of what the heavy perfume had been trying to mask.

The stink of putrefaction.

"Gangrene?" I asked.

She snorted. "No. Or maybe yes. I always thought gangrene was the process of death in living tissue. If a limb is already dead . . ." She shrugged.

"But a transplant—"

"Do you mean from a living donor?" She smiled a ghastly smile. "My dear Christopher, I thought you would be more squeamish about the medical ethics involved. Besides, my flesh from the neck up remained well preserved *without* the assistance of the good doctor's nanobots. It seemed logical that the transplantation would work well with a million tiny machines working day and night to keep my tissues oxygenated and under constant repair."

She peeled off the other glove with greater difficulty; the fingers of her left hand were noticeably clumsy. Her right hand was black—not with advanced necrosis but with the pigmentation that denoted a Negroid donor. "This arm was harvested more quickly and attached more recently. It will last longer but, eventually, it will need to be replaced, too." She ran those dark fingers over the ridges of the even darker straps girdling her torso. "If we had time I could show you a woman who epitomizes the melting-pot concept of America. The stitchwork is very fine; nothing like those old black-and-white horror movies on the late show."

"My blood," I said. And stopped. I didn't know what to say. Or, rather, I couldn't quite figure out *how* to say it.

"It brought me back from the dead, the first time. Kept me alive from the neck up, upon the second. I believe it could keep my body from rotting under me and sending me back to the operating room again and again and *again and*—"

Deirdre walked back into the living room and Theresa immediately composed herself. "Did I miss something?"

Theresa turned away and pulled her gloves back on. "I have to be going. Will you spare a little for my sake? Or should I go back to Pipt and see if a *living* transplant works a lot better?"

I ignored the implied threat. "I could give you a transfusion right here and now. No need to go back home and do it."

She shook her head but kept her back to us. "Not now. Not like this." Her voice was unsteady. "My body isn't quite . . . right. At the moment. I wouldn't want to 'preserve' it in its current state."

Little alarm bells went off in the back of my mind but they became distant as she turned and smiled. "I'll have to come back, then," she said as if finding new resolve. "Or hold out for a few more weeks until you can come and visit us on terms that you are comfortable with."

"Theresa, I am sorry—"

Her smile grew in intensity. "How quickly you've forgotten, Christopher. Call me 'T.'"

"I wish—"

"I do have to go, now. I must return the boat, check in at the airport, and return the rental car."

I frowned. "There are no commercial flights out until six a.m."

"Private jet. Will you walk me to the boat? You could at least do that. For old times."

I wasn't sure what old times she was referring to but I nodded.

"We'll both walk you," Deirdre said.

"There's no need to go to all the trouble."

"Don't worry, honey. As long as Chris is armed, I'll hang back at a discreet distance. You can whisper all the endearments you like as long as I can keep him in a fifteen-foot line of sight."

Theresa looked back at me. "I must say, Chris, your

fiancée is either very open-minded or very secure in your relationship."

"Uh, Deirdre is not my fiancée."

Theresa's eyes widened. She looked over at my Security Chief. She looked back at me. "Really? That's . . . interesting . . ."

"Isn't it?" Deirdre opined. She turned to me. "Check your clip."

I pulled the Glock from my shoulder holster. "How many times do I have to tell you, it's not a clip, it's a magazine. Clips are loads for the long bores."

"Long bores, huh? Well, that would be you."

I ignored that but ejected and reinserted the ammo magazine so she wouldn't keep on. Deirdre picked up her shotgun as we headed out the door.

Outside, the air smelled fresh and clean, washed clear by the showers of the morning before. The combined stench of T's perfume and decay evaporated but I felt a shiver as her black-clad body disappeared in the darkness, leaving her head to seemingly float through the night like a glimmering apparition.

"So, who is the lucky lady?" Theresa asked over her invisible shoulder.

"How about an exchange of information? I'll give you a name if you give me an address."

In spite of my attempts to match her stride, she still managed to walk just ahead of me. "I'm sure the doctor will send you directions shortly."

"Tell him to send it snail mail; I seem to be having trouble with my ISP." We reached the end of the front lawn and she started down the stairs.

I hurried to catch up. One flight down she slowed and leaned back against me as I matched her pace. "Are you sure there's nothing I can do to persuade you to come with me?" she murmured suggestively.

Maybe her brain had starved for oxygen: that approach hadn't worked back when she still had her original body. And, while I might confess to one or two mild kinks in the boudoir, borrowed, putrefying flesh just sort of kills my amorous inclinations.

"The steps are kind of slippery with the night dew," Deirdre called down. "You might want to use the handrail."

Theresa took the hint and hurried down the stairs. Mostly to annoy my Chief of Security, I hurried after her.

The boat moored next to the dock was larger than I expected, certainly larger than a lone individual required for crossing the river for a hasty visit. Suki and her entourage had been lucky: there was plenty of space aboard for them and room to spare, as well. The craft was twin-hulled for stability and that gave her the added advantage of a shallow draft, allowing her to berth so close to the river's bank. A tarp covered a pile of something amidships and I remembered our visitors' luggage. It looked like Suki and Co. had left some of their gear behind. Which meant Deirdre and I would probably have to hump it all up the stairs if Theresa was in as big of a hurry to depart as she claimed.

The problem was the tarp covered a *big* pile.

Worse, the pile was getting bigger.

The tarp rose into the air until it was as tall as a man standing erect.

And it didn't stop there!

"Chris!" Deirdre bellowed. "Get back!"

Like to where I once belonged and you can call me Jojo: I moonwalked back up three steps as the tarp fell away and I looked up at a vaguely man-shaped silhouette. Imagine Arnold Schwarzenegger and Sylvester Stallone's love child, bottle-fed on steroids and beaten daily with an ugly stick for thirty-some-odd years . . .

This thing might have been his scarier, older brother.

"Fall back to the house and I'll cover you!"

"Nothin' doin', Red," I growled as I squeezed past her and grabbed her belt from behind. "We're gonna run this like a three-legged race!"

She twisted and shoved me up to the top of the first landing. "Then don't slow me down! Run!"

We ran but I couldn't keep from looking back. As it stepped over the side of the boat, the dock settled low in the water as if the creature weighed a ton.

"What the hell is that?" I asked as we turned onto the second landing and started up the final flight of stairs.

"It came here on that psychopathic bitch's boat," Deirdre grunted at my hip. "She kept it hidden until she could lure you down to the dock. That means it's something very bad!"

"That's it," I puffed, "she's officially off the guest list for the wedding."

The thing was on the stairs now, bounding up toward us, taking three steps at a time. The wooden treads cracked like gunfire beneath its ponderous feet.

I pulled the Glock from my shoulder holster and fired a couple of rounds into the air.

"What are you doing? It's behind us, not above us!"

"Thought I'd let Suki know company was coming." We reached the top and nearly stumbled making the transition to softer ground. "Besides, shooting it might make it mad."

"Let's test that theory." She turned, shoving me behind her, and pumped a shell into the chamber. "Stop or I'll shoot!" she bellowed as the thing reached the top of the stairs.

The creature stopped and you could see the fear reflected in its eyes—the fear on our faces, that is. It wasn't hesitating; it was merely posing for effect, giving us a chance to really see what we were up against.

Mary Shelley's description of the creature in her magnum opus remarked upon "its gigantic stature, and the deformity of its aspect, more hideous than belongs to humanity . . . the wretch, the filthy daemon, to whom I (Victor Frankenstein) had given life."

This thing was bigger and uglier. It wore clothing of sorts, pants and a shirt of some gray canvas material. Its color and the creature's misshapen form were such as to make it impossible to discern where one left off and the other began.

Then it opened its mouth and displayed a pair of three-and-a-half-inch fangs.

"Holy shit!" I cried. "Frankenstein meets Dracula!"

Deirdre discharged the shotgun and the phosphorus load dazzled us with its actinic, bright flash. As my eyes recovered I could see patches of the thing's bare flesh where the ragged shirt had burned away to reveal a crazy quilt of stitch lines and multihued patches of skin.

It casually swatted at peppered patches of smoldering hide as if the fiery pellets were mosquitolike annoyances.

She jacked another shell into the breech but the monster was upon her in two quick bounds and closed its massive hands around the smoking barrel. I saw the muscles bunch in her arms as she tried to twist the weapon out of its gray-green grasp.

"Guess . . . what?" it intoned in a deep funereal voice.

"Uh," she said. "Hulk smash?"

It shook its great, blocky head. "Hulk . . . splash!" And flicked the shotgun to the side so fast that Deirdre didn't have time to let go. She was suddenly airborne and disappeared over the edge of the bluff before she could even scream.

"Crap!" I said, hoping that *saying* the word would keep me from *doing* it. I turned and ran for the house as fast as I could.

It *let* me get there first.

I slammed the door behind me, turned the bolt and knob locks, and slid the restraint chain into position with a fumbled flourish. Technically, it was all unnecessary as vampires cannot cross a private threshold without an invitation—even if the door is wide open. But I wasn't thinking rationally. Something that big and that hideous was bad enough. The fact that it possessed a quick wit and matching reflexes suggested that it was even more dangerous than it looked.

Maybe it was pen pals with Madame LeClaire, as well.

I closed my eyes and tried to think past my panic: Deirdre was still out there and, even if she survived the fall with minor injuries, the thing was still between her and sanctuary. How could I help her? "I . . . hate . . . monsters," I sighed.

"Well, you're not always so lovable, yourself," Suki said from behind me.

I opened my eyes and looked over my shoulder. She was standing in the doorway wearing an abbreviated silk robe. Her hair was damp and she was barefoot.

"I took a quick shower," she said in answer to the question in my eyes. "I thought I heard some kind of racket. Where's Deirdre?"

"In the river, I hope. Where's your security goon squad?"

As if in answer to my question, Lance came hurtling through the glass window adjacent to the front door like—well—a lance.

Suki's face changed.

I had seen her in inhuman form before, but only as a cat. Some Japanese vampires can manifest in feline form, the extra tail being the one characteristic that tends to separate them from the rest of the breeds. But this was different. Asian vampires have a more demonic aspect in their arousal state. Her face contorted into something resembling an ancient ceremonial mask with teeth and tusks and eyes that glowed like fanned embers. Her fingernails grew into curved talons and her robe parted to reveal a Picasso-like distortion of the human form.

"Who dares?" she roared in a voice that was suddenly an octave below my own. "Who attacks my human servant?"

I was trying to think of an abbreviated response when the other nightmare voice chuckled just outside the door. "Little pig, little pig, let me in . . ." it singsonged.

Beau walked into the room wearing a shoulder rig with a handgun that would've made Detective Harry Callahan envious. "What's going on?" he asked.

"Disney's Fangtasia," I wheezed. "And you're gonna need a bigger gun."

"How many?" Suki growled.

"Uh, one." I didn't count Theresa. Hell, the thing out there could have brought a pack of rabid Dobermans and I wouldn't have counted them, either.

"Then why are we standing here?" She ran across the room and leaped through the broken window.

"Save some for me!" Beau yelled as he made a detour to the door in order to follow. He should have had his weapon out before he opened the door. That way he might have been ready when the gigantic arm with camo-colored skin reached in and the huge gray-green hand closed around his face. Then again maybe nothing would have made him ready enough: the hand twitched and there was an audible crunch as Beau's skull imploded. As he dropped, I pointed the Glock at the mismatched mass in the doorway and emptied the magazine.

It must have done some damage. The creature bellowed and hunkered down, turning back to peer in at me as the hammer repeatedly clicked on the empty chamber. Then a guttural but ululating battle cry erupted behind it—someone had been watching way too much Xena. The thing turned around and there was a wet smacking sound that cut the cry off in mid yi-yi-yi.

There was a serious weapons locker in the basement with a bazooka, rocket launcher, and a couple of heavy-caliber machine guns. I was turning in that direction when the monster turned back and began squeezing through the open door.

"Hey," I said, "you can't do that!"

"I can't?" it purred. Purred like a lion, that is.

"I didn't invite you in!"

"File a claim with the grievance committee." It was taking some effort: seven-foot doors do not easily accommodate nine-foot monsters. Still, it would be on top of me before I could reach the basement stairs.

I made it as far as the den, picked up an end table and tore off a sturdy wooden leg. I turned as it crouched to work its way through the interior doorway. As the one arm was momentarily positioned behind him to push against the frame, I darted forward and drove the splintered end of my makeshift stake into the center of its massive chest with all the preternatural strength I could muster.

It should have pulped the creature's heart. Instead, there was a muffled "clank" and the chair leg rebounded in my grasp. The monster paused and waggled a finger at me as if to say "naughty, naughty." I glimpsed the glint of metal through the ruined patch of flesh in the middle of its chest.

There was no way I could get to a weapons locker in time, unlock it, and load something that had a prayer of stopping this thing. If I lured it out and into the cemetery it would only make a puree of The Neighbors. I could blow out the pilot-light in the stove, turn up the gas, let it build up, and blow us all to kingdom come—if the monster was willing to wait around for a half-hour.

Indecision had paralyzed me and now the thing was through the doorway and reaching for me with impossibly long arms. I leaned back and it staggered on its next step forward. A slimy beige band encircled its neck and it grew a second, smaller head beside its own: Deirdre's. Her face and hair were spattered with river mud and a steady trickle of brackish water dribbled behind the monster's massive legs as though her arrival had rendered him suddenly incontinent.

I grinned through my terror. "What kept you?"

"What do you mean, what kept me?" she gritted. "Who invited it in?"

The thing sniffed. "Ah." It grinned. "Smells like team spirit . . ."

Deirdre moved higher on the creature's back and her other arm came up, a hunting knife in her hand. Before I could open my mouth to warn her, she leaned across its huge shoulder and plunged the knife into its chest.

The blade snapped off and dropped to the floor.

"Now that's interesting," she said—just before our Goliath threw himself back against the interior wall. Oak planks covered with plaster snapped like a string of fire-crackers and, as it leaned forward, I could see Deirdre was embedded in the wall, pushed halfway through the other side.

I didn't call to her, asking if she was okay. If I couldn't find a way to stop this thing in the next few minutes, none of us were ever going to be okay again. I turned and ran for the library.

Kyle was coming toward me from my study, a pair of automatic weapons in his clenched hands. "Down!" he shouted, and I dropped into a home plate slide across the hardwood floor as the Uzis made a thunderous, tearing sound.

He stepped past me as he emptied his magazines and I scrambled on into the next room. I had no faith that bullets or even grenades could stop our fanged juggernaut. *Think!* my brain screamed as my gaze darted around the room. *How do you stop a two-legged freight train?* The bookshelves mocked me. I checked the desk. Letter opener? Scissors? That was it: if I could just get the thing to run through the house with a pair of scissors . . .

The fireplace was cold: not even a winking ember much less a burning brand to wave in its face. I reached for the heavy iron poker just as the Uzis fell silent and Kyle screamed. It was a short scream, terminated by a sickening crunch. I looked back through the doorway just in time to see his bloodied face hurtling in my direction.

I went down with his mangled corpse on top of me. He was wadded up like a crumpled piece of paper and it cost me precious seconds to extricate myself from his wet and tangled remains. I was up on one knee and suddenly looking into the face of my own death. It smiled. "Goodness, gracious," it rumbled in a happy voice, "that was thirsty work! I need a drink . . ." Its cavernous mouth opened and its three-and-a-half-inch fangs *actually moved*, growing another inch!

Even worse, the daggerlike teeth had the color and reflective qualities of stainless steel, not the ivory hue of natural dental enamel.

This time there was no war cry, just an abbreviated roar as an Oriental lion stuck its demonic head between the monster's massive thighs. It twisted its fantastic visage upwards and its fanged and tusked mouth snapped shut on Frankenvamp's crotch.

The monster stopped and stood very still for a moment. Perhaps it didn't have a heart but it did appear to have balls. "That hurts," it announced conversationally.

As if the rest of its scorched and punctured flesh was mere illusion.

"Then maybe you should lie down!" Deirdre announced from behind it.

The thing suddenly pitched forward and only my enhanced reflexes got me out of the way in time. It crashed, facefirst, into the floor. Deirdre stood just beyond in the den, holding the bunched end of the carpet runner that led from the den to the study. She glared at me. "If we survive this, promise me that *I* get to kill that body-swapping bitch! But, in the meantime, *run!*"

I didn't run. Where was I going to go? And while I like to think I was loath to leave Deirdre and Suki, it was more likely I was too pissed off to retreat any more. I started whacking the thing with the heavy iron fireplace poker, smashing it down on Gargantua's shaggy head again and again. "Why? Won't? You? Die?" I grunted, delivering what should have been a killing blow with each syllable.

There was the muffled clanking sound with each blow and the creature's skull retained its general shape despite the repeated punishment.

Then it started to rise.

"The question is," the thing rumbled, "why won't you? I have come to gather data and specimens to assist in researching this issue." It reached down between its legs and pulled Suki away. She came reluctantly and with her toothy maw full. As it threw her through the side window I saw a freshet of gore where its groin used to be. The fluids that dribbled forth looked more like antifreeze than blood.

"Now," it said turning back to me, "we can do this the hard way . . . or the easy way."

I looked at the trail of gore and structural damage behind it. "The *hard* way?"

It nodded. "Thou sayest."

"Nooooo!" With a banshee wail, Deirdre leapt back onto the aircraft carrier expanse of its shoulders as it reached toward me. She had no weapons and her own superhuman strength was clearly inadequate as she grasped its blocky head and tried to snap its tree-stump neck. I tried to thrust the poker into the wound where its heart should be and was rewarded with another metallic sound as the heavy tool met heavier resistance.

The creature ignored its redheaded jockey and focused on me. That was its first mistake. As it plucked the poker from my shock-numbed grasp, Deirdre's hands flew to the monster's face, curving into fleshy claws just below its heavy, shelflike brow. Faster than it could reach up to grasp her hands, she plunged the index and second fingers of each into the thing's eye sockets.

It roared like a wounded elephant and bucked like a rabid mustang. Deirdre and the poker both went flying. My computer preceded her as she skimmed the top of the desk, both ending up impacted against the outer wall, just below the shattered window. The poker smashed through the heavy glass of the giant aquarium like an elongated bullet and the whole thing exploded. A miniature tsunami of water swept me off my feet and just out of the monster's reach.

But only for a moment.

Kneeling on the newly made beach of rocks and sand and broken glass, I gazed across the tableau of flopping, dying fish and gingerly reached for the red, brown, and white striped *Scorpaenidae* that some aquarists call a lion-fish. The *Pterois volitans* looks like a three-dimensional lace doily with candy-cane coloring and fins of gossamer. I picked it up by its fragile tail, careful to avoid the Tinkertoy scaffolding that spread its saillike appendages in multiple directions. The spines were barbed and hollow and capable of delivering painful if not lethal doses of poison and neurotoxins.

I looked up at the monster's blind and bloody face towering above me. "Stay for dinner?" I hissed. "We're having fish!" And I snapped the lion-fish up so that it imbedded in the creature's right cheek like a giant sticky burr.

The monster instinctively swatted at it with its hand which only made matters worse. It howled and I scrambled, pulling myself up to the fireplace and reaching for the glass jar with the heart, sitting on the mantel. I figured a shattered glass jar was better than no weapon at all.

Then I looked a little higher.

I caught the jar one-handed as a battering ram shaped like an arm smashed into the brickwork just below the mantel. The other arm was thrusting forward just inches to my left. "Scraps!" it yelled: "*Scraps!*"

I danced a complicated two-step, trying to avoid the deadly grab and sweep of those giant limbs as I reached up with my free hand and grasped the hilt of Brother Michael's great sword. The monster cocked its head as the blade came free of the scabbard with a serpentine hiss. A moment later I was knocked on my back and sliding across the floor as one of its flailing arms connected. It was hard to tell whether the broken glass from the aquarium was doing more damage to the hardwood floor or my nether regions in the process. I suspected both would require refinishing if I survived.

The jar was still intact as I'd cradled it to my chest with the fall. The sword clattered off to my right, just out of immediate reach.

The thing cocked its head again, listening for anything that would give away my position or disposition. I lay still, fighting to get my wind back and trying to reach for the sword without making any further sounds. The jar against my chest was a hindrance and the sword was just out of reach. The back of my shirt was in tatters as, I was sure, was my skin past the subcutaneous layer. The floor was already wet so it was tough to tell how much blood I was losing.

"Scraps!" it bellowed again. "I need visuals! Help me or the precious blood is lost!"

If it were possible for this to get any weirder, well I just didn't want to know. I turned my attention to slowly setting the jar down off to my left.

"Scraps! To *me*! Tick-Tock is winding down . . ."

I twisted just enough to settle the jar a couple of feet to my left and then started twisting to the right to reach for the sword.

There was a sound from the front of the house.

The front door closed.

Then the sound of footfalls as someone followed the trail of destruction toward the library.

It smiled in anticipation of reinforcements, the curve of its fanged lips ghastly on that sightless, ruined face.

I turned further, my fingers brushing the sword's hilt . . . and a small shower of loose coins fell from my pants pocket to chatter and roll across the hardwood floor.

Its head snapped forward and I scrambled amidst the loose change and glass debris to grab the weapon and get out of reach.

"What the hell is going on?" asked the wrong voice as a massive hand clutched my ankle. "Some big boat down by the dock takes off like a bat out of hell as I'm makin' my approach. Then I come up here and find someone's started a party without me. The door's off the hinges, there's a bunch of fresh stiffs littering the joint, and *oh shit!*"

The Kid had finally noticed the monster.

"Betrayal!" the thing hissed as it turned toward the new arrival, dragging me with it. "Father was right; she could not be relied upon. May each piece of her rot on earth and again in Hell!"

"Hey, it talks!" He produced his ancient .38 police special like a magician's card trick: one moment his hand was empty, the next it was pointing a blunderbuss of a revolver at the fearsome intruder. "Put 'em down and dust, High Pockets, or I'm gonna start squirtin' metal!"

"Get back, Kid!" I yelled. "This thing's fast!"

"So'm I. An' I ast ya: how fast can somethin' that big—"

These were the last words The Kid ever uttered in the flesh. The creature's other great hand fell upon J.D.'s head, enclosing it in a giant five-fingered cage. The Kid was fast, as well: he got off four shots, the large-caliber slugs notching grooves across the massive torso as they were deflected by something denser beneath the outer sheath of gray flesh. Then the hand clenched and, like Beau's, the scrappy little vampire's head was crushed. It and then the rest of him dissolved in a silent explosion of chalky dust.

"Nooo!" I shrieked. I was still on my back, my leg trapped in the creature's bear trap grasp, but I'd kept the sword. I pulled a sit-up and swung the blade down across the forearm that held me prisoner. The bright metal sheared through that tree trunk of muscle like a hot knife through whipped cream. The monster screamed, raising its stump of an arm that was now spouting greenish ichors like a Halloween drinking fountain. I screamed along as the hand that was still locked around my lower leg spasmed, crushing my tibia and fibula.

"Ruin!" the monster moaned, clutching the dribbling stump to its armored chest. "I should kill you but my master needs your blood."

"Where?" I gasped, struggling to my knees. "Where can I find your master, you son-of-a-bitching fiend?" I didn't think it was any more likely to give up that information than Theresa, but hey, as long as I was still talking I wasn't blacking out.

"High above the world, O wretch," it answered. "In his eagle's aerie he watches over us all. You need not search for it: he will come to you, soon. Or bid you come to him. And you will, you know."

"Count on it," I hissed, shuffling forward on my knees. "Just give me the address."

"He will send it with your wife and daughter." He leaned toward me. "His power will remake the world."

He was close enough. I whirled the sword and chopped off the creature's loathsome head. "Not if I rock his world, first," I said as the huge head went bouncing across the room.

Somebody put hinges in the floor: it suddenly rose up to hit me in the face.

I slept and dreamed of bat-headed demons.

Chapter Eight

ASIDE FROM FEELING ravenous, waking up was not the nightmare I expected it to be.

I was in bed. I was clean. And the only immediate discomfort associated with my crushed left leg was that it was encased in a makeshift traction-splint.

Deirdre was sleeping in a chair next to my side of the bed. The other side of the bed was still empty.

I turned my head and studied her face as she slept. She must have washed up hurriedly for there were still flecks of river mud here and there and she had failed to get all of the twigs and leaves out of her tangled auburn tresses. There were shadows on her face, neck, and arms, as well—the last remnants of bruises that would have lasted for weeks on human skin. A faint line marked the divide where her lip had been split. An eye that had started to swell and close now appeared to have nothing more than the casual application of eye shadow.

The sound of footfalls on the stairs woke her and her

eyes fluttered open as Dr. Mooncloud entered the room carrying a pair of goblets on a bed tray.

Taj was short, round, and brown. Her jet-black hair and eyes reflected the fusion of her American Indian and East Indian heritages. Likewise her professional pedigree was a fusion of medicine and mythology with a degree from Johns Hopkins and an internship in her father's medicine sweat lodge.

Nothing about her suggested that she worked for a vampire enclave in the Pacific Northwest.

"Ah, you are awake, finally."

"How long have I slept?" I asked, trying to sit up. Deirdre reached behind me and arranged the pillows to give me some back support.

"Two days."

"Two—?"

"You were in a healing trance," she explained, settling the tray across my lap. "You should be very hungry, now. I didn't know whether to bring you warm or cold, so I brought you both."

I looked down at the goblets, both filled with blood. It took all of my self-control not to grab one and start greedily gulping it down. "How's Suki?"

"Sleeping. As is Dr. Burton. I've got the day shift, he's got the night. Now, drink."

"Have you seen Lupé?"

"A Ms. D'Arbonne is going to take me to see her this afternoon. You need to drink before your body pulls you back down into shock."

"I have questions."

She nodded. "I'll talk while you drink."

She anticipated nearly every question so I didn't have to ask them. The bodies of Kyle, Lance, and Beau had been cremated in the backyard. Clay was currently laying brick to replace the scorched earth with a barbeque pit. The windows and the doors had been repaired or replaced. There was still some work to be done on the fireplace in my study and the wall separating the living room from the den. A new fish tank had been ordered—acrylic instead of glass—and Deirdre had picked up a new computer for me—a laptop. She had spent the better part of the last two days watching over me and reinstalling software and files from her bedside post.

Kurt was insisting on our immediate relocation to New York or he was coming down with a small army to fetch me.

And the dusty remnants of The Kid had been gathered and placed in an urn. They now waited on the fireplace mantel downstairs in the study. Billy Bob Montrose was coming by after dark to discuss funeral arrangements.

I felt an unaccustomed surge of emotion as I thought about The Kid. Was this what grief felt like? I couldn't quite remember. Since I parted from Lupé a big hollow bubble had swelled inside my chest, numbing all feelings except for a slow pulse of anger. That pulse was quickening, now.

Anger was a fine emotion. Strong and sharp and pure. It motivated. It sought results and resolutions. Grief paralyzed. It muddled the mind. I couldn't bring the little twerp back but I could avenge his death. This Dr. Pipt might be some sort of mad scientist but now he was dealing with one very pissed off lab rat!

"And the monster?" I asked as I finished off the second glass and dabbed at my mouth with a napkin.

"Gerald and I performed crude, sectional autopsies in the downstairs bathtub. You, um, might want to use the upstairs shower for another day or so." She pulled back the covers and began to unfasten the splint around my leg. Apparently two days were sufficient for my accelerated healing factors. "I think it will be easier to show you, than tell you," she said, extending her hand to help me up.

The damn thing was a cyborg—a creature that was half living organism, half machine. Well, not half and half, actually; more like seventy/thirty. But that thirty percent of hardware made all of the difference.

"I've sent tissue samples back to Seattle for more detailed workups," Mooncloud said as I considered the sectional samples encased in Tupperware in the basement freezer. Other components of metal, plastic, and wire— grafted with bits of flesh and pieces of bone—were laid out on available surfaces. Deirdre wasn't going to be using the weight bench or the tanning bed for the next couple of days.

"Organs, skin, limbs," she catalogued as I closed the lid on the gruesome assemblage. "I also sent on some of the finer cybernetics and implants but I wanted you to see this." She handed me a skull. Once upon a time it had been a human skull; large, but not large enough. Surgeries had been performed to enlarge and reinforce it with steel bands and plates. And the jaws had been outfitted with hydraulic fangs. Fangs that were actually extendable hypodermic needles.

"The plastic tubing ran from here," Mooncloud used her pen to tap the nozzles at the back of the hollow spikes, "through twin pumps surgically implanted beneath the pectoral muscles. From there they would carry . . ."

"My blood," I offered.

She nodded. " . . . your blood down to collection reservoirs in the abdominal cavity. The actual containers were plastic but they were shielded with steel and Kevlar."

I handed the rebuilt skull back to her. "So, this thing wasn't really a vampire of any sort. It was just a giant syringe on legs."

Mooncloud nodded. "Sent to collect, store, and safely transport your blood."

"And I guess its vital organs were shielded with armored implants. No wonder it was so hard to kill. There must have been a half-inch steel plate in front of its heart!"

"Well, not exactly . . ." She handed me a metal ovoid the size of a cantaloupe with four nozzled openings. "This was its heart."

I hefted the mechanical pump and turned it over in my hands. Something was stamped along a nearly invisible seam. "What's this?"

"Do you have a magnifying glass?"

"Up in my study."

"Let's go."

We went.

Pulling a small magnifying glass from my desk drawer, I placed the artificial heart under a lamp and moved the lens until I had the best resolution. The stamped letters read *Ozymandias Indust.*

"Ozymandias Industries?" Mooncloud said when I showed it to her.

"Like the poem?" Deirdre asked. She had shadowed us all the way but hadn't spoken until now.

"Poem?" Mooncloud repeated.

"By Percy Bysshe Shelley," I explained. "It tells the story of a traveler in a distant land who comes across a giant statue, shattered and half obscured by the desert sands. The face on the statue is cold and haughty; the inscription on the pedestal is haughtier still."

"Look on my works, ye Mighty, and despair," Deirdre murmured.

"It is quite an accomplishment," Mooncloud said, picking up the mechanical marvel.

"The point of the poem," Deirdre elaborated, "is that this great king's mighty works were already forgotten, disappeared into time's oblivion."

I had nearly forgotten that Damien had first met Deirdre in a library.

"So," mused the good doctor, "does this Pipt fancy himself the great king? Is he supposed to be Ozymandias?"

"If you'd seen the email he sent me, you'd be thinking more along the lines of Ozzy Osbourne." I felt my lips twitch toward a smile in spite of my mood.

"Or maybe Oz, the great and powerful?" offered Deirdre. "Pay no attention to that man behind the curtain!"

"'Oz never did give nothing to the Tin Man,'" I muttered, "'that he didn't, didn't already—'" My blood suddenly ran cold. Given my unique biochemistry, that phrase was probably more than a euphemism. I set the magnifying glass down very carefully.

"What?" Deirdre wanted to know. "What is it?"

I fumbled for the chair behind me so I wouldn't end up on the floor. Again. "I think I just cracked the code."

"You see, the problem is that most people's familiarity with the works of Lyman Frank Baum is relegated to an MGM musical motion picture released back in 1939." I spread a series of colorful booklets across the dining room table and picked up the first one. "That movie was loosely based on the first Oz book, *The Wonderful Wizard of Oz*."

"When I was a little girl," Deirdre said, picking out a volume from the latter third of the series, "I always wanted a pair of ruby slippers."

"Hollywood revisionism." I laid the book back down. "They were silver slippers in the book but Metro-Goldwyn-Mayer wanted to make the most of the new Technicolor process. That change was just one of many." I began sorting the books into distinct groups. "There are forty official Oz books, dating from 1900 to 1963. Baum wrote the first fourteen. Confining ourselves to the official oeuvre alone presents us with hundreds of characters. The Scarecrow, Tin Man, and Cowardly Lion seem pretty normal once you get deeper into the series."

Dr. Mooncloud picked up a copy of *The Magical Mimics in Oz* by Jack Snow, published back in 1946. "I didn't realize you collected children's books."

"Professor Cséjthe teaches American Lit," Deirdre said without raising her eyes from her 1937 copy of Ruth Plumly Thompson's *Handy Mandy in Oz*. She turned another page.

"I'm on sabbatical this semester. Hope it's not permanent. Anyway, I kept thinking this name Pipt was familiar but I just couldn't place it. The first association that always came to mind was Pip in Charles Dickens' *Great Expectations*."

"And then there's Gladys Knight," the redhead said absently.

Taj smiled. I just ignored her. "But it just occurred to me that there *is* a 'Pipt'—a Dr. Pipt—and he's a character from Baum's Oz stories."

Dr. Mooncloud cocked a skeptical eyebrow. "Coincidence? What does he do?"

"Well, he's more of a sorcerer than an actual doctor. His main claim to fame is the Powder of Life, a magical residue that bestows living status on any inanimate object it is sprinkled on."

"Any inanimate object?"

"Well, it worked on his phonograph. Made it dance around the room. More notably, it was responsible for animating some significant citizens of Oz: Jack Pumpkinhead, the Sawhorse, the Gump, the Glass Cat, and—" I held up the seventh book, "—the titular character of this adventure."

Deirdre glanced up, did a double-take, and grabbed the book for a closer study of the cover. "It's her!" She jabbed a finger at the young woman frolicking on the tattered book jacket. It's a caricature, of course, but it's her!"

Dr. Mooncloud moved to where she could read the title: "*The Patchwork Girl of Oz*?"

I nodded. "She was created to be a servant for Pipt's wife, Margolotte. Her name was supposed to be Angeline . . ."

"Angeline?" Deirdre asked.

"Yeah. But the Glass Cat called her Scraps."

I was lying on my bed, waiting for sunset.

Even though I had slept for two days, a healing trance was not the same as a restful repose.

And, according to Dr. Mooncloud, I was clinically depressed, as well.

She said it wasn't unusual for those who found themselves living the vastly altered life of the nosferatu. The fact that I was stuck between the worlds of the living and the undead made my depression all the more inevitable. She gave me a bottle of pills she called "mood elevators" and urged me to come back to Seattle for some head sessions with a Dr. Melder.

I guess vampires need shrinks since the confessional was clearly out of bounds . . .

Maybe I was having difficulty coping. And maybe the biochemical changes in my cerebral cortex were coloring my point of view. But the emotional lassitude that had settled over me like a heavy dark shroud wasn't mysterious at all.

The Kid was dead. Well, by most definitions, he had been dead for approximately eight decades. But now he was gone, as well. Suddenly. Savagely.

Because of me.

Others had died. Because of me.

My wife and daughter were dead because of me.

My unborn child might die because of me.

Lupé had almost died—was keeping her distance now—because of me.

I had spent the past year worrying that the necrophagic virus in my system was going to turn me into a monster someday. If the rules of cause and effect were to be believed, I was already there.

I had promised myself oblivion before it came to that, a sacrifice rather than a suicide, for the good of the world. What further purpose could my existence serve other than to bring more pain and death to others around me?

Kurt seemed to think I had a higher destiny. That my occupation of that twilight realm between the darkness and the light was a pivotal point for bringing change. But change to whom? And what kind of change?

Could I marshal the forces of darkness and lead them, like an army, into the light? How could I lead, much less entice, them when I seemed incapable of finding my own way?

Come to New York, he insisted. Confront the power-hungry traditionalists in the East Coast enclave, face them down. Show them that the Children of the Night can peacefully coexist with their Siblings of the Day.

But there was no peace in my own heart now.

And the "opposition" was bigger than that. The opposition was widespread. Most of the true opposition didn't know my name or that I even existed. The struggle wasn't really a personal one: by its very nature, my existence was a gauntlet thrown down to both realms, the light and the darkness. And since I couldn't take refuge with one side to resist the other, I was merely fighting a holding action. And that, not for long, given the size of my battered little faction.

How could I make a moral stand when defeat was

inevitable and everyone around me was certain to die? How could I ask—how could I *allow* them to discard themselves for a hopeless cause? What point would be served other than to prove my values wrong and needlessly fatal while cementing the position of the darker status quo?

I had two choices.

I could run and hide. In a sense, that's all that I had been doing since the accident that had killed my wife and daughter. Gee, look at how well that strategy had worked out.

Or I could switch from defense to offense. No hope of winning there, either. And more of the people around me would die before it was over.

More of the people around me would die whichever way I went.

So, the first order of business was to divest myself of my human—and not-so-human—shields.

"'It is only as a man puts off from himself all external means of support and stands alone, that I see him to be strong and to prevail.'" Deirdre was standing in the doorway. "'He is weakened by every recruit to his banner. Is not a man better than a town?'"

"Now," I said, "you get out of *my* head."

"I'm not psychic. It's Emerson, not telepathy."

"And you quote Ralph Waldo because . . . ?"

She came into the bedroom, partially closing the door behind her. "You've been reading his essay 'Self Reliance' a lot lately."

"So?"

"I think you're prepping for New York."

"Prepping?" I decided to sit up. Discovered that I lacked the will to do so.

"Psyching up." She walked over and pushed my legs over so she could sit on the side of the bed. "I think you're getting ready to make a run for it."

I put my hands behind my head. "That would be the smart thing to do."

She shook her head. "I mean from us. You've always worried about putting other people in danger and this latest attack has just underscored all of your fears."

"The Kid is dead. If you or Suki were human, both of you would be just as dead as her badass trio. Lupé thought the wedding was going to be problematical but just getting engaged damn near killed her!"

"And when you look around, do you see her?"

"No."

"Do you see me?"

Yes, I saw her. She wore a turquoise shirt, unbuttoned to show the curve of her throat, descending to the swell of her bosom. My eyes were not held by the shadowy hillock of cleavage but by the faint ticking of her carotid as it slipped along the side of her neck. I forced my gaze back up to her face. I was still in trouble there. "Yes."

"Tell me to go away."

"Okay. Go away."

She smiled. Her lips were slow and lazy: "No." She leaned over me. "Did you tell Lupé to stay away?"

"No. But I might have. Should have."

She shook her head. "Doesn't matter. She's an adult. She chose not to come. I'm an adult. I've chosen not to go."

"She was seriously injured, Deirdre. She couldn't be moved."

"Maybe that same day. But she's a lycanthrope, Chris. She's been up and around since. She *chooses* not to be here."

"That's her business."

"Yes," she said, "yes it is. So don't be playing head games over how everything that happens is your fault. We're all grownups. We all make our own choices. You're not some complicit puppeteer."

"Okay . . ."

Her smile changed. I thought it grew wistful though it was hard to see as her proximity was now blocking the light. "Don't run . . ." she murmured.

I said nothing.

"Don't run," she whispered, "from me . . ." Her face came down and her lips brushed mine.

"Deirdre," I said quietly, "I'm not feeling very well right now and neither are you. We've lost friends and colleagues. We're battered and bruised on the inside as well as the out."

"We could help each other feel better . . ."

"I love Lupé."

"But does she love you?" She read the hesitation in my eyes. "Can she love you the way you need to be loved? Can she do this?" Her lips crushed mine. Her mouth was hungry and I felt the suggestion of her tongue against my teeth. "She can't even bear to have you touch her!" she gasped against my mouth. "What could she offer you even if she was here? Could she give you this?" She grasped my hand and guided it to her left breast. Belatedly I realized her shirt had come unbuttoned. *When did that happen?* There was no bra—neither now, nor, apparently, during the times she went sunbathing. And, aesthetically speaking, her bosom was about as perfect as any you might find outside of what we euphemistically call a men's magazine.

But it wasn't Lupé's breast.

"Kiss it," she murmured.

"No. Deirdre, I—"

"Then bite it!" Her hand was suddenly before my eyes, my fanged dental appliance resting in the cup of her left palm. Even though I didn't possess the half of the recombinant virus that grew the preternatural incisors, modern dentistry had found ways to compensate. "Put your teeth in your mouth," she whispered, breathing heavily, "and then put them in me!"

"No."

"You've done it before."

"I'm not thirsty."

"You're lying!"

I *was* lying. I was thirsty. I was more than thirsty, I was *hungry*. I was hungry a lot these past few days and never so aware of how everyone's pulse seemed to throb against the sweet, sloped sides of their necks. Deirdre's sudden shift from sex to food had caught me off balance and it took me longer than I intended to just say: "No."

She swore softly as she took the razor-sharp fangs between the fingers of her right hand. "They should take your picture and put it in the psychology texts under 'passive-aggressive' . . ." She brushed her hand across her breast and suddenly there were two red lines tracing the inside curve of her cleavage. Blood, red and warm and

ripe with promises began to well up along the cuts and
drool towards her midriff. "Dinner's on me," she said,
pulling back the sides of her shirt and leaning toward my
mouth.

I opened my mouth to say "no" again. But I didn't. We
both paused, holding ourselves very still. The only movement was the blood (*the blood! oh, the blood!*) turning to
rivulets, crimson streams of life and power, trickling to the
roughened delta of aureole, circumnavigating the globe in
search of southern latitudes, until two streams converged.

A third tributary formed.

The convergence grew, swelled, formed a second, liquid
nipple, tumescent to the tweaking of gravity. It grew heavier
and finally dropped down on a thin ruby strand like a one-
way bungee jump of blood, falling onto my lips.

My self-control was a trembling house of cards, collaps-
ing in all directions. I pulled her down and pressed my
mouth to the river's source.

Perhaps it was Deirdre's blood that overwhelmed my
resistance—its unique alchemy made it stronger and
sweeter than the nectar that ran through human or vampire
veins.

Certainly living blood, hot and pulsing from its nursery
of flesh and bone, was more compelling than my usual
fare. Long-dead plasma and platelets—stored and frozen
in plastic and warmed over to simulate its former live-
liness—were pale, watery substitutes when offered
honeyed ambrosia.

Still, I had resisted live blood-offerings before. But this
time the need, the Hunger, had grown beyond all previous
demarcations. I was surprised by its new depth of urgency,

catching me in a sudden, heady undertow. I barely heard the footsteps coming down the hallway. The pounding of my heart reverberated in my head, revving its four-chambered engine to match the hammerstrokes of Deirdre's own. The whisper of the door was lost in sighs from her throat, the gasps in my own as I nursed at the red spill of life across her bosom.

The voice, however, was crystal clear both before, when it called: "Oh Chris! I came as soon as I heard—"

And then after, when Lupé said: "—I guess I did not come soon enough." There were autumnal tones in her voice, promising a deep and endless winter.

I didn't push Deirdre away nor leap from the bed to claim that it wasn't what she thought. I didn't hurry down the stairs in her wake, apologizing and begging for her to hear me out. I didn't even move until I heard the front door slam like the last beat of a cardiac muscle in final arrest.

Only then did I carefully, gently, but implacably, move Deirdre aside and rise from the ghost town of my bed.

"Where are you going?" Deirdre asked softly.

I wiped my mouth on my sleeve, dabbed at my chin. "To make a phone call."

"To Kurt?"

"Yes."

"The sun hasn't set, yet."

"Here," I answered. "In New York it is already dark."

I walked out of the room.

Sometimes *it* looked like a man. *It* was not a man and if you looked into *its* eyes, you knew this immediately. The soldiers who encountered *it* near the road instinctively gave *it* a wide berth and little more than a sideways glance. Anyone who looked closer or longer, felt his bowels loosen and an unaccustomed scream building up in the back of his throat.

Off the road and deep in the green hell of the jungle, *it* appeared to the peasants as a great shadowy jaguar by day and a great, winged darkness by night. The peasants would cross themselves in obeisance to modern catechism, then invoke more ancient prayers upon the altars of their ancestral hearts.

Something had awakened. *Something* walked among them. *It* had not stirred from the dark depths in twenty-five hundred years but now *it* was come forth.

It was hungry—as hungry as anything might be that fed on villages, snacked on armies, dined on pestilence and plague. But *its* hunger was as nothing in comparison to *its* need!

Blood!

It must have the *blood!*

It did not stop to feed. *It* turned neither to the left nor the right. Only one certain kind of blood would serve.

The demon moved relentlessly, heading north by northeast. Day and night *it* traveled. Implacably, tirelessly, until *it* came to the ocean.

The Gulf of Mexico would lead *it* in a great, arcing approach, through Mexico, then Texas, and finally into Louisiana. *It* weighed the advantages of velocity versus distance and decided against the speed bumps of human population centers. *It* gazed out over the gray-green swells of the Atlantic Ocean and then walked forward into the water.

It was heavier and denser than a human so first the breakers and then the undertow had no effect as *it* moved deeper and deeper into the pounding surf. Soon *its* head disappeared beneath the waves as *it* continued its long walk toward the man *it* had glimpsed in *its* own fearsome dreams only a brief decade before.

Soon, it thought, *very soon . . .*

One final, bloody sacrifice for Camazotz, Lord of the Underworld, and then eternal silence and endless darkness.

Forever and ever.

Amen . . .

☠

Chapter Nine

I AWOKE FROM the dream as the landing gear of the 737 bounced on the runway. One minute I was dreaming that the waves of the Atlantic Ocean were rolling over my head, the next I was descending to earth from a sojourn in the skies.

I had expressly forbidden Deirdre and Suki to come to New York with me. That's why they were sitting three rows behind me instead of occupying the seats on either side.

I tried to ignore them but it finally became necessary to fake a trip to the restroom so I could lean over and speak to the Asian vampire. "Stay out of her head," I whispered. "Out of respect for me if not her."

Deirdre's distress level dropped a little after that but Suki's amusement only grew. Bad enough that the blood-bond made me sensitive to the redhead's emotional state; I had no idea why I was tuned in to Suki's broadcasts, as well.

The rest of the flight was uneventful except for the dream. Nightmares are bad enough when you're asleep. When you wake up you should be able to shake it off, dismiss it as a bad dream, and know that you are safe in the bright light of day.

I couldn't do that. *Something* was stalking me. The dreams were merely progress reports, reminding me that the Darkness was drawing closer, even when I was awake.

At least I had two small consolations.

First, this trip was buying me time on the demon front.

And second, I hadn't embarrassed myself by screaming during my in-flight nap.

There was no avoiding my two shadows as we deplaned at La Guardia. It was just as well. A limo driver was wandering about holding a placard with my name written on it.

I grabbed Deirdre's hand before she could point. "No, dear, a limo isn't for us," I murmured. "We'll take a cab." We ambled past the chauffeur and I exerted all the mental influence I could muster to keep Deirdre's and Suki's attention diverted until we were out of earshot.

"That driver was looking for you," the redhead said as soon as I released my grip, both mental and physical.

"A lot of people are looking for me," I said. "Not all of them are friendly. Ah, here we go . . ."

Another limo driver had come into view. This one wore mirrored sunglasses and held a placard with the name HENRY CLERVAL printed across it. I steered in his direction.

"Mr. Clerval?" he asked as we approached. He was shorter than me, slighter of build, and I could probably knock him down and run before he could get a weapon out. He didn't seem old enough to grow the moustache and goatee that narrowed his already narrow face. Adding to the oddness of his appearance was his apparent lack of an Adam's apple.

"No," I said, "the name is Murnau. Friederich Wilhelm Murnau. But you can call me Fred."

He looked at me uncertainly. "That's not part of the password."

"Yes, it is."

"Not the Fred part."

"Okay, call me Mr. Murnau. Listen there's another limo driver back there holding a card with the name of Chris Cséjthe on it. Who sent him?"

"I don't know, but we expected this might happen. Follow me."

We followed him out to a black stretch limo with black SUVs parked in front and behind. All had their engines idling. Five other people followed behind us: two businessmen, a woman pushing a baby stroller, a college student with a backpack, and a kid who looked like he was lost but wasn't. They flanked us as the heavily tinted passenger window rolled down in the back.

A very angry master vampire sat inside just beyond the sunlight's reach. "I am not pleased," Kurt Szekely announced with a scowl.

Actually, he was furious.

Furious at me for coming with no more than a moment's notice. Furious that I was flying commercial with next to no security precautions. Furious at the ladies for letting me.

And, I suspected, for necessitating his traveling about in the light of day.

The risk was relatively nil, however. Back in Louisiana the expected high was a balmy sixty-four degrees under sunny skies. Here in the northeast the sun hadn't made an unshrouded appearance for days. A storm front had dropped a foot of snow from the Canadian border to the Jersey shores and the wind chill was rumored to be in the minus twenties. I should have brought a coat—more for camouflage than comfort as my transformed flesh was becoming less sensitive to temperature variables.

Sitting in the car, we were treated to a detailed explanation of his ill temper while our luggage was attended to. The limo was stretched and armored, outfitted with a wet bar, and occupied by another familiar face. Stefan Pagelovitch sat across from me, wearing a dark double-breasted suit, dark shirt, dark tie, and very expensive wingtip shoes.

"Hello, Dennis," I said as the girls slid in next to me.

Pagelovitch's face began to sag, melting and rearranging itself until Dennis Smirl sat across from me in the Seattle Doman's place. "How did you know?"

"The outfit's too monochrome for one. Stefan likes color; he wouldn't wear black to a funeral much less a business meeting. Those shoes? Nice, but not imported. Stefan favors the Italians. And, as a master vampire, he has a palpable aura. You? You're surrounded by—" I sniffed. "Brut?"

"Hai Karate."

I blinked. "You're kidding."

"You're one to talk, Old Spice boy."

"But how? Where do you get—?"

"There's this warehouse—"

The door opened again and the limo driver passed Kurt a note while the hired muscle stood around outside with their gun hands inside their jackets. The snow had picked up again and it looked like Paul Bunyan had flicked his cigar ashes over their heads and shoulders.

"Nothing like a low-profile meeting at the airport," I said as the ambiguously gendered driver closed the door and walked around to sit in the front seat.

Kurt gave me the look. "Do you think your arrival here is a secret? Under the circumstances this is the best I could do with short notice. Besides, we must demonstrate a level of security befitting your status."

"I'm impressed."

"The idea is to impress your enemies." He turned the lapel of his overcoat and spoke into a tiny microphone. "As soon as the luggage is secure, we drive."

Kurt Szekely could have been a Doman, himself. He had spent over a hundred years in the service of a Great Evil—an ancient demon who had pretended to be the bloodthirsty Countess Elizabeth Báthory. When I unmasked her perfidy he executed her physical body, himself. Then he and the Szekely Clan swore fealty to me, declaring me the new Doman of the New York demesne. It was an honor Kurt might have taken for himself. Instead, he assumed the role of majordomo and ally as other fanged wannabes stepped forward to contest for the throne.

I still was unsure of his motives at times.

But I was pretty much out of alternatives.

The fact that he was out and about in the day—albeit under a ton of sunscreen despite the solid cloud cover— bespoke his age and power.

He wasn't especially tall—just under six feet—but I had met undead with a six-inch or hundred-pound advantage that didn't exude half the menace that Kurt put out. As we used to say in the broadcasting biz, he had a face made for radio. It wasn't that he was ugly or even unattractive; there was just something about even his most casual expression that made you want to look away. And you didn't turn your back on him without that unpleasant prickling sensation between your shoulder blades.

The funny thing was I seemed to amuse him. When you've spent the last couple of centuries scaring the hell out of everyone you met, it's a refreshing change of pace to run into someone who actually goes out of his way to irritate you.

At least that's what he once told me.

As far as I'm concerned, that assurance belongs on the list of other trusted expressions which include: "I'll still respect you in the morning," "the check is in the mail," and "I'm from the government, I'm here to help you."

"So," he said, fixing Suki with a jaundiced eye, "you are the Oriental vampire."

"Asian."

"What?"

"Asian." She refused to be intimidated. "'Oriental' is a misnomer."

"Misnomer?"

"It's her politically correct way of telling you that 'Oriental' is politically incorrect," I said. "She's Asian."

He waved his hand in dismissal. "I was curious as to your ability to move about after sunrise. How old are you?"

She favored him with a smile. I knew Suki's smiles: there was nothing behind it except teeth. "One should never ask a lady her age, Kurt-san."

"Asian vampires differ from the European," I offered. "The differences are more than just cultural."

"You saved her life, too," he said, changing the subject abruptly.

"Um. Not really. At best, we all saved each others' lives—it was sort of a tag team approach."

"I speak of before. When she was helpless, with a broken back, in the lair of your enemies."

I pointed at Smirl. "More his doing than mine."

"It proves my point," Kurt said as our limo, flanked by the SUVs, caravanned away from the loading zone and began plowing through ripples of miniature snowdrifts. "Your greatest strengths lie in marshalling the talents and abilities of others. A Doman is more the general than the lone warrior."

"How about 'distant figurehead?'"

He didn't bat an eye. "Figurehead, perhaps . . . in the best sense of the word. Distant . . . under certain conditions. But, for now, you must prove yourself a diplomat and formidable adversary. At tonight's reception—"

"Tonight?" Suki protested.

"Do you have any idea of how difficult it is to run security on a room full of people?" Deirdre demanded.

The temperature in the back of the limo dropped a good ten degrees. "First of all," Kurt said quietly, "you are in *my* demesne, now. I act as seneschal for the Doman and administer all matters in his name. As you are guests here, I extend certain courtesies but those courtesies have limits. If you are here as Christopher Cséjthe's consorts, you may enjoy a greater degree of informality with him . . . but not with me.

"If, for example, he takes Darcy Blenik as another consort while he is here—and through ignorance or design she brings him harm—I will be obligated to kill her and go to war with her family. Do not presume that I would treat you any differently."

"Uh, Kurt," I said, being careful not to look at either Deirdre or Suki, "neither one is a consort . . ."

Kurt addressed Suki and Deirdre directly, saying: "Then I am even less inclined to cut you any slack." He turned back to me. "Please keep your *friends* on a short leash until the formalities of the next three nights are concluded."

Deirdre was not sufficiently cowed. "I'm your Doman's Chief of Security," she told Kurt.

"Not here you're not. Here, you are an unnecessary complication. All security matters are my concern, now. Tonight Christopher Cséjthe will meet with representatives of other enclaves and factions who will offer tribute and seek alliances. Tomorrow night he will address the families of this demesne and settle any challenges to his succession as Doman. Your only real value lies in your unique biochemistry and which clan alliance he might purchase by offering you for their study."

"I would never do that," I said.

Kurt answered me by continuing to speak to Deirdre.

"He has not sufficiently transformed to consider sacrificing you for his own personal gain. Yet." The last word hung out there in midair, resonating with all of its implications. "However the time may come when he must choose to sacrifice one life—or two—to save many. And that time may come quickly."

"So," said the shapeshifting gangster from the Chicago demesne after the silence had lengthened, "how have you been?"

As I opened my mouth, Deirdre asked: "Who's Darcy Blenik?"

We took the Queensboro Bridge into the city and drove down 60th Street, skirting the boundaries of Midtown and the Upper East Side, passing by Bloomingdale's. I knew that the enclave owned a number of properties from Morningside Heights and Harlem all the way down to Lower Manhattan. Kurt briefed us on the various "safe houses" in hotels, churches, synagogues, office buildings, brownstones, warehouses—even a bank. We didn't go to any of those. Instead, we took a right on Madison Avenue, passed by the Museum of American Illustration, then a left on 81st Street, and another left on Fifth Avenue. We drove into the parking garage for the Metropolitan Museum of Art at 80th Street as a parade of snowplows passed by, flanked by a pair of sand and salt spreaders.

Our driver produced some sort of pass and we drove in and eventually down. We parked on an underground level that had no painted slots and was occupied by a few old service vehicles.

"How can you have a vampire safe house in a church?"

I asked as we exited the car and entered an elevator set in a bare concrete wall.

Kurt slipped a plastic card into a slot below the panel of buttons as Deidre guessed: "I suppose you defile all visible icons and religious symbols." She steadfastly refused to act abashed in Kurt's presence. I liked her all the more for it.

"Actually, a simple unconsecration ceremony is sufficient for most of us," he answered grudgingly. "As long as the demesne recognizes its ownership of the property, the décor is muted, and no actual handling of consecrated materials is required, we are able to pass through such edifices and access the prepared habitats below. It's the synagogues that are the challenge . . ."

"More potent iconography?"

He shook his head. "Observant Jews. *Too* observant. The orthodox congregants notice the least little discrepancy even if they've never been in the building before." He contemplated the concert-tour tee-shirt she was wearing as she slipped out of her light jacket. "Slayer," he read across the swell of her bosom. "Do you fancy yourself a 'slayer', Ms—?"

"Just call me Deirdre, Kurt," she answered, working her own brand of intimidation. "After all, we're all family, now. And no."

"No?" His eyebrow underscored the question but also suggested he wasn't sure of exactly which question it was.

"I don't fancy myself a slayer. Buffy's the Slayer."

"Buffy?"

"It's television," I whispered. "Ask her if she fancies herself The Executioner."

"It's a comic book," Suki coached.

Smirl shook his head. "You're thinking of *The Punisher*."

"Anita Blake is The Executioner," the redhead said.

Kurt sighed. "Then, thankfully, you are not subject to delusions of grandeur."

"Oh, I wouldn't say that," I said as the elevator stopped five floors down.

"What would you say?" he asked patiently, as the doors opened and he led us into an underground corridor as wide as a suburban street.

"Well," Deirdre took the ball, "I'd say that I'm not Buffy and I'm not Anita and I'm not Sookie, either . . ."

Kurt looked at me.

I shrugged.

" . . . I'm just Deirdre . . ."

We entered an electric tram that seated six plus luggage.

" . . . the undead ass-kicker."

Which pretty much ended that conversation.

The driver joined us while the other security personnel were taking the elevator in shifts and bringing the luggage. We started off with the understanding that he (or, as I suspected, she) would return with the vehicle to get the rest of our belongings and the handlers.

There were side tunnels heading off toward Central Park, but Kurt drove us toward the museum's location. Underneath the massive structure's subbasements, he explained, were living quarters as tastefully appointed as any five-star hotel.

We pulled up to an unloading zone and Kurt led us through a set of doors and into a nicely appointed hallway as the driver began to turn the tram around. Eventually we arrived at a large oaken door.

Kurt produced a large brass key from his pocket and inserted it into a plated keyhole.

"What?" This time it was Suki asking the questions. "No electronic passkeys? No biometrics? No retinal scans?"

He pushed the door open. "Biometrics can be hacked, electronic passkeys jacked. Sometimes the old ways are the best ways."

I was about to say that keys could be duplicated. Then I got a second look at the key as he extracted it. The design looked old but the brass gleamed as if new. And the teeth—or prongs—angled off the circular barrel in three different directions. It couldn't be copied on any known key duplication machine that worked with prefabricated blanks. Likewise a sideways mold impression would not capture the three-dimensional configuration. No lock and key system was completely foolproof but this would come closer than anything.

He handed me the key, saying: "Don't lose it."

"What about us?" Deirdre asked.

"Why would either of you need a key?" he asked.

"Well . . . you know . . ."

"No. I don't. Why would you need to leave unless it was to accompany the Doman? And if you are with the Doman, he *has* the key."

And with that, he ushered us into the suite.

Actually, it was more like a house than a suite. A house with five bedrooms, each with its own private bath. It was really a small underground mansion with living and recreational space sufficient for a small army. And that wasn't counting the staff and servants' quarters.

Kurt gave us a "quick" twenty-minute tour, introducing us to the service personnel and acquainting us with the amenities and the security systems. He concluded by inviting us to unpack, rest, and refresh ourselves while he finalized preparations for the pending reception. Then he left, promising to return around seven p.m. for a pre-meet strategy session.

The house chef stuck his head in while I was unpacking and asked if I would care for an aperitif.

That was a big affirmative. The Hunger had kicked into overdrive since I'd been shot. One or two blood packets from the blood bank every week or so was all I'd needed up till now. Suddenly, a couple of warmed over meals in a pouch—even on a daily basis—seemed woefully inadequate.

"And what would the master prefer?" the chef inquired, sounding more like a wine steward at the moment. "A generous 'O'? A dry but slightly sweet 'A' or a fruity 'B'? Or shall I bring you something exotic from our rare stock?"

Okay. This was weird, ordering blood by type as if it were like differing years and vintages of wine. But, hey, it beat going out into the streets and hunting mystery meat at night. . . .

I shook my head: *Where did that thought come from?*

"Do I take that as a 'no,' sir?"

"Sorry, just thinking." *Or not thinking* . . . "I'll tell you what; I've never had any AB. Do you have any in stock?"

"Positive or negative, sir?"

"Negative if you have it." AB negative was the rarest of the ABO groups and existed in less than one percent of the population. The fact that I wasn't that concerned about how they came by it was a little disturbing. Perhaps the mood elevators that Dr. Mooncloud had prescribed were blunting my conscience along with my angst.

Or maybe it was finally eroding under the transmutative onslaught of the virus.

He nodded. "Very good, sir, I shall send something right up." He disappeared as I closed my empty suitcase and set it in the walk-in closet. Then I flopped on the tennis court–sized bed and ran down my mental checklist.

The Kid's ashes were now in Billy Bob Montrose's custody. He wanted to postpone any sort of memorial until I got back. I left him with instructions as to what to do if I didn't come back. It was a distinct possibility and I wanted things done right by the little twerp. With me or without me, his ashes were to be taken to California and spread across the intersection of Routes 46 and 41 just outside Cholame at precisely 5:45 p.m.

The house, property, and most of my secret bank accounts were deeded over to Lupé in the event of my death or disappearance. I had arranged for some tidy sums to be forwarded to Deirdre and Mama Samm. Also a charitable bequest to Father Pat's missionary work—if anyone could find him. Olive would become full owner of After Dark Investigations.

Had I missed anything?

There was still my to-do list on the adversarial front. Several individuals or families in the New York demesne were trying to kill me and would keep trying until they either succeeded or I did something to discourage them. Back home I could only keep dodging. Here, I could explore the old football maxim—the best defense is a smashing offense.

If I could just figure out who my enemies were and how to do that before the game went into sudden death overtime.

And then there was this Dr. Pipt. The not-so-good doctor had gone to a lot of trouble to make his Frankenstein monster into a walking autolancet. To what lengths might he go on his next attempt? And how did Theresa, the Patchwork Girl of Ozymandias Industries, figure in?

It didn't seem likely that I was destined to lead a long and happy life. But I'd settle for short and scrappy if I could take a few of the bastards with me.

I was musing on the theme that Dr. Mooncloud's happy pills should be renamed "Jimmy's Cracked Corn" when there was a knock at the bedroom door.

Come, I thought.

The knock sounded again.

Come!

Oh.

"Come," I said.

A woman entered the room. Her hair was white. Her skin had that fish-belly, glow in the dark, had-to-lie-out-in-the-sun-just-to-neutralize-the-blue-tones kind of whiteness. All she lacked were the pink irises to be a true albino.

If she was one of the maids, she wasn't dressed for it.

Her strapless evening gown was an eye-catching claret that was all the more fascinating as I couldn't see how it stayed up. She was thin and angular, no bosom and very little hip to provide anchor points.

She extended a white arm as she approached the bed. "Master Cséjthe," she said in a surprisingly husky voice, "I am Bethany."

I sat up and noticed three things.

First that the hair on my arms—and apparently all over my body—was starting to stand away from my skin.

Second, Bethany was human, not undead.

And third, the vein that ran along the side of her neck was very prominent.

"Yes," I said, not sure of what I was saying yes to.

"Chef said you requested AB negative," she said, leaning toward me.

"Yes?" Her hands were empty, neither a bottle nor a pouch in sight.

"Where would you like me? On the bed?"

Oh God . . . "You're it. Her. You're AB . . ."

"Negative."

"Negative?"

"AB negative," she clarified with a twinkle in her eye. She reached behind her and I heard a zipper clear its throat. "I hope you like me. I've always feared that I might be an acquired taste."

The dress came down and she was white marble with blue veins.

"You must be under some compulsion," I whispered as she crawled onto the bed and rolled into my lap.

"I am here of my own free will," she answered. "I'm not

a fang-banger . . ." she looked up at me with pale blue eyes, " . . . but for you I'll make an exception."

"Why?"

"You are the Doman, for one reason."

"No, I mean, why are you . . . a willing occupant of my wine cellar?"

She gazed up at me with eyes so pale they almost seemed empty. "The money is very, very good. Especially since I am a statistical rarity. And there are benefits . . ."

Before I could find out about the benefits there was another knock at the bedroom door and Deirdre started to come in. "You forgot to pack your—" She stopped as she took in the tableau. Her face colored in stark contrast to the feminine snow sculpture lying across my lap.

"I thought you might need—that is, I brought . . ." She walked quickly forward and handed me a familiar inlaid wooden box. "Here. Bon appetit." She turned and left as hurriedly as decorum would permit.

I opened the box as the door closed behind her.

"What is it?" Bethany asked.

"My teeth," I answered as I pulled the fanged dental appliance out of its velvet-lined case.

"They told me that you didn't have—that you weren't fully transformed. There's a small knife in the bedside drawer if you would prefer."

I looked at the ivory points in my hand and then down at Bethany, her head thrown back, her neck a creamy arch of pale flesh and blue veins, her small breasts pulled taut and flat like a boy's.

What the hell was I doing here?

It was hard to think when I was so very, *very thirsty*!

Her snow-white hand took the fangs from my untanned but darker palm. She began to hum as she drew the twin points across her throat. Her skin was not broken but two faint, parallel red lines followed in their wake. She turned her head and drew the teeth up the side of her neck . . . and then back down again.

"Bethany . . ." I said hoarsely.

She dragged the incisors down over her chest, across her breasts until a sharpened tooth caught on a nipple. It rose, tumescent, a pinkish pencil eraser, and a drop of blood formed, like crimson mother's milk.

I snatched the fangs back and hurriedly set them in my mouth. To delay now was to risk a dangerous loss of self-control: I slid an arm beneath her and raised her snowy neck to my icicled mouth.

Bethany was subdued when she left. I soon found out why.

Chef appeared as I was cleaning up. He knocked hesitantly and I found him standing nervously, fingering his white hat, as I emerged from the bathroom. "Yes?"

"Did the master find his selection to his taste?"

"What?"

"You ordered AB negative."

"Yes. Bethany. Well." *To my taste?* The truth of the matter was I had not yet come to note the differences in blood and donor types to be any kind of a gourmand. Part of me was still not over the ick factor. And, until recently, I had only required small amounts of blood on an irregular basis. But Bethany had tasted . . . different. How much of that was the blood and how much the vessel?

"Bethany is one of the rarest flowers in our hothouse," he continued.

"I know. AB negs constitute only one percent of the population."

"Oh, she's rarer than that. Bethany's also a Lutheran."

I was trying to figure out what her religious affiliation had to do with anything when the antigen association clicked into place. "LU-a or -b?"

"A."

I whistled. "That makes her a double neg!"

"Then you know what I'm talking about?"

"Hey, when you find out you have a rare blood disorder, you tend to do the research. Lutheran, Kell, Lewis, Duffy, Kidd, Fisher—even some of the antigen classifications that just use the alphabet. LU-b is rare enough; LU-a drops her off the population charts and onto the Endangered Species list."

He nodded. "All of our consensual donors are precious to us. We treat them well and make sure the symbiotic relationship is a rewarding one. I think you can see why an exotic like Bethany is particularly special in our eyes . . ."

"And upon our palettes," I said. "Now, I know I'm the new boss and most of the staff is anxious to mind their *p*'s and *q*'s—but you really need to stop beating around the bush and get to the point. What seems to be the problem?"

"Well, that is . . ."

"Come on, I don't bite." I felt a bead of moisture at the corner of my mouth, touched it with my finger, and looked at the remnant of Bethany's blood on the tip: I had missed a spot.

"Well, it's just that she seemed dissatisfied as she was heading back to her quarters."

"Dissatisfied?"

"Master . . ."

I flinched inwardly. It was a hateful appellation and far too reminiscent of really bad, two-a.m.-on-the-telly monster movies. I forbade anyone to use it in my presence back home. Kurt, however, had repeatedly impressed upon me the need to establish my dominant status here. Reform, he argued, was best administered from a position of strength.

" . . . it is just understood that the donor will be pleasured in exchange for the wine of their body."

I stared at him. "Pleasured . . ."

"Yes, sir."

"You mean, have sex with her?"

"Only if you wanted to, master."

I frowned. "Well, I didn't want to. So, I didn't. So, what's the problem?"

"The problem, sir, is that *she* didn't enjoy it." He bowed his head. "I'm terribly sorry, sir."

"Well, why should she enjoy it? I put my teeth into her flesh and drank her blood! Being on the receiving end is not my idea of a good time. But I did try to be as gentle as possible and stop that bowing and cringing! I'm not going to kill the messenger." Unless he continued to drag this conversation into further obfuscation, that is.

"Well, some do engage in physical coupling while feeding . . . and there are some donors who relish the pain, the restraints, the slow, excruciating—"

"Yeah, I get the picture. So what does Bethany expect in return? What's her kink?"

He looked up at me, his face blank with astonishment. "Didn't you read her?"

"Read her what? A menu? A bedtime story?"

"You entered her throat without entering her mind?"

Oh.

"Master?" he inquired after a painfully long silence.

"Chef, please send for Bethany and tell her to return to my quarters. Tell her I was . . . tell her I will . . ."

"You cannot drink from her again, this day, unless you mean to bring her over."

"I won't." Another file drawer opened in the back of my head. "Chef," I asked as he turned to go, "does part of Bethany's contract include the promise that she will be turned someday?"

"But of course," he said, hesitating at the doorway, "and therein lies another reason to treat the donors with special care. For if you mistreat them while they are still human, what sort of monsters will they be when you finally give them like power over others?"

Nearly a half hour into Bethany's orgasm there was a knock at the door.

"Come," I called, careful not to take my hand away from the small of her back.

Dennis Smirl walked into my field of view. "What are you doing?" the Chicago shapeshifter asked, looking first at me lying on the bed and then at Bethany sitting primly on the side, fully clothed and facing away from me.

"Tipping the waitress."

He circled around where he could see her vacant, empty stare. He took in the perspiration that misted up from the white flame that burned beneath her skin, the tremors, the clenching and unclenching of her hands, and then listened to the soft gasps and quiet moans that punctuated the paragraphs of silence.

"What is she seeing?"

I shrugged, careful again not to break physical contact. "I'm not a mind reader, yet. I can make suggestions. Force them, if necessary, through mental domination. And my psionic influence is greater if there's a blood-bond, even if it's only a one-way sharing. I'm not really privy to Bethany's fantasy life. I just probed a little to find her pleasure centers and she seemed happy to have me stimulate them."

He grinned. "Probed, huh?"

"Talking above the eyebrows, Dennis. What are you doing here?"

"Do you mean here in New York or here in your bedroom?"

"Both, actually. Though it looks like you're attempting psy-*coitus interruptus* at the moment."

"Well," he said, pulling up a chair, "as you may have heard, a new Doman is being elevated to the throne of the New York demesne and all the other enclaves are sending representatives to the ceremony—"

"Or bloody coup."

He nodded as he sat. "Obviously, whoever sits on the throne when the dust settles will be a power to reckon with. So, there're going to be a number of ambassadors lining up to reckon, negotiate, and curry favor. I'm just presuming on our friendship to push my way to the front of the line."

I nodded. "And?"

"And," he reached inside his suit coat and pulled out a thick envelope, "my Doman sends this with his compliments. He hopes you will find the information useful and will remember Chicago favorably in any future business dealings."

"What is it?"

"Intel on your enemies."

I broke contact as I reached for the package. Bethany fell back across my lap with a gasp as I took the envelope and opened it. There were thirty or forty pages, typewritten, all on very thin, slick-feeling sheets.

"Flash paper," Smirl said as Bethany heaved and thrashed a bit. "A match, a candle flame—and the evidence is all gone." He snapped his fingers. "Just like that!"

Bethany sat up, startled at her emergence from the interior world to the exterior.

"Just in case I don't come out on top," I observed.

"Might be safer for you if your enemies don't find it in your possession."

"Yeah, that's Chicago, the city of altruism."

"I wouldn't be comparing urban reputations if I were you."

"Where am I?" Bethany gasped.

"New York, New York," I said, "it's a hell of a town."

Chapter Ten

I READ OVER the material and tucked it away before Kurt returned for my briefing. If I could trust the intel—and there were at least a half-dozen reasons why I shouldn't—my best hope lay in playing the various families against one another. The pages contained psychological profiles of both known and suspected leaders as well as lists of closeted skeletons, literal as well as figurative. It was a blackmailer's dream.

This wasn't what I signed up for, however.

I wasn't risking my neck to be monster-in-chief like Vlad Dracula or Elizabeth Báthory. Maybe it was a fool's pipe dream but, if I had to rule through terror and bloodshed, I might as well turn the reins over to the rest of the fiends. Unfortunately, idealistic missions to change the system all too often end with the system changing the idealist. What shall it profit a man that he gain the whole underworld but lose his own soul?

But then, I hardly thought of myself as an idealist any more.

Kurt, ignorant of my Chicago cheat-sheet, provided much of the same background material, drawing most of the same conclusions in terms of viable strategies: undermine the strong, elevate the weak, divide and conquer. And the iron glove for my hand of power would be the Szekely Clan who had historically served as the demesne enforcers and was presumably loyal to me.

Through Kurt.

Who was most concerned with my positions on the issues. He kept pressing me for details on what I would tell the various clans and ambassadors when tonight's meet and greet began.

He was not alone in his concerns. By signing on as the new ringmaster for this circus of the damned, I was gambling that mostly human me was still the best chance for the rest of humanity. Better, anyway, than something whose blood had cooled to below room temperature. But mostly human me wasn't as human as I'd been a few months ago. And getting less human as time went on. How much longer would I remain a preferable choice to the other monsters?

What would happen when my blood cooled sufficiently?

"You understand," Kurt was saying, "that you simply can't order an entire species to voluntarily starve itself to death."

"There are blood banks."

He shook his head slowly. "It has worked in isolated situations, serving a few here and there. You are suggesting soup kitchens to serve hundreds on a nightly basis."

I planted my elbows on the table and rested my forehead against my palms. "Supply and demand would be problematic. And the volunteer wine cellar—"

"Even more impractical," he finished for me. "And it's not just logistics and delivery issues. We are, by nature, hunters. Predators. It is our nature and cannot be permanently denied."

"Yeah, yeah; it's your inalienable right to keep and bare fangs. But the demesne system has managed to restrain that so-called nature. There are laws. There are rules. The demesne sets limits on the hunters as well as on the hunt. You're not even allowed to sire more family members without the Doman's permission."

"Which the Countess granted quite liberally as long as she was assured of clan loyalty. The rumor is that you intend to impose a policy of zero population growth."

I rubbed my chin. "Now there's an interesting idea: undead birth control. What other rumors are making the rounds?"

"Almost anything that you can imagine. The more popular ones suggest you are a 'Sin-eater.' That you will return the dead to life, that you will teach us how to walk in daylight—pseudo-religious nonsense and wishful thinking. The more troubling ones claim that you will take away their rights to hunt and reproduce, that you will free the lupin from their servitude, and that you will trigger the great Apocalypse between the People of the Day and the Clans of the Night."

"Which reminds me," I said, sidestepping several issues at once. "How come I haven't met any lycanthropes, yet? Are they all on vacation?"

Kurt's eyebrows raised a couple of millimeters. "How do you know that you haven't?"

I looked him in the eye, waited the requisite six seconds,

and said: "I *know*." I didn't add that, when you're marrying into the family, you learn to pick up on a number of things the furophobes don't.

His shoulders twitched in a negligible shrug. "The first three nights are scheduled around meetings with the families, private audiences—nothing pertaining to the underclasses. It was deemed less volatile to send them away until basic issues get sorted out."

"You mean safer than putting them in the position of having to choose sides in the event that my coronation suddenly goes south."

Now it was Kurt's turn to give me the long stare. "I think I know you better than most but there is a great deal that I still do not know. I know that you resist violence and abhor killing. I believe that you still feel a greater loyalty to the living than the undead—though I expect that to change with time. I know that you do not seek power and that the only reason that you are here must be to protect the living as best you can.

"Be careful, Domo. Many are glad that you are not the monster the last Doman was. But even they will turn on you and destroy you if you seek to deny them their nature."

"Nature, red in tooth and claw? Tennyson spoke of animal nature. Are we not men and, therefore, may rise above animal nature with will and reason?"

"Are we truly men, Domo? We possess the teeth and claws of the predators. Man does not but even he may echo the poet, red in bomb and bullet. No, my dear Christopher, you may be a kinder, gentler ruler but you must content yourself with what accommodations the clans are ready for. Do not expect evolutionary leaps: you are Doman but you are not God."

The meeting ended with little resolved beyond the fact that long, involved policy decisions should wait until the clans and I had become better acquainted. For Kurt that meant I might be better persuaded of the futility of my vision. For me it meant a chance to peruse the battlefield and scout the enemy for weaknesses.

For both of us it meant avoiding major unpleasantness for just a little bit longer.

To that end, I put off asking more nosey questions, such as how the enclave acquired its immense wealth.

No question I had stepped off of the high ground and was wading into a moral morass. If there was a path between losing my life and losing my soul it was a very narrow and convoluted one. Too bad I hadn't the opportunity to have said a proper goodbye to Lupé before coming here to play the part of Napoleon Custer at the Little Waterloo.

As I adjusted my cummerbund and checked my tux in the mirror I felt something brush against my leg. I looked down and saw a tan-and-brown cat. It might have passed for a Burmese breed except for one thing—if its possessing two tails counted as "one" thing.

I reached down and picked her up. She was heavy for a cat. "Hello, Suki; long time no meow." She purred as I scratched her behind her ears. "Let me guess. You have nothing to wear?"

"Actually, she thought she could serve you better in cat form," Deirdre said from the doorway. "She'll dress if you prefer." Deirdre wore a green satin gown which, with her red hair, made her look all Christmassy and like an elegant present ready to be opened on an intimate holiday eve.

I set the two-tailed cat down on the bed. "A man always feels that he has more status if there are two beautiful women on his arm." The cat purred loudly. "But I fear I would be twice as distracted and I am already distracted enough."

"Oh my." The redhead sauntered over and took my arm. "You're *very* good at this diplomacy thing! You honey-tongued devil, you!"

"That's silver-tongued devil," I corrected as we started toward the door and a waiting army of bodyguards. The cat jumped off the bed and padded along behind us.

"Teach your grandmother to suck eggs, Chris. I know a sweet tongue when I taste it . . ."

I had no comeback. As far as Lupé was concerned, I *was* a silver-tongued devil.

And all of the connotations were negative.

A phalanx of security types—some even human— escorted us to an underground ballroom several city blocks away. My best guess was that we were under Central Park now.

Over the previous century and a half some eight-hun-dred-and-forty-three acres between 59th and 110th Street had been repeatedly dug up and laced with a succession of conduits, tunnels, chambers, and underground passages for channeling a succession of lakes, lagoons, aquifers, flood plains, water supplies, fountains, telephone cables, electrical conduits, and maintenance access routes. As new landscaping projects were developed, old drains and tunnels were closed for new channeling systems. At present there were more forgotten and unused channels under the park and museum than there were official passageways on the current city blueprints. Stories were told and legends grew about what might creep through the subterranean paths beneath the city. Truth be told, the stories averaged out to be half right. There were few beauties but many beasts. And, while there were no such things as Teenaged Mutant Ninja Turtles, there was a monster under Greenwich Village that the inhabitants had nicknamed "Shredder."

Tonight the population under the Great Lawn had trebled even as half of the subterranean residents had fled in terror. Vampires and Monsters and Weres, oh my!

Except there were no Weres: they had been sent away.

Just as well. If I was to believe my beloved's dire warnings, I could well be fighting a battle on two separate fronts when they returned.

Our entrance to the cavernous ballroom went unnoticed. The lights had been dimmed and images were playing out on a large screen at the far end of the room.

Familiar images.

The monstrous creature with the steel fangs was frozen in mid stride, bashing its way into my dining room. A small readout of numbers designating the date and time was displayed in the lower left-hand corner. It was a freeze frame from my home's video security system.

"Best estimates put the creature's height somewhere between eight and nine feet," a woman's voice was saying, "its weight somewhere in the twelve to fifteen hundred pound range." Her voice emerged from speakers all around the chamber so it took me a moment to locate her up on the dais, standing behind a podium to the right of the screen. "A cybernetic organism, or cyborg, it appears to be a reengineered human. Surgical enhancements are confirmed. Genetic enhancements are presumed though we are waiting to obtain tissue samples for confirmation."

There was something about the woman—even at a distance—that seemed strangely familiar. I moved forward to get a better look, pushing at my forward guard to break a path through the crowd.

"In addition to steel and Kevlar implants and skeletal augmentation, the creature may have had its strength and reflexes artificially enhanced. As you can see from selected portions of the security video, it is as fast as it is strong."

On the screen a series of herky-jerky edits showed it selectively taking out my security personnel as well as my home's structural architecture.

"Even though the creature killed one vampire and three humans and injured another vampire with ridiculous ease . . . your Doman managed to defeat it single-handedly . . ."

I was pissed off to find security video from my home being shown to a bunch of strangers, some of whom were heavily invested in getting rid of me. And I was grieved to see a replay of the deaths it had caused, particularly that of The Kid.

And I was majorly annoyed that Deirdre and Suki's parts in the battle were largely left out.

But I had to admit I was impressed with the spin.

The editing of the video and the narration worked to underscore the monster's invulnerability and then my parts were intercut to make me appear heroic and invincible. Either Kurt had just discouraged the next assassination attempt or he had convinced my enemies to multiply their efforts by ten.

"And so," the speaker was concluding, "there is an unknown entity in the game, which has moved against the interests of New York. We are fortunate to have a Doman who has experience in dealing with what even *we* would call the unusual and extraordinary!"

The audience response to that seemed evenly split between the mutterers and the murmurers.

"The Doman has authorized a one-million-dollar reward for information leading to the identity and location of this mysterious Dr. Pipt."

Deirdre leaned toward my ear and whispered: "Does that include me? I've done some more research."

"Research?" I whispered back. Given the background noise, whispering was easier to hear than muttering or murmuring.

"I've read more of *The Patchwork Girl of Oz.*"

"And?"

"Am I eligible for the reward?"

I shrugged. "I didn't even know there was a reward until just now. But I don't see why not."

She nodded. "Well, I found out that this Dr. Pipt gave away a whole batch of his Powder of Life to Mombi the Witch in exchange for a Powder of Perpetual Youth. Only the Powder of Youth was a fraud. It didn't work."

"Of course."

"So Pipt had to make more powder—Powder of Life, that is, since he had given it all away to the old witch."

"And what did she do with her portion?"

"Made Jack Pumpkinhead, for one."

"And how does any of this relate to the real Dr. Pipt?"

She looked at me. "I don't know. Yet. I'm still research-ing."

"By reading an old Oz book?"

"It beats what you've been doing this afternoon."

I was spared having to come up with a reply by a blar-ing introduction from the sound system. "And now I'd like to introduce the new Doman of the New York demesne, Christopher Cséjthe!"

Showtime: the queen is dead, long live the king.

The security team hustled me up on stage and I was escorted to the microphone. The podium gave me the illusion of a shield. Likewise the two large bodyguards flanking me to either side. A large, Plexiglas screen served as both a teleprompter and a bulletproof barrier for my upper torso. The only way I could've been better protect-ed was to have addressed the crowd from another room. I looked down at the audience. Anyone harboring thoughts of taking me out right here, right now, could see the futil-ity of making such an attempt. They would either be exposed or need to use something that could harm the other occupants of the room, thus negating the political advantage of such an act.

I pulled the microphone out of its cradle on the stand and stepped around the podium. "Go sit down, boys," I said to my bodyguards, "I won't be needing you in this room."

The guards were in a quandary: Kurt had given them specific orders to be all over me like white on rice. Yet, their Doman was giving them a direct counterorder. And to disobey me in front of the clans was as dangerous to me as it was to them. I helped resolve matters by giving them a little mental nudge. They stumbled out of my way.

"Good evening, ladies and gentlemen," I said as I walked to the center of the dais. "I think I'll dispense with the teleprompters. If a leader can't speak from his own heart, he shouldn't presume to speak for anyone else, either. And I don't think I want anything to come between me and you. If we can't work in harmony, bulletproof glass and armored barriers aren't going to solve the problem."

Kurt was hovering stage-left looking positively apoplectic. He shouldn't have been surprised. It was no secret by now that I was no good at following other people's scripts.

"I apologize for not coming to New York sooner but I have had other business to attend to." I paused. "Part of the delay has been due to unscheduled visitors interrupting my work. While the mysterious Dr. Pipt sent this most recent emissary, there have been other intrusions as well. Some by representatives of people within this very room."

The mutter-mutter/murmur-murmur volume rose to a new level. I let it build and then pulled the microphone in close for more volume.

"I must admit I was amused by the first seven attempts on my life—" Actually that was a lie but the first rule of intimidation is to never let them see you sweat. My smile turned into a frown. "—but my patience has its limits and I find that I am no longer inclined to be so tolerant. Any further assassination attempts will be dealt with harshly.

With penalties assessed for the clan and family as well as the perpetrator." The mutters and murmurs had faded away. "I just want to make sure that we're clear on this point before continuing."

A tall, aristocratic-looking vampire was standing at the edge of the stage, his handsome features framed by a silky mane of chestnut hair that fell past his shoulders. He stood head and shoulders above the crowd and was able to lean an elegantly cuffed arm across the edge of the elevated platform without stretching. "I have a question," he said politely.

I stepped closer and said, "Yes?" And lowered the microphone to make his query audible to the room.

"If I *kill* you," he said, reaching out and grabbing my ankle, "how will *you* enforce *that*?" He yanked and I fell backwards. The back of my head smacked the stage and I was as momentarily stunned as my security team. He dragged me into his embrace and his mouth was on my throat before anyone else could take a single step.

He didn't just bite me; he tore my throat open with his razored teeth: it was his best hope of killing me before anyone else could reach him.

It hurt like hell and probably would have hurt a lot more if I hadn't been coasting on the edge of shock. As it was, the pain seemed to revive me and I began to struggle. Not that struggling was going to do me a lot of good. As I've pointed out before, I'm no match for a full-fledged vampire in either the strength or the speed department. The word had gotten around and this guy knew it. I felt a gush of blood and his mouth was on my wounds, greedily slurping all the high octane Doman blood he could suck down.

Maybe he was too greedy: he started to choke on the third swallow. As his mouth came away, I licked my palm and slapped my hand over the bloody gash on my neck. My assailant released me and it was all I could do to keep from falling to the floor like a sack of spilled groceries. The stage was against my back and helped to prop me up. The crowd pressed in on either side, cutting off my escape routes and providing additional support. And my attacker was in front of me. I wasn't about to fall down because I had no intention of getting any closer to him than I was now, total exsanguination or not. I locked my knees, kept a tight grip on my neck with my left hand, and waved at the thickening haze with my right.

Then the screaming started.

It started all around me but it was the loudest just in front of me.

I waved my hand all the more, trying to fan the smoke aside to see what was going on. My attacker stumbled against me and it was suddenly obvious why there was both smoke and screaming.

His face was gray and black, his mouth a bubbling ruin. White-and-gray fumes issued from his lips, vented from festering sores on his throat, and leaked from a growing red-and-gray stain on his shirt above his cummerbund. His eyes were bulging in their sockets, reflecting a kaleidoscope of confusion, fear, and pain beyond imagining. His hands gripped the folds of my jacket. "It . . . burns . . ." he wheezed, more noxious vapors issuing from his scorched mouth.

Powerful pairs of hands grasped my shoulders and hauled me back up onto the stage. My attacker held on with a death grip and came along for the ride. We were pried apart and he fell back on the stage where he writhed and moaned.

Kurt pushed through the semicircle of security people and threw an arm around me. "Let's get you out of here."

I shook my head. I had lost a lot of blood but I could feel my accelerated healing factors kicking in. I might still pass out but I probably wouldn't bleed to death now. "Not yet." I nodded at the dying vampire. "Who is he?"

"Yuler Polidori."

"The Polidori Clan?"

He nodded.

Oh great. I carefully bent down and retrieved the microphone cord, pulling the mike toward me. It wasn't easy using just one hand. A bodyguard assisted. "Yuler," I said, kneeling over the writhing vampire, "Yuler Polidori. Who is your master?"

"No . . . man . . ." he gasped, "no . . . *man* . . . is my . . . master . . ."

In other words, not some fangless wimp who was a pretender to the throne of the New York demesne.

"Then who is your Sire?"

He shook his head. "I acted . . . alone . . . saw . . . my chance . . . took it . . . no plan . . . kill me . . ."

I looked at Kurt. "Can he be saved?"

Kurt stared down with a face of stone. "What would be the point? This one would not talk."

An alpha vampire with close-cropped gray hair shouldered his way through the crowd and leapt onto the stage. The security team moved toward him but Kurt waved them back. "Friederich," he said.

"Domo Cséjthe," Friederich Polidori said, inclining his head to me.

I gave him a slight nod in return. I was afraid that if I moved my head any more than that, I would reopen my jugular.

"I am mortified, my lord. Yuler has always been wild and headstrong but I never suspected him capable of treasonous behavior. Had I had any inkling, I would have killed him myself."

Funny. It was a nice little apology but curiously flat in the sincerity department. An accomplished liar might have put too much emotion into the speech, punctuating his sentences with exclamation marks. Polidori recited the words without any inflection, as if reading cue cards in an emotionless monotone. Then I got a look at his eyes and felt the prickle in my parietal lobes: ole Freddy was trying to *glamour* me. He was putting all of his efforts into sugarcoating the message telepathically.

I turned to my seneschal, who looked a little unfocused himself. "Isn't that a little odd, Kurt?"

"Hmm? What?"

"That a Sire doesn't know what his Spawn is thinking?"

"That is true," he answered, his gaze hardening.

I turned back to Polidori. "A clan leader knows he has a hotheaded Spawn who has positioned himself right next to the stage where the new Doman is going to speak? A Doman who has been the target of repeated assassination attempts by powerful foes within the enclave, itself? Who then attempts to use mental domination on the Doman and his First while trying to offer an embarrassment of an excuse?"

"It appears to have all of the markings of a conspiracy," Kurt growled. There was apparently no love lost between the Polidori and Szekely clans.

"On the other hand," I continued, "it may be nothing more than a series of errors in judgment. Of course, for the head of a clan, so many mistakes and misjudgments could spell ruin for the families that follow him—even if he was loyal and true."

Polidori scowled. He was angry that a member of his family had been caught in the act of trying to assassinate me. Perhaps he was angry that the attempt failed. He was certainly unhappy to be dressed down in such a manner. But what probably pissed him off the most was the fact that the microphone was still on and our little exchange had been overheard by everyone in the room.

Perhaps he was tempted to attack me, himself.

And perhaps the grisly result of the last attempt that smoked and bubbled at his feet was giving him pause.

"My lord—let me be the instrument of your vengeance."

"What? Oh, I see. You wish to prove your loyalty by killing one of your own who is suffering and likely to die anyway." I shook my head. "That is no gift to me."

"Doubtless it would safeguard any secrets you might wish to keep," Kurt observed.

Stay out of this, I sent to my majordomo.

He glanced at me, a flicker of surprise appearing and disappearing across his stony face.

"Here is my gift to you and your clan, Polidori: I give Yuler back to you alive. I give him to you with the charge to *keep* him alive." *If "alive" was the proper term for an undead.* "Heal him as best you can. That will be your apology and gift to me. Your clan's atonement is to heal Yuler."

Friederich Polidori was aghast. Well, technically, he *was* a "ghast" anyway. But this was so outside the pale of his expectations that he didn't know how to respond.

"I shall expect a progress report when we meet again tomorrow night."

"Tomorrow? But our appointment is for to—"

"Tonight. I know. I'm rescheduling you for tomorrow."

"But we are first! This is an insult!"

There was no way I could outdominate a master vampire. The best I could do was take a tone with him. "No, Fred; *this* is an insult," I said, pointing at the gurgling, hissing Yuler. "And he's going to occupy your attention for the remainder of the evening. Now, do you need help getting him back to your domicile?"

He seemed to come to a decision. "No."

I almost said: "No . . . what?" but maybe I needed to cut Polidori some slack. And maybe I also needed to *not* push my luck past the breaking point.

He turned and his clan moved as one toward the stage. As Yuler was lifted down and carried toward an exit he turned back to me, clicked his heels and executed a short bow. "Until tomorrow, Domo."

"Buh-bye, Fred." Well, some pushing is instinctual . . .

As he strode away, head held high, a haughty expression frozen on his aristocratic countenance, Kurt leaned in and whispered, "We can reschedule all of tonight's appointments."

"Don't be silly," I murmured. "Just push back my

appointments an hour or so. I need to clean up and replace a couple of gallons of blood, that's all."

I walked back to the podium with Kurt and a half-dozen security personnel hovering around me like the Marines bent on raising the flag on Iwo Jima. "Sit down, gentlemen," I said pleasantly.

They looked at each other as if I had just asked them to do headstands.

"Sit down," I said pointedly. I had to make the fact that I was still on my feet work for me or I would be resting permanently before the night was over.

They returned to their seats and the standing posts just offstage.

"Now then," I said, turning back to the audience, "where was I before I was so rudely interrupted?"

"You were saying," answered a woman's voice from the floor, "that 'any further assassination attempts will be dealt with harshly. With penalties assessed for the clan and family as well as the perpetrator'."

There was a ripple of nervous laughter that turned to murmurs (no mutters) as I turned away from the podium and went down the steps from the dais back to the floor again. A conga line of bodyguards scurried after me as the crowd hurriedly parted and I made my way to the dark-skinned woman who had just spoken. She appeared to be a mix of Eurasian and Negroid stock and her accent suggested that she might be a recent immigrant to these shores. She stood her ground as I arrived, refusing to take a step back as I walked right up and into her face. Neither of us spoke and the room fell silent. I removed my hand from my throat. Blood oozed in a sluggish trickle from tears that were already on their way to forming pink weals. Reaching out, I cupped her chin with my right hand and put my left behind her head.

"What—" she finally said, and I suddenly wrenched her head from her shoulders before she could speak a second word.

Tucking it under my left arm, I licked my right hand again and pressed my spittle-soaked palm to my neck. As her headless body collapsed to the ground, I turned and began making my way back to the stage. "Get that off the floor," I said to the last security man and ascended the stairs again.

I placed the head on the podium so that it was looking up at me. Then I looked out over the stunned assemblage and smiled. "She was correct." I patted the head, whose entrails dribbled down the front and side of the podium like gory party streamers. "And I should be grateful to Yuler Polidori for assisting me in making my point." Confusion suffused some of the faces of those nearest me in the crowd. "What? You think that killing him would have been harsher?"

"No, my lord; killing him would have been a kindness!" It was another woman who spoke now. A tall, raven-haired beauty, equal in aristocratic bearing to Friederich Polidori: Carmella Le Fanu. "Nor, I suspect, are you finished with the Polidori Clan in this matter."

Everyone held their breath to see what I would do next.

I inclined my head and pulled my hand away from my neck. A hundred pairs of eyes focused their greedy attention on the bloody hamburger effect between my jaw and my ruined collar. "They'll be getting my bill for the tuxedo tomorrow."

More laughter now and less nervousness.

"However, as Madame Le Fanu points out, the matter is not yet closed," I continued. "Perhaps you are used to Domans who rule through violence and intimidation. Perhaps you have had leadership that equates brutality with strength. Make no mistake; the guilty *will* be brought to justice. But a rush to judgment often punishes the innocent. And a Doman's responsibilities are, first, to protect and serve the welfare of his people . . ."

"The vampires . . ." I heard someone mutter.

"*All* of his people," I said. "Wampyr, were, demi. Natural, unnatural, supernatural, preternatural."

I felt hundreds of eyes glance toward the head by my right hand.

"Oh, very well," I said, "bring me the body."

A couple of the security team trotted up, bearing the headless corpse. They hadn't been too far away.

I lifted the head and gazed into its eyes. "Woman," I said, making sure we were both close enough to the microphone to pick up the sound of my voice, "I adjure you from the realm of the living to speak from the land of the dead! Tell me your name!"

Her eyes fluttered open and I had to fight a momentary flashback to Theresa Kellerman's decapitation as her mouth worked like the Tin Man's as he prepared to speak his first words after standing rusted for a hundred years.

"Jhojie Selangor," she finally croaked. I made sure the microphone picked up every syllable.

She shouldn't have been able to speak at all. Never

mind being technically dead, the problem, once again, was the disconnection between larynx and lungs. Among the dangling entrails, however, several bladderlike appendages pulsed, pushing enough air through her voice box for a short answer or two.

"And do you swear fealty to me as your Doman and promise to serve me faithfully?" I pressed.

"I . . . swear . . ." she gasped.

I turned and, as the bodyguards held the headless body erect, I eased the entrails and, finally, the head, back into the gaping wound created by her cranium's sudden departure. Waving my bloody hands in what I hoped looked like sufficiently mystic gestures, I muttered incoherently and hoped that snake oil was in season.

Stepping back, I cried: "Release her!"

Everyone stepped back: the security staff, the audience. Jhojie Selangor blinked, reached up to give her neck a minor adjustment, and stepped forward. Somewhere in the back of my mind, Colin Clive was shrieking: *She's alive, alive!*

The audience wasn't much less restrained as I returned to the podium.

"I will be looking into a great many matters," I said, continuing as if my little exercise in head games hadn't even happened. "Perhaps this will make some of you uncomfortable. Just remember that we are banded together for our common welfare. Our strength and security lies in our combined numbers, our combined efforts, our common purpose. But nothing is ever achieved without sacrifice and the one truism of mutual effort is compromise. To *get* something you have to *give* something. If we are all to benefit, we must all be willing to temper our individual and family desires with satisfying others' needs as part of the bargain. It is my job as your Doman to see to it that the enclave benefits . . . so that you all may benefit.

"That is one of the main purposes of my meeting with your representatives and ambassadors from other demesnes over the next three nights. To better acquaint myself with your needs and concerns so that I might serve you all.

"I look forward to meeting with all of you during the nights ahead. I shall go now and change into something more comfortable and begin my visitations for this night. I urge you all to stay, enjoy the refreshments and the music, party and, perhaps, use this opportunity to renew old acquaintances and make new ones. Good evening, my friends."

Scattered applause broke out as I backed away from the podium, turned thunderous as Kurt and Jhojie came to my side, and continued as I was escorted off the platform by the small army of Bodyguards-R-Us.

Out in the corridor I sank gratefully into a cushioned seat on the electric tram.

"Are you all right?"

I closed my eyes. "I am so *thirsty*."

"I'll call ahead and have fresh blood waiting. Any preferences?"

"Yeah. Have it sent up in a bucket. Tonight I'm not sure I would know when to stop with a living host."

We started off with a lurch while Kurt radioed ahead. "You departed from the script tonight," he said when he finished the call.

"I hadn't counted on Yuler."

"I'm talking before young Polidori. When you told the bodyguards to sit down and you stepped away from the podium."

"I'm not one of them, Kurt. I have to do it my way. This brings me to a couple of things. Just before Yuler's Sire stepped in, I asked if Polidori could be saved. You didn't answer my direct question. You presupposed my purpose in trying to save him. *Don't* second-guess me. Give me the answers I ask for, not the answers you think I need."

"I think you need more than you ask for," he argued. "As your advisor, it is my place to give you advice. Again I must make the point: because they are stronger, faster, older—"

"Wiser?"

"—more powerful, it is all the more reason that you must demonstrate your power."

"I thought I just did that."

"Your destruction of the young Polidori was most impressive. But you should be demonstrating power instead of mercy."

"Abraham Lincoln said: 'I have always found that mercy bears richer fruits than strict justice.'"

"Yes? Well, Shakespeare wrote that 'nothing emboldens sin so much as mercy.' Show them your power first. You can then afford mercy later."

"Mercy *is* power, Kurt. In showing the Polidoris mercy, I was showing everyone else my strength. I don't think ole Freddy felt I was being kind. And I doubt anyone getting a good look at Yuler thought he was getting any kind of charity, whatsoever."

My seneschal nodded grudgingly.

"I'm not going to play the role of brutal dictator here. If I can't do it my way I'll walk away."

I could feel him shaking his head inside the pounding of my own. "You cannot walk away."

"I won't be another Elizabeth Báthory. I won't become Vlad Drakul the Fifth."

"No," he said sadly. "You are somewhat cleverer than either in your own way. And, in a sense, they are both your parents. You are already turning into a monster. Someday you will be more terrible than the two of them joined together."

Now there was a happy thought. I had come to New York to face down my enemies. With apologies to Pogo, my most dangerous foe waited for me in the future.

Myself.

Chapter Eleven

"AN HOUR'S REST," the doctor was saying as he closed his medical case. "And I want the lights off. You'll heal much quicker in the dark."

I nodded absently. I had the telephone receiver to my ear and was having a simultaneous conversation with another doctor, Dr. Burton, who was inexplicably back in Seattle.

"It sounds as if the silver compounds in your tissues and bloodstream have intensified in their toxicity," he was saying. "Some unique quality in your hemoglobin appears to be transmuting its properties in ways that human or vampire or lycanthrope blood wouldn't. Perhaps when you ingested the blood of Elizabeth Báthory—"

"She wasn't the Countess Báthory," I corrected, "she was a demon posing as my great-great-ancestor. And it wasn't her body that I drank from; it was one of her meat-puppets."

"Yes, I know," he said. "But as the demon moved from host to host, that body was physically transformed, right down to the cellular level. She was onboard and fully invested when you drank from Chalice Delacroix's body. You drank demon's blood, once removed, charged with preternatural essences that we can't even begin to dream of, much less categorize. Perhaps your body is utilizing the silver as a defense mechanism."

"Against Lupé? Look, Doc, mixed marriages are hard enough without us not even being able to touch each other. You gotta do something!"

"I can't come to New York without my Doman's permission. Why don't you ask Stefan? But I have to warn you, I'm really operating in the dark, here. And New York has labs and doctors—"

"Yes, we do," agreed the other doctor who was standing by the door. "And we'll be happy to start working on your problem once you've fully recuperated. Now hang up the phone and rest before your first appointment."

I held up my hand to show I was getting there. "What about Lupé, Doc? How is the baby?"

There was a long pause. "We don't know."

"What do you mean, you don't know?"

"She's gone. And we don't know where. We think she's gone back to her pack, her family." I saw the New York physician's highly sensitive ears prick up at that.

"Just a moment." I turned to the doctor standing at my door. "Is there anything else, doctor?"

"I—er—that is—I just want to say that you were very clever in stopping your own bleeding tonight. The clotting sacks under your tongue are unusually developed and your enzyme output must be triple that of any vampire I've ever examined."

"Yeah, well, that's because Mother Nature has designed us to make things bleed. Rudimentary clotting sacks are just an evolutionary afterthought if you ask me."

"Well, you are unique. And it was sheer genius to use your own saliva to accelerate the mending of your throat. I'd like to study—"

"I'd like to finish this call," I said harshly. "Please turn off the lights on your way out, doctor. And I'm sure I don't have to remind you that anything heard inside this room is privileged information."

"Oh, yes. Patient confidentiality is a staple of the medical oath."

"It's more than that, Sawbones. It's the most powerful member of your enclave giving you a warning."

"Yes. Yes, sir! Good night!" He flipped the wall switch and closed the door, plunging the room into darkness.

I put the receiver back to my ear. "Gerald . . . don't leave. She's not hereslf right now and I'm not sure her family is really going to help her."

"Ask Pagelovitch. He'll be visiting in the next day or two."

"I will. Tell her . . ."

There was the sound of breathing on the connection—mine, not his.

"Christopher?"

"Just call me if you hear anything." I hung up.

I stared at the soft glow of the phone's touchpad floating just above the nightstand and considered fumbling down, next to it, for the bucket on the floor. They had taken me at my word when I requested a pail of blood. I had spoken in hyperbole but I ended up drinking most of the contents like a man dying of thirst. How anyone could ingest that much at one sitting was beyond my understanding.

But not, apparently, beyond my need.

And I was still thirsty!

I no longer felt weak, just tired. There was a difference. And I no longer hurt, I just ached. Another difference. Like Bilbo Baggins, I felt thin and stretched, only instead of butter I felt like strawberry jam spread across too much toast. Once a healing blanket, the darkness was now like an empty vacuum, a starless void in the deepest regions of space. I felt nebulous, dissipated in entropic heat-death. Fading into eternal oblivion.

Only there was a star.

A single point of light that flickered and grew like a distant nova.

The star became a nebula, a nebulous display of the Northern Lights.

Lime green . . .

Rippling into a distortion of . . . a suit and tie and broad-brimmed hat!

The Kid was materializing in the darkness like the midnight reflection of neon lights in a dark puddle. My subconscious guilt manifesting on the borderline of consciousness? An undigested bit of blood, a blot of plasma, a crumb of platelets? Manifestation of gravy or of grave?

"How now, spirit," I croaked, "whither wander you?"

The apparition made no answer but flickered at the sound of the door whispering open. It disappeared and all was darker than dark as I heard the door close again with a quiet click.

Bare feet padded across the floor and I was momentarily distracted by the fact that I could actually hear the difference between shod and unshod footsteps on the carpet.

Now another sound: a rustle. Clothing, sliding, dropping to the floor.

An intake of breath.

And the rich, warm smell of blood!

I could still detect the scent of the cold, coagulating remnants of the bucket's contents. This, however, was a heady brew of meaty odors, the juice of life, still living, still vital, immediate and hasty from the vein!

It drew closer and the edge of the mattress depressed as another body joined mine on the bed.

Deirdre had come to offer me the enhanced healing properties of my untainted blood, my former gift that now circulated in her transformed body.

Her hand touched my bare chest and she moved to straddle me, both of us performing a blind dance in the dark, our hands scouting ahead to show us the way.

She pulled my head to her throat and I licked at the flow that had already collected in the hollow between her collarbones.

The blood filled my mouth, washing over my tongue like a tsunami of napalm. I swallowed liquid fire and, for a moment, I recalled Yuler Polidori's contorted face, his steaming mouth blistered and bubbling as my own blood burned him from the inside out. But this was different. This blood was potent and cleansing, like a whiskey astringent, revving up the tiny motors of each cell it touched. I felt like a volcano erupting in reverse and knew that this was something that passed beyond the psychosexual excitations of undead bloodlust. A steady diet from these veins would either burn me up in six months or keep me young and vigorous for a thousand years!

And that is when I realized that I couldn't be tasting my own recycled blood in Deirdre's body.

That blood had its own potency. Mine had resurrected the dead and turned the undead back into the living. It was powerful and unique and, according to some, even sacred.

But *this* was something different. It had a different brand of potency. It tasted forbidden. Felt secret and nearly unattainable. It was an elixir untasted by the wampyr or they would have kept stories about it. Hell, they would have written songs about it, fought wars over it, razed empires to acquire it.

It wasn't human blood.

And it wasn't Deirdre that I was drinking from.

It took every bit of willpower I possessed to pull my bloody lips away and gasp: "Who . . . ?"

"Meow," answered Suki's voice.

Jhojie Selangor was nervous. She kept looking around the private reception room at the security guards that Kurt had insisted on posting.

"Don't worry about them," I said, smiling and trying to put her at ease. "They're just here for show. They're really nothing more than Teletubbies with fangs."

Deirdre smirked. She lounged in a chair to my left. Kurt was ensconced in the chair on my right, trying to suppress a scowl. I had agreed to their presence on the

condition that neither would speak unless spoken to. I
wasn't worried about the two-tailed cat that was curled
beneath my chair. She had plenty of room to stretch: if I
ever got back home I would have to tell Boo that the
whole "throne" issue was literal as well as metaphorical.

I knew I wasn't endearing myself to my bodyguards
with the Teletubbies remark but I had other people's
feelings to consider. The Szekely Clan had served as the
demoness Lilith's enforcers—sort of an undead Gestapo
who kept the malcontents in line and performed whatever
unpleasantness was required to prop up her reign of terror.
Given the fact that the New York (or any other) demesne
was made up of scary creatures, it naturally followed that
the enforcers had to be even scarier.

Now that ole warm and cuddly me had taken the place
of the Blood Countess from Hell, there was still the issue
of the Szekely reputation. The junkyard might have a
kindler, gentler owner, now, but the junkyard dogs were
the same old, rabid pit bulls.

To a certain degree that worked in my favor. As long
as I could trust the Szekely oath of fealty, that is. But it
also had its drawbacks. As long as my subjects suspected
that I was nothing more than a puppet or a tool of the
Hungarian mafia, they weren't about to get real confi-
dential. So my first order of business was to work at
gaining the trust of the various clans as I met with their
representatives.

This wouldn't be easy with the head of the Szekely Clan
sitting at my right hand.

I had to convince some that I wasn't the Devil
incarnate.

I needed to assure others that I could be utterly ruthless when necessary.

And I had to figure out when to be what to which.

As a succession of private audiences with the various clan and demesne representatives progressed through the early hours of the morning, I found it necessary to wear a number of different faces and take a diversity of different tones with my various supplicants.

Right now I was trying to be all reassuring. The last time I had been this close to Ms. Selangor, I had stepped in and yanked her head off. Of course we had rehearsed the whole thing a couple of hours before the reception, but she still wasn't quite sure what sort of a devil she was making a deal with.

Jhojie Selangor had been born in Malaysia back in the early 1960s. She had immigrated to the United States as a young woman—the result of one of the Internet's "foreign brides for American men" services. She had listed on her application form that she wished to marry a "nice, clean American man who needed plenty of care and loving."

Even though she was less photogenic than some of the other Malaysian brides-in-waiting she had her pick of responding pen pals. She didn't mention that her main reason for leaving the country of her birth involved persecution. Or that she had been driven out of three different villages by the time she was nineteen.

Jhojie Selangor was a *Pênanggalan*.

The undead of Malaysia fall into five groups derived from three different species. There are the *Langsuyar* and the *Pontianak*, who are distant relatives of the Greek *Lamiai*. The *Polong* and the *Pelesit*, who are small, animallike blood drinkers. And the *Pênanggalan*, who are as unique a creature as you are likely to find in the vampire kingdom.

A *Pênanggalan* is always female. By day she appears to be a normal woman and has no fear of the sun. At night, however, her true nature is revealed as soon as she finds a secluded spot for her body to rest. Her head then separates from her body and flies off, trailing its entrails like some horrific jellyfish, in search of prey. The head must return and rejoin its body before sunrise or it will be destroyed. Granted, not your typical East European undead profile, but it made her an ideal clan leader and representative for the Morlocks.

Not to mention our little guerrilla theatre during tonight's reception.

Other immigrant undead had largely folded themselves into the ethnic communities of their human origin: the Mamuwaldes were based in Morningside Heights and Harlem, the Tlahuelpuchis in El Barrio and Jackson Heights, the Aluka on the Lower East Side as well as Borough Park and Williamsburg, the Chiang-shih in Chinatown and Flushing while the Kyuketsukis favored the more exclusive Riverdale area. Then there were the Bavas in Little Italy and Bensonhurst, the Dearg-dul in Hell's Kitchen and Five Points, the Rakshasis and Vetalas in the East Village with some encroachment on Flushing, the Nachtzehrers in Yorkville, and the Upír who had moved from East 97th Street out to Brighton Beach. The Loogaroo, Sukuyan, and Asema clustered along Eastern Parkway between Grand Army Plaza and Utica Avenue; the Gronnskjegg in Bay Ridge and Sunset Park. The

Vjeszczi preferred Greenpoint while Atlantic Avenue and Midwood was home to the Oneidas. Astoria, Queens was overrun with the Vrykolakas.

The "family" clans varied a little more in ethnicity and, to some extent, species. The Polidoris' turf was the Upper East Side. The Le Fanus slept in penthouse coffins in Upper Midtown. The Szgany were Gypsies and had spread throughout The Village and Soho. The previous Doman had called the Szekely Clan to be her pit bulls of the damned and their kennels were now on the Upper West Side.

And then there were those clans who did not identify themselves by a particular ethnicity. There were the gangs like The Deads and The Hammers. And The Ladies of the Night who were actually, as you might suppose, "ladies of the night."

And, of course, the Morlocks.

Jhojie Selangor presided over a microcosmic melting pot of those immigrants and cast-offs that had no single ethnic, cultural, physical, or metaphysical tribe with which they could find fraternity or commonality. With no single neighborhood in which to blend, they had taken their place beneath the streets of the city, dwelling underground much like H.G. Wells' fictional troglodytes from which they took their name. At once feared and scorned for their differences, their leader explained that they most longed for a sense of legitimacy. They wanted recognition from the other clans that the Morlocks had equal birthrights among the families of the night. She hoped that the new Doman would make a place for them at the big boys' table.

It seemed a reasonable request, an agenda I would push regardless. But it didn't hurt that I owed her one for the head-popping turn at my coming out party.

My next appointment, Silvanio Malatesta, had trained most of his life to become a monster. He just spelled it with a *b* instead of an *n*.

As a kid he had run with a succession of street gangs until he was old enough to attract the attention of the mafia (which, like vampires, doesn't really exist either). He worked his way up through the ranks until he became an underboss for one of "those families." Back in the hey-day—the Forties for Silvanio, when he was still Warm—he had discovered the inhabitants of another underworld.

These *piazzaiollos* were worse than the Sicilians—they had no fear of the gun or the knife and he lost several good men and more than a few street punks before he learned their dark and terrible secrets. Silva did not understand how such creatures came to be but he did understand power. These Bava had it and he wanted it. You gave up certain things to acquire power, everything in life is a trade-off: *Non c'è rosa senza spine.*

But what would he really be giving up? Silva worked nights and preferred to sleep late anyway. The priests had said he was going to Hell while he was still a young boy and, by the time he became a made man, he had long said goodbye to his own soul. Near invulnerability to bullets, superhuman strength and speed, the power to cloud the minds of the simple and superstitious—why would anyone not accept this Dark Gift? Not that it was being offered, you understand; it had to be bargained for. But Malatesta was a man who had learned how to get what he wanted regardless of the cost or what others wanted. He was brought over.

The Family should have considered him their greatest asset. Instead, they feared and loathed what he had become. Old World superstitions and Catholicism were arrayed against the advantages he felt he had to offer.

But the division ran deeper than that.

The Dark Gift had changed him in ways he had not reckoned. A cataloging of the physical transformations did not take into account the mental and emotional changes that were taking place, as well. He had thought himself a "cold-blooded killer" before, never imagining how the literal version of those words would remake him and all of his future plans. The Dark Gift does not serve humans; it is humans who must serve the Dark Gift. Silvanio Malatesta gave up his position of underboss for La Costa Nostra. He severed his ties to his former Family by severing their jugulars. Now he was godfather for the Bava, gangsters with fangs. Fangsters. The New York demesne had its own mafia now. And Malatesta came to our audience wanting to know if the new Doman was going to muscle in on his turf.

Likewise Dante Inferno (don't you just love the names vamps come up with when they rename themselves?) and Blackstar Sabertooth. Only Dante and Blackstar weren't asking any questions. They had come to do me the favor of explaining how it was with The Deads and The Hammers, the two major vampire street gangs in the city. They weren't looking for anything from me and I shouldn't be looking for anything from them.

I told them pretty much what I told everyone else that

night: I was just looking to get acquainted for now. No promises, no pitches, no deals—just a little turn out on the dance floor and we'll do lunch at a later date.

My next appointment was from out of town. The representative of the Northern Wilderness Clans arrived in traditional Native American garb. Her buckskin dress, leggings, and moccasin boots were adorned with beads, bones, and shells. Her eyes were as black as her hair and implied age far beyond her appearance as a maid of, perhaps, seventeen summers.

"Morning Star," she addressed me, bowing low as she approached the throne.

I promised myself to replace the furniture before continuing with tomorrow night's appointments. While the Doman of New York City couldn't very well conduct business from a folding chair or ensconced in a giant beanbag, the throne motif was a little too surreal for my tastes. Eventually I was going to succumb to the growing urge to bellow "Off with their heads!" as the audiences progressed.

But for now: "Greetings," I said, glancing down at the typed itinerary, "Wah—wuh—"

"Please, call me Wendy." She smiled and her teeth were as bright as the moon in her brown face.

I returned the smile. She was a delightful contrast to my previous audience with Hackle and Jackal. "And please call me Chris."

She sat upon the chair across from me as her ancestors might have sat around their council fires, cross-legged with her feet tucked under her.

"Tell me of your clan, Wendy."

"My people are the Forest Folk and the Spirits of Water, Wind, and Stone." Her fingers fluttered. "I do not speak for them, I speak on their behalf."

"I'm not sure I understand."

"I am not their leader. Some tribes have their own, others not," she said, gesturing with her hands. "We each have our own ways. In one way only are we all alike." Her hands were eloquent and I wished I could divide my attention between her words and her gestures so that I might attend to both. Unfortunately I was tired and my earlier blood loss was taking its toll.

"We are the Spirit Peoples, bound to Mother Earth in the secret places. We swim in the lakes and rivers . . ." Her fingers were schools of fish wriggling through shallows and rapids. " . . . we creep through the tall grass, lurk at the edges of the glen . . ." she said with a stealthy palm, " . . . we rest between the stones, and leap upon the high places . . ." Her hand swept up and my head lolled back as my eyes tried to follow its trajectory. " . . . we soar with the eagle . . ." My eyes fluttered and then cleared as I beheld the great mountains to the west, beyond the Alleghenies. " . . . we bathe in the fountains of the dawn and move across the land at the speed of night . . .

"Do you see?"

"Yes," I murmured, the outlines of Bokwus, Hino, and Adekagagwaaa appeared in the background as the shadow-shapes of the Ohdow, Chenoo, Nagumwasuck, and Inua passed through earth and tree and brook and stone.

Mother Earth is our flesh and bone, Mother Nature our blood and breath.

We are tied to the land.

We are of the land.

As long as the land is well, we are well.

"Well . . ." I mumbled.

But the land is being poisoned. The land is polluted with a cancer.

Somewhere in the back of my mind—down in the root cellar, actually—a little voice was clearing its throat and suggesting I take a step back. It was also warning me about getting involved in public health concerns.

An enemy has come among us, a fierce and terrible enemy!

High up, among the cloud-wreathed mountain peaks, a castle appeared.

He has brought his dark sorceries upon the land and has poisoned the streams and fields with his potions and elixirs. He has snared the Forest Folk and twisted their offspring into demonic shadow things—just as he has made twisted things of his own shadows.

He destroys in the name of life. He distorts and corrupts the ladders of time and task. He mangles the forms of creation in his unending combat with the Creator.

There were things in the water with extra eyes, no eyes, feelers, and worse.

Things in the forest that gave birth to abominations, things that should not have lived but did.

Things that were kin to Yog-Sothoth and the Nameless Ones.

Things that were hungry in obscene ways.

That mocked God and spat in the face of sanity.

Darkness, once more, was coming upon the face of The Deep.

He is The Mangler, also called Nikidik, whose True Name is nearly forgotten. The inhabitants of his first kingdom have passed through the Gates of Fire or of Time and few survivors remain who remember the horror of his reign, the foul designs of his Master.

We ask you to gainsay him!

His power has grown in the secret years that passed since he was presumed dead. But he did not die! He became fruitful and multiplied!

Soon he will be Legion!

It was as if a great shadow overcast my mind. Through the darkness I caught glimpses of victims waiting in long lines, and of fires and pits and dark smoke dissolving the sun. White flakes falling in a parody of snow on warm summer afternoons. Steel tables and surgical tools and notebooks bulging with data on what the human body might endure and what the human mind might not.

You must withstand him, kith and kin.

You must destroy him in all of his parts so that no portion of his works may remain or return.

Let no hostage deter you.

Do not let Death bind you.

Trust in the unborn and the undying.

Why . . . me . . . ? He seems far away . . . beyond the borders of my demesne . . .

Your demesne lies between the borders of light and shadow. And his hand is stretched out toward you, even now.

Awake . . .

My eyes snapped open and I was momentarily dazzled by the light in the room.

The chair across from me was empty.

The guards appeared to have dozed off. They were on the floor, leaning back against the wall or slumped over on their sides. Deirdre was snoring. Kurt's chin had dropped to his chest.

"I see the Four-fold Man," wrote William Blake, "The Humanity in deadly sleep / and its fallen Emanation, the Spectre and its cruel Shadow." I wondered how Blake would have rendered our little naptime into scansion and verse.

"Can it get any weirder than this?" I muttered.

You'd think I'd learn to keep my big fat mouth shut—even the rhetorical questions get me nothing but trouble. The problem was I didn't even have a clue as to how much trouble I was in before the door opened again.

Two large toy soldiers marched into the room.

"Large toy" sounds a little oxymoronic—like "jumbo shrimp" or "military intelligence"—but these apple-cheeked, white-trousered, red-bloused, black-capped automatons were the size of children. Or dwarves.

They goose-stepped in with their spike-bayoneted muzzle loaders strapped across their backs and each carried a small chest in his white-gloved hands. The chests were as identical as the pair transporting them. As they drew closer I could see that they more closely resembled miniature caskets—coffins, about fourteen inches long and shaped proportionally with ancient brass fittings.

The little soldiers came forward and placed the little caskets on the floor just inches away from my feet. They then saluted and turned and marched back out of the room.

I stared after them and then down as the door closed behind them. Someone had used a wood-burning stylus to inscribe the same words in German on the lid of each casket:

Schlüssel zum Erfolg ist verfügbar

Rough translation: "The key to success is at hand." This made a wee bit more—if not complete—sense when I picked one up. It was locked. *To prevent someone from getting in?* I wondered.

Or something from getting out?

The ceremonial gifts from the clans and families were all carefully X-rayed before being delivered to me so I figured it couldn't be too dangerous. But if the key was at hand, it wasn't immediately evident. I set the mini-coffins aside for later examination: my next two appointments had arrived and I had a roomful of protectors to wake up.

Kurt was loath to leave me but he needed to find out what had happened to his much vaunted security systems. He particularly wanted to know why his backup team hadn't come running when the hidden cameras showed us passing out.

I waved him off, assuring him that we could fall asleep equally well, with or without him. That neither reassured him nor improved his mood. He muttered into his lapel mic while Deirdre resumed her smirk. After all of his high-handedness, she was enjoying the fact that his security had fumbled the ball twice in one night and both times it had happened on his watch. Kurt was learning that I wasn't an easy guy to protect.

Come to think of it, maybe I should take note of that issue, as well.

The door opened and a young woman entered. She looked like a fresh-faced, well-scrubbed college sophomore or junior reporting for her first internship. She wore a baggy pullover of midnight blue over a pair of tight black slacks and sensible, comfortable shoes. Her chestnut hair was pulled away from her face and dropped into a ponytail of Clydesdalean proportions. She preceded a big, dangerous-looking vampire whose fangs actually curved over his lower lip. Worse, he was a mouth-breather. The tux that barely fit him didn't do anything to suggest an air of sophistication, it was actually counterintuitive. His long black hair hung to his shoulders in twisted greasy locks. He had more hair on his knuckles than I had on my chest.

They were an odd pairing, this vampire and his human servant. Or maybe he was simply bringing his lunch to work.

Kurt headed for the door. "Spook and Carol will take my place until I get back," he said over his shoulder. "Be careful. And don't be a pain in the ass."

Yup, Kurt was finally learning what my security detail *really* entailed after all this time.

I turned to the big vamp as the door closed behind my majordomo. "So, Spook, huh? I'm guessing you weren't ever in the CIA." I gestured to the empty chair on my right. "Have a seat."

The coed stepped up and sat down. "I'm Spook," she

said with a smile, "that's Carol." The big vampire moved to her side.

Oboy.

I turned to the two vampire envoys that were waiting for their appointment to begin. One wore a skullcap, the other a shemagh. Both wore beards. "And you are . . . ?"

The Aluka and the Oneida were a treat, of sorts. Their numbers were the smallest among the clans as they never sought to bring others to their state of damnation. Vampire Jews or Muslims had to be made by vampires who had no stake in either religion. No pun intended.

The more orthodox Jews and devout Muslims who woke up undead invariably tried to destroy themselves. Their beliefs wouldn't permit them to continue their existence as an unclean thing. Where their doctrines forbade suicide, many found clever and elaborate ways to exploit scriptural loopholes and have "accidents." Sometimes they would force fatal encounters with overwhelming numbers of other unclean monsters. Only a few of those on either side of Father Abraham's family tree found ways to reconcile themselves with their newfound thirst for blood.

You might suppose those survivors would wage holy (or unholy) war on the other side of the Middle East equation. Surprise! Their most violent clashes were heated arguments over the definition of kosher blood and whether the uncircumcised and the infidel fell within the proscriptions of lawful prey. As long as they weren't inclined to blow each other up I was happy. Don't fix what ain't broken, I always say.

Next.

Carmella Le Fanu wasn't a treat, she was the entire candy store.

Tall and elegant, she was graceful, projecting an aura of irresistible beauty with almost no effort. Which meant she was at least a hundred years older than me though she appeared to be somewhere between her second and third decade. She sat across from me, looking me up and down as if she was the one in the candy store, while her brother did the talking.

Valentine Le Fanu was the poster boy for those who like romance novels with teeth. His hair fell about his shoulders in silky waves like a dark curtain. He wore ruffles and lace beneath a velvet frockcoat and his skintight breeches tucked into expensive riding boots at mid-calf. He had a pretty-boy face made less girlish by a strong jaw and intelligent eyes that suggested that he was no fool nor did he tolerate any gladly.

"As much as I would love to see the Polidori Clan reduced in influence and prestige," he was saying, "I feel that it is only fair to warn you that Yuler was most likely acting at another's behest."

I did not take advantage of his timely pause to ask "who?" I merely smiled and waited.

"There is a vampire named Cairn who makes no secret of his ambitions to rule the city. He has been responsible for a number of political assassinations over the past fifty years. Lately he seems to have turned his attentions to the most powerful among the clans and we suspect he seeks to turn the clans against one another, starting a civil war that would destroy the demesne from within."

"If he presents such a serious threat," I asked, "why haven't you dealt with him before now?"

"Because they don't know who he is," Spook said from the chair on my right.

"Why, Darcy," said Carmella, also speaking for the first time, "still awake? I thought it was long past your bedtime."

"I'm sorry, Carmella. I wouldn't have interrupted if I'd known you were actually following the conversation. You were staring so hard at Domo Cséjthe that I thought you had drifted off into some little daydream."

"Vampires don't daydream, my dear."

"How sad for you. Sleeping must be so much more boring for you than it is for me."

Carmella opened her mouth to reply but Valentine laid a hand on his sister's arm and said: "She is but a kitten, Mella; do not play the ball of yarn for her."

Deirdre leaned over and filled the ensuing silence: "*You're* Darcy Blenik?"

"When Kurt mentioned your name I assumed you were a vampire," I said climbing into the passenger seat of the tram.

Spook—aka Darcy Blenik—climbed behind the steering wheel. "Oh, Uncle Kurt. He thinks of me as one of them since I am family."

"*Uncle* Kurt?" I stifled a yawn: it was getting close to dawn.

"Well, he's actually my great-great-great-grandfather but it's so much easier to close the multigenerational gap and call him uncle." We started off down the tunnel with a jerk. "Carol," she called over her shoulder, "send a note to maintenance and tell them either the battery isn't holding its charge or we've got an intermittent short somewhere in tram two."

"Yes, miss," he rumbled from the seat behind me.

"So, what is it that you do around here?" Deirdre asked her.

"Not a whole lot, actually. Whatever chores Uncle Kurt gives me to keep me out of trouble. I've kind of been at loose ends since my father died."

"You were the speaker at the podium, this evening," my Chief of Security observed. "You were making the presentation with the security video."

I looked and could see it now: with her hair piled on top of her head and wearing an off-the-shoulder evening gown, she had appeared to be much older.

She nodded. "Yes and I must compliment you, Ms. . . . ?"

"Just Deirdre, dear. I left my last name behind with my past life."

"Well, Deirdre, you handle yourself well in a fight. It was a shame to edit out some of those moves but Uncle felt it best to make Domo Cséjthe appear as formidable as possible." A pause. "I also met you at the airport."

"You were the chauffeur," I said, mentally putting the moustache, goatee, and mirrored sunglasses back on her face.

"Call me Spook," she answered agreeably.

"Call me Chris."

"Oh no. Uncle would insist on proper formalities with the Doman. One half of maintaining respect is in observing the formalities."

"I'm not big on formalities."

"So I've been told." She turned the tram down a side passage. "What I haven't been told is how you are both human and wampyri. Are you dhampir?"

"Technically, no."

Deirdre was perplexed. "Dompeer? I've known a couple of occasions when Cséjthe has put a real *damper* on the festivities . . ."

"A dhampir," Spook explained, "is the son of a vampire. That is to say, conceived by a wampyri father and birthed by a human mother. He is born with attributes of both the living and the undead. By tradition he's the perfect vampire hunter."

"My parents were human, my condition—"

Suki yowled loudly in cat form and Deirdre hastily interrupted. "I think the details of Chris's condition are best left a little hazy, at present. The less that is known about his strengths and weaknesses, the better his chances of surprising his enemies."

"Of course," our driver said. "You certainly surprised Yuler tonight. And I daresay a great many others. Of course your reputation was quite formidable even before the evening began. If Cairn has sent assassins after you in the past, he will most likely be a little more thoughtful before doing so again."

"So, tell me about this Cairn," I said as we turned down the passage leading to my quarters.

"First, you tell me what that is . . ."

Something was crawling down the middle of the passageway toward us. Something that looked like a lizard under the uncertain light of the intermittent fluorescents—or maybe a very large spider. Except that it was hunchbacked and, for either, it had the wrong number of legs.

"Aw no," I said as we drove nearer. "No, no, *no*! Who thinks up this crap?"

"More importantly," Spook observed as she eased the tram to a stop, "who is able to make this sort of thing work?"

A severed hand crawled into the illuminated spill from the headlights. The lump on its "back" contained an eyeball that rolled around and blinked as the stronger light dazzled it.

"Ohmigod!" Deirdre stuck her head between ours. "It's Cousin Itt!"

Spook turned to her, wide-eyed: "It belongs to your cousin?"

"Noooo." It was a scary voice and echoed around the confines of the tunnel, disguising its source for a moment. Then I realized it was behind me: Carol the Vampire had spoken his third word of the evening. "It iss character from Addams Family, yah? Only you mean Ting. Co-sin Eet iss all hairy mit liddle hat."

"Oh." Spook looked back at the hand which appeared to be looking back at us. "Wasn't that a movie?"

Deirdre shook her head. "TV show."

"Noooo. Vas cartoons in *New Yorker* magazine."

I sat there and considered screaming but I wasn't sure whether it was because of the "thing" in front of me or the conversation all around me.

Chapter Twelve

HIS TEETH ARE TERRIBLE round about. His scales are his pride, shut up together as with a close seal. One is so near to another that no air can come between them. They are joined one to another, they stick together that they cannot be sundered. By his neesings a light doth shine, and his eyes are like the eyelids of the morning. Out of his mouth go burning lamps and sparks of fire leap out. Out of his nostrils goeth smoke, as out of a seething pot or cal-dron. His breath kindleth coals, and a flame goeth out of his mouth. In his neck remaineth strength, and sorrow is turned into joy before him. The flakes of his flesh are joined together: they are firm in themselves; they cannot be moved. His heart is as firm as a stone; yea, as hard as a piece of the nether millstone. When he raiseth up himself, the mighty are afraid: by reason of breakings they purify themselves. The sword of him that layeth at him cannot hold: the spear, the dart, nor the habergeon. He esteemeth iron as straw, and brass as rotten wood. The arrow cannot make him flee: slingstones are turned with him into stubble.

Darts are counted as stubble: he laugheth at the shaking of a spear. Sharp stones are under him: he spreadeth sharp pointed things upon the mire. He maketh the deep to boil like a pot: he maketh the sea like a pot of ointment. He maketh a path to shine after him; one would think the deep to be hoary. Upon earth there is not his like, who is made without fear . . .

I sat straight up in bed, eyes wide and staring into the darkness.

The dream was bad enough. That it came with new installments every time I slept made it worse: the demon continued to plow through the ocean like a torpedo with teeth and claws and spines. But with subtitles from the Book of Job it was assuming apocalyptic proportions.

It was coming for me, moving purposefully. Without sleep. Without rest. Without pause.

But what awakened me, what chilled my already tepid blood and pulled my eyelids wide in the darkness of my bedchamber, was the touch of the hand upon my foot!

It had escaped Darcy Blenik's custody and crawled through miles of air ducts to enter my quarters and attack me in my bed.

I felt it creeping past my ankle and over my shin like a slow and crafty spider. It hesitated upon my knee as if plotting its final trajectory. Would it go for my throat? Attempt to gouge my eyes out? I braced myself for its attack . . .

"Oh, you're awake." The voice was vaguely familiar and sounded vaguely disappointed.

oh. Is this a bad time?"

Carmella Le Fanu was stretched out on the bed beside

me, her hand on my knee. She appeared to be naked. I blinked, adjusting to the glare from the doorway. She was still naked.

"Ms. Le Fanu," I said slowly, "you and your brother have already had your appointment with me."

"That was business," she said with a slow smile.

*had*In the dim light Carmella's smile was reminiscent of the Cheshire Cat's. "It is understood that the Doman will be taking consorts soon."

"And you're auditioning, right?"

"Let's just say that I am doing some research."

"How do we know you aren't another assassin, come to kill him in his sleep?"

"Because, for one thing," Suki's voice answered, "she's not carrying any weapons. And, for another, I wouldn't allow it."

We all looked toward the far corner of the room where the voice came from. Suki sat in a chair, still wrapped in shadows, but finally visible. She held a slightly curved katana across her thighs. It was still sheathed but two inches of the blade were drawn, reflecting the light so that it momentarily dazzled Carmella.

I turned back to Deirdre. "You were saying something about Kurt?"

"He wants to see you as soon as you're up."

"I'm up."

"What about my research?" Carmella wanted to know.

I reached down and patted her on the head. "I'll arrange for some handouts to be distributed at a later date. Now, everyone out. Shoo. I want to shower and get dressed."

Carmella smiled and sat up. She was working extra hard on her projecting. "Wash your back?"

"Security protocols would require that one of us be present at all times," Deirdre answered.

Carmella's smile grew. "That could be fun . . ."

"No, it wouldn't," Suki said.

Kurt, himself, came to chauffeur me through the tunnels to the demesne's lab facilities. As he steered the tram through a bewildering maze of tunnels, I asked what we knew tonight that we didn't know this morning.

"Not enough," he grumped, driving with his shoulders hunched. "There's nothing on the security video of your appointment with the woman who put us all to sleep."

"Does that, in itself, tell us anything?"

"No. It's not really so unusual. Many of us exert a peculiar effect upon electromagnetic media."

"Do we know where she is now?"

He shook his head. "It is as if she came and went like the wind, itself."

"Everyone knows it's 'Wendy.'"

He looked at me blankly.

"And Wendy has stormy eyes," I tried, "that flash at the sound of lies . . ."

The look intensified.

"Never mind. How about the toy soldiers?"

"Also gone." He held up his hand. "And please do not quote meaningless poetry to me; I have a headache."

"Maybe you shouldn't be driving, then. They say most accidents occur within twenty-five miles of the crypt."

He grunted. "You sound awfully chipper for a man who was nearly assassinated last night."

"What? Yuler? He was just the warm-up act. Carmella Le Fanu made a run at me this evening."

"What?" The tram screeched to a halt. "She tried to kill you?"

"Worse. She was trying to sleep with me."

"Oh." He started to smile. "This is maybe a good thing. If you take Carmella as one of your consorts—"

"Yuler's less intimidating. Did you finish your examination of the boxes?"

He started the tram again. "Yes."

"What did you find?"

"Nothing."

"There was nothing inside?"

"No evidence of explosives or booby traps were found. The chests have not been opened, yet."

"Why not?"

"You are the Doman. We require your permission to open your personal gifts—even if we do suspect they are potentially dangerous."

"You could have awakened me."

His shoulders hunched a little higher. "Security spent hours examining the chests. I was not about to have you awakened in the middle of the day to open some presents. I need you sharp, tonight."

Deirdre, who was sitting in the back with Suki, cleared her throat and spoke for the first time. "Um, a moment ago you said 'are' potentially dangerous."

"What?"

"The absence of evidence denoting danger," Suki

observed, "does not guarantee that danger does not exist."

Deidre bristled a bit. "Well, big *duh*!"

"Sorry. I wasn't sure that you understood the context—"

"I understand a lot more than you think."

"What does that mean?"

"I think it means somebody is cranky and needs a nap," I said, rubbing my temple where a migraine was starting to wake up.

"If anyone needs a nap, it's Miss Pussy Gabor. She's the one who was apparently up all night."

Kurt glanced at me for a translation.

"Guard duty," I said.

"I'm not the one who's cranky," Suki replied.

"Speaking of cranky," I said, speaking a little louder than necessary, "I'm sensing a diminishment of enthusiasm on your part, as well, Kurt. Are you sorry I made the trip?"

"You cannot remain as Doman—you will not even survive—unless you deal decisively with your enemies." His first words were hesitant but the rest turned into a verbal stampede. "So far, you have reinforced your reputation for being soft and indecisive. You cannot rule the clans unless your enemies fear you and your allies believe you to be strong!"

I stared ahead, half-expecting another disparate body part to creep into the headlights of the tram. "So, what do you suggest? Round up some enemies and make an example of them? Do you have a list, Kurt? Whom do you want me to kill?"

He scowled as we turned a corner and coasted to a stop beside a steel door. "A great deal of difficulty could be avoided if you eliminated this Cairn."

"Yeah? Well, who is he? What does he look like? Where does he live? How do I find him?"

His hunched shoulders drooped. "I don't know."

Great. If I wanted to keep my job as top monster in the fang factory, I had to do battle with an invisible man.

And I wasn't all that crazy about my job to begin with.

Maybe just crazy . . .

The laboratory facilities in New York were far beyond the resources that the Seattle demesne boasted. Perhaps I should have sent Theresa's head here, when I had the chance. But I trusted Doctors Mooncloud and Burton while I was less sure of the East Coast's cast of characters.

The hand scuttled around the inside of a Plexiglas tank like a pink, hyperactive lizard. Its single eye cast wildly about until it fixed on me. Then it moved toward me as far as the clear walls would permit. It began scratching at the barrier with a single-minded patience that was more unnerving than its own grotesque appearance.

"Why does it do that?" I asked.

The question, to my mind, was largely rhetorical: I didn't really expect an answer. Spook provided one anyway. "It's programmed to," she said, slipping a series of X-rays into a row of clips on a backlit panel.

"See? Here are the CPU and memory modules." She tapped a dark, shadow array nestled between the back of the hand and the hump of the eyeball in a series of exposures. "Power source. Servos and a secondary endoskeleton," she indicated a series of jointed lines parallel to the natural bones and joints, "enhance and provide backup for the primary system of bones, nerves, and musculature. It's a simple robot in a flesh-and-blood glove, using an organic camera in place of a metal-and-plastic sensor."

"How does it stay alive without a working circulatory system?" I asked. "Why isn't it decomposing like any other severed hand?" I thought of Theresa's rotting limbs.

Spook pointed to a lump near the wrist on the X-ray. "I think this is a miniature pump and it's circulating the blood past this membrane that's grafted over the stump. I suspect the artificial skin is a permeable membrane like those developed by the Navy. It allows oxygen to enter the bloodstream through an adjacent vascular system. Still, even hypothesizing the implantation of protein seeds for fuel and nanobots for cellular maintenance and repair, this is not a viable organism. It is not designed for extended operation and is probably starting to break down even now. The hardware could have been fabricated and programmed to find you at any time. The surgical implantation, however, most likely took place within the past two to three days—just before it was brought here and released in the tunnels."

"And what was it programmed to do?" I wondered. "Kill me?"

"I don't think so," Kurt answered from a lab stool. "Assuming it's Pipt—"

"Oh, it's Mr. Ozfest, all right!" I walked around the translucent box while the five-fingered cyborg scrabbled to keep pace with my movement. "Who else could come up with something like this? It's not as sophisticated as the Frankenvamp but I don't know of anyone else capable of this kind of bioengineering." I looked at him. "Unless there really is a Doctor Frankenstein . . ."

Kurt held up a hand. "Please, Christopher. I believe the phrase you Americans use is 'get real.'"

I looked at the centuries-old vampire. "Yeah. Sure. What a silly idea." I looked at the other silly idea doing five-fingered pushups in the Plexiglas tank. "Did the Countess ever dabble in this sort of thing when she was mapping the human genome?"

"Not to my knowledge. It was mostly cells, bacteria, and viruses. Very little in the way of surgical procedures and those seemed pretty straightforward. This . . ." His face went blank—wrestled with an unfamiliar emotion—and composed itself again so quickly and smoothly that I almost missed it. " . . . this is more like something I once saw in a Bavarian hospital . . ." His voice trailed off.

"Yes?" I wasn't inclined to let the moment pass. "Tell me."

He shook his head and his voice was gruffer than usual. "It was more than seventy years ago, halfway around the world. The living may call us monsters but they still write romantic novels about the vampire. No one writes romances about the Nazis and their medical experiments. Butchers invoking the Dark Arts to create a race of supermen—*ptah!* Those who haven't forgotten, know better. Those who are too young to remember . . ." He shook his head again. "There are many times and places in my long existence that I would as soon not recall to memory. The Nazi madness is something the world should not forget . . ." His voice trailed off and he stared at a distant, dark memory before whispering, " . . . but would also do better not to remember too well."

He got up and went over to the tank, opening the lid. "Anyway, what I was starting to say is that someone capable of creating this"—he caught the hand with his own and lifted it out—"could certainly create something deadlier to send after you."

"Like the Frankenvamp?"

"That creature makes my point. It was apparently sent to draw your blood, not destroy the repository of your flesh. If this Pipt values your blood, he certainly would not want to kill the goose that lays the golden eggs." He carried the hand over to a counter and switched on an ultraviolet lamp.

"So," I pondered, "if Tall, Dark, and Destructive failed to retrieve my precious bodily fluids, what did he expect to accomplish with the hand job, here?"

Darcy, walking over to the lab's entrance, snickered softly. She flipped the light switch and the room went dark except for the ghostly purple illumination of the UV lamp.

"He's trying to lure you to come to him."

"But I don't know where he is."

"You do now." He held the hand beneath the violet bulb, turning it palm up. Glowing lines appeared amid the whorls and creases of the hand's palm: a contour map, tattooed in phosphorescent ink, visible only in the black light's peculiar wavelength.

"Where is that?"

Spook spoke. "I've scanned a photo of the pattern into the computer and we're running a cartographical search now, hoping for a match. Blowing up the photo reveals elevation numbers narrowing our search to mountainous regions around the world." She held up an antique skeleton key. It had been sewn onto the back of the hand with a couple of stitches, found when we captured it. "But we're hoping for some additional clues."

"So," I asked, "can I open the chests, now?"

"You? No," Kurt answered dourly. "One of my people will do it while you observe from the next room."

A humanoid shape appeared in the doorway beyond. It wore yards of heavy padding, monstrous gloves, and a gas mask. Spook handed it the key and we moved to a monitor showing the two chests behind a blast wall, surrounded by sandbags.

"As Uncle probably told you," she said, as the muffled security guy shuffled into the camera's view, "we found no evidence of booby-trapping. No trace elements of explosive compounds. But both caskets are opaque to X-rays. And the locks don't appear to have any kind of a tumbler system that would interface with a key, either."

"So you did try to open them?" I asked.

She shook her head. "I would not open either one without you present, Domo Cséjthe. I did, however, use a fiber-optic scope to examine the interior of the lock. I've never seen anything like it."

"Yeah?" I looked back over my shoulder at the thing in the terrarium. "Well, I've never seen anything like the beast with five fingers outside of a couple of a couple of B-minus horror movies—and they didn't have eyeballs."

"Which is why a chest containing mundane explosives might well be the least of our worries." She tapped a button and moved a slide switch with her right hand while operating a joystick with her left.

The screen zoomed in on the key entering the lock on the first chest.

We held our breaths.

Nothing happened.

The technician turned the key.

Still nothing.

We watched as he made several attempts to unlock the first chest. Unsuccessful, he turned his attention to the other casket. We eventually stopped holding our breaths: it was evident that nothing was going to happen.

Five minutes later I was examining the key with a magnifying glass. "This is the same key that was attached to the creepy-crawly over there?"

"The same," Spook promised.

"And the messages on both chests connect the key to the hand." While I intended it as a statement, it came out sounding more like a question.

"Not necessarily."

Everyone looked at Deirdre who was looking at the chests on the monitor.

"How good is your German, Chris?"

"Rudimentary. I dated a language major in college." I didn't mention my German-born great-grandfather: I was learning to keep my family antecedents to myself.

"I see," Deirdre said. "Well, you got the first part half-right. *Schlüssel zum Erfolg* can translate as 'the key to success' or 'the secret of success.' The 'key' in question doesn't seem to be very successful."

I looked at her. "I didn't know you spoke or read German."

"I minored in Romance languages."

I cleared my throat. "So maybe we're not actually look-ing for a key? What about the rest of it? I wasn't sure about 'at hand'."

"'At hand' would be *ist verfügung*, not *verfügbar*. On the other hand—sorry—if you wanted to say that the key was *on* hand you would say *vorrätig*."

"But the chests don't say *vorrätig*, they say *verfügbar*."

Deirdre nodded. "Yes. *Verfügbar* means 'on-hand.'"

I stared at her. "Okay, I thought you just said *vorrätig* meant 'on hand.'"

"Yes. But without the implied hyphen. *Verfügbar* sort of inserts a hyphen in the English translation. *Verfügbar* may also translate as available or allocatable or at your disposal."

"Italian," I said slowly. "Portuguese, Spanish, French . . . the descendents of the Latin dialects. Geman isn't a Latin derivate, so it isn't a Romance language."

The redhead shrugged.

"Dammit!" I threw the key back onto the table. "I wish this guy would make up his mind! Does he want to be Doctor Frankenstein or The Riddler?" I stomped into the next room.

Everyone chased after me with the obligatory cries of "wait" and "what are you doing" and "it's not safe."

"I don't have time for this crap," I said, stepping around the wall of sandbags. "I've got a demesne to run, a political minefield to navigate, assassins to dodge." I picked up one of the boxes and carried it to a counter on the other side of the room. "Some vampire named Cairn is working overtime to kill me but he's not half as distracting and annoying as the Lord of the Things who keep dropping by to borrow a cup of blood."

I crouched down to examine the lock with a critical eye. It stared back, seemingly unimpressed. "Bring me the key."

Kurt puffed up. "I forbid you to take this risk!"

"What risk? As we've discussed before, this guy doesn't want to kill me. He's *baiting* me."

"The bait may cover a hook that is both sharp and barbed," Suki said, speaking for the first time.

"Yeah?" I reached out and touched the brass lock plate. "Well, he may be a master baiter but—"

I shut up as I heard an audible click from inside the lock.

"What did you just do?" Spook asked as I took a step back.

"I touched the lock plate."

"Why would that do anything? The lock plate, the entire mechanism, has been touched a number of times."

I cocked my head. Stepped back. Turned and fetched the other casket. "Somebody want to touch this lock plate?"

Spook walked over and pressed her finger, then her thumb, to the lock on the second chest.

Nothing happened.

I reached out and touched the lock. There was another audible click.

I stepped back. "Fingerprint recognition?"

your"How would this guy have my DNA sample?"

Deirdre harrumphed. "How about that head case Kellerman? She probably had sticky gloves to pick up skin sheddings or something when she paid her little social call."

Spook turned and gave me a long speculative look. "This seems like an awful lot of bother just to collect a couple of pints of blood."

"His blood is worth a lot of bother," Deirdre said.

I turned back to the first chest. "I doubt Yuler would think so." I pulled at the lid and it opened easily.

The inside of the casket was lined with satin cushioning. There was probably lead sheeting underneath to block any X-ray examination. Nestled in the pillowing was a glass vial, maybe two inches wide and five inches long. Suspended in a clear solution was a pale kidney bean.

Or it looked like a kidney bean until I picked up the vial and looked more closely.

It was a fetus.

I turned to the other chest and opened it with a trembling left hand.

Another vial, another fetus.

I turned to Kurt. "Take these to the genetics section and run their DNA."

"We don't even know if they're human—" Spook started to say.

"Run it! Stat!"

I started to shake and had to grip the vials carefully: too much pressure and they would shatter, too little and they would slip through my suddenly damp hands.

"*Now!* I roared.

"Your first appointment is in one hour," Kurt announced to my back as I unlocked the door to my suite.

"Cancel it."

"Why?"

"Because I've got to pack."

"Pack?"

Chef appeared as I stalked through the foyer. "May I prepare a suitable repast before you depart, Master?"

"No!" I said. And realized I was ravenous as I said it. "Yes. I'm thirsty."

"What would you like?"

"Something to calm him down," Kurt interjected. "And what do you mean, 'pack'? Where do you think you are going?"

"At the moment? My best guess is Germany, so I'm going to need travel arrangements, maps, currency exchange, and a bilingual guide. Also a passport. If you can't fabricate one for me on short notice, get Malatesta on the phone." I turned to Chef. "Whatever you send me, make it a double. It may be awhile before I can hit another blood bank."

"Male or female, Master?"

"What? Oh. Uh, female . . ." Intellectually, I knew that it shouldn't make any difference: food was food. Still there was a sexual subtext and that made me doubly uneasy with the whole predator/prey issues.

But it didn't seem to bother me as much as it used to.

"Human or unhuman, Master?"

"Huh? What do you mean?"

"Do you wish to sample another human? Or would Master prefer the potency of vampire blood?"

"You didn't mention the fact that there were undead vintages in the wine cellar last night, Chef."

"I am afraid Bethany has been a little too effusive in

praising your technique, Domo. There have been—ahem—volunteers, if you are so inclined."

I looked at Kurt. "These wampyri volunteers wouldn't be potential consorts, would they?"

He shrugged. "Why Germany?"

"Because this guy has a faint German accent. Because the writing on the chests is in German. And because of something you said about Nazi experimentation. If I can believe what he told me, this Pipt would be old enough to have goose-stepped about the Rhineland back in WW Two. Germany has mountains. Until your niece comes up with a topographical match, it's a place to start." I looked at Chef. "Send up half a dozen of your best stock and I'll make my selection in my quarters. Throw in a little variety." I caught Deirdre and Suki's exchange of looks out of the corner of my eye. "What?"

"You seem a little upset," Suki answered evenly.

"Good point." I turned back to Chef. "Tell the volunteers that I'm upset. See if they still want to volunteer under the circumstances."

"You still haven't answered my question," Kurt said as Chef hurried out of the room. "I thought we agreed that this Pipt was not as high a priority as establishing your authority over the demesne and dealing with more immediate threats like this Cairn."

"Priorities change."

"How could they change? Cairn will keep trying to kill you. All this Pipt seems to want is a couple of pints of your blood."

"He may want more than a couple of pints of blood," Suki observed.

"But, as I said before, you don't kill the goose that lays the golden eggs."

"No," she agreed, "you lock the goose up so it will always lay golden eggs for you and you alone."

Kurt turned back to me. "All the more reason for staying here, then."

"I can't."

"Why not?"

"Because this Dr. Pipt has hostages," Spook answered from the front door. "The DNA checked out. He has cloned Domo Cséjthe's dead wife and daughter."

Chapter Thirteen

THE BLOOD IS THE LIFE—so sayeth the Old Testament.

Genesis, Leviticus, Deuteronomy, all have strong prohibitions concerning the "eating of blood."

But the concept is older than written language. This simple, basic axiom comes down to us from a time before.

Perhaps before there was even a spoken language.

Our distant forebears believed that drinking the blood of your enemy, or eating his heart, bestowed the blessings of strength, courage. That such transferred the essence of his vitality to your own blood, your own heart, your own vitality.

If you think that we've moved beyond such primitivism perhaps the difference is more a matter of scale, today, with corporate raiders replacing the barbarians at the gates: "Chainsaw Al" Dunlap in for Genghis Khan, companies dismembered, gutted, and consumed by conglomerates. Resources, inventories, labor pools, payrolls—corporate life-forces consumed upon the economic fields of battle. Thousands of hoplite livelihoods are sacrificed to feed the glutted stock options of boardroom chieftains. Before you pronounce the economic "sciences" the superior belief system consider the pyrrhic victories of corporate raiders: the slash and burn trails through the regional economies as the Wild Hunt passes "buy."

Give me the good old *mano y mano* primitive any day. . . .

The ancient Hebrews recognized the dangers of developing appetites that turned other humans into prey. Even the blood of animals was proscribed in their codex of law and ritual.

Too bad I wasn't Jewish.

In fact, I wasn't even sure that I was fully human anymore.

There was, however, enough humanity left for me to get upset over this latest visitation from the Pipt Plaguebook. Never mind the complex biochemical changes wrought by Dracula's transfusion; my ingesting human, werewolf, and demon blood. There are worse offenses than personal attacks upon one's personal flesh. Back when Kadeth Bey used the Dark Arts of necromancy to raise my wife's and daughter's corpses from their graves and reanimated them with ancient and evil spirits, I was appalled.

But now I was beyond furious.

Why was this worse?

The sciences of medicine and biology were giving my loved ones a second chance at life via cloning. Wasn't that a good thing?

Why, then, did this seem more heinous than their previous, demonic resurrections?

Was it because Pipt had casually used their cloned fetuses as bait? That he could keep copying them for any number of monstrous projects and purposes? Our mad scientist had to get his raw materials for Fangenstein and that five-fingered creepy-crawly from somewhere. Back in Mary Shelley's time he might have procured his parts from the gallows and the grave. Now, in the third millennium, he was more likely to spend his time exhuming DNA instead of whole corpses.

Beyond biology, beyond science, was the ineffable question of the soul. As in: one to a customer? What happened when there were more soup cans than soup? Did other sinister brews appear in the canning process? Or was the broth progressively thinned and watered down until it lost all flavor and identity, eventually evaporating altogether?

Kurt and the others were right: I wasn't thinking clearly just now. I *couldn't* think clearly. The only thing I could be sure of was that Pipt's reassembling my wife and daughter in the lab was no mere happenstance: it was both message and threat.

Anger was turning to rage—bad enough—but my increasingly aggressive Thirst was piggybacking on it and ramping up to an unbearable level of need! I paced my quarters like a caged predator, waiting for the food—the *volunteers*—to arrive.

It only took twenty minutes for the first to be delivered but it seemed like an eternity. It felt like days, weeks, months had passed since I had last fed.

☠ ☠ ☠

Before my Thirst was slaked, I drank from seven different volunteers—four of them blood-drinkers, themselves. I started by telling myself that, by drinking a little from each, I didn't take too much from any.

By the time I was sated I knew a different truth. I had multiplied my victims.

I spread the pain.

And there was no way to give each the time and care they deserved in exchange.

At least some of them liked it.

Those that didn't? Well, that was their lookout. They were volunteers, right? Maybe they should seriously reconsider their positions in the food chain. Say: "Ciao, babe," not "chow."

I found myself wondering how Carmella would taste.

And I wondered if Darcy Blenik's sweet, tight husk had ever felt fangs pierce her well-scrubbed skin. Would her blood taste virginal? Would she be like a glass of cool water after shots of whisky, snifters of brandy, steins of ale, and goblets of wine?

I shook my head. I was full to bursting with new blood and I still wasn't thinking clearly. I climbed out of bed, pushing at the lethargic bodies that surrounded me in a fleshy tangle. I had started out fully dressed but friendly fingers had unbuttoned and unzipped during the feeding frenzy and impatient hands had ripped and torn everything that didn't immediately slip off or fall away. It was just as well: the blood would have never completely washed out, anyway.

I stumbled to the shower and turned on the hot water.

I felt cold and dirty. I used half of the shampoo and a complete bottle of liquid soap, fogging up the bathroom like a night on the Scottish moors. When I was done I looked presentable on the outside.

Inside I still felt cold and dirty.

Back in the bedroom no one had moved. Nor did they stir while I dressed. I wondered, briefly, if one or more of them had died from exsanguination. Decided it was unlikely. More specifically, it seemed unimportant. I exited without checking.

Deirdre looked at me as if I still had blood smeared across my face. Suki considered me with a greater impassiveness than usual. Kurt, at least, seemed pleased that I had topped off at the pump. "Are you feeling better?" he asked. "You have a big night ahead of you and we are already behind schedule."

"Are we?" I breezed past him and opened the outer door. "Where's my passport?"

"It has been ordered. But these things take time. Tonight you should concentrate—"

"Let's get something straight, Igor: *I* am the Doman, *you* are the 'Do' man. As in 'do what I say.' You've made your suggestions. I've heard them. Now we will *do* what *I* think is important. I don't give a flying flip about several hundred walking corpses under Gotham City while my wife and daughter are being held hostage. You can just reschedule their twenty-minute lap dance with the grand fanged Poobah *and*, if anyone gets their panties in a wad, well they can just sit on a stake and rotate. Got that?"

As Kurt stalked to the door, Deirdre sidled up to me and whispered: "I can't believe you said that!"

"Said what?"

"Flying flip."

Although irritated and reluctant, Kurt was obedient. He drove me to the lab and dropped me off before heading off to check on my passport forgeries.

The computer was still trying to find a match for the topography tattoo on the hand but Spook wasn't there. A couple of technicians were puttering around the lab. A little boy sat on a stool beside the Plexiglas tank, studying the hand.

The hand, in turn, was studying him.

I asked one of the techs about Spook.

"Still asleep," he answered. "She pulled an all-dayer."

"Well," I said, looking at data scrolling down the monitor screen, "it looks like she's running matches for the Alleghenies at the moment. Has she already eliminated Central Europe?"

He shrugged. "I really don't know."

"Well, who would?"

"It's Miss Blenik's project, sir. No one else is allowed to touch it."

"How long before she's up?"

"I don't know, sir. She left orders that she wasn't to be disturbed."

"Yeah?" My whole body was thrumming with tension. I couldn't just stand around, waiting for something to happen. "She can sleep later. Disturb her."

He nodded and stepped to a wall phone.

There was a tug at my pants' leg.

"Mister?"

I looked down. It was the boy, suddenly off of his stool and across the room at my side.

"Are you the new boss-man, mister?" he whispered.

"What?"

"Are you the new boss-man?"

"Um. Yes."

"My name's Tommy. What's yours?"

"Chris." I watched the tech dial a number and wait with the receiver at his ear.

"*Chris?*" Tommy repeated my name like it was the punch line of an extremely silly knock-knock joke. "That's a *girl's* name!"

"It's also a boy's name."

"It's a *funny* boy's name."

I finally turned my attention to the little towheaded kid. "Isn't it past your bedtime?" I hadn't seen any other children so far nor had I expected to. Still, the possibilities weren't so farfetched. With human servants, biology was bound to have its way with a pair of them sooner or later.

"Are you lookin' for Darcy?" he asked, ignoring my question completely.

"Yes. Where are your parents?"

"I know where to find her."

Which was more than the lab tech seemed to know. He was still on the line, waiting.

"She's in her room, sleeping. Which is where you should be."

The boy went all wide-eyed. "In Darcy's room?"

"No. I mean in your own room."

"She's not there, either."

The lab tech turned to me and said: "She's not answering. Her phone is probably unplugged."

"Or she's out," I said.

"She may be on her way here," he agreed.

Another tug on my pants' leg and I looked down. The boy shook his head.

"Where is she, Tommy?"

He crooked his finger, motioning me to bend down. "I don't know how to tell you," he whispered in my ear, "I have to show you. 'Sides, it's a secret!"

I gave the tech my cell phone number and instructions for Darcy to call it if she arrived before I returned. It was only after Tommy took my hand and led me to the door that I remembered that the Gator-man still had my mobile. My family, my humanity, my fiancée: after working my way through the important stuff I was down to losing the inconsequentials, scattering them in my wake like Hansel and Gretel's breadcrumbs in the ever-darkening forest.

The hand with the eyeball seemed to wave bye-bye as it scrabbled at the side of the tank.

After about two dozen turns and tunnel changes, I was starting to wish I had brought some breadcrumbs so I could find my way back. Even that would have been impractical as we moved into a sunken corridor with dripping pipes and an inch of water flowing sluggishly along the floor. There were no intermittent fluorescents now and the glowing lichen that oozed from the ceiling barely provided enough illumination for even my enhanced night vision.

As we splashed through a crumbling intersection where concrete met brickwork met stone, I asked: "How long have you lived down here, Tommy?"

"It seems like forever," he answered in a gee-whiz voice.

"I'll bet. You look like you're about seven. Is that how old you were when you died?"

He turned his head and gave me a long look but didn't break stride.

"Your hand is cold, Tommy—if that's your real name. You haven't been ninety-eight-point-six for a long time."

"Nineteen fifty-three," he said. "I was nine—small for my age. And my name is Thomas."

"So you don't really think Chris is a girl's name."

He released my hand and grabbed a rusted iron rung set in a mossy oubliette. "We'll find out soon enough." He started climbing.

"And are you really taking me to Darcy Blenik?"

"Darcy will meet us," he said over his shoulder. "She didn't want you to know but some of us felt it was better to ask your blessing than seek your forgiveness."

His small form was becoming smaller as he climbed upwards. I could stand here, go back and wander around the tunnels for a few days until the search parties found me, or I could follow not-so-young Master Thomas and see what game was really afoot.

I was inclined to climb. The sound of footfalls back down the tunnel, stealthy but for a slight splashing echo, encouraged my ascension. I climbed.

We came out through a manhole in a clump of shrubbery on the far side of the park. Thomas gave me a curious look as I hurriedly dragged the metal cover back and dropped it into place. "Wouldn't want any squirrels to fall in," I explained.

His expression suggested this was unlikely when the squirrels were hibernating and the biggest nut had just followed him up here. "Come on," he said, slipping through the foliage and out into the open. It took me a little longer to ease through the curtain of evergreen branches but he waited patiently. As I joined him he grabbed my hand and said: "C'mon, Dad! Mom's gonna get mad if we're late!"

That's when I noticed one of New York's Finest ambling down a path in our direction.

"Okay, uh, Junior. Lead the way."

And he did. Right by the cop. Who nodded pleasantly to the "father and son" hurrying to a family rendezvous somewhere across the snow-dappled grounds.

The snow had half melted, the clouds were gone, and the air was still, but the temperature was back below freezing. Even though I was less troubled by the cold, I needed to start dressing like temperature made some kind of difference if I wanted to blend in.

A limousine idled at the curb a couple of blocks away. The kid made for it directly, splashing through slushy puddles and plowing through crusty clumps of snow. Ice-crusted grass crunched under my shoes as I tried to keep my feet dry by following in a circuitous route. Since my legs were longer we arrived at the curb at the same time. The door opened and we climbed into the back.

Two platinum blondes sat across from us, red sequined dresses up to only here and fur stoles only down to there.

In between, their barely restrained bosoms threatened to break free and rise like twin pairs of dirigibles straining toward the heavens.

"Jeepers," said Tommy, "look-it them piggybanks!"

I blinked and realized our fellow passengers were Marilyn Monroe and Jayne Mansfield. Or, at least, looked like them. I didn't know which was scarier, the real deals back from the grave or things that could pry your head open and pour the images over your gray matter like maple syrup.

"Oooh, Tommy," Marilyn breathed, "you brought us an extra playmate!"

"And he still looks warm," cooed Jayne.

"Sindi, Sassy," the kid said, "this is Christopher Cséjthe, our new Doman."

"Ooooh, Mr. President—I mean, Domo Cséjthe!" Sindi/Marilyn extended a satin gloved hand. "This is such an honor!"

"Likewise," added Sassy/Jayne, "I'm sure!"

I briefly took each of the gloved hands in turn and released them. They felt strange, like the size and angle were wrong. "Ladies . . ." I turned to young Master Thomas. "Playmate?"

"Would you like to play with us?" Sassy inquired brightly.

"You look like a perfect gentleman," Sindi observed on the verge of breathlessness. "I hear that gentlemen prefer blondes . . ."

"Uh, sorry . . . no."

"Maybe he's hungry, sister. Would you like a menu, Domo?"

I looked back at Sassy. "A menu?"

"Do you like Italian?"

The interior of the limo was not well-lit. The women leaned back in their seats so that the shadows concealed their features for a moment. When they leaned forward, the Marilyn and Jayne were gone, replaced by Sophia Loren and Gina Lollobrigida. The outfits were different, too: dark material, sleeved, but still exposing ample décolleté.

"Mama mia!" exclaimed Sophia.

"How about-a some spicy meatballs!" Gina chimed in.

Both threw their shoulders back and shook their "charms" like a bad burlesque act while cackling like drunken chorines.

I looked back at the kid. "Playmate?"

Thomas grinned like a kid turned loose in Disneyland and I had to remind myself that he was even older than I was.

"So," said one of them, starting to lose a little focus, "tell us what you like."

"Why?" I asked, feeling the hairs on my arms start to rise.

"We understand that you're going to be auditioning consorts," said the other, also losing face and figure. "We'd prefer more comfortable quarters—"

"—but we'll take what we can get," added the first. "Just let us show you what you can get!"

"Tell us what—"

"I'll tell you what," I snapped, cutting them off. "Don't *show* me anything. Just sit there for a moment."

While the human parts of me might be susceptible to

the full vampiric mind-twist, the transmuted portions of my brain had proven resistant to previous attempts at all-out mental domination. Perhaps I could filter these glamours as well. I stared back at them, trying to peel the illusion like an onion.

Underneath the outer shell of 1950s' icons and 1960s' screen legends were more identities from the '70s, '80s, and '90s: actresses, models, singers, even a couple of princesses—one still living, one dead. Before I knew it I was sitting across from pop royalty: Britney and Christina.

"Hubba-hubba," said Tommy. "Too bad we can't pick up Madonna!"

I looked at the kid. "Oh, please. Nobody says 'hubba-hubba' anymore. I'm not sure they ever really did." I looked back: now I was sitting across from a pair of Paris Hiltons. "Okay, now I'm starting to get scared."

She/they morphed into the Olsen Twins.

"Now I'm really, really scared."

I blinked. And, for the briefest of moments, Mary-Kate and Ashley became twin girls who appeared to be on their way to their sixth birthday party. Long, blonde hair framed identical round, cherubic faces and huge, blue-gray eyes gave them the appearance of sixties kitsch waif paintings or, maybe, nineties anime heroines. Somehow, in spite of the other glamours, I got the uncomfortable impression that this was pretty close to their true appearance.

They had to be very old and very powerful to project multiple appearances so convincingly. Not that they didn't really inhabit prepubescent bodies but, while their flesh had stopped aging, their minds and appetites had not.

The one on the right licked her lips.

Ew!

I turned to "playmate" Tommy. "You said you were taking me to Darcy Blenik."

"Darcy?" The one on the right wrinkled up her little button nose. "But she's so . . . young!"

"She's practically a baby," agreed the other. "You'd be wanting something a little more mature."

"And diverse . . ." The one on the right started to blur.

As did the one on the left.

Now I was sitting across from Faith Hill and Shania Twain. Who promptly broke into a very bad rendition of "I wanna be loved by you" and sounded more like Marilyn and Jayne as they stumbled into the "Boop-boop-ee-doop" part. Either I was very resistant or there were just some illusions that could not be fully managed on all levels.

I felt the bright coppery taste of dinner rise in my throat. As I tried to swallow it back down, the window separating us from the front seat slid down.

"Domo," the turbaned chauffeur said, "why don't you sit up front with me?" His dark complexion and long curly beard were not familiar but the voice was.

"Hullo, Darcy," I said.

"What's with the hide and go Sikh outfit?" I asked as she drove north.

"As a human, I don't have the advantage of being able to mind-wipe witnesses or cops." She had raised the tinted window so that we had a bit of privacy. Judging from the sounds in the back, maybe the privacy wasn't so much for us. "Sometimes it's best to leave a false impression in the event that things go south."

"And how far south might things go tonight?"

"Depends."

"Past the Mason-Dixon line?"

She gave me a sideways glance. "Maybe all the way to the equator."

"That far? Tell me more."

"If I did, I'd have to kill you." The accompanying smile was weak.

"Everyone back at the ranch thinks you're in bed."

"Good."

"So, why aren't you?"

"Got things to do."

I looked over my shoulder. "Your night to baby-sit?"

"In a manner of speaking."

"You have a very limited manner of speaking," I said after another three blocks of silence. "As your Doman I find it a little unsettling that secrets are being kept from me."

She sighed, but the tension remained in her arms and shoulders. "Did it occur to you that perhaps your ignorance might also be your protection?"

"Nope. I'm surrounded by potential enemies. The more I know the better off I am."

"Maybe in the wild," she said, "but politics is a different jungle. Ever heard of plausible deniability?"

"Plausible deniability is an abrogation of a leader's responsibilities. It suggests that he is either willing to sacrifice his underlings for decisions he won't own up to—or he really isn't in control of the people around him. Either way, it's a damning indictment of the guy in charge."

She shook her head. "Oh boy. Uncle was right: you aren't going to last long here."

"Not if I don't know what is going on."

"See, here's the problem: no one really knows if you're going to be a good fit to the demesne—"

"Because I'm part human?"

She nodded.

"Kind of a racist attitude, don't you think?"

"It's a question of policy, not biology. I'm human but I'm not Doman. I don't make or break the rules that affect the lives of everyone else in the demesne. The concern is that you are gonna be 'ethical man' when what's really needed is 'practical man.'"

"And ethics is a bad thing, right?"

"It comes back to how human are you?"

"Human or humane?"

"I guess the words are interchangeable."

I shook my head. "Not really. When we are treated like animals, we say: 'Hey, I'm *human*.' When we behave like animals, we say: 'Hey, I'm *only* human.'"

She smiled. "Nice. But the question remains. Can you rule a pack of predators who must hunt, who must kill, to survive?"

"I'm not convinced that killing is necessary. A symbiotic relationship—"

She slapped her hand on the dashboard. "There are too many carnivores who will *not* submit to those limitations. If you try to impose a vegan lifestyle on vampires you will have civil war. At best, they will all rise up and depose you. At worst, there will be a bloodbath as the clans are torn apart over leadership and loyalties—a bloodbath that could well spill over into the human neighborhoods. Weak and ineffective leadership could be worse for your ideals of mercy than having another monster like Elizabeth Báthory rule!"

"And the assumption is my human side will make me weak and ineffectual?"

"So far you're an enigma. You've survived assassination attempts, destroyed two former Domans, and chosen not to form any political alliances, yet . . ." She paused. "Well, there is that little rumor that you're forging ties to the Were community. I'm assuming that one is just as ridiculous and ill-founded as all of the others seem to be."

"That's me: Mr. Urbane Legend."

She ignored that with a shake of her turbaned head. "The point is, my uncle respects you and you have allies in the Seattle and Chicago enclaves. This gives you political clout that no former Doman has had in living memory. And living memory around here goes back several hundred years."

"But there's still that niggling little problem of my humanity," I said.

"So, as I said, we're all watching to see how you do on your first tests."

"Tests, plural?"

She nodded.

"Like Yuler? How'd I do there?"

"The jury is still out. While many feel it would have been more merciful to kill him—points for you—you did imply a death sentence for attempts on your life just before Yuler made his."

"I believe I said 'dealt with harshly' with consequences for the families and clans involved, as well. Ask Friederich

Polidori if he and his clan emerged from the evening unscathed."

"Social humiliation is not the same thing as harsh punishment."

"Depends on who you are and where you're from. But, rest assured, ole Freddy and I aren't done yet. Not by a long shot. Now, you said 'tests' plural. I figure I'm in the midst of another exam tonight. I'm assuming it isn't 'open book' since you've avoided any worthwhile explanation of your errand, tonight."

"And then there's the matter of your dead wife and daughter."

Sometimes people light the fuse of my temper and it's a short one. In this case, it was a hand grenade and Darcy Blenik had just pulled the pin. I counted to three: "You want me to take tests? Fine! Sharpen up a woodpile of number two pencils and stack the little blue books to the ceiling! After that, I'll pee in a cup! I guess for every day that I survive around here as the head tooth fairy, there is going to be a fresh round of exams.

"But let's get one thing clear: my family is *not* a test! And I will demonstrate to anyone who thinks to make them one that they are dead wrong—heavy emphasis on the words *dead* and *wrong*!"

She let the silence build in the car before answering softly. "No one wants to bring your family into this, Domo. You know that this is not our doing. But it cannot be anything but an indicator of your priorities, of your loyalties, if you choose to leave New York at this crucial time."

I didn't respond so, after a moment, she spoke again. "You can't afford to be distracted with side issues—"

"My wife and daughter are not side issues." My volatility was downshifting into implacability.

"The lives of two weighed against the lives of many."

"Obviously you never saw *Star Trek III: The Search for Spock*."

"What?"

I glanced at the side mirror and thought I saw something following behind us in the dark. Should I mention it to Darcy?

No, said a voice in my head.

"Look, I'm not saying your wife and daughter aren't important," Darcy was saying, "but let us handle it. We can send a team. You are needed more here."

"As what? A rubber stamp? Kurt seems to have done all right in my absence."

"He cannot hold things together indefinitely. And he cannot act as seneschal for a Doman who would abandon all of his people for two that have already died."

There was no point in continuing the debate. My wife and daughter were more "my people" than a thousand strangers in an unfamiliar city—strangers who were likely to kill me if I didn't measure up to their expectations. They had all managed their affairs without me to this point while I was responsible for Jenny's and Kirsten's deaths.

And it wasn't just that my poor, dead family was being used, once again, as preternatural hostages. Pipt had sent the Tell-Tale Heart, the Frankenvamp, and the creepy-crawly thing back there in the fish tank. Pipt was now using the twice-deceased Theresa Kellerman as his emissary. She had been tenacious in pursuing me while still alive and after her first death. Now that Pipt was acting as her personal necromancer there was no reason to believe she would back off now. Screw politics: this was my number one priority. And if I couldn't deal with one presumably human madman, I certainly couldn't hope to rule several hundred undead ones.

"So what about Cairn?" I asked abruptly.

"What?" The question caught her off balance and seemed to fluster her.

"I get the fact that the average Joe and Jill Vampire are wondering about my human agenda. I take it this Cairn sees this as an opportune time to make a power grab."

Her face was like stone. "That would seem logical."

"So what's his campaign slogan?"

"What?"

"What's his political platform? 'Vote for me: I really suck?' 'Go Undead, Not Half-Dead?' Has he addressed vampire social issues?"

"The ascension to the throne is not a democratic political process—unless you count character assassination, disinformation, and dirty tricks campaigns." A small smile cracked her frozen façade.

"Yeah, I get that, too. But what about the vamp, himself? What does he promise to those who support him?"

"Power, I suppose, just like any other political movement. As for specifics, you would have to ask one of them. That's assuming you could identify one, capture him, and make him talk."

"It just seems an odd kind of campaign," I mused. "No one seems to know who this guy is or what he stands for. I'm told this Doman wannabe has been taking out the opposition for a half century or so and yet he's still a back-room boy, no closer to the limelight and making a popular bid for public candidacy. That's a long time to keep to the shadows."

"Not if you're an elder vampire," she said, her eyes narrowed against the glare of passing headlights. "Their lives are measured in centuries the way yours and mine are counted in decades. Fifty years is a relatively brief span of time in the bigger political picture. And you forget that Dracula and Báthory were the ruling powers during those years. Any opposition was dealt with swiftly and brutally during that period."

"Maybe," I conceded. "But the door's been wide open these past several months. It's been a perfect opportunity for an established member of the New York community—a political freedom fighter by some accounts—to step forward and challenge a fangless outsider for the throne. The enclave is all abuzz with rumors that I will impose moratoriums on breeding, hunting, and killing."

"Perhaps he prefers to do that from behind the scenes for a bit longer."

"My intel suggests that he's more interested in seeding chaos than consolidating a power base."

Her lips were compressed in a straight line beneath the faux moustache and beard. "Who knows? Insanity is not uncommon among the older vamps."

"And those who serve him?"

"As I said, you'd have to find them to ask them. *Our* intel suggests that secret cadres exist which denounce Cairn in public but serve him in secret. And that's as far as we've been able to get."

"Ever try to infiltrate one of these cadres?"

She snorted. "Despite my nickname, I don't have any disguises that good." The car angled up to a curb and stopped. "We're here."

"Here" was a side street lined with old brownstones dating back a century or more. Lights burned in some of the windows dispelling the first impression that the crumbling buildings were long abandoned.

Darcy flashed the headlights twice and killed the engine.

"I still don't know what we are doing here," I said.

"We are here to perform a little surgery. Our demesne has developed cancer and tonight we're going to remove a tumor."

"Really? Why didn't Kurt brief me about this?"

"Kurt doesn't inform you of every little administrative detail. And just as he doesn't micromanage what he delegates, so I don't pass along every little detail of my work, either. He trusts me to do my job so he can concentrate on doing his."

"Sounds reasonable," I said. "Except everyone thinks you're still in your room. So stop dodging the question and tell me what we're doing and why you're running it like a covert ops mission. And why you're hauling the three leg-biters with fangs."

One of her eyebrows went up. "Leg-biters?"

"Leg-biters, shin-kickers, ankle-grabbers, cookie-crumblers, yard-apes, curtain-climbers, thumb-gummers . . ."

"I am taking Tommy, Sindi, and Sassy to see their Sire."

"And that is?"

"Malik Szekely."

"Any relation to 'Uncle' Kurt Szekely?"

"His brother."

"Ah. Kurt never mentioned having a brother."

"He wouldn't."

"Family history?"

"Isn't family all about history?"

I nodded. "And I'll bet the Szekelys have oodles of it."

"You are a quick study, Mr. Cséjthe."

"Yeah? Then how do you explain the lapse of judgment that brought me here?"

"You can wait in the car, if you wish."

"What? And miss the father and child reunion?"

"You are upset."

"What makes you say that?"

"You're working very hard at keeping your face and your voice neutral."

"You think?" I asked calmly. "Maybe I just don't give a shit."

"You prove my point. If you didn't care, you might say that you didn't care. You're not a vulgar person, Chris. When you say you don't give a shit, you are telling me that you are upset."

"Are you?"

"Upset? No. I have grown up surrounded by vampires. One of them was my father. I have served them since I came of age. I understand them. And I know my place. And my destiny."

"How nice for you."

"Yes," she said, "how nice for me. You are still trying to figure out your place. You think you know, but you don't.

You think that having more information will make your choices easier. It won't."

"And why is that?"

"Because information is more than just cold, hard facts. It is also about people. And people are about relationships."

"Emotions," I said.

"That too. But relationships are about family. About tribes. Clans. Group identities. Loyalties." She shook her head. "Relationships subvert our greater morality. We defend our children when they are in the wrong. We make excuses for brothers, sisters, parents, lovers, kith and kin. Our country, right or wrong. Our friends and mates, before all strangers. You and me against the world."

"It is only as a man puts off from himself all external means of support and stands alone that I see him to be strong and to prevail," I recited.

"Is not a man better than a town?" she finished. "But it's more than Emersonian morality. It's about how even your enemies begin to transform as you come to know them—from threat and danger to equations of misunderstanding and lapses of tolerance. Evil becomes enigmatic, a puzzle to be dissected and deconstructed, not fought and eradicated. You shake your head as the world burns around you and say: 'Why can't we all just get along?' No, Mr. Cséjthe, the problem with fact-finding missions is they substitute information-processing for action, the illusion that thinking about something or talking about something is the same as *doing* something. You become Hell's bureaucrat, assisting evil by obfuscation, all in the name of further observation and analysis."

"And that's what you think I'm doing here?" I asked.

"Why don't you tell me what you think you're doing here?" She opened the car door and got out.

I followed suit and leaned across the roof of the limo. "Among other things, to answer your last question, I'm trying to figure out why Kurt never told me he has a brother and why this visit is such a secret."

"How about we make a deal, Domo? You tag along, keep your eyes and ears open, your mouth shut, and I will answer all of your questions when the visit is over. I'll even throw in three complete surprises. Agreed?"

"I don't agree to conditions blindly."

"Try being nearsighted for the next thirty minutes, then. If you do as I say, no humans will die tonight. Interfere, and the blood of innocents will likely be spilled. I don't say this as a threat. It will be the result of our failure."

I looked into her eyes. "You're asking me to trust you. What if I'm wrong? What if you're wrong?"

"You don't know if you can trust me," she said. "But how will you ever know if you can trust me until you *have* trusted me and weighed the result?"

Damn, now there was a logical conundrum. I gestured in surrender. "Lead on, MacDuff."

Surprise suffused her hirsute features. "Another myth busted."

"What?"

"You're supposed to be Mr. Literary Quote-Master and yet you just misquoted Macbeth."

I shrugged. "I was quoting pop culture, not Willy Shakespeare. You want me to say: 'Lay on, MacDuff. And damn'd be him that first cries, "Hold, enough!"?' I just figured we were on the same side, here. But if you want to invest in the whole *Macbeth* scenario . . ."

I was suddenly distracted by the sight of the other children: they were almost invisible in the darkness—even in the infrared spectrum. The fact that Sindi, Sassy, and Tommy were cold wasn't surprising. It was the twenty-odd kids—some coming down the street, others huddled on the stoops of the neighboring brownstones—who were giving me pause. It wasn't only past their bedtimes, it was past their lifetimes: *these children were beyond cold, they had no body heat whatsoever!*

Then I noticed something else. A cat crouched atop a battered garbage can. It, too, was cold. Darcy Blenik and I were the only warm things out on the street.

And I was no longer that warm.

Darcy walked over to huddle with the kindervamps and a spirited discussion developed. Heads turned my way and then back to the huddle. A consensus seemed to emerge. The huddle broke up. The children melted back into the shadows.

"Come," Darcy said. "Remember what I told you. And try to follow my lead."

I followed her lead up the street and onto a stoop another three buildings over. She climbed the steps like an old man and rested a moment before pressing a buzzer.

While we waited I looked around. The kids were all gone. The cat was crouched two steps below. Ahead of us, iron bars backed the glass in the door and the side windows like idealized Belgian waffles. Never mind burglars, an army couldn't get into the lobby without heavy artillery. On the other side of the barred glass, a video camera stared back at us. A little red light came on beside the lens.

"What is it?" rasped an ancient voice from the tiny speaker next to the buzzer.

"It's Darcy, Uncle Malik," she answered sweetly. And raised her hand in a girlish wave.

"What? I don't see any Darcy," the rusty voice grumbled. "All I can see is some kind of Shriners' mascot and a smudgy-looking fellow."

The smudgy-looking fellow would be me. True vampires do not cast shadows or reflections. They have a similar effect on photographic film and videotape. As my brain chemistry changed I, too, began to project a subconscious electromagnetic field that affected cameras and recording equipment.

I was still visible for the time being, just not very photogenic.

Darcy wore a voluminous greatcoat of royal blue that looked like it belonged to a Cossack officer of the Napoleonic era. Gray-white pantaloons and the curved end of a cutlass scabbard were visible below the skirtlike hem of the overcoat. Her feet were ensconced in red satin slippers with pointy toes that curled upward.

"Good gracious, girl," the voice growled, "I haven't seen a getup like that since your grandmother was a baby!" I think it was attempting a purr and the vocal cords would only compromise so far. "I know you like to use disguises but aren't you more likely to attract attention running around like that?"

"This is New York, Uncle. If you got out more you'd know I could pass quite handily for a cabbie."

"Did you come here in a taxi?"

"We came in a limo."

"Then you should have dressed to pass for a limo driver. What about him?"

"I'm dressed to pass for a tourist on his first visit to the Big Apple," I said.

"A tourist who forgot to wear his coat in the dead of winter?"

I nodded. "Convincing, huh?"

"Uncle, this is Christopher Cséjthe, the new Doman."

There was no immediate response.

"Uncle Malik?"

"Why did you bring him here?"

"To discuss your petition for amnes—"

The ancient voice cut her off: "Why did you bring him *here*? Such things are best discussed at a neutral location. Now that he knows where I dwell, what are my guarantees that he will not return with reinforcements?"

"Uh, I've come in good faith," I offered, trying to wing it without cue cards.

"Bah! They always come in good faith! And then they come with the stake and the torch . . ."

"You've heard the stories about this one," Darcy said. "He is not like the others. He is merciful to his enemies. He only kills in self-defense."

Another long pause. Finally: "Weapons?"

"He's clean."

"Also trustworthy, loyal, helpful, friendly, courteous, kind, obedient, cheerful, thrifty, brave, and irreverent," I quipped.

Darcy gave me a look that said *Don't help*.

"Precious is coming down to escort you up. I'll buzz you in once he gets there."

I looked at Darcy. *Precious?* I mouthed silently. I started to smile.

"Book cover," she replied.

As in don't judge by, I decided as Precious descended the stairs and came into view.

He was huge. Six-six and nearly half again as wide. His bald head gleamed in the light of the foyer and his skin had the appearance of having been recently oiled. Gold rings, large and heavy, drooped from paper-punch piercings in his ears and nose. He looked like a cartoon cannibal from deepest, darkest Africa even though his voluminous flesh was the color of dirty chalk.

"Let me go first," she whispered. "Hang back. And don't let the door close behind you."

Precious fairly minced his way across the lobby and nearly arrived too late to catch the doorknob as the lock buzzed open.

"Good evening, Miss Darcy," he trilled as he pulled the door back.

I noticed three out of four things as he ushered us in.

One, Precious had the falsetto voice of a long-time castrato.

Two, his teeth had been filed to triangular points.

And three, his breath smelled like the back end of a slaughterhouse.

Precious noticed one out of two things as we entered: "Are you wearing a sword under your coat, my dear?"

The scabbard had shifted upwards under her greatcoat:

a good nine inches now protruded from between her coat-tails like a friendly tail.

"It's part of the costume, Precious. Plastic and rubber."

"May I see?" It wasn't really a question. There was no doubt that we weren't going anywhere until her uncle's hulking companion was satisfied.

"Fine," she said, unbuttoning her coat from the top down as I caught the door to keep it from closing behind me.

"What are you doing?" Tall-White-and-Gruesome demanded, turning toward me.

Darcy turned as well. "Here, block the jam with this." She tossed a crumpled pack of cigarettes to me.

Precious took a step, reaching for me, and was thrown off balance as Darcy's greatcoat burst open.

Sindi, Sassy, and Tommy rushed out from the parted material like schoolchildren released for recess. They charged the big man and attached themselves to his lower extremities like Velcro Cabbage Patch dolls. Sassy and Tommy each sank their fangs into a meaty thigh. Sindi went for the crotch. Precious began to scream like an operatic soprano on helium and danced like a sumo wrestler on meth.

I dropped the cigarette pack but the door stopped two inches from closing. It began to swing open again. The other children were storming the porch and the first wave was breaching the door.

Darcy had her sword out now and it wasn't plastic and rubber. The blade was silvery steel and looked very sharp. Sharp enough to sever the big man's head from his shoulders. Which it did as she went all Uma Thurman on him.

A tide of children swept across the foyer, trampling over the fallen mound of twitching flesh and starting up a game of rugby with the razor-toothed head. A couple of them slipped in the spreading pool of blood, one of them taking a knee. Another executed a running lunge and belly-surfed across the crimson tide with a squeal of glee. The others were businesslike as they spread about, producing crowbars and wicked-looking tools of indeterminate origin. Some began attacking doors down the hallway, others started up the stairway.

The pitter-patter of tiny feet never sounded so chilling.

"Tell me, Domo, do you believe in evil?"

I looked at Darcy. This had to be a trick question.

"Or do you believe in theories of social injustice?" She turned and started up the stairs.

I didn't follow. It felt wrong. What was I doing here?

Besides playing hall monitor to the children of the damned, that is?

That's when a cold and clammy hand fell on my shoulder.

Chapter Fourteen

"GOOD GOD, GIRL; you scared me half to death!"

A disturbingly nude Suki gave me a half-smile and said: "Only half?"

"What are you doing here?"

"Following you. What are *you* doing here?"

I looked around at the prepubescent bedlam unfolding about us. "I don't know yet. Trying to figure out what's really going on in my new demesne."

"Typical. You blunder about like a blind man in a china shop and get your bearings from the sound of broken glass."

It wasn't a bad analogy: orderly chaos surrounded us. A pent-up group rage was unfolding from the ground floor up but it had the appearance of anger with a purpose. Kids were breaking locks and forcing their way into other apartments. Screams began to erupt anew from inside the other rooms.

No one took notice of the new Doman or the cat that had turned into a naked lady.

I glanced at an uncomfortable expanse of bare skin and turned my attention to the stairs leading to the second floor. "I'd offer you my coat but, as you can see, I forgot to bring one."

"Stop blushing; I'll put my fur back on in a moment. I just wanted to know if there was a plan. Not that you usually have one. Or that you'd let us in on it if—"

"Here's what I know so far," I snapped. "Kurt has a brother whom he has never mentioned, who appears to be the black sheep of the family . . ."

The tiny lobby elevator dinged and the dial above its diminutive door indicated that it was on its way down from the fourth floor.

"That's interesting. If Kurt's the *white* sheep of his clan—" Her voice stopped in a shiver and I didn't think it was due to her lack of attire.

"Anyway, Darcy's apparently organized some sort of a raid here and she doesn't want Uncle Kurt to know about it."

"And what's your place in her scheme of things?"

"I get the feeling I'm along for an evaluation."

"Hers or yours?"

"I started off thinking it was mine. Now I think it's the other way around."

"With you, it usually is. So, are you helping or just hanging?"

"Good question."

"Bad answer."

The elevator dinged again, signaling its arrival.

"Either way," she said, "I've got your back." Her voice squeaked up past the human register on the last word. It was followed by a distinct meow.

The door slid open revealing an empty two-person lift.

Darcy arrived seconds later, swooping back down the staircase, her billowing greatcoat giving her the appearance of a giant bird of prey. "Where is he?" she bellowed. "Did he get past you?"

"Nobody got past me. The elevator was empty."

The door was starting to close again and she darted forward to catch the edge before it could slide shut. She stuck her head inside and something large and dark fell out of the ceiling. She went down beneath a billowing black cloak. The sword went skittering across the floor of the lobby as it bore her to the floor. As the curved blade came to a stop against the toes of my shoes, a seven-year-old boy ran down the stairs and rushed toward the front door. He was naked and half covered in blood, twin streamers of silvery chain trailed behind him from leather cuffs about his wrists. Two little girls, no more than four or five were in hot pursuit, one brandishing a hammer, the other waving a butcher knife.

I had seconds to make a decision as I bent to retrieve the sword. Something seemed to click behind my eyeballs as I switched over to infravision but the lobby lights and welter of confusion made it difficult to read multiple targets as I lifted the curved blade.

The boy squealed and changed course to avoid me but I was close enough to take a step and drop the blade back down across the path of his pursuers. One good glimpse finally told me that both were cold and I sliced the closest one in half as she bore down on her victim.

She burst like an exploding Dustbuster, scattering ashes in a three-meter radius. The thing was not a child; it was an undead predator—possibly decades older than even Tommy and the twins. There was no question in my mind that I had just destroyed something that was inhuman and evil but, as I turned to her companion, I suddenly found myself down on my hands and knees, retching up the remnants of my evening's repast and casting a bloody Rorschach across the lobby floor.

By the time I wobbled back to my feet, the boy was backing into a corner as the other kindervamp stalked him with a claw hammer raised in her chubby little fist. He hissed at her and I almost dropped the sword as his quarter-inch fangs became visible. A second look confirmed what I had missed with the first glance: he was as cold as the children from the street.

Not my fight, I decided and turned back to the elevator. Darcy was still down, her legs kicking at the tiled floor of the lobby and failing to gain purchase, but now she was mostly inside the lift and was being drawn further in.

I charged, clapping a hand to the side of the door as it began to slide shut. A young man with long golden hair had one knee pressed between Darcy's shoulder blades and the other on her right arm as she desperately tried to reach up behind her with her left. He had her right leg twisted up behind her with the pantaloons pushed back to expose her calf and ankle and was lowering his mouth to her skin when the tip of my sword intervened.

I tapped him under the chin with the flat of the blade and said: "Ah, ah, ah?"

He looked up, his smooth, young face looking like an undergrad's who has just been informed that he must enroll for Advanced Calculus instead of Speech 101.

Then something moved under the planes of his face; he lunged.

He was fast enough to beat a human's response time but I'm about half again as fast and the sword was already in position. The tip caught him between ribs and collarbone as he ran up the blade. I rammed the hilt of the sword against his upper chest and drove him back against the elevator wall, embedding the first third of the blade in the metal behind him. He was neatly pinned for a moment, his toes barely touching the floor, as he struggled like a dying butterfly.

The problem was, he wasn't a butterfly and he wasn't anywhere near dying. In a moment he was going to find a way to dislodge himself and playtime would be all over.

I grabbed Darcy and dragged her back out of the lift as the door tried to close again. It would have been a little easier if she had cooperated but, as I dragged, she fumbled with the interior of her rumpled greatcoat. The elevator door bumped my hip and reversed its motion. Malik had already loosened the sword sufficiently to get his feet flat on the floor. We had maybe ten seconds.

Darcy brought forth an M61 fragmentation grenade from an inner pocket and deftly thumbed the pin one-handed. The lever snapped open and our time was suddenly cut to four seconds. She held on to it for almost three of them. Then, as the door started to close again, she snapped it off in an underhanded throw. The metal ovoid disappeared through the narrowing slot and clattered around the inside of the lift like a golf ball inside a spin dryer.

The door was barely closed when an awful, tripart noise

shook our eardrums: the sound of the blast, the *spang* of metal walls warping out of shape, and the hailstorm rattle of steel fragments ricocheting throughout the elevator's interior. Greasy black smoke simmered out of the crack in the split door.

"That was easy," Darcy murmured as I helped her to her feet. I hated to think what she might consider difficult.

Tommy and the twins appeared beside us as if by magic. "Everything's set," he announced.

"Good. Wait for me in the car." Darcy turned to me. "You saved me."

I was tired and it was taking me extra seconds to come up with my "shucks, ma'am, twarn't nothin'" speech when she continued: "And in doing so, helped me kill Malik Szekely. I trust you won't be discussing this night's events with Uncle Kurt."

The girl had a deft way of turning a front-end good deed into a back-end obligation.

We exited the building as the bedlam inside was reaching a crescendo. I started to turn left—the limo lay in that direction—but Darcy turned right. I reversed direction, still trying to reconcile the ancient, raspy voice on the intercom with the youthful visage in the elevator and almost missed the small device that Spook was pulling from her pocket. "You know, the funny thing about life is that it is a schoolroom in reverse," she said, opening the cover. "It gives the tests first and the lessons afterward." The device appeared to be a small electronic controller, two switches, two buttons.

I didn't like the looks of it: I had used one very similar to it once and my fuse box assassin had carried another very much like it. "Yeah? Well, I hope this test is over because I'm still waiting for the lesson."

"The lesson is always the same. Evil always wins."

I walked around to stand in front of her. "So what are you saying? That we weren't the good guys tonight?"

"Oh yes, we were the good guys. And we did what we had to do. To have done nothing . . ."

"Edmund Burke," I said. "'All that is necessary for evil to succeed is for good men to do nothing.'"

She nodded. "But often good men must do terrible things to thwart great evils . . ."

"And thus are more evils born," I concluded. "Aristotle said we must, as second best, take the least of the evils."

"Yep. You *are* big on the quotations. The problem with using other people's words is no one knows where you, yourself, stand."

"Okay, if you're asking about evil, I'm against it."

"Good to know," she said curtly. "Now the question remains: What does the Doman of the largest undead enclave in the Western Hemisphere consider evil?"

"Well, pedophilia is high on the list. Undead pedophilia even higher."

"Textbook. Pick another P-word."

"Another P-word?"

"Preemption," she elaborated.

Ah. "The question is what lesser evils I am willing to commit in the name of what I consider good?"

She nodded. "Does your heart bleed for Malik's little victims? Or for the future victims of his little victims?"

"Are we talking about breaking the chain of molestation? Or killing vampires?"

"You tell me."

I shook my head. "One evil is not the same as another."

"Isn't it?" She glanced back at the shadows flickering between the iron bars on the windows of the old brownstone. "Malik was captured by the Turks during the fifteenth century. He was ransomed back after a year of captivity. A year does not seem very long in an existence that has spanned centuries. But when you are a child, suffering unspeakable indignities, the acquisition of power and the passing of generations may amplify—rather than bury—the bruises of the soul. And what goes around . . ."

"Comes around?"

"Just keeps going around and around and around until a way is found to stop it." She flipped a switch on the remote. "I promised you three surprises." She pressed a button. "Surprise . . ."

The initial explosions sounded like distant mortar fire. The charges were apparently set in the basement to breach the gas main. Which was ignited by the initial blasts. The follow-up was a blast that blew out the glass and loosened the bars, cracked the stone, and rattled my fillings. The old apartment building was instantly turned into a giant Coleman lantern, a glowing white-hot mantle that encompassed a jet of purple flame turning winter's night into summer's day for a couple of blocks in every direction.

I grabbed her arm. "There were children in there!"

"You know better than that," she said wearily. "There were only things that looked like children. Things that might have been children, once. He took their innocence from them and he took their lives. He remade them in his own image. Undead and unnatural."

"Not every molested child becomes a child molester! It's the exception, not the rule!"

"No," she agreed. "But the statistics are not promising when you give them eternal life and power over innocent flesh. Malik has created hundreds like himself—only he granted them the dark gift while they were still unfinished. Malik, himself, was not turned until he reached physical maturity. He offered no such completion to those he transformed into his undead playthings."

I stared back at the inferno that was cleansing the world of Malik and his terrible legacy. "Your little coconspirators planted the charges while the neighborhood kids went about attending to the newest victims. I guess they thought they were preventing the curse from spreading. But it was just a convenient way for you to bring them all together while your 'mini-mes' turned the whole building into your final solution."

She nodded. "As I have said, a quick study."

"So how are the three in your limo any different from the others? Why should they live while the others are given the shake-and-bake solution?"

She flipped the second switch. "Surprise number two . . ." She pressed the second button and a thunderclap went off under the limousine where Tommy, Sindi, and Sassy waited. The car rose eight feet off the ground and turned into a fiery version of Darcy's grenade in the elevator.

I could feel my eyebrows starting to singe in the blast-furnace breeze that washed over us but I only felt colder down deep inside. "You're out of switches," I said after a long moment. "What's the third surprise? That we have a long walk back to the park?"

"Nope." She put the remote back inside her coat pocket. When her hand reemerged it was holding a SIG-Sauer P226 auto-pistol. Up close, it looked a lot bigger than it actually was. The black eye of the barrel was positively huge.

"Okay," I said, "you really are a dhampir. Even though all the legends say a dhampir is the son of a vampire, you're a credit to your gender. You outslay the Slayer and are cuter than the Executioner. But I'm the good guy, remember? Reforming the fanged, protecting the fangless . . ."

"The thing about evil," she interrupted, "is that it is incapable of sustaining itself indefinitely. Deal enough death, impose enough indignities, and even the sheep rise up against the wolf. Báthory was only months away from an open revolt. Never mind the living; the undead had had enough of her excesses. Unambiguous evil is self-correcting."

"Maybe," I said, "but I think it's always best to speed up the process."

"Except people like you don't. You're another Chamberlain."

"Richard?"

"Neville. You'd rather negotiate with evil than destroy it. Evil perpetuates itself through the cooperation of the willing. You find yourself in the belly of the beast and, instead of trying to cut your way out, you redecorate and distribute throw pillows! Worse, you're the Typhoid Mary of the Stockholm Syndrome!"

I was more annoyed than afraid. "Let me get this straight. I've been in town two days, trying to figure out how to keep hundreds of undead killers from turning all of New England into their own coffin-and-breakfast while dodging assassins so that I can live long enough to institute some positive change. And you, Miss Lived-Among-The-Vampires-All-My-Life, take a few minutes off from your job as PR flack for Uncle Kurt to lecture me on collusion with the enemy? If that isn't a case of the pot calling the thimble black, I don't know what is!"

"If they knew that I was working against them, I wouldn't live long enough to accomplish anything."

"And it's beyond your comprehension that I might be working from the same script?"

"There are obvious differences between us, Cséjthe. I do not traffic with the dead. I have never acted to save nor had physical congress with the undead. Despite maintaining my cover for many years, I have never been seduced by it. I know who I am and what I stand for. The Hunger and the Bloodthirst have never had a foothold on my soul. I have passed through the fire and have not wavered."

"Yeah, unthinking fanaticism is like that."

"If you really want to bring down this evil empire, take solace in the fact that your death will accomplish more toward that goal than an entire lifetime of administrative Mickey-Mouse."

"Oooh, nice turn of phrase. But you're not thinking clearly. I offer more advantages as an ally than a lever for political instability."

"At least you're not out and out begging. I like that. You're presenting a cool and reasoned argument for what you believe are logical alternatives. But that just underscores how dangerous you would be as Doman. You would find all sorts of intellectual justifications for the evil that would flourish under your benevolence. You lack passion. You are already becoming undead, yourself. You accept what other humans would not. I'm doing you a favor by pulling the trigger now: you may not yet possess a hell-bound heart."

"And so you kill me and, of course, another powerful wampyr takes advantage of the resulting paranoia to make his move. Will your cause be better served if Cairn becomes Doman?"

She shook her head. "You still don't get it, do you? Like my mother before me and hers before her, *I* am Cairn!" Her finger tightened and a hissing, spitting, somewhat singed cat leapt upon her as she squeezed the trigger. Her arm was moving off trajectory as the cat became something else but an express train was already smashing into me, knocking me off my feet. Thunder roared and I smashed into the wall of the tenement building beyond the sidewalk like a rag doll hurled by an angry child.

A giant bubble of pain swelled and burst in my chest.

Bloody red-shift to white and I was asleep in the light.

I awoke in rainbow-spangled darkness.

Dark and mysterious shapes encompassed me, their dim outlines refracting the available light in spectral shifts like the event horizon of ghostly prisms.

FLASH!

The world was suddenly ablaze in hellish red, as if the great dragons of Hiroshima and Dresden and Nagasaki had arrived to breathe their benedictions on my soul.

FLASH!

The blue ice of Ragnarok sucked all warmth, all color, all hope from the world in the vicious name of Entropy.

FLASH!

Red.

FLASH!

Blue.

FLASH!

Red.

FLASH!

Then blue . . .

Then red . . .

Blue . . .

Red . . .

I turned and found direction.

Dirty basement window.

Outside, on the street, a police car strobed the fire-lit night with its red and blue light bar. A cop stood over huddled shapes, speaking into his transceiver. Another knelt next to Suki, adjusting a blanket about her shoulders as she hunched over like someone caught in the bitter throes of *mal de mer*.

A banshee keened in the distance.

I was numb.

I was in shock.

I had been knocked into the building when the gun discharged . . . fallen through the basement window, down into the cellar.

I tried to climb back out but I couldn't get the proper purchase on the window frame to boost myself back up.

I turned to look for another way out, wondering what had happened to Darcy Blenik. Had she escaped? Had she shot Suki and run away instead of coming after me?

The banshee wailed louder.

I staggered through an obstacle course of barrels and boxes, shelves and racks, finally finding an old staircase leading up to the first floor. The treads seemed mushy with age and I hesitated as an odd sound penetrated my mental haze.

Not the squeak of a stair but the susurrus of whispered voices.

I turned and scanned the basement, looking for infrared signatures in the hazy, flickering dark.

Nothing.

Nothing *warm* that is.

Something purple-dark, maybe.

Something *colder* than room temperature . . .

I went up the stairs backwards, stumbling on the mushy treads but unwilling to turn my back on whatever whispery things there might be scuttling about in the musty shadows.

The floor in the lobby was just as old and rotten as the

cellar stairs. It was like walking on pillows and feeling that one misstep, one overly rotten plank, could send me crashing back down into the basement.

I went through the front door and staggered to a stop on the front stoop. Malik's brownstone was engulfed in flames down the street and fire engines circled it like stalking lions.

There were two fires, however.

Within the red, yellow, and orange jets of flame another conflagration roared. Tattered flames of blue and green and purple fluttered and flashed, their rhythms and patterns reminiscent of negative film stock run in reverse.

Dark shapes frolicked at the fire's core. Distorted silhouettes chased one another about though the inferno like children running through a cool fountain on a hot summer's day. Distorted faces, like blackened *commedia dell'arte* masks, peeked through curtains of hot gasses, grinning or grimacing as they sought and fled from one another.

"Scary, ain't it?" asked a familiar voice.

The Kid sat on the limestone-capped brick sidewall that ran alongside the steps.

The multihued blaze, the red/blue flashing strobes of the fire trucks, cop cars, and ambulances, seemed to make no impression on the electric lime green zoot suit that he wore. It seemed to glow in the predawn light with a radiance all its own. He wore a broad-brimmed hat of matching color tilted back on his head and his chalky hands were clasped below one knee, pulled up toward his chin, as he took in the organized pandemonium with me.

"You're dead," I said, unable to articulate the various imports that implied for my current circumstances.

"Well, natch, Daddy-o. Been dead for close to a century, now."

"I'm. Dead," I managed, coming closer to the core issue.

"Hmmm." J.D. turned his attention to me and appeared to ponder. "Maybe. But there's dead and then there's dead. And then there's dead again."

"'Death is but one and comes but once / And only nails the eyes,'" I quoted.

"Yeah? Who wrote that?"

"Emily Dickinson."

"She must've wrote that while she was still alive because she don't know from nothin'."

"Really."

"Look-it, she might be the bee's knees in certain literary circles but I sure wouldn't ask her to inventory Shineola in the afterlife. Now that guy what wrote *Peter Pan*, he got a much better idear when he said 'To die will be an awfully big adventure.'"

"You've *read Peter Pan?*"

He shrugged. "Guy wrote about boys who never grew old. Seemed relevant." He unfolded himself from his perch next to the steps. "But instead of jawing about a bunch of literary know-nothings maybe you ought to be thinking about copping a ride." He pointed at the nearest ambulance. "They're loading your body on now."

I turned and the world spun about me. By the time I could orient myself, the back doors on the emergency vehicle were slamming shut and an EMT was climbing into the driver's seat. "Hey!" I yelled, "Wait!"

I ran down the steps, stumbling a bit on their mushy surfaces, and sprinted toward the ambulance. The siren whooped and the van chugged forward just as I caught the back door handles. I managed a short hop and glimpse through a rear window before slipping and falling into the pavement. What was strapped to the gurney inside didn't look like me. There was a lot of blood and pads and an oxygen mask, and a paramedic was working feverishly to do something. Suki was sitting on the other side, huddled in a blanket, staring at all of the blood as if she might never want to taste any again.

Darkness.

Pulling myself up out of the pavement was like falling facedown in a sea of mud and trying to drag myself free of the tremendous suction of muck and mire. I got my head up just in time to see the ambulance turn the corner several blocks down. "Hey!" I yelled. Like it was going to make any kind of difference.

Now what should I do?

The ambulance was gone and I could spend days walking the length and breadth of Manhattan trying to find the right room in the right hospital in an utterly alien city of 8 million people. And if I was dead what would be the point?

I looked back at The Kid. "I could use a little help here."

His mouth twitched. "Sure." He got up, ambled over and reached down as if to assist me. "Take my hand," he said.

I reached up and grasped his hand. Or tried to. My fingers passed through his without even a tingle. "I'll be damned."

"Could be," he agreed.

Chapter Fifteen

IT TOOK US TWO hours to walk two miles. Something about being noncorporeal and being disconnected from the physical plane seemed to put us into a different time/space continuum and bollixed up moving from one point of reference to another. We made deep sea divers look like Olympic sprinters.

There were other issues as well.

"Okay," I said as I looked up at the predawn sky, "I think I've got the basics down: noncorporeality versus surface tension, electromagnetic radiation versus synaptic cohesion, dimensional overlaps."

"Really?" The Kid thrust his hands into his Captain Kangaroo pockets and shook his head. "And here I thought I was giving with the lowdown on how to make the haunty scene."

"If you really want to give me the lowdown, you could tell me where I'm supposed to go now. Heaven? Hell? Purgatory? Paradise?"

"Hey, just because lots of people told me where to go when I was undead don't make me no tour guide now that I'm all phantomy. Dead ain't the same as undead."

He was plainly spooked—no pun intended—and I figured that if someone like The Kid could be afraid long past the point of having a life to hang onto, my chances of R.I.P.ing were sure to get ripped up before the ectoplasm settled. Still, there was no point in getting grave before the grave was actually dug. "Don't fret, Junior," I said, trying to clap his nonexistent shoulder, "you're still the ghost with the most."

He brightened. And I mean that literally. "Thanks, Big Daddy. It's been rough trying to work this out on my own. Now that you're here, I figure on having some kind of purpose."

"Besides annoying me for eternity?"

"Aw, man . . ." He grinned but the smile faded in reverse Cheshire style and he looked away. "See, here's the thing. I been around almost a century, alive and undead, but when I finally get dusted, I dunno whether to be pissed off 'cause I'm so mad or piss on myself 'cause I'm so scared."

"I can relate," I said, thinking that the reality of my own demise had yet to sink in.

"You? You're in a smooth groove. Don't nothin' rattle you even when you buy the big one. Here you're dead without even cashing your three-score-and-ten and you're just as cool as a cucumber. What's your secret, Stan?"

"Spook softly, Junior, and carry a big shtick." I didn't explain that this was a euphemism for maintaining denial and stalling for time.

"Good advice," he decided. "Especially since the sun will be coming up soon. We need to find some shelter and hunker down."

"Why? Do the dead undead burst into flame?" *Dead undead?* Sounded better than "undead dead . . ."

"What? No. At least I don't think so. It's just that we ghostly types get all watered down and fadey when the sun comes up. Go blind and can't hardly move. Kinda like Superman and kryptonite, ya know?"

"That's what I meant when I said electromagnetic radiation. Maybe I should have called it photonic sensitivity."

"No matter how you dress it up with the fancy language, Chief, daylight can mess with you real good!"

"But does it destroy us? Or just stun us until nightfall?"

"Don't think I want to find out. 'Specially since there's worse things—" He was interrupted by pale fingers of sunlight sliding between the buildings to our left. The night was turning into dark bars of shadow—slabs of darkness that were starting to seep back down into the cellars and basements around us. The Kid stiffened. "Oh crap! It's later than I thought!"

He grabbed at my hand and tried to pull me off the street. His fingers passed through mine again and he staggered through a lamppost. "We've got to get inside!" he said.

"Hey, if I'm dead, what's left for me to be afraid of?"

As if in answer to my question, someone started screaming off in the distance—two or three someones. One of the voices abruptly choked off but the volume of the remaining terror continued to grow. Something came around the corner three blocks ahead of us.

The Kid was doing everything he could to grab onto me and tug me toward the nearest building. "Come on, we gotta scram! They're coming!"

"Who's coming?" The sudden flash of sunlight was dazzling me, making it hard to think.

Two men were coming toward us, running full tilt, but moving in slow motion like the inhabitants of a languid dream. They wore rumpled suits of indeterminate color, the hues bleached out by their flickering transparency. While they moved like film stock slowed down to half-speed, the shrieks emanating from their open mouths were high-pitched like audio set on fast-forward.

"Cséjthe!" The Kid bellowed. "Run!"

I took a step. My foot came up like it was coming loose from hot tar.

Something else came around the corner. It wasn't moving in slow motion.

"Get off the street!" The Kid was shrieking.

The thing that was coming around the corner was joined by two more things. "Things" were the best I could come up with at first. Perhaps they were a trio of creatures, perhaps three distinct "swarms" of many creatures. Whatever they were, they were as scary as hell!

Although the man in front wasn't moving particularly fast, his companion was falling further and further behind. The creatures were gaining on both.

"Cséjthe, don't look at them! Look at me! Run toward me!"

The Kid's words barely penetrated. I was seized with an overwhelming urge to run in the opposite direction. I took another gummy step.

The Old Testament prophet Ezekiel described heavenly beings which resembled wheels within wheels, amalgams of eyes and wings. As they whirled closer, these creatures looked more like the cartoon Tasmanian Devil in full spin mode, only with red eyes and green talons and flashing silver blades.

They caught up to the slower of the two runners in moments, surrounding him like a trio of unholy dust devils. The shrieking intensified, the sound coming from dozens of throats instead of just two. A sound like the howling of the wind—containing multiple velocities, the din of horn and bone and metal all rubbing together with a high-pitched chittering overlaying all. The spinning accelerated and the creatures began tumbling like multilayered gyroscopes made of teeth and claws and spines of rust-spattered iron. Faster and faster they fluttered and flashed, tightening their orbits. Then they rushed together like colliding cuisinarts and the runner at the center disappeared in an explosion of fog and vapor, his screams fading down a long invisible tunnel.

My equanimity evaporated, as well: I turned and began a sticky, slow-motion sprint toward The Kid and the dubious shelter of a flimsy steel and stone building.

The howlingwhirlingshrieking sound off to my left intensified and began to grow in volume as I pushed my feet against the gummy pavement and clawed at the air in an attempt to pull my way forward. With each step my feet seemed to sink a little deeper into the gelatinous asphalt and I fancied I could feel the hint of a breeze against my neck, the backwash of air from the razored Turbines of the Damned as they closed in for their second kill.

The Kid was backing into the outer wall of the building, merging with the stone surface like an entertainer taking his final curtain call. Only there was nothing entertaining in his eyes. They were wide and haunted, eyes that had seen many deaths over the long decades and looked as if they were only really seeing it for the very first time now.

The shrieking intensified behind me and I knew that they had caught up with the second runner just as he was catching up with me. He began to gibber and howl as my toes sank through the edge of the sidewalk and I knew that I had less than a minute before they were upon me, as well.

Don't listen

    Don't think

       Focus

          See the ground as solid

             Believe yourself to be as solid as you are real

The voice inside my head wasn't my own but I wasn't inclined to argue. I pushed against firmer ground and accelerated toward the wall where J.D. was submerging into a sea of rock and mortar.

The screaming began in earnest as I leapt across the sidewalk and hurtled into the stone wall.

Except I didn't pass *into* the wall, I smacked up against it! I had gained the advantage of a more substantial reality, only to find it shutting me out just short of the finish line.

Okay, okay; not solid! Not real! I thought furiously as I scrabbled against the side of the building. *I am such things as dreams are made of . . . a shadow of a thought . . . a fog . . . a mist . . . the reflection of fog or mist!* This time the voice in my head was my own and much less convincing. The wall seemed a bit soft but still impenetrable. The sounds of vorpal blades behind me went snicker-snack!

Lemme in! I mind-shouted, pummeling the marshmallow stones with transparent fists. *I'm Casper the Friggin' Ghost! The Phantom of the Grand Ole Opera! The Spirit of X-Men Yet To Come!*

The screaming dissolved into tatters of sound that echoed like an army of mice falling down a deep, dark well. The whirring and clicking grew louder and now there was an unmistakable disturbance in the air against my back.

I leaned into the wall, unwilling to turn and face the horrors that were closing in on me.

Something tugged at my left wrist and I lost my balance.

I fell into darkness.

I stared at a multitude of feet as they padded around on the carpeted floor. I stared because they were at eye level for me and I wasn't quite ready to leap to my own feet, yet. J.D.'s feet were just a couple of feet away. But they were turned the wrong way. I knew they were his feet because nobody else was wearing transparent two-tone broughams. The rest of the feet in the room were bare but solid. They were also feminine—for the most part. I looked up.

We were in a ladies locker room.

"Which explains," I observed, "why you're paying no attention to me even though I've just narrowly escaped death."

"How can you escape death—narrowly or otherwise— when you're already dead?" he asked, concentrating on the new arrivals from the shower room.

"Aye, there's the rub."

"What? A massage?"

I ignored that. The Kid was probably pulling my leg. Probably, but I couldn't be completely sure, given our current issues of corporeality. "What the hell were those things?"

Perhaps I should have been more specific: The Kid obviously had other "things" on his mind, now. But, after a moment, he grunted and said: "Threshers."

"What? As in bringing in the sheaves?"

He shrugged. "I dunno. Maybe. I thought they was angels the first time I seen 'em."

"As well you might," I said. "'As for their rings, they were so high they were dreadful; and their rings were full of eyes round about them four. And when the living creatures went, the wheels went by them: and when the creatures were lifted up from the earth, the wheels were lifted up.'"

"Now yer scarin' me!"

"Because you think they're angels?"

"No. Because you can quote chunks of the Old Testament right outta thin air. I already figured they might be the Big G's huntin' dogs. And if they're angels, well I don't figure on ever going into the Light. I'll take my chances with the Dark."

"So what do these wheelie things do exactly?"

"Exactly? Look-it . . . all I know is they come in the sunrise. They sweep through the open spaces like the Wild Hunt, looking for disconnected spirits—those who haven't moved on to wherever it is that we're supposed to go next."

"Earthbound spirits?"

"Yeah. If you ain't tied to your body, you're fair game. They tear you up and some of 'em even burn the pieces! I seen 'em do it a couple of times now! It's horrible!"

And that was all that he knew. Or wanted to know.

Me? I was wondering if they were intelligent beings with a higher purpose—like sending unanchored spirits on to their final destinations. Or maybe they were just something feral, bestial, stalking the afterlife for the remnants of consciousness like dire wolves of the damned. While I had never bought into the cartoon depictions of clouds and harps and halos, I had scarcely imagined the flipside of "Life After Life" being "Death After Death."

The Kid had cause to be scared. Apparently I did, too.

I sighed and started to get up. It wasn't easy with barely dressed women walking about. Even harder when one walked through me. Woooo: a pulse of warm darkness, a flash of a boardroom meeting, and a condensed internal debate over the office politics of looking too good or not looking good enough. She passed on and so did my little trip down Memory Lane Bryant.

"Unlax, Doc; you're safe now," he said as I staggered to my feet. "The Threshers won't bother us in here. We're safe as long as we stay put until nightfall."

"Nightfall?"

"Yeah. Ain't it a bitch?" A couple of towels hit the floor.

"Too bad we can't go anywhere without risking afterlife and limb." His tone belied his disappointment.

I stumbled over to an unoccupied bench. I sat down and promptly fell through it to the floor. Why didn't I keep on falling? As that thought coalesced I felt the floor start to give beneath my derriere. *Solid! Solid! Very hard floor!* I thought furiously as I bounded to my feet.

And a solid bench, too!

I sat again—gingerly this time—and stayed in place. "So, these—Threshers—you call them?"

He shook his head. "I don't call 'em, Chief. That's what some other spook was tellin' me—hey now, pretty mama! No need to be shy! Just us girls in here so why don't you turn around?"

"Come on, Junior." I snapped my fingers but they made no sound. "A little focus, here. What are they? Where do they come from? Where do they go? How do you know they won't come in here?"

"Don't know much." He came over and sat beside me as most of the exposed flesh disappeared beneath street clothes. "I mean, how do you research things like that? They come with the light, disappear with the dark. They're the reason we go bump in the night instead of haunt around the clock. The only way to be safe is to stay out of the light."

"Don't go into the light, Carolann!" I mimicked in a falsetto voice.

The Kid stared at me.

"It's—um—a movie. *Poltergeist?* There's this—okay, never mind. How do you know we're safe in here? We're still in the light."

The Kid gazed up at the fluorescent tubes that hummed overhead. "I dunno. Don't think it's the same thing as that sailor photography."

"Solar photonic sensitivity."

"Whatever. Besides, I don't think they can pass through solid walls."

"Hmmm." I stared down at the floor. Dipped a translucent toe in the concrete. "Hey, Junior?"

"Yeah?"

"I gotta point out that 'don't think' isn't the same as 'know for a fact.' But here is something that I *do* know for a fact: women don't pass through solid walls."

"So?"

"So, there were close to a dozen in here a little while ago. How did *they* get in and out?"

The Kid's eyes grew big as the concept of doors and windows jumped into the equation. Then he forced a smile. "H-hey, Big Daddy, I don't think these things can fit through any human-sized openings."

"Again with the 'don't think'."

"Look-it, they haven't followed us in or they'd have been here by now. We're safe and sound, right where we are. Nobody can see us. Nobody can hear us. Nobody can mess with us!"

I grunted. "That's what Polyphemus said."

"Poly who?"

"The Cyclops. He learned that, in the country of the one-eyed giant, Odysseus was king."

"I don't get it," J.D. said as the last of the ladies closed her locker and exited the changing area. "I thought it was supposed to be something about the one-eyed man bein' king in a country full of blind men."

I thought of spending eternity babysitting The Kid. Maybe this was Hell nor was I out of it. "Look, Junior, the floor show's over. Let's move on. I got a body to catch up to and time's a-wasting."

He scowled—maybe at me, maybe at the emptiness of the room. "Now who's not payin' attention? We can't go nowhere during the day unless you want to get up close and personal with one of the ghost grinders out there!"

"Maybe," I said. "Maybe not. There might be some ways of getting around without risking exposure. We could try some things."

"We could end up deader than we already are!"

"Look," I insisted, "I am not going to spend the rest of the day cowering in a ladies' locker room."

"Who's cowering?"

"Leering, then. Having slipped the bonds of the flesh I'm surprised you still have any vestiges of its appetites."

He looked at me as if I was from another planet. Maybe I was. "Hey, the day I stop looking will be the day that I'm—"

"*Dead?*"

We both turned toward the sound of the new voice. Something crouched at the end of one of the benches. It was dim and shadowy and suggested something vaguely manlike.

"Er," The Kid said, "hello. Come here often?"

"Best peepshow in this part of town," the new scrim shady murmured. It had a low, smooth voice that lapped against one's ears like an oil spill. "You can't beat a woman's locker room for balancing quantity and quality."

"Come again?"

"Would that I could," the voice purred. "You can't beat the meat when there's nothing left to greet."

"Come on, Junior," I made a grab for his arm with all of the success of Anna Kournikova taking on the Williams sisters at Wimbledon, "let's go."

"Do you know what Hell is?" There was a shadowy movement, the suggestion of a dim head being shaken as if to imply *of course you don't; you're still too new at this to understand anything.*

"Sartre suggested that Hell is other people," I said.

"Yeah. Yeah! That's it exactly. Hell is other people. Take my harem . . ."

The Kid perked right up. "Harem?"

"I start my rounds at 4:30—in the a.m., you know. Brunette, a couple of blocks from here."

"Handy," I murmured.

"And leggy," he agreed. "I think she's a stockbroker. Wears these businesslike suit-and-shirt tops but likes the short skirts. And boy, do they like her! Shaves her legs every morning in the bath. And it takes awhile because her legs go all the way up to her—"

"Okay," I said, "we get the picture."

"Oh, it's more than a picture, my friend. It's perform-ance art. A 3-D movie with Sensurround seating and unrestricted viewing. Everything else is choice. But the legs are the main attraction. Best I've ever seen and I seen a lot—hundreds before and tens of thousands since—"

"You died . . . ?" I offered, filling in the blank.

"Just sayin' I know what I'm sayin'."

"Because you're a connoisseur."

"Damn right. I'm normally not here this early because it takes so long for her to slide that razor all the way up from her ankles to her—"

"So you travel after the sun comes up?" He had my full attention now.

"What do you think?"

I wanted to know how he moved about in daylight without fearing photonic paralysis or the Threshers. I think I wanted to follow him out of here whistling "Me and my Shadow" . . . so I wasn't about to tell him what I really thought underneath it all. Still, if I had been in full possession of my flesh it would have been crawling by now.

"—called in sick this morning and went back to bed so no early show today. At least I can always depend on the health clubs. The old and fat ones are automatic no-shows. Perfection is rare but at least these broads are trying to refine the product."

"The product," I said.

"And even if there's a fair number of skanks, the volume of members guarantees a few worthwhile shows each day."

"Shows," I said.

"For lunch I head down to The Village where this lezbo couple get together every day for a nooner. The strawberry blonde is actually bi and married and gives it to her old man every Friday night after dinner out on the town—it's pretty much like clockwork, a sure bet. But I digress . . ."

"Early evenings I like to drop by Blondes-in-a-Box. It's what I call this apartment over—well, that's a trade secret. Two secretaries, both blondes, share the rent but they're straight so they got their own beds. They actually time-share with a stew who comes in and uses the fold-out couch two to three nights a week. She's blonde, too. After work, it's time to come home, change, bathe, shower, shave—three pairs of legs that can't hold a candle to the stockbroker but, hey, a little variety is a good thing and the razor always moves toward the same destination. By the time the bathroom is empty, the strip clubs are kicking into high gear." The shadow seemed to turn to The Kid. "Hey, I know what you're thinking . . ."

Looking at Junior's face it would be difficult to not know what he was thinking. If "thinking" was truly the appropriate term, here.

"Anybody can go to a strip joint. The real action, as the Silver Fox used to sing, is what goes on behind closed doors. That may be true but I bet ole Charley never watched a pole dance from ground zero. And the bouncers tend to keep the backstage area off limits to anybody with a body. Hey, let me give you the real tour tonight! I can show you who's hot and who's not—especially after the stage show!"

"Actually, I'm more interested in the daylight tour," I said.

"Sorry. The daylight tour's private. Strip clubs, health clubs—open memberships. When it comes to private residences, you gotta collect your own petting zoo."

That did it. "Look, you pathetic sack of ectojism, I could care less about your perverted little corner of Hell—"

"Hell?"

"Hell, yes! Hell! Filling your hours, your days, your

own little corner of eternity with an endless round of peep shows. Never mind that you're violating the privacy of the living; is *this* how you plan on spending the rest of your afterlife? Always looking backward? Always lusting after what you can't have? What you can't touch?"

"Well, if you don't like it," the dark space shot back, "just take your snooty friend, there, and leave."

"Watch who yer callin' snooty," The Kid snapped.

"Not you. The other one. Behind him."

We both turned. If there was someone behind me, he was invisible. The three of us appeared to be alone in the ladies locker room.

But not for long: the outer door eased open. A little Hispanic girl entered, dragging a pink backpack by a broken shoulder strap behind her.

"Okay, look," I said, "I just want to know how you get around the city while the sun is still out."

"I don't know how I could explain it to you, you being so superior to me and all."

I sighed and closed my eyes. It didn't work so well when your eyelids—assuming you still had any—were all transparent. I wondered, briefly, if I might be able to concentrate on visualizing myself and our shadowy pervert as being a little more corporeal. That way I might be able to kick his dim ass until he told me something that I actually wanted to hear.

"Um, chief?" The Kid was making an equally ineffective attempt to tug on my noncorporeal sleeve. I looked where he was looking.

The little caramel-colored girl was standing a few feet from the door, staring at the space we occupied as if she could either hear or see us. She couldn't have been more than six, maybe a precocious five.

"Do you think—?"

I shrugged. "I'm the newbie, here. You tell me."

The door opened again and the child's mother came in, toting a large tote bag.

She had high cheekbones suggesting Aztlan blood in her Spanish heritage and a thundercloud of black hair that crackled with a storm of static electricity. Her eyes tilted in a mysterious, exotic fashion and she had an elegant air that seemed at odds with the sweatshirt tucked into the overalls that lapped over a pair of cheap sneakers.

"Yeah! Now that's the kind of thing worth waiting around for!" the spook enthused. "I may have just found me a new addition to Merve's Harem!"

Which meant he'd be following her home when she finished her workout.

Now I was in a quandary. I had pretty much reached the limits of my tolerance for keeping company with Merve the Perv. It wasn't just the "ick" factor; there was something also infinitely sad about his voyeurism, a succession of libidinous peep shows that occupied his every waking minute, encounters without hope of any possibility of physical consummation. Not exactly Sartre's take on "Hell as Other People" but a perverse twist of French existentialism all the same.

That was Merve's Hell. What Hell waited for me now that I had shuffled off this mortal coil? And how long before I recognized it? Or was I already caught in its embrace and doomed to be as eternally clueless as Merve?

In addition to my growing desire to quit our shadowy companion's company was my growing discomfort with our present hideout. Despite the purity of our motives—or mine, at least—I was vastly uncomfortable loitering in the ladies locker room.

But if spooky ole Merve was going to follow his latest obsession home through the bright light of day, I needed to hang around to see how it was done.

As mom opened the locker, the shadow moved in closer for a front-bench seat. I retreated to the far end of the room to weigh my options. The Kid followed. "Hey, chief," he murmured, "maybe we should check out the rest of the building."

"Really." I gave him "the eye." At least I think I did. I wasn't sure about any of the physical business anymore.

"Hey, I like to look at the ladies as much as the next guy but I ain't no pedal-file!"

"Good point, junior. We can always cover the exits and follow him when he leaves." I looked back at the Hispanic woman as she unhooked the straps of her overalls. If motherhood had enhanced her figure, trips to the gym were keeping it from becoming too enhanced. Her cinnamon skin practically glowed with health. I blinked. And, for a moment, saw the traceries of veins and capillaries, pulsing like threads of golden light, a subdural doily of toaster wires carrying the burning essence around her body again and again as her heart stroked the ancient rhythm of the dance of life.

I was powerless to move as she pulled the sweatshirt up and over her head. Her hair crackled with additional lightning as the collar combed her thundercloud tresses into an expanding nimbus of dark energy. But my eyes weren't drawn to the private lots of flesh, the secret places kept hidden from the purview of the world and the gaze of strangers. Don't get me wrong: I could certainly appreciate this sculpture of muscle and skin and feminine ripeness—this Venus de Milo in ochre and burnt umber. But I would admire that as an aesthete, beauty for beauty's sake, sans the passion of carnality.

Sans the lust of the beast.

Or so I thought as my gaze moved from the private to the public sector, traveling over swell and then up slope, across incline, and climbing the shelf, the wall, the cliff, the side of the neck. A pulse fluttered there like a plucked string, the echo of life's sweet music, an eddy in the swirling lights of her flesh.

And something *did* seem to stir in my own depths. Through dimensions I thought left behind, elements that could only be nonexistent, came a feeling that was impractical—even blasphemous—for anyone and anything inhabiting this plane.

Perhaps I had left elements of my humanity behind.

But I had brought the *Stain* into the next world with me.

Merve might spend eternity with his nose pressed to the metaphysical glass of every peepshow in town but where must I eventually be drawn? Back to the demesne where I could watch my fellow blood-drinkers dine? Or, perhaps, haunt the night shift at various hospital emergency rooms? If my spectral thirst grew, perhaps I would head south, looking for the killing fields of some Central American junta . . .

Perhaps the Threshers were God's mercy to the deceased, after all.

"What is it, Honey?" The mother didn't actually say that. Or she did, but she said it in Spanish. Which I suddenly understood a lot better than I should have, given the years that had passed since my grade school language lessons on the classroom TV.

The little girl continued to stare as if she could actually see us, turning her head here and there as if she were following our conversation, as well. Now that my attention was turned back to her, I could see that she glowed, as well. Only she was enveloped in an outline of blue light. It surrounded her like a second skin.

"Are they here?" the mother asked.

The little girl nodded. "Only not the same ones. These are different."

"Are they like the others?"

She cocked her head, regarding the bench where Merve perched, then the far corner where J.D. and I had retreated to. "One is. The others are kinda sad. Except for the fairy."

"Well," said her mother, in that matter-of-fact way that parents have of discussing monsters in the closet and boogie men under the bed, "you just do what your grandmama told you." She reached into her tote bag and pulled out a spray bottle.

It looked like one of those brand-name cleaners with the label torn off. It was a white plastic container with a nozzle and a pull-trigger handle. A decal of the Virgin Mary was pasted lopsidedly on the side so that only the original letters FOR and 09 were visible to either side.

"Go away!" the child shouted in our direction. "You shouldn't be in here! It's just for girls!"

"That's why I'm here, darlin'. Tell your mommy—"

Merve was under the impression that she couldn't actually hear him any more than she could see him. I certainly hoped not considering the miasma that was pouring out of this man-shaped sack of darkness. But she made a face as if she actually could and said: "You're nasty! Go away!" And then she pointed the spray bottle right at his misty mug as if she could see him and gave the trigger a couple of confident pulls. The spray hissed through the vague shadow of his head like he wasn't even there.

A moment later he wasn't.

He was up and running around the room, shrieking like one of those car alarms that invites a sledgehammer solution at two in the morning.

Just before he went barreling through the outer wall I noticed something. While his outline hadn't been too distinct to begin with, his head was even less so, now. As a shadow fades with the coming of the sun or a fog disperses into wisps of vapor, his cranial area seemed to be dissolving like a blot of grease in a cleaning commercial.

Although he passed from sight, we could still hear his cries through the muffled barrier of brick and steel. I started to follow him but stopped as his shrieks turned to screams and the deadly whines of multiple Threshers became audible.

So much for learning the secret of Merve's Voyeurs to the Bottom and go See . . .

"Are they gone, honey? Did grandmama's philter work?" the mother asked.

"The nasty man's gone but there's still three others."

I looked around, did a hasty head count, only came up with two including myself. "The girl can't add," I murmured.

"Mebbe not, chief," The Kid observed, "but she sure knows how to subtract. I vote we blow this joint."

I nodded. "Since she's between us and the door, we're gonna have to make our own. But inner walls, only! The coffee grinders of the gods are still outside."

We took a step toward the inner row of lockers but the girl said, "Oh, no you don't!" and twisted the nozzle. This time she shot a stream of liquid instead of a misty spray. I looked at the wet line that was drawn across the wall and the floor. I blinked and it suddenly seemed to glow orange with a pulsing viciousness. I blinked again: a clear fluid, maybe water. Blink: the orange juice of death. Blink: water.

"I think we're in trouble, here," The Kid said.

"My mother always said the company I kept would get me into trouble."

"Nyuk . . . nyuk. I'm thinking we're not going to do any better in trying for the door."

"Doubtful. How about the basement?"

"Basement?"

"Yeah," I said as she gave the nozzle another twist, "I think our best bet is down."

He shook his head. "Not if there ain't no basement!"

The nozzle tracked our way. "Well, we can't stay here!" I dived into the floor thinking, not solid, *not solid*!

It was like jack-knifing through marshmallow paste.

Then emptiness.

Solid, I thought, solid!

I came to rest on the basement floor. The Kid was right behind me.

"Shit!" he said. "She nearly got me! If there hadn't been a basement here . . ." He shuddered.

"What?" I managed to wobble back up to my feet: no easy feat when nothing else is solid enough to use as leverage. "What if there hadn't been a basement here?"

"Think about it, chief. You got imagination enough."

I thought about it. Passing through a foot or so of wall or floor was disorienting, difficult. But, being wider than a foot, myself, I wasn't likely to lose my way in the process. Dropping into the earth, however . . .

Now I repressed a shudder. Maybe I couldn't suffocate but the idea of wandering through the earth—lost, blind, deaf, disoriented, searching for a way out and possibly working your way deeper—swimming through stone and sand and dirt for days or months or years, not knowing which way was up and whether you were pulling an Arne Sacknussemm instead of finding your way back out. No more floor-diving without a look at the blueprints, first!

"Hey," said The Kid, "I think I just found Merve's tunnel o' love."

He was pointing at a manhole cover.

Chapter Sixteen

IF THE SEWERS were ideal for specters like Merve to move about the city, sheltered from the harsh light of day, they were also ideal for a broad spectrum of other things—organic, inorganic, extraorganic.

Had we been corporeal we would have been wading up to our waists in waste by now. Fortunately for our delicate sensibilities, the sludgy waters passed right through us like smoke pouring through a screen. Unfortunately, we were up to our eyeballs in extradimensional critters, some human-shaped, most not, who were more like pudding than smoke on the dimensional density meter.

"What *are* these things?" The Kid groused as a chartreuse pollywog slithered between the memories of his fourth and fifth ribs.

I pushed past a sparkly slug the size of my arm with two rows of multiple eyestalks down its back. "It's life, Jim, but not as we know it . . ." It looked like an upended centipede covered in glitter.

"These things give me the creeps!"

"I guess it's got to be hard," I said, "after so many years of being the creep-er, making the transition to the creep-ee."

"Hey, you watch! I can handle bein' creepy just fine! You just—hey! What are *you* doin'? Get off'n my leg you little two-headed freak!" The Kid commenced to dance a little jitterbug. "There's one thing I don't get, though," he said as he finally dislodged some bifurcated gremlin made of glow-in-the-dark silly putty. "If this is how ole Merve the Perv gets around during the day, how does he follow these dames home the first time? Phantom periscope?"

"He probably gets a gander at their driver's license, overhears them give out their home address—maybe to a cabbie . . ." I swiped at a huge cobweb with my hand. Missed completely as the web was real, more real than me apparently. " . . . shoot, he probably just goes out to the front office and checks the gym's membership records when nobody's looking."

"Yeah? Well, he still has to know how to get there from here. I don't know *where* we are or *which* way we're going now. In fact, we wouldn't even be able to see where we're going down here if it wasn't for that little bit of swamp gas there."

I looked up at the glimmering blue marble that drifted just above our heads and a little ways ahead in the tunnel. "Hmmm. Well, I wanted to put a little distance between us and the health club before sticking my head out and getting my bearings."

"I can dig that, Big Daddy, but I ain't so sure that following William, here, is such a good idear."

"William?"

"That's what I've taken to callin' him," The Kid said. "William. For Will. As in Will-o'-the-Wisp."

"You're such a sentimental old softie, coming up with pet names for swamp gas."

"Well, now, that's the thing, see—*crap!* I ain't *never* getting *that* outta my shoe! These so-called marsh lights ain't just your natural phenominu—pheninan—stuff! The legends all say that they liked to lure travelers to their deaths in the swamps. How do we know that our Willy ain't tryin' to do the same thing with us?"

"Um . . . because it would be redundant?" There was a three-way split in the tunnel and I stopped to consider our new options. "Besides, how do you know that it is a 'he'?"

"Well, it sure ain't no 'it'! He's intelligent—some, anyway. An', right now, he's listening to us."

I shook my head. "Which goes to show he can't be *that* intelligent." There was the sound of running water far off down the left tunnel so maybe that wasn't our first choice on the Highway to Hell Tour. "Besides, maybe he's really a she. And maybe not a ball of swamp gas after all. Actually, she looks like one of those stage-play versions of Tinkerbell in Peter Pan. Maybe she's really a fairy."

"Oh yeah. Sure. Clap yer hands, boys 'n' girls, if you believe in fairies."

The urge to sigh was overwhelming but I was making a conscious effort to cut back. "Well, aren't you a Mr. Grumpypants."

"Bein' dead twice over has that effect on me."

"Listen, if you're going to spend eternity in a mood . . ."

"Look who's talkin'!"

"Hey," I snapped, "you've had a little time to get used

to all this. Me? I'm still adjusting. *And* being chased by the Texas Chainsaw Massacre Times Three on rollerblades! *And* vanquished by a six-year-old wielding some serious homemade spook remover! And now I'm wallowing around in the gutter—literally, figuratively, transdimensionally—and probably headed in the opposite direction of where my body was actually taken!"

"You're still thinkin' of lookin' for your carcass?"

"Yeah. Why? You got more pressing appointments?"

"No. I mean, I don't see the point. You're dead. It's just so much useless, rotting tissue. Another day or two and it'll get dumped in the ground. Or cremated." He brightened. Visibly. "Hey, if they do that, we can go back to Merve and see about gettin' yer ashes hauled!"

"Don't try to cheer me up."

"Why? You like being so gloomy?"

"No. I *want* to be cheered up. It's just that you're so bad at it."

It shut him up but only for a moment.

"Seriously . . . what are you lookin' for, chief? Closure?"

"I don't know what I'm looking for. I just feel this overwhelming urge to get back in touch with my inner viscera."

He waved a translucent hand. "That's normal. Like amputees feelin' their toes after their leg's cut off. Yer so used to havin' a body that it takes a while to get used to it bein' gone once it goes 'poof.'"

"Well, I didn't go 'poof'," I said. "I went—"

Away.

There was a ghostly tug and I suddenly found myself burrowing through suffocating darkness.

I popped into daylight.

In the middle of a street.

A cab smashed into me!

Well, smooshed through me, actually. Followed by a bus: I was treated to a kaleidoscope of thoughts and impressions as a double row of passengers zipped through my dimensional interstices.

I turned and fled for the curb in requisite, daylight slow-mo.

"Hey, chief?" The Kid's head popped through the pavement near my original exit point. "You okay? What gives?" A garbage truck rolled through his head but he gave it no notice.

"I don't know . . ." I was up on the sidewalk now but the pedestrians were worse than the traffic. Every other second someone passed through me and a stray word or image flashed through my head with each intersecting encounter. "It was like something yanked me up and out of the ground."

J.D. crawled up out of the street and scurried toward me in a desultory fashion, looking to the right and the left as if checking for traffic. He wasn't checking for traffic, however: it continued to plow through him like so much smog and he paid it no mind.

He was watching for Threshers.

"We can't stay out here, like this," he said, finally reaching the curb. That seemed to be as far as he could go. When he took another step toward me, he bounced back onto the street.

Meanwhile, I was standing in the middle of the sidewalk with a stream of pedestrians passing through me. A parade of mind-flashes dominoed across my mind like a tuner being run up and down the radio dial.

"How're you doin' that?"

"What?" It was hard to concentrate with a stream of consciousnesses doing *A River Runs Through* Me.

"The sharing-the-same-space-with-the-living trick that you seem to be doing."

I looked around. "I don't understand. What have we been doing all this time—walking through walls, sinking through floors—?"

"That's inanimate matter, Big D; people are different! You can't just occupy the same space as someone who's actually alive! Not unless you're one of them demons that's workin' some kind of possession mojo!"

"Really? I didn't know it wasn't allowed. Again, some kind of rule book or instruction manual would be helpful when one passes over."

The Kid made another attempt to reach me but got spun around by the heavy foot traffic and knocked back into the street. "It's not so much that it's considered bad form," he said, regaining his balance, "as it's just not supposed to be—well—*possible*."

"Except for me," I observed.

"Except for you."

"Interesting."

"That's putting it mildly."

"So, maybe I'm not a ghost . . ."

"Not a typical one, anyway," he agreed.

"Maybe I'm some sort of demon, now. After all, I did drink some of Chalice Delacroix's blood after it had become charged with demonic essence."

"Maybe . . ." He kept moving back and forth, looking for an opening. " . . . but you just don't strike me as the demony type. Rule breaker, yes. Ever since I met ya it's been like Rebel Without a Pause."

It seemed hopeless: even if he could find an opening that could reach me, the crowd would just sweep him on past in no time. I began working my way back toward him.

The problem was similar in reverse: the people weren't entirely transparent to my own passage, either. It was like wading through a school of fish, all sorts of disturbing little tugs and twitches in strange and uncharted places.

"Yeah?" I said, "Well, I'm ready for a little time-out right now until someone can set me straight on what comes next."

"C'mon, chief; you should know better. When you get born, no one's waitin' in the delivery room with a personalized copy of the Owner's Manual. There ain't no guided tour of the universe. And your best bet for a personal destiny map is as likely to turn up in a fortune cookie as in some prayer book. Why should things be any different after death than before it?"

The street was closer, now, but the next question was: where did we go from here. "Got me there, Junior. I just figured that once I was dead I'd have better things to do than wander around aimlessly."

"Yeah, well, my motto is be happy that you even get to do that once the curtain comes down."

I was almost to the curb when I was jerked off my feet again. I flew down the street and smashed through the outer wall of a building. Or smooshed. No damage was apparently done to the masonry or myself.

I found myself at the bar of a quaint little tavern. The interior was all done up like one of those elegant English pubs from the turn of the century—the nineteenth century, that is. Lots of teak and mahogany and leather, with green-shaded lamps and brass rails and fittings. And spittoons, by God!

I watched as the bartender filled a great glass stein with a dark and foamy lager and proceeded to slide it down the bar toward me.

Through me!

The mug continued on several feet and into a one-handed catch by a gentleman who was giving more attention to his newspaper than his just-now-arriving drink. His two companions only had eyes for the new delivery.

I stepped back out of the bar, bemused by the impression that I had gotten a ghost of a taste as the beer went sliding through my midsection.

The gentleman wore a gray, double-breasted suit and the shoe that was visible on the gleaming brass rail was polished to a mirrorlike shine. His wingmen were quite shabby in contrast. Their clothes were rummage sale mix-'n'-match, their hair unkempt, their eyes wide and wild. As he calmly lifted the stein to his lips they grabbed at his arms from either side, each attempting to pull the mug and its contents toward their own desperately straining mouths.

His arm completed its arc and he took a quaff with no visible reaction to the tug-of-war that was seesawing back and forth across his beverage.

The stein returned to the counter and the man's gaze

never broke its lock on the racing form folded in his other hand.

The two barflies settled down once the beer was back on the bar but the one on the left made another swipe at the glass that clarified the situation at once. As his hand passed through the drink I could see that he and his partner were as transparent as The Kid and myself.

I turned and considered the crowded room.

It was too early in the day for any real bar business yet the tavern was packed. A closer look, however, revealed three—maybe four humans. The rest weren't really there.

But they were trying really hard to be.

They crowded around bottles and glasses. They paced behind the bar and tried to sip from the taps when a drink was poured.

And every time a flesh and blood hand hoisted a glass, they clutched at it as a drowning man scrabbles for a lifeline in a churning sea. Well, why not. Merve's particular obsession was but one possibility among hundreds. Maybe thousands.

Somerset Maugham nailed it in *Rain*. Desire *is* sad.

The Kid caught up with me as I beamed back out via the big glass window.

"What was that all about?"

I shrugged. "Again, looking for the Cliff Notes, myself."

He looked up at the signage. "Starting a little early in the day, ain't ya?"

I looked behind me. "For a bunch of the regulars I'd say it's a little late in the life."

He nodded, suddenly solemn. "We need to find shelter.

But let's look a little farther along." We started off down the sidewalk and I could swear, for a moment, I could hear him humming "In Heaven There is No Beer."

It had an uncharacteristically mournful sound to it.

Then I jerked a little and stumbled. This time the tug felt more localized. And centralized. As I placed my hand over my midsection I discovered that a portion of my topography had changed.

"Hey, Junior!"

"Aw man . . . promise me that yer not gonna be hangin' that moniker on me for all of eternity!"

"Do you have an umbilicus?"

"An what?"

"A navel. A belly button."

"Listen man, I got all of my equipment," he said, cupping his groin. "Not that any of it does me any good now."

"But it's the same as before, right?"

"You mean other than the see-through, now you touch it, now you can't qualities?"

"Yeah. You got an innie?"

"What? My belly button?" He looked around. "Chief, this ain't the kind of thing that two guys stand around, outside a bar, talkin' about—even if nobody else can see or hear 'em. Ya know?"

"In or out?"

"In! Okay? Now let's change the subject. Better yet, let's get back to shelter before the Ghost Dusters show."

"I used to have an innie," I said, rubbing around my midsection. "But all of a sudden I seem to have developed an outie. A way-outie . . ." I felt where the surface of my abdomen used to dimple and, again, encountered a protrusion. Not just a lump. Way more than navel lint. More like . . .

I looked down. Not so easy to focus in the harsh light of day. I was indistinct. There was just a general suggestion of form but I was more blurred translucence than demarcated outline.

What I could see was vaguely humanoid but it was impossible to tell if I was a naked ghost or outfitted with phantom duds like J.D.

On the other hand there was that protuberance from my abdomen about where my navel should have been. Instead of an umbilicus, I seemed to have an umbilical cord. It appeared to be composed of a faint, silvery substance, was about the circumference of my little finger and snaked off into the distance like a glowing lifeline.

"Hey," I said, as the transcendental implications fell into place. "Maybe I'm not dead after all!"

"Denial," The Kid mused. "That's how most of the hauntings start, I hear. *I'm* not really dead; this is *still* my house . . ."

"But I'm not really a ghost and my belly button proves it!"

"Yeah? So what are you? The Invisible Man?"

"Actually," I replied with a grin, "I think I'm an astral-naut."

Explaining the concept of astral projection to The Kid was both easy and difficult.

On the one hand he had no difficulty in accepting the idea of consciousness operating independently of the flesh. After all, he had no flesh and his consciousness was still hanging around.

On the other hand, the idea of differing planes of existence stalled out for him the moment it got more complicated than "Life"/ "Afterlife." The nuances of astral travel versus the ethereal plane totally eluded him. The closest analogy that made any sense to him was the Phantom Zone projector from the old *Superman* comic books.

You work with whatever tools are at hand.

Even so, he was pretty much of the opinion that I was dressing up the issue of departed spirits with a bunch of pseudoscientific mumbo jumbo. As far as J.D. was concerned, there seemed to be no significant difference between "astral travel" and "dead and haunted."

"Except," I tried to explain, "astral projection is practiced by the *living* through transcendental meditation: TM. The body remains alive while the astral self travels to other levels of existence and returns again, via the silver cord. It anchors the astral consciousness to the physical body so it can find its way back."

"And you've done this T and A before?"

"TM. And no, I haven't. But I've read about it—"

"Yeah? And I've read about brain surgery but I don't go around callin' myself a doctor."

"You don't seem to be very happy for me."

"You want to believe a little spooky plumbing makes you still alive at the other end?" He shrugged. "Okay by me. We got time to kill. So's the plan now is like you follow the cord to find where they've taken it?"

"Got any better ideas?"

"Just one."

"And that is?"

"Run!" he screamed.

The Threshers were coming, rolling down the street, rebounding off the sides of buildings and vehicles like a trio of pinballs loosed on the bonus round.

The Kid jumped through the big glass window of the bar. I tried to follow but came up short: the silvery cord had caught up the slack and wouldn't let me move more than a couple of feet in that direction. It wasn't enough!

I began a slow-motion run for the building across the street.

More cars, more cabs, several trucks, and a bus: a kaleidoscope of thoughts and emotions tunneled through my mind as drivers and passengers drove through my astral essence.

By the time I was approaching the center line I could see that I probably wouldn't make it to the other side in time. One of the Spinning Tops of Doom was no longer rebounding off of the approaching traffic but rolling up and over the hoods and roofs of the outside line of vehicles. I might reach the sidewalk but it would catch me before I could make the building beyond. An SUV rumbled through with The Stones wailing "Gimme Shelter" on the radio.

Maybe the Threshers had no power over astral bodies. If I wasn't *technically* a ghost—i.e., disembodied spirit by reason of physical death and full detachment of the soul— then, perhaps, they'd leave me alone.

Or be unable to affect me in any way.

On the other hand, most operative systems function on the basic level: if it looks like a duck and walks like a duck and . . .

"Quack!" I said, and changed direction, dodging toward a manhole cover some twenty feet away.

It was close: grabbing my cord and using the circular metal cover as a bull's-eye, I bungee-jumped into the sewers just as one of the Ginsu gyroscopes sliced and diced its way within five feet of me.

I crouched in the dark for long minutes. If I had possessed a heart I would have needed a good half hour just to get the pulse back down to a good seventy beats a minute. As it was I had trouble catching my breath and—hey—I didn't even seem to have a set of ectoplasmic lungs! If I ever got back to my body and recovered from this I was going to have to avoid funerals for the rest of my life. Why? Because the next person who used the phrase "eternal rest" in my presence—I was going to seriously kick his ass!

After a while I noticed a light hovering over my shoulder. "Will, you son of a gun! Decided to tag along? Or were you down here all the time, waiting for us to come back?"

The faerie light bobbed a little and wove a vague pattern in the air.

I fingered the silvery cord that snaked off into the dark and passed through the sewer wall and into the dense earth beyond. I could try pulling myself, hand over hand, along my lifeline, traveling blindly through the midnight ground toward my body. Besides the risk of losing my grip and getting lost, there was the problem of losing The Kid. Or the possibility of climbing back up out of the ground too soon and getting pureed. Best to hunker down and wait.

"I think we're gonna be here awhile," I told my Will-o'-the-Wisp. "Too bad you're not a sparkling conversationalist."

I didn't mean it in an insulting way but Tinkerbell reacted like I'd thrown down the gauntlet. The light spun around three times and smacked into my forehead like a bullet.

I went out like a light.

The front door to my house in Louisiana stood ajar. More than ajar—it was half off its hinges. It had been repaired after the Frankenvamp's visit but now it was all *Tool Time* demo again.

A *dream?* I wondered. I didn't like this: any dream where you can ask yourself if you're dreaming is bound to be something more and this didn't look none too good . . .

Dr. Mooncloud sat in a big, stuffed easy chair that had been dragged to just inside the entryway, a sawed-off shotgun across her lap. All of the other shotguns from the house arsenal were stacked around the chair, their barrels given the shortening treatment, as well. Outside there was a soft "huffing" sound and the tread of delicate footfalls on the porch. "I'd shoot to wound if I could," Mooncloud called, "but sawed-off shotguns don't give me that option! I see another furry face—another furry *anything*—and I'm going to fill that with silver shot, as well! So you just settle down out there and be patient! Your pack leader behaves himself and he'll be back out as soon as he's done!"

Sprigs of some sort of plant were nailed to the door frame—wolfsbane? The other windows were boarded up from the inside. I was finally beginning to understand why mad scientists preferred castles over split-level ranch styles in the suburbs.

Another standoff was taking place upstairs in my bedroom.

Lupé was propped up in bed against a mound of pillows. She was bristling, dark hair sprouting beneath her eyes and trailing down the sides of her neck. Fingernails were becoming talons where they clutched the bedclothes in front of her. Dr. Burton stood next to the bed, fully vamped out, his fangs extended, his eyes red, muscles tensed and ready to spring. Both stared at a tall, hirsute man in the doorway.

"I can save you if you come with us, now," the man was saying. His hair was brown and bushy, streaked with gray. It swept back from a widow's peak set low on his forehead and swept over large and curiously angular ears.

"Save me from what, Grandfather?" she argued. "Myself?"

"You should be with your people. You should be with your family!"

"This is my home, Grandpére. I have a new pack, now."

"I did not stand in your way when you left The Pack to seek your fortunes in the West. We do not always serve where and whom we'd choose. But this . . ." He shook his shaggy head. "You have nothing but an empty house and two abortionists from a rival vampire enclave to look after you!"

She reacted as if he had slapped her but sat up a little straighter after a moment. "I think you are mistaken. It is you who does not want me to have this child."

"*No one* wants you to have this child! The thing that grows within you is an abomination! Ask this vampire, here, what his orders are! Do you really think his master would send him here to midwife a child that would foster a genocidal war between our peoples?"

"The Seattle demesne is not involved," she said.

"Then why is he here?" he spat back. "No enclave meddles in another's business unless it is their business, as well!" He raised a sharp-nailed finger as she opened her mouth. "And do not mouth the word 'friendship' to me. I know the wampyri, and their ways are not warm-blooded nor are they kind. Your upstart, half-breed Doman has upset their ordered balances of power and very soon now they shall snap the slack out of his shortening leash and stop his run altogether."

"And what do you care?"

"What do *I* care? For *him*? *Nothing!*" His deep-set green eyes shifted to Dr. Burton and seemed to flare. "I do not care to discuss pack business before an Outsider, much less one of the wampyr. But candor, perhaps, serves me better than diplomacy in this matter.

"Do I admire this Cséjthe for standing up to the Families, for the skill and cunning he has shown in defeating many fearsome enemies? Yes, yes, I do. Do I take delight in the discomfort of the other wampyri and drink toasts to their befuddlement and confusion at the bizarre interloper in their midst? Most certainly." He made a mocking half bow in the direction of the black vampire. "Would I throw my lot with his? Lead my pack in support of his cause? You *must* be mad!"

His eyes suddenly went dark, shifting from glowing

emeralds to submerged mossy jade. "He will die and die soon, granddaughter. And though I do not wish for you to die with him, that is *your* choice to make as you wish . . ."

Like burning copper, his eyes reignited with green flames: "But you will *not* take the lives of the pack with you! None of us should be expected to pay a price for *your* folly!"

"No one's asking—"

"The blood-drinkers do NOT ask! They will see your growing belly and they will learn that a wampyri—half-breed or no—has grown seed within a living womb! They will not make 'an example' of you! They will make it as if you and the abomination never even existed! They *would* make an example of your family—except they *will* destroy all of your blood kin lest the fertility of your flesh extend beyond the province of your own fecundity! Then—and only then—will they turn and make 'an example' of every remaining member of the pack!"

His voice softened. "The child will not be born. Too many others will not allow it. *My* concern is that if—*since* this must be so, why compound the tragedy with your death? Or the deaths of others?"

Lupé turned to Dr. Burton. "Is this true? Are you here to help me keep this baby? Or are you under secret orders to abort it and make it look like an accident?"

"Let us help you, child," the pack leader interrupted. "We have the herbs that will help you terminate this—this—"

"Pregnancy," Mooncloud said from behind the tall, furry fellow.

"—it would earn the pack protection from wampyr

wrath," he continued as if aware of her presence all along, "and grant us a measure of good will. And, more than any of the others, *we* would have your health and safety at heart, as well."

"Yeah? Well, tick-tock, Gramps and the whole debate may be moot in a moment." Mooncloud slide-cocked the shotgun in her grasp. "Your pack just hightailed it out of here."

"What? Why?"

"Could have something to do with this Really Big Ugly that climbed out of the river down by the docks and is headed this way."

The house suddenly shook as if struck by a giant mallet.

"I think that's him."

As quick as thought I was back downstairs and watching the frame of the front entrance ripped out of the wall by a grotesque giant that made the Frankenvamp look petite and effete.

The demon Camazotz had arrived.

I blinked as the light flew back out of my head and the darkness closed in around me.

No!

"Will!" I yelled. "What was that? Is that happening now? Get back in here!" I thumped my head. "Come on! Give me another look!"

It just hovered there in the sewer's eternal night. Other than a little quiver or two, it didn't respond at all.

"Come on!" I yelled, the close echoes giving me a headache. "I gotta know what's happening!"

Or what had happened.

Was this a memory?

A dream?

Or another kind of astral connection giving me broad-band ghostcam access to the here and now, back home?

What could I do?

"Oh man, this can't get any worse . . ."

There are a number of things you don't do.

You don't tug on Superman's cape.

You don't spit into the wind.

And you never never ever say: "It can't get any worse . . ."

Why? Because as sure as you do . . .

There was a yank on the silvery cord and I was hauled up out of the sewer and into the street like a trout landing on the bank of a river.

The chittering hum of a Thresher buzzed behind me.

Chapter Seventeen

THERE WAS ONLY one of them left. It was about thirty yards behind me, patrolling the area in front of the bar where I had gone to ground.

It didn't appear to notice me at first.

I had time to register a couple of extraneous facts. First, the sun had passed its zenith and was now noticeably lower in the sky. Time flies when you're having fun . . .

And J.D. had poked his head through the outer wall of the bar. His mouth was open. "Run!" he screamed. "It's behind you!"

Now the creature *was* aware of my presence. Thanks, Kid.

It was clear to both of us that our act was still splitsville for the time being. "If we get separated," he yelled, "I'll meet you back at your new digs!"

"No!" I yelled back. "Get back to the house in Louisiana! Lupé's in trouble!" The last was said over my shoulder as I turned to flee: Ezekiel's Wheel had started to roll.

I did a little Lee Majors, Six Million Dollar Mojo sprint and dived back into the asphalt. Instead of slicing into darkness I skimmed along its surface like a Slip 'N Slide from Wham-o. The astral cord had taken up the slack as I moved. I was still exposed.

I jumped to my feet and saw that the Thresher had closed the distance from thirty yards to thirty feet. I turned and headed for the curb knowing that there was no way I could reach shelter in time.

As terrifying as this thing was, there was a touch of ignominy in being destroyed by something that bore more than a passing resemblance to the Looney Tunes Tasmanian Devil in full spin mode. In my final moments I had to ask myself: What would Bugs Bunny do?

Perhaps I should have asked what Wile E. Coyote would do: as I crossed the center line a bus smashed through me, multiple passengers crowding the last thoughts in my head with snippets of their own.

Fortunately, there was still room for one very important thought of *my* own!

Solid! I thought furiously: *Very solid bus!*

And I was on my way uptown, kneeling on a seat and staring out the rear window where the Thresher churned over my point of departure with impotent fury. "Oh man," I said, when I felt like I could finally breathe again, "this sure beats the hell out of traveling through the sewers."

The Thresher followed after the bus, bumping up against the rear a couple of times but, true to The Kid's theories, these things seemed to be strictly outdoor operators. The bus appeared to be as good as a Sherman tank in the ectoplasmic realm.

I eventually turned around and sat more comfortably. I was sharing a seat with a man in his late thirties or early forties wearing oversized Ray-Bans. Snuggled up at his feet was a German shepherd wearing a harness with a specialized grip: a seeing-eye dog. The seeing-eye dog was staring up at me like he was seeing me pretty well.

"Nice doggy," I said.

The nice doggy growled softly.

"Max?" the blind man inquired, "What's wrong?"

No point in ruining anyone else's day. I got up and climbed over several seats till I found one that was totally empty. I might've tried just walking through the seats but I wasn't sure enough of my control and didn't want to end up falling out the bottom of the bus altogether.

Now that I had time to catch my breath (such as it was) my thoughts returned to Lupé. The whole issue of her pregnancy and the positions of clans and enclaves was suddenly secondary. The demon Camazotz had come to my home looking for me. What horrors would be visited upon those it found there? Would my beloved escape? Could any of them survive?

There was no question of any of them being able to stop such a thing. So what would it do when it didn't find me there? Would it take prisoners to gain information? Torture them to learn where I had gone?

What could I do?

Even if I could return right now?

The Kid had died in that house but his ghost had traveled to New York by using me as a focal point—a personal haunting, if you will. That was how he was on hand to meet me when I "died." Or got knocked out of my body, at any rate. I didn't know how or how long it would take him to get back to Louisiana.

Or what he could do to help, either.

Meanwhile, I was just riding a bus around Manhattan.

Or not.

The bus turned a corner and I remained behind, the tension in the silver cord making course deviations a rather limited variable.

The Thresher had fallen back in its pursuit or it would have had me right then and there. That was the good news.

The bad news was that it had been joined by another. I scrambled for the curb and this time I made it. And there was enough slack to dodge into the building proper.

The floors were a green-and-white marble polished to a high sheen with alternating columns of green and white every hundred feet or so, soaring to a second-story ceiling of white, scalloped domes. It took a few moments to figure out that I had actually stumbled into a "store."

Excepting the grand columns, the space was cavernous; the counters of jewelry or unguents and *parfums* and scarves and belts and accessories but small, lonely islands in a vast ocean of marbled openness. Around the vast perimeter were the cycled stations of fashion: garments for the morning, outfits for midday, ensembles for afternoon, gowns for evening, apparel for night— elegant ladies' clothing for all points of the clock and compass.

The Threshers might be shut out but there were other invaders.

Zombies had breached the doors, spilled into the lobby, fanned across the mezzanine, shambled to the counters, and lay siege to the salesgirls who struggled valiantly to face the ancient forces that confronted them!

I blinked.

No. Not zombies. At least not like Boo and Cam and Preacher. These ladies were still alive—though the thick layer of makeup troweled over ancient flesh made it hard to tell at first. The hair that refracted unnatural bands of color from the light spectrum still grew from their scalps. Their lips and nails had been dipped in dye, not blood or entrails, to achieve the presumably desired effect. They were old and rich. The young couldn't afford to shop in a store whose inventory equaled the GNP of a small Mediterranean country.

This place catered to those who could afford a scarf that cost what most women earned for two months and overtime. It offered dresses that the owners would only wear once even though a lifetime at minimum wage wouldn't be sufficient to pay the freight.

Don't get me started on the shoes.

As the matrons performed the shuffling dance of commerce and consumption, I saw each joined by a veritable entourage of fashionistas, style mavens, and clothes fetishists who practically fell all over each other as dresses were considered, footwear slipped on and off, scarves draped, belts slung, and accessories compiled and recombined. What am I saying? They not only fell all over each other, they fell through each other. Like Merve and the bar spirits, the store was infested by the lingering after-taste of fashion's hunger. The Apostles Matthew and Luke made it sound pretty bland when they said: "where your treasure is, there will your heart be also." They should have said: "where your heart is, is where you're trapped when your time runs out."

In other words, what matters most to you is the cheese on the mousetrap of eternity.

Nice. The Gospel according to Stephen King.

I wondered where my heart would turn up on the Post-Apocalyptic-Alley-Alley-Oxen-Free-O-All-Souls Tour . . .

For such a big, empty store it was a very crowded space. Like a kaleidoscope of reflected wheels and patterns, each living soul participated in the allemande-left and the do-se-do of shopping while their ghostly compatriots orbited them like phantom solar systems on crack. And, after a time, I could make out third parties in the grand farandole across the great marbled floor.

Creatures that were human and yet weren't, ghostly yet not dead, circled the outer edges of the dance and held out their arms. In their clear and shining grasps they held gowns and dresses that gave off a light of their very own. Fabrics that were not of this world shimmered in subtle patterns that flickered like heat lightning, shimmered like trout in shallow mountain streams, pulsed like quasars deep in the Orion nebula, and shone like the stars at the world's first birthday. They made gowns of silk and satin look like scorched burlap and each promised sensations of power and peace and healing and grace. Nothing hideous could wear such a garment and not be beautiful, nothing lame could don such material and not dance, nothing small could be adorned with such and not become large, anything was possible in these robes of light.

But the dance did not cease. No one hesitated. All eyes were on the sacks of silkworm spittle or bags of cotton pulp or tubes of reprocessed hydrocarbons. No one glanced at the raiment woven from sunbeams and early morning mists, apparel spangled with fireflies and glowing eyes of the Dwellers of the Deep, or the robes that pulsed like the long, slow heartbeat of the volcanoes. Vestments of light were offered and ignored. The blindness of the living continued in death. It was a Maypole dance around a tower of rotting wood while crystalline galaxies spun just outside the mud-trampled circle.

There was something . . . a mantle . . . a djellaba, a hooded serape, or something of spun moonlight, pleated with the aurora borealis. It came toward me, proffered in alabaster hands and I touched its hem briefly.

How can I describe the sensation of that contact? Not in terms of tactility or texture. It was not a question of thread count or weave—though the garment was more real than anything that ever touched my skin when I still walked the earth clothed in flesh. It was more like the smell of soft summer rains and early morning mists. The taste of fresh summer strawberries and icy-cold spring water on a hot summer's day. It was the sound of wind in the trees—a whisper amid a small orchard and a mighty exhalation through a great forest, the chimes of children's voices as the last lesson book is closed, and the peaceful song of the hearth cricket on a warm winter's night. But, more than anything else, it was the feeling of home—home for the hunter weary from the hill, for the sailor worn from the sea.

For me . . .

"For me?" I asked. And the clothing of eternity began to gather into my hands.

FLASH!

And I was stumbling out into the street, again.

No.

The shock of disappointment was greater than the shock of sudden translocation.

"Noooo!" I cried, and tried to claw my way back toward the green-and-white marbled crossroads.

The cord brought me up short.

And, a block away, a trio of Threshers rotated on their multiple axes and began to roll and spin toward me.

For maybe two hours I played Dodgem in traffic with the ghost grinders. I moved mechanically, only half caring about some of the chances I took. I was getting better at jumping from one vehicle to another, despite the unpredictable bungee contractions of my astral connection. To be fair, the spinning tops-o'-doom were having more difficulty as the sun inched its way down the western sky. Maybe they were solar powered: they seemed to lose steam as they crossed the shadows from the taller buildings, shadows that lengthened and grew more potent as the daylight waned.

As for my vehicular assistance, there were taxis and cop cars and delivery trucks and automobiles and limousines and even a fire truck. Now and then I'd jump out and run into a building, sometimes emerging two blocks down after a lengthy tour of stores, banks, and offices. There was a church along the way with a christening. The baby was surrounded by family and the family was surrounded by—well—it was difficult to tell, especially since the older ones were less distinct, but I was guessing more family with ancestors going back seven generations, at least.

And there were other . . . people. I hesitate to call them "creatures" but they were and weren't like you or me.

And they floated. Not that everyone's feet were firmly planted on the floor—or that everyone's feet were even visible at times—but these beings hovered over the whole assemblage like traffic copters preparing reports for the five o'clock news.

The feeling was different from most of the other haunty scenes I had visited so far: a sense of peace, of hope, even. But hanging around was out of the question as another strong yank landed me outside, again.

No Threshers in sight for the moment. I had emerged some distance from my entry point, the sun was lower in the sky, and I was walking into deeper shadows from the buildings across the street, now. I decided to risk staying outside for a block or two in hopes of finding a street sign to get my bearings.

I watched both ends of the boulevard, figuring the Threshers couldn't pass through any of the buildings and would have to remain in the light as much as possible. So I wasn't paying any attention to a dark alleyway and that is why the thing caught me by surprise as it barreled out and into me like a deranged cave bear.

It looked like a rabid grizzly. Matted, coarse brown hair, snaggly teeth, red-rimmed eyes; it staggered erect and advanced like some trained circus bear, paws waving before it, grunting and chuffing and growling. "Lil buddy!" it roared, spreading its massive arms for a crushing bear hug.

There were other people on the sidewalk. Without giving the creature any particular amount of attention, they gave it wide berth. New Yorkers are well acquainted with such phenomena: street people are like intermittent showers—you open your umbrella and keep walking.

"How long's it been?" the bushy-bearded giant bellowed. "I thought you bought the big one outside of Baghdad!"

I took in the green field jacket that seemed inadequate for a New York winter and considered the lines radiating from the wild eyes to the dark mysteries of hair that covered half of his face. Too old for Gulf War Two—maybe GW One?

"Or was it at Chipyong-ni?" He staggered and a pint bottle slid from a pocket to smash on the sidewalk.

Chipyong-ni? That was in North Korea—the Eighth Army had made a stand there against the Chinese communists back in '50–'51 . . . "Whoa, Sergeant Rock! You wanna do the spare-some-change-for-a-vet routine, I suggest you get a more believable back-story. Or at least settle on a particular war."

Our veteran for all seasons looked down at the shattered bottle. "Oops! Outta antifreeze!" Looked up. At me. "Buy a fellow soldier a drink?"

I looked around. No one else was standing still or making eye contact. This afternoon the role of Wacko Street Person's Imaginary Friend will be played by Christopher L. Cséjthe.

"Okay," I said. "Assuming that you can actually see me, is it possible that you can hear me, as well?"

"Uh-oh!" he said, "Charlie's here."

"Charlie?" I followed his gaze as he turned his head back toward the direction I had come.

A Thresher was rolling up the street behind me.

"It's Damn-Nang all over again!"

"Pick a war," I muttered, "any war—just stick with it." And started to run. The problem was Section Eight was in my way: I was between Sergeant Rock and a hard place.

"We'd better run for it, Sparks," he said. Then bellowed at the top of his lungs: "Retreat!"

I was already in the process of running through him, headed for the nearest wall, when he turned. It was like sinking through warm cookie dough that was suddenly flash-fried with a crisp, outer shell. "Hang on, Li'l Buddy! I'll get us outta here!"

And just like that, I was hitching another ride uptown. Only, instead of riding inside a two-ton truck, I was a passenger inside a three-hundred-pound refugee from Bellevue: *Bogie on Board.*

I tried to hop off. Jump out. Disengage.

I couldn't.

I was trapped in a psychic headlock, a prehistoric bug locked in amber. For all intents and purposes, *I* was the psychotic homeless guy, running down the middle of the street now. The fact that I didn't have anything to say about it was secondary. There was a storm of steel and chrome headed toward us and a Whirlwind of God nipping at our heels. At any moment now, this was going to end very badly for both of us.

Relax, kid.

Yeah, enjoy the ride.

And the warm.

Not to mention the room.

Yeah, you'd think six would be four too much, but Pauly's got a bigger skull and a smaller ego than most.

The voices belonged to more than one entity but, because they did not come from differing tongues and voice boxes, they were almost impossible to tell apart. Did I say *differing* tongues and voice boxes? There was nothing organic about the things chittering away in my—um—"ears."

Don't worry, son, Corporal Barrett is a veteran of rush-hour Ringalevio.

Yeah, he may not be much on the social interaction but he's Fran Tarkenton when it comes to broken-field running against crosstown traffic.

Fran Tarkenton? Try Johnny Unitas.

Yo, old timers! Try bringing it into the twenty-first century.

Yo? How about 'Yo Mama?'

Yeah, there ain't no quarterbacks worth discussin' since Joe Montana retired.

You talking before Kansas City or after?

I tried to look behind me.

Hey, don't do that!

Leave the body alone.

You don't want to mess him up while he's playing in traffic.

Like we said, relax and enjoy the ride.

As long as he stays off the bumpers, we're all safe.

The Proud Marys can't touch you as long as you're suit-ed up.

"Proud Marys?" I asked.

And suddenly realized that Pauly was bellowing at the top of his lungs as he worked his way through cars and trucks like a salmon surging upstream to spawn: "Big wheels keep on turnin'! Big wheels keep on turnin'!"

Over and over and over again.

It wasn't long before we were running from the cops, as well.

We can run . . .

But Pauly can't hide.

Yeah, they know where he lives.

"Where does he live?"

In a packing crate.

No cardboard boxes for our boy.

Which makes it hard to move about.

Good thing he's big and strong.

No one's allowed to permanently stake out a grate, you see.

But they cut Pauly a little more slack than most. He's good about sharing. Especially on the cold nights.

Pauly's a prince.

"If Pauly's such a prince, what's he doing out here?"

You mean, cleaning windshields at red lights, panhan-dling for change, and sleeping in alleyways?

Our man Pauly took Unca Sammy to heart when he wuz told to be all that he could be.

And this is all that he could be once they taught him what they taught him.

"What did they teach him?"

Twenty-seven different ways to kill a man with your bare hands, for one thing.

Is it up to twenty-seven, now? They only taught me fifteen.

Poor Pauly: so big and so strong. You'd think God made a better killing machine when he super-sized those hands . . .

And backed them up with arms and shoulders that could snap bones with shrugs and gestures.

That's what the D.I.s thought.

D.I.s don't know nothin' about God, though.

Poor Pauly.

He wasn't cut out for killing.

Not like us.

No.

We're so good at it.

Were so good at it. Not so good at not being killed.

Yeah, at least Pauly's still alive.

Even if he ain't in one piece no more.

Me, I lost an arm at Guadalcanal. Pauly lost his mind in Hobo Woods, east of Binh Buong.

Good thing he's got us to look after him.

"Is that what you call it? Looking after him?"

What? You think you know us?

There's a lot of things that would move into someone's head if they could and cause all kinds of mischief.

Mischief would be a sad understatement.

Make The Exorcist *look like* My Dinner With Andre.

"So what kind of help are you giving him right now?"

What? This?

Pauly needs the exercise.

Especially since he's going to be locked up again for a while.

"You can't help him escape?"

Escape?

Evade the authorities?

Now who's crazy?

Pauly gets hauled in every so often for his own good.

Yeah, it's not like they lock him up and throw away the key.

It's more like a "catch-and-release" program.

He'll get deloused. A warm bed. Three squares. Medical attention.

They won't hurt 'im.

They like Pauly!

Pauly's a sweetie!

He's kind of a celebrity.

Or we are.

Yeah. We like to chat up the docs and they get all excited and write papers on multiple personality disorder.

Haven't you been paying attention? That's so out of fashion. It's DID, now.

DID?

Yeah. Dissociative . . .

Disassociative Identity Disorder.

That's it.

I thought we were multiple personality manifestations?

We are. It's just that they have different words for it, now.

What difference does it make?

Well, go back a few hundred years and say Pauly's pos-

sessed, instead. See what kind of difference that makes.

"So, you guys are ghosts, not demons?"

What's in a name?

Add up some of the stuff my country ordered me to do in a buffalo pasture half a world away . . . well . . . maybe the demon gig ain't so diff.

Hey, you follow orders—

Ours not to question why, ours but to do and di—

Put a sock in it, O'Rourke. All the crap the brass told us to do didn't make no goddam difference to whether good little American boys and girls grew up quoting Chairman Mao. You wanna give the Nazi bastards running the ovens at Auschwitz a pass because they were just following orders?

Why not? It's all just a cosmic circle-jerk anyway. We spend five decades fighting the Communists only to elect 'em to office and appoint 'em to the bench once the Evil Empire is finally brought to its knees. You can die for that flag, G.I. Joe, but your kids aren't allowed to pledge allegiance to it any more.

Not under God at any rate.

Hey, don't get me started on God!

What's your kick? God didn't command you to collect Gook ears and make necklaces.

I'm talking about the bigger picture, asswipe. Man's inhumanity to man.

Free will, baby.

Free will's got nothing to do with the Service.

Yeah? Well, neither does God.

Trouble is you're still looking for order in the universe. It's chaos theory all the way, Cappy.

"Are you sure," I asked, "that Pauly's the crazy one and you all are just along for the ride?"

There was a cop car up ahead and one of New York's Finest was exiting the passenger side.

What's this guy thinking? He's going to bring Pauly down bare-handed?

Yeah, a net or a beanbag gun would be a good idea. It took four guys the last time.

And we don't want to hurt nobody.

Or get Pauly hurt.

Better start steering or we're in for another verse of Sgt. Pepper-spray's Lonely Hearts Club Banned.

"Steering?"

Yeah. We can, you know.

Sometimes we have to.

Pauly don't always make the best choices when it comes to his own self-interests.

"Good thing he's got you guys on board to look after him."

Hey, if there's one thing they teach you in the service, it's you always got your buddy's back.

I think the new guy is being ironical.

Yeah? I thought he was one of us.

You mean as in "military" or as in "dead-and-gone?"

Military, natch. We're all D and G in here.

I'm not so sure, Gunny. This guy's still plugged into something.

What?

Sure as shit! What is he? Wired?

Maybe he ain't dead.

Yeah? And maybe he ain't human, neither.

"Hold on, boys. It's just the difference between you upgrading to dish while I'm still stuck with cable."

Maybe. And just maybe you're the next upgrade to the Devil's Armor—a stealth Proud Mary that can get under the skin and do its shredding from the inside.

Only you ain't dealing with no confused, newly dead civilian who's still calling out for his mama.

Naw.

The U.S. military taught us twenty-seven different ways to kill with our bare hands—

. . . they only showed me fifteen . . .

—and we faced scarier things than you before we died! As well as after!

The darkness inside Pauly's head began to thicken and grow close with menace.

"Hold on, fellas. No need to go all Sergeant Fury and His Howling Commandos. I'm just a footloose guy on the astral plane trying to get back to my body before someone decides to pull the life-support plug at the hospital."

What's an astro-plane? Sounds like some kind of Russian space vehicle.

Body, huh? What hospital?

"I don't know. They hauled it off in an ambulance and I haven't seen it since. I just figured out I've got a lifeline I can follow a few hours ago. That was after the Threshers showed up and complicated everything."

Threshers?

"Proud Marys."

And I ended up repeating the story of my presumed demise and subsequent scavenger hunt for my mortal remains.

Sounds like a pretty tall tale to me, Maggot: vampire ghosts and intelligent swamp gas and such.

"Oh yeah. And six disembodied military vets riding around in the skull of a Section Eight AWOL is so SOP."

He's got a point, Sarge.

And a new mission would be a nice change of pace.

Yeah, running evasion maneuvers with the NYPD and playing PSY-OPS over at Bellevue gets old after awhile.

And even if an actual extraction or retrieval is out of the question for Pauly, we could still steer him enough to follow the cord and get you a little closer to the target.

Yeah, if you're telling the truth, it could be kind of interesting to see.

And, if you're not, it ain't gonna be pretty.

"I know. You know twenty-seven ways to kill with your bare hands."

Is he being ironical, again? That sounded like he was being ironical.

Now it was a white-knuckle combination chase, game of hide-and-go-seek, and treasure hunt as Pauly's barracks' buddies steered him to follow the now-you-see-it-now-you-don't astral cord that presumably led to my body. All the while we had to avoid the cops and mental health workers who were trying to work their way close enough to manage a bag-and-tag on the crazy street person who kept darting out into traffic.

By now we had picked up four Threshers who were rumbling along beside and behind like an honor guard. An honor guard waiting to shred me as soon as I popped outside of the crazy vet's carcass. The crazy vet, meanwhile, was humming "As Those Caissons Go Rolling Along."

The trick to steering is to firmly plant yourself in the driver's seat.

"Uh-huh."

Not that it's that simple with most people. The conscious mind does not willingly admit to other consciousnesses, much less share motor control. It's hard to get a grip unless the other's grip is kind of loose to begin with.

Drugs, alcohol—sometimes that's enough—

If the original will was weak to begin with.

Yeah, but the psych wards are usually the best places if you want a seat at the front of the bus.

"What are you saying? That the Middle Ages had it right? Mental illness is nothing more than demonic possession?"

Watch who you're calling a demon, Bub!

Like I said, not always proud of what I was ordered to do—

I still have nightmares!

—but those it was done to did far worse to me and mine!

Let me tell you something, kid. When you've been around a little longer you'll discover that nothing is all of one thing or another.

If there is a Devil, there are guys locked up in some upstate hospitals that even he wouldn't want in Hell with him!

Yeah, there are things that will get inside your head— some of 'em real, some imaginary. But there are guys who come out of the womb missing chromosomes that make the rest of us human.

Those, they don't need no trauma and they don't need no psychic hitchhikers to make 'em dangerous. They're just royally fucked up even before they're potty-trained.

Which way, now?

Left. Go left.

Shit! The damn thing goes right through the wall!

Whoa! Whoa! Whoa! Slow down!

Stop! Stop!

Pauly ran into the wall and rebounded. And fell backwards and hit the pavement.

A pair of Threshers loomed to our right, a couple of cops to our left.

Damn! So near and yet so far!

The wall was adjacent to a hospital emergency entrance.

I said my goodbyes quickly. The cops had cuffed Pauly and were in the process of hauling him to his feet. With the Threshers hovering just beyond, I would have to dash for the wall while I was still close. A few extra feet and I would lose my narrow margin of proximity.

Stop by and drop a twenty in Pauly's can if you can.

"How will I find you?"

Ask around.

Everyone on the street knows Pauly.

Yeah, they'll keep us locked up for observation for a few days but eventually we'll be back on the streets.

It never lasts too long.

And what is time when it's already run out, once?

"Good point. See you guys around. Semper Fi!"

What?

Oh crap! You weren't a Marine, were you?

"No. Coast Guard."

Good. For a moment we were afraid we were gonna have to make Pauly strangle himself.

Yeah. Demons are one thing, jarheads are something else altogether.

The cops pulled Pauly away from the hospital.

I pulled in the opposite direction.

There was a popping sensation and the Threshers rushed in.

I jumped and staggered, trying to dislodge my insubstantial foot that was momentarily hung up in Pauly's departing backside.

At the last minute I stumbled loose and fell through the wall.

And into the basement.

There must be dozens of storage rooms in hospital basements. Cleaning supplies, medical supplies, other supplies, parts, tools, equipment, furniture, linens.

Of course I landed in none of these. I ended up in the room with a wall full of stainless steel filing cabinets.

Filing cabinets with very wide drawers.

Drawers that weren't designed for manila folders, hanging folders, or any other kind of paper management system.

These drawers were designed for storing dead bodies: I had dropped into the hospital's morgue.

And the silvery cord that erupted from my hazy midsection snaked across the floor and into a drawer that was on the bottom row.

Chapter Eighteen

MAYBE I WASN'T dead, yet.

Maybe the cord continued on through this wall of corpses like it had through a hundred other walls today, and I would find my body somewhere upstairs recovering nicely and receiving a sponge bath from a pretty nurse.

Hell, I'd settle on getting my rectal temperature taken by a homely intern, just as long as I was still alive!

Only one way to find out: follow the cord.

Just walk up to the drawer and take a look inside.

Yep. It's just across the room, now.

Gonna start walking any minute now.

Any minute.

Real soon, now.

And then two people slammed into the morgue making enough noise to wake the dead.

Nothing seemed to stir inside the steel drawers so maybe that was a good sign.

The two appeared to be a teenaged boy and an older

man. It was hard to get much in the way of details as they were on the other side of some frosted glass partition. Their voices carried clearly enough, though. Especially the older man's: he was bordering on hysteria. The boy was following him around, trying to speak in a reasonable voice.

The man began grabbing at the stainless steel drawers set in the wall and trying to tug them open. "Where did they put her? Where is she? I want to see her!"

"What's the point?" the teenage boy asked. "She's gone."

"Gone?"

"Gone on ahead."

"But she should still be here!" the older man shrilled. "They took her! They've put her somewhere! Help me find her!"

"What would be the point?" the boy asked again.

"We should be together! They shouldn't have taken her!"

"It's not that they took her," the kid tried to explain, "it's just that she's gone on ahead. You're not going to find her here."

"But she is here!" the older man screamed.

"No, no she isn't. She's gone on. You're not going to find her here."

"I have to see her!"

"Well, you can't. Not really. She's gone. Gone on. All that's left is her body. And that's no good any more."

"Why? Oh, God! Why?"

"I don't know why." For the first time the boy's voice took on an audible edge. "Why do you drink and then get behind the wheel of your truck? Did you think the odds would never catch up with you? Anyway, red lights don't care if you're drunk or sober! It was stupid! Just stupid!"

"I don't remember any of that! Help me find her!" None of the drawers would open for him.

"Yeah, well, she's not here. She went first. She's gone on. And we should go, too."

"Go where?"

"The next place. One of 'em, anyways."

"I'm not ready."

The boy shrugged and it was as if the frosted glass that he was standing behind was becoming more opaque. "Who is? Look, I gotta go. It's pulling at me and I'm afraid of what might happen if I resist while the welcome mat is still out."

"I'm afraid!"

"Of what? The bare little bit I can see from here is bright and beautiful! It makes my eyes burn and my chest ache! I've never imagined anything like it!"

"I don't see anything but darkness."

"You have to look—"

And the boy was gone.

The man remained, moving from drawer to drawer. Giving up on opening up the body storage units, he began poking his head through the steel front pieces to examine the inner contents. "I can't see. There isn't any light. There isn't any light!"

Suddenly the darkness inside the drawer where my cord led wasn't half as frightening as the blindness outside in this room. I grasped the cord and, once again, used it as a lifeline as I pulled myself, hand over hand, along its faintly glowing length and into the filing cabinets of death.

The cord extended into the darkness and I passed bodies stacked at various levels and passed through and out into storage rooms of a more benign nature.

Eventually I found the stairs.

But I was well on my way to the first floor before I stopped hearing the anguished cries of *"There isn't any light!"* echoing in the empty bowels of the basement corridors.

The emergency room was on the first floor but there was no point in loitering there. If I wasn't in the morgue, yet, I would have been moved to the intensive care unit. I left the stairwell and went looking for a wall map to get my bearings and chart my course.

I found the hospital chapel, first.

I needed a moment to think.

And to rest.

I was exhausted. Even without physical muscles and tendons and ligaments, I ached and found it an effort to put one noncorporeal foot in front of the other. And what was I going to do once I got back to my physical shell? Climb back inside and try to wake up? Sit at the bedside and wait to see if I lived or died? I had spent the better part of the day working my way back toward my mortal remains and figuring out a few more aspects of the afterlife. But I hadn't spent much time figuring out what I was going to do next.

What *could* I do next?

I slipped through the blond wood doors and entered the cool, darkened room.

Candles glimmered in alcoves and on a bare, nondenominational altar. Most of the light, however, came from the outside, filtered through stained glass windows depicting doves and healing hands and medical symbology: all faiths welcomed here including those who had none.

Another interpretation: the medical profession as God.

A half-dozen people were scattered throughout the pews. Some praying, some meditating, one sleeping. Two were joined by creatures who might've been cousins to the otherworldly clothiers back in the green-and-white-marbled store. One individual was surrounded by a fog of darkness. The darkness made a hissing, whispering sound and the woman who sat at its malevolent core wept softly and shuddered.

That didn't seem right.

Correction: that seemed pretty fucking wrong!

Like anybody who wasn't here on account of a paycheck needed any additional grief.

My own troubles were momentarily forgotten as I considered the cloud of sorrow and fear that enveloped the woman like a sour stain. "Hey!" I said, emboldened by the fact that no one alive was likely to hear me. "You, Dark Shadows; leave the lady alone!"

No one moved except the weeping woman, who gasped as if stung by a sudden, vicious ache. The shadowy mantle that encompassed her like an ouroborous of darkness twisted and writhed like a living thing.

"Yeah, I'm talking to you!" I shouted. "We don't like your kind around here! This is a place for people to think good thoughts, hopeful thoughts. You go whisper your poison to the people who go where they *want* to hear your shit! Capeesh?"

It hissed and began to unwrap its anaconda embrace of the weeping woman.

"That's right! This is a hospital, Bog Breath! People come here for healing! Go haunt a crack house, you toxic piece of sh—"

The misty fog crackled off of the woman and snapped across the chapel like black lightning, knocking me through the blond wood doors and back out into the corridor. Even though I had passed through the wood like an empty illusion, the sensation was like being knocked through a very solid wall by a pneumatic pile driver. I felt like one very solid ectoplasmic bruise.

And more: part of me felt singed, scorched where the darkness had struck me.

I got to my feet with the sobering thought that there might be deaths beyond death. And that, as vulnerable and fragile as the flesh might appear, it may be what insulates us from the greater shocks and dangers beyond our temporary, cocooned state of existence.

I stumbled to the chapel entrance and cautiously poked my head through the wall next to the doors.

Play Misty For Me was back and swarming about the woman in the pew. So much for being a good spookmaritan. I was a newbie in a very ancient realm and hardly qualified to mind my own business, let alone anyone else's. I started to pull my head back out but hesitated as I heard a soft sigh.

The woman had stopped crying.

Granted, she still looked well down the road to Despairsville but, even from the back of the room, she seemed a little less tormented. And the bands and strands of negative energy that roiled and coiled about her gave the impression of struggling to find a foothold.

Maybe that's all it took under some circumstances: a chance to catch your breath. Or a foot momentarily struck from the stirrup, the saddle loosened from your back . . .

Perhaps some hospital chapels would be better served by moving the candles off the altar and replacing them with cable television showing Comedy Central or Cartoon Network. God may loose the fateful lightning with His terrible, swift sword but some kids in the oncology wards might be better off watching Gallagher loose the fateful melon with his terrible, silly sledgehammer.

I looked over at the two luminous creatures who seemed distracted from their little tête-à-tête with a pair of humans holding hands. Maybe they were consulting God or, perhaps, just each other but I figured it was way past time for them to join the party. "You guys work strictly on assignment or are you allowed to freelance?"

They looked at me like I was a little mad.

I was more than a little mad; I was edging into seriously pissed-off territory. Maybe I could feel proud that, in distracting the Thing, I might have helped this situation. Maybe I could withdraw, now, and go on my way, having learned to keep my mouth shut until I knew more about the stuff I was tempted to mess with.

Maybe I could have.

But I didn't.

"Hey, Creepshow," I called to the miasma of malevolence that was trying to renest about the mourning woman, "why don't you pick on someone of your own dimensional corporality?"

It bunched up like a gathering thunderhead and suddenly arced across the chapel to go splat against the wall. Leastways, that was what it sounded like on the other side as I jerked my head out just in time. Lucky for me the wall wasn't as permeable for the Shadow-thing as it was for me.

Or was it?

Wisps of dark smoke began to bleed through the outer wall and into the corridor. The Thing had readjusted its focus. Now it was time for me to readjust mine: I started off down the hall at a lope.

"Thanks for the help, fellas," I muttered at the chapel doors as I passed by, "or ladies." Or whatever the hell they were supposed to be. If they actually were angels, then to hell with them. There was a hissing, sizzling sound in the corridor behind me.

Time to get the hell out of here.

I worked my way up two floors via the stairways. I didn't trust the elevators. I wasn't fond of them when I was technically living and now that I was technically dead I could finally understand why.

Trust me, you don't want to know: you'll find out in your own good time.

By now I was running across more people wandering the corridors. Well, what used to be people, anyway. Most were in transit and all but a few were recent sojourners. A couple, however, looked like they had been wandering about the hospital for a very long time and were more than a little spooky.

But nothing as unsettling as the Darkness that strode along the passages behind me. It was showing no sign of giving up the pursuit though the well-lit hallways seemed to slow it down a bit.

I wasn't exactly running the decathlon, either. Fluorescents aren't in the same league as solar radiation but the flickering phosphors were exerting a leadening effect on my arms and legs all the same.

I snuck a look over my transparent shoulder. The Darkness was vaguely man-shaped now, loping along on two shadowy legs, swinging a pair of shadowy arms with a rhythmic determination that was somehow more frightening than the inhuman spin of the gimbaled Threshers. Was it the vague anthropomorphism that made this thing more threatening? Or the really strong impression that, with the Threshers, it wasn't personal . . .

. . . while this Thing was *anxious* to hurt me.

And I was running out of hospital.

Even if I could stay ahead of Mr. Route 666, my body was presumably somewhere up ahead and, sooner or later—around the next corner or maybe three more floors up—I was going to arrive. And then what?

Maybe I could crawl inside and use my flesh like a bomb shelter. Hunker down and wait for Tall, Dark, and Nasty to go away.

If he'd go away.

Maybe he'd follow me in—like poor Corporal Barrett's barracks mates.

And then it would be a battle over who got to sit in the driver's seat.

Uh-uh.

I was going to have to lose this joker or have it out with him right now.

I stopped.

Turned.

Raised my fists.

"Okay, Donnie Darko; that's it! No more Follow-the-Leader. Let's play a new game. It's called—"

The Thing was so anxious to play that it didn't wait to learn about the new game or any of the rules. It rushed toward me. When it smacked into where I was, I was already gone.

I had gotten pretty good at this "now it's solid/now it's not" approach to walls and floors. I essentially dropped down a floor, hoping that Satan's Little Helper would miss the direction of my sudden departure. It should have worked. I found myself down in an OR with full-blown surgery going on all around me.

"Suction," said the surgeon.

"BP is going up," a nurse announced.

"What are you doing in there?" a balding little man demanded. "Get out of my wife's chest."

I looked down. I was standing in the middle of the operating table and the patient. I looked up. The little, bug-eyed, balding guy was somewhat indistinct. So was one of the surgeons.

"See that?" said Dr. Invisible, standing at the surgeon's right shoulder. "Just to the right of the aorta. You'll need a little more light."

"A little more light here," demanded the surgeon.

"And ease the tissue back a little for a better look," murmured the ghost doc in the surgeon's ear.

"Get out of there!" the little spook insisted. "Have you no respect!"

"Sorry," I said, trying to step out of the table and patient without walking through an actual human being. The surgical team had me pretty effectively hemmed in. "I'll be out as soooooooon—"

I was out, up, and away.

My through-the-floor dive had just turned into a delayed bungee jump: the silvery cord jerked me back up through the floor I had just departed. The Darkness was still there, casting about, trying to figure out where I had gone to. We got a quick gander at each other as I was jerked on upward through the ceiling and into the next floor up.

And the floor above that.

And then two more.

I came to a stop halfway through the sixth and seventh floors. It took a little squirming—mental and otherwise—to get the rest of the way up and back on my feet. I was in the middle of another corridor. Now which way do I go?

How about toward the sound of familiar voices?

"Why would I lie to you now, Uncle?"

"That is a very good question, my little spook," I heard Kurt answer. "Unfortunately, you did lie to me. You told me you didn't know anything about the Doman's where-abouts last night nor my brother's death. Then I find out that you lied about both!"

"And I've told you, Uncle, that the Doman swore me

to secrecy. I had no idea he was going to kill Uncle Malik."

"The Asian demon claims that the plan and its execution were your doing. That Cséjthe didn't even know that I had a brother."

"Of course she would say that; she works for him! She is his creature! She would say anything to protect him!"

"And what would you say to protect yourself, eh? You've already lied once to cover your tracks. Have there been other occasions? And are you still lying to me now?"

"This is ridiculous! I have ever done your bidding."

"Except bring me the ashes of the traitor Cairn."

"No. And I haven't quite mastered the knack of walking on water, either. Look, I thought the Doman had business with Uncle Malik. When he suddenly turned around and assassinated him, it caught us all by surprise. If I hadn't sworn a blood-oath right then and there, I would have been next!"

"You are a Tween, Darcy. Blood-oaths have no power over you."

"But he doesn't know that."

"I doubt he even knows what a blood-oath is. The point is you covered for him against your own flesh and blood. And don't tell me that you feared for your life: he was already in a coma when you claimed you had been asleep in your room."

"Since there was nothing I could do to bring Uncle Malik back, I thought it best to bide my time until I could discern the Doman's true intentions."

"Then you should understand what I must do now. Give me your gun."

"What? Why?"

"Why? You ask me why when my Doman lies near death in a room down the hall with a bullet in his chest? Of the two people that I know were present near the time and place of the shooting, one of them is 'his creature' who 'would say anything to protect him' and the other is you. So, I'm sure you understand why I must ask for your weapon until more is known about this incident."

"And if I hand my weapon over to you, Uncle, who will protect our Doman from his real enemies while you hallucinate me as an imaginary one?"

"Sundown is minutes away. There will be an abundance of security around his room and about this floor within the hour."

"And until then?"

"He is in a more secure location than the ICU and in the hands of his own people."

"Perhaps, Uncle, your motives are the ones that are impure in all of this."

"We've already had this discussion, Great-grandniece. As divisive as Cséjthe's ascension is proving to be, his assassination could be disastrous, triggering a bloody war for clan power and political advantage that might destroy us all. Particularly if the other demesnes perceive us as vulnerable at this time. I have no ambitions to rule over the shattered remains of a once great empire."

The cord gave a strong tug and I was suddenly propelled down the hallway, my seneschal and my murderer flashing past like highway markers on the autobahn. Suki and Deirdre were at the far end of the corridor having their own huddled conference.

"—lost contact. All they can get now is that the lines are down or the phones inside the house may be out of service."

"What?" the redhead asked. "As in ripped out of the walls and marinated in body parts?"

"Pagelovitch is putting together a team to go down there and check it out but there's a dearth of willing volunteers. The word's gotten out that uninvited guests have a history of not returning from Domo Cséjthe's hospitality. If Burton and Mooncloud have met something nasty— well, then, not even the Doman's friends are safe, are they?"

Deirdre looked like she was trying to decide whether to laugh or cry. "Safe? It's funny now that I think about it. I suppose I've never been less safe than these past few months and yet, never felt more so." She turned and looked at the door that they were standing beside. "Even now I keep thinking that he's going to wake up and figure out a way to turn this all around. Not because he's especially clever or smarter than everyone else. Just because he has the damnedest . . . luck . . . of anyone . . . I know . . ."

And then she made her decision: she started to cry.

"He may pull through this, yet," Suki said, folding her cell phone back into her purse and reaching out to hug Deirdre. "Vampire hearts don't function in any way like a living human's would. And the fact that the EKG says he's brain dead doesn't necessarily mean anything either."

"Why? Because he's neither living nor undead? Just because he can get away with breaking some of the rules doesn't mean that the laws of physics can't catch up with him. He's been living on borrowed time and now time has run out! If he was a vampire, that bullet in his heart would kill him just as surely as a wooden stake would. If he was alive, his heart would tear itself apart around the bullet's fragments. What did the surgeon say? That it appeared as though the cardiac muscle was paralyzed between heart-beats."

"The key word is 'appeared'," Suki reminded.

"Oh, yeah. Because if the blood wasn't circulating at all then he would be dead instead of in a permanent vegetative state! That's not good! But as bad as that is, if God ever takes His finger off the pause button on the VCR, he'll tip one way or the other and end up as a pile of rotted meat or in a permanent dust-itative state!"

Okay, this wasn't helping. Time to go and form my own opinion. I squeezed between them and pushed on through the door into the room on the other side.

There were curtains around the bed. After walls of steel and stone, I slipped through these without even blinking.

Inside the circle of linen, the treatment station area was dark except for the phosphor ribbons on the readout monitors and a small, soft spotlight that framed the patient's upper torso. All else was in shadow.

The body in the bed looked dead.

The ventilator pushed air in and out of his (my?) lungs with a mechanical single-mindedness. The monitor *eeped* and showed a sine wave that bore no resemblance to any kind of a heartbeat I'd ever seen on ten seasons of *ER*. Other than that there were no signs of life connected to the body in the bed.

The arms and the parts of the face that weren't

obscured by the ventilator were as white as the sheets of the bed. The skin, waxy and almost translucent.

I was as pale as a ghost.

Okay, there's a potentially redundant analogy . . .

So, what now?

Duh! Get back in my body, of course!

I crawled up onto the bed and rolled over onto my carapace of flesh. Then, relaxing my tenuous cohesion a little, I willed myself to sink down into my body like a spa patron sinking into a luxurious mud bath.

Unlike a luxurious mud bath, however, the clay was cold. And brittle.

I submerged into darkness. Into a grave of sorts.

Unlike my previous melds there were no shared thoughts, no internal tastes or touches or smells or memories. Did the experience recede because the mind was my own? Or because the mind was shut down?

Or brain dead?

I tried to move an arm. I felt nothing.

I twitched my leg. Nothing moved.

My eyes were glued shut.

My body encased in lead.

Dimly I heard the mechanical rasp of the respirator from afar but I could draw no breath. I was suffocating in the dark!

I sat up out of myself with a cry of horror. Poe was an overrated hack: getting sealed up inside a wall was nothing in comparison with being entombed in your own dead flesh! I slid out of my body and off of the bed. I had to catch myself on rubbery ghost legs before I sank through the floor.

All of that effort to return to my body, risking the Threshers and losing The Kid . . .

"What's the point?"

"That," said a strangely familiar voice, "is the central question of existence. And the answer—no matter how good or how true—never seems to satisfy for long."

I turned and peered into the darkness on the other side of the bed.

A figure began to emerge from the gloom. Someone hunched over in a chair. Doctor? Nurse? The white clothing was loose and draped like a robe instead of a hospital uniform. Patient? The massive head came up slowly revealing a stonelike visage.

A large and scary patient?

His face was human . . . and it wasn't. You noticed this after another moment. It came close but it was too proud. And too fierce. And the planes and angles came together as the result of a geometry that wasn't entirely of this world. The nose was prominent, beak-like. The brow like a mountain cliff. The eyes like lava flares in deep caverns.

And, of course, the great white pinioned wings that arched up from behind his shoulders were a dead giveaway.

"Michael!"

The owner of the otherworldly sword that hung above my fireplace inclined his leonine head. "Cséjthe. I see you have returned from your wanderings."

"Yeah, and don't think it's been easy!" I said, getting over my abashment very quickly. "Next time you get a chance to chat with the Big Guy? Tell Him that a few little kiosks with 'You Are Here' maps would be *muy* helpful."

I was really happy to see him though you wouldn't know it from the tone of my voice.

If he was happy to see me, you wouldn't know it from his tone, either. "Perhaps it would be best if you told him in person."

"Is that why you're here? Are you pulling repo duty now? Gonna Swing Low, Sweet Chariot me?"

"Actually, I am here to place my finger on the scales." And his arm moved into the light. The sleeve of his robe was pushed back to above the elbow and, as I watched, his alabaster flesh took on a solidity that made even the furniture seem indistinct. His right hand came into view holding a syringe. "There is not much time and the vessel must be brought back into balance."

"Not much time?"

"The helicopter is landing on the roof even now. I must depart within minutes." The needle slid into the perfect flesh inside his left elbow.

"Oh, no you don't! I've got about two days' worth of questions. You can't just pop in and then rush right off again. Unless you're taking me with you. *Are* you taking me with you?"

He shook his head slowly. "You cannot go where I go."

"Well, then let's start with where I'm supposed to go."

That massive brow rose a little at one corner. "Would it do any good to try to tell you?"

He had a point. Once, long ago, in Sunday school the teacher had asked me if I knew where bad little boys and girls went. "Sure," I had told her. "Behind Fogherty's barn." And it seemed like people had been unsuccessfully telling me where to go ever since.

Or maybe not so unsuccessfully given my current state of affairs.

I watched the barrel of the syringe fill with a milky substance and wondered if this was the final hallucinatory result of the brain decaying from oxygen starvation: an angel doing drugs at my bedside while I played Twenty Questions on the theme of Life, the Universe, and Everything.

"It's just that I'd like to know if I'm going to Heaven or Hell or just supposed to pick out some real estate to haunt . . ."

"You want to know about Judgment Day," the archangel intoned.

"Judgment Day?"

"'And I saw the dead, small and great, stand before God; and the books were opened,'" he quoted. "'And another book was opened, which is the book of life: and the dead were judged out of those things which were written in the books, according to their works.'"

"Actually," I said, "I've never bought into that whole Book of Revelations courtroom-drama-at-the-end-of-time story."

"Oh?" His eyebrows rose and he fixed me with that piercing look that bore more than a passing resemblance to a bird of prey.

"Well, at least in terms of an end-of-the-world trial and a big book filled with your life's deeds and such."

"You don't believe there's a big book?"

"Not a literal book. With covers and paper pages and such."

"It would be comforting to think there are no files, no records of your past misdeeds . . ."

I shook my head. "Oh, I know there's a record—there's a file on everything I've ever done, not done, felt, thought, imagined . . ." I tapped my chest. If you can call nonexistent fingers passing through nonexistent pectorals "tapping."

"Right here. I'm my own book, my own filing cabinet: my own record of accomplishments and failures, dreams and nightmares, graces and sins. It's all written down, line for line, inside of me. You want to know who and what a man is, you don't look it up in some book on a shelf. You go inside him and see what graffiti is spray-painted on the innermost walls of his heart."

"So," Michael pursed his lips, "when the Day of Judgment comes, you are your own record of what you are, for good or for ill."

I nodded. "Except I don't believe in that, either."

"In what? A Day of Judgment?"

"Nope. Not a final, let's get out the calculator and add up the plus and minus columns to close out the books kind of event. I figure every day is judgment day: hour by hour, minute by minute, you are what you are and who you are based upon the latest, up-to-the-second totality of your choices and experiences. The balance changes constantly and your fitness for this life or the next is a moment-by-moment affair of existence. Life doesn't decide who and what you were after the fact, only dusty historians."

The angel pulled the syringe from his arm and stood. "You have an interesting perspective on metaphysical imagery. I would be interested in how you interpret the afterlife when your time comes." He took a step and leaned over my carcass in the bed.

"What do you mean 'the afterlife *when* my time comes'? I've been doing the Kiefer Sutherland with the spooks and spirits for the past twenty-four. Doesn't that count even if I'm just visiting? Uh, I am just visiting, aren't I?"

Michael shook his head and positioned the syringe over my chest. "This isn't the afterlife, Cséjthe. You haven't sojourned out among the vast interdimensional interstices of creation."

"So what have I been doing all of this time?" I eyed the needle positioned over my heart. "And just what do you think you're doing there?" Leave it to Mama Cséjthe's baby boy to second-guess an angel when there's no one else to turn to.

Before I could get an answer to either question there was a sizzling sound and the darkness that had dogged me from the chapel downstairs came boiling through the wall like a wronged lover on the Jerry Springer show. Malevolent energy washed in with it like a black tide and I felt a vicious undertow grasp at my supposedly nonexistent lower extremities. I staggered.

Michael did not even look up.

"You have no business here," he murmured. "Go back to the Darkness and hide in the Greater Shadow until the Light finds you at the appointed time."

And, just like that, it was gone. No struggle. No contest of wills or powers. One moment the shadow was present, the next it was gone. No muss, no fuss.

"Penn Station," the angel said.

"Uh, what?"

"You wanted to know what you've been doing since you

were dispossessed of your vessel, your body. Try Penn Station."

"Penn Station?"

He nodded. "Penn Station isn't the world or a country or even a city. It's a place, an area—one of many within one city of many—where people come and go as they make the transition from one place to another."

"It's a train station," I said.

"That is one way to look at it. Albeit a rather narrow one. And all that you have really done is to wander around Penn Station for a few hours. While thousands of souls are catching trains and hopping taxis to towers of glass or fields of green out beyond the city's stone and metal sprawl, you have wandered about the cold stone and brick lobby and mezzanine. Instead of traveling with the other travelers, you have squatted with the few dispossessed."

"The who?"

"You can find them in any train or subway station: the mad and the homeless who sleep in the maintenance tunnels and come up briefly to panhandle for change. Do not look into their empty eyes nor heed their senseless babble. They are the fading echoes of life squandered and ill-used. They are not guides to the truth that lies behind the curtains of this world; they are the lost and the Deceiver's sleight-of-hand to turn others from their paths."

"And what was the dark cloud? Give me a Penn Station analogy for that!"

"Do you think terrorists are confined to the world and politics of the living? Hatred of life and light go hand in hand. That is why I am here." He plunged the needle into the chest of the body on the bed.

"To do what? Stick it to me? Why not? Everyone else has."

The angel depressed the plunger, presumably sending the milky substance into my heart. "Poor traveler. So busy counting the quantity of his enemies that he does not measure the quality of his allies."

"That include you, Mikey? Or are you here on someone else's orders?"

"Does it matter?"

"We didn't exactly see eye to eye the last time our paths crossed. Just curious to know where you stand now. And why we seem to be blood brothers all of a sudden."

"It is not yet your time. The blood of the Eloihim may buy you the time you need to complete your mission."

"Mission? What mission? And you didn't answer my first question."

"Is it not enough to know that I and my kindred possess free will? And that the essence which now seeks to repair the contamination of Marinette Bois-Chèche's demon-tainted blood flowed in my veins before it entered yours?"

"Yeah, yeah, I hear your words, Mikey, but I'm still not sure this is anything more than 'the enemy of my enemy is my friend' kind of deal. Not that I'm not your grateful dead, you understand, but I would like a better handle on the sitch before it unravels any further."

"I am not a fortune-teller, Cséjthe."

"Man, you're not even a guy by the side of the road who'll give directions to the nearest Gas'N'Go. All I know is that everyone seems to want my blood and yet I'm the guy who seems to be getting everyone else's. I'm supposed to be undead but that hasn't worked out. Then

I'm supposed to be dead—can't get closure here, either. If this is God's plan then He must be a cosmic-sized Forrest Gump. On the other hand, what if this action isn't officially on the game board?"

"You don't believe in books and courtrooms. Why would you believe in game boards?"

"Irony? Sarcasm? Good God! Who are you and what have you done with Mikey?"

"Very funny, Cséjthe. But I must leave you, now."

"What am I, winged one? The spook who comes in from the cold?"

His brow twitched. That was unnerving: it put one in mind of a landslide waiting for one good temblor. "Perhaps you are not as dense as you pretend."

"Tell me more."

"Tell you what? That there are forces for good and for ill in the world? In the worlds within worlds and the worlds that encompass this and those beyond? That the laws that bind and shape and define reality and creation at every level hold us locked in eternal conflict? A never-ending battle?"

"For truth, justice, and the American way?"

He closed his eyes. "I do not know why I even try."

"And that's just my point: why do you try? With me? Why are you here? With me? Why are you sticking your—um, blood—in me? I'm nothing! I'm not alive anymore! I'm not dead, yet! I'm no damn good at following the rules!"

"That is precisely what you are good at," the angel interrupted with a smile. The curving of those so solemn lips was like a sunrise in the gloom.

"Following the rules?"

"*Breaking* the rules." He laid the syringe on the tray of instruments next to the bed and pushed the wheeled table away. "Last year, while you were being pursued by mortal enemies, you had a conversation with the red-haired woman who stands outside in the hallway now. You told her that there was a difference between laws and rules. That true laws could not be broken . . ."

"Only superceded by higher laws," I murmured.

He nodded. "Most people—here and even where I come from—do not understand the difference any more. We are all bound by the laws of our various kingdoms. That is the reality of creation at every level. But, in the meridian of time, we have become equally bound by the rules we have come to believe in as legitimate as though they were laws themselves."

I stared at him. "And I'm special because I'm good at breaking the rules."

He nodded. "Dead and yet not dead. Human and yet something more—and less. Rule-breaker. Warlock."

"Warlock?"

"By the original definition, which meant 'oath-breaker.' The breaking of oaths was once tantamount to the breaking of laws—sacred laws."

I shrugged. "And this is important to you?"

"Perhaps much ere the struggle between light and shadow is played out to finality."

"And you're here, doing the milk-it-does-a-body-good spot because I have a role to play in the game. Is that it?"

"Everyone has a role."

"Everyone doesn't have angels popping into their hospital rooms to give them a bolus of angel juice in the heart."

"There are a relatively low number of 'players' who are the head of the second-largest vampire enclave in the world while harboring elements of vampire, werewolf, Loa, and demon blood in their body without yet being mastered by any."

"And now I have something else in the mix."

"As I said, I've come to place my finger on the scales."

"Sounds like cheating."

"To bring you back into balance?"

"To tip me in any direction."

"What if you've already been tipped?"

I sighed and tried to rub my aching eyes. It might have helped if they had really been there. "I'm not saying I don't need help here. And don't think I'm not appreciative—though it would help to know what I'm supposed to do so I could appreciate my situation a little better. But if the other guys start tipping me one way and you and your posse start tipping me back the other—well, pretty soon I'm nothing more than one of those round-bottomed inflatable punching bags, getting knocked one way and then the other, swinging and swaying back and forth until entropy brings blessed relief. What's the point of having free will and personal agency if I'm just a collectable action figure for the shelf of the Almighty or a paperweight on the desk of the Devil? What's our purpose then? Heroic, moral poses while they wave us at each other and make appropriate combat noises?"

"Perhaps coming here was a mistake," he said.

"Aha!"

"Aha?"

"Now we come to the heart of it! Are you here in an official capacity or are you kibitzing?"

"I can stay no longer. Others are coming." His wings fanned out behind him and spread as if he would take flight by crashing through the drop-panel ceiling.

"Well, if you won't read my tea leaves, tell me what I can do for The Kid!"

He looked at me strangely. "The one you call J.D has twice survived his destiny. Let him go. You have enough worries."

"Let him go where? Into the light? I wouldn't hold him back if that was the case. But he's got some free will, too. And I'm in need of a little backup until this whole thing gets settled out."

"Trust your son," Michael said, starting to glow with an unearthly radiance. "He's saved you twice so far."

"My what? I don't have a son, I have a daughter." An unexpected surge of grief and I was suddenly close to tears. "Had a daughter."

"Had, have, will have . . . you'll find that tense doesn't matter so much when you step outside of time." The light increased to a painful intensity. "The fact that your daughter died doesn't make her any less your daughter even now. The fact that your son has not been born yet doesn't make him any less your son even now. Who do you think pulled you through the wall of the gymnasium when the creatures you call Threshers were right behind you?"

"Who?"

"I do not know his true name. Nor his birth name. You have taken to calling him Will."

And, like a flash of lightning, he flickered with a bright and terrible light.

And disappeared.

Chapter Nineteen

THE DOOR OPENED and a parade entered my hospital room before I had a chance to recover from Michael's flashbulb exit or digest his allegations about our will-o'-the-wisp companion. A pair of doctors and a nurse entered, the men carrying white, hard-shell briefcases and the woman pushing a draped crash cart on noiseless casters. Deirdre and Suki followed behind trying, in vain, to get an update on my prognosis. Kurt trailed behind, dragging Darcy. Or was she holding him back, trying to avoid a confrontation with Suki? I wasn't sure because I was still trying to put Michael's parting words into some kind of comprehensible perspective.

And figure out why the Indian—excuse me, Native American woman now coming through the door looked so familiar.

The representative of the Northern Wilderness Clans was still arrayed in her traditional Native American garb. I figured the buckskin dress and moccasin boots were

409

diplomatic garb for the formal reception a few nights back but the outfit seemed a bit out of place for traipsing about the Big Apple otherwise.

"Cséjthe," Wendy said. "The Mangler will wait no longer." She was looking at ghostly me, not at unconscious, pile-of-meat-in-the-hospital-bed me.

"I demand to know what you are doing," Kurt was saying. He was speaking to the doctors, not to Wendy. "I am supposed to be consulted and kept up to date on any and all treatment decisions!" No one was paying any attention to Wendy.

"They cannot see or hear me, Cséjthe, any more than they can see or hear you," Wendy explained.

"We are preparing the patient for transport," answered Doc Number One.

"We are medevacing him to NYU, where they are better equipped to treat unique cardiac trauma," added Doc Number Two.

"Why?" I asked. "Are you a ghost?"

"Out of the question," Kurt argued. "I'm bringing in my own specialists. They should be here any minute!"

"Not a ghost. A spirit," Wendy said; "you still do not know who I am, do you?"

Doc One opened his briefcase and pulled a syringe out of the foam-lined interior. "That leaves us no time for checking vitals," he said. The syringe wasn't like any hospital-issue instrument I'd ever seen. It looked like something the Klingons would have used for executing criminals.

"Does it matter?" asked Doc Two, opening his case, as

well. "We would proceed with the infusions regardless."
He produced another syringe that looked like it was
mating with a fuel injector.

I pulled my eyes away from the nightmare needles long
enough to notice something else: there was something
familiar about these two . . .

"I am Wendigo," Wendy was saying, "and my patience
is at an end! We must depart now!"

"Now hold on, baby sister . . ." I moved in to get a better look. " . . . these bozos are messing with my flesh and
something's not right here . . ."

"What is in that syringe?" Kurt demanded.

Maybe the doctors reminded me of each other. Upon
closer examination I could see that they were twins.
Identical twins.

"Let them work, Uncle," Darcy whispered. "If you're
moving Domo Cséjthe back to the demesne for his recovery,
you may as well let them continue to prepare him for
transport."

"Your flesh is useless for any practical purposes,"
Wendigo said. "We will leave it behind and find more suitable flesh for you."

"I'm not so sure that NYU isn't the better option,"
Deirdre was saying. "I mean taking a helpless and mortally
injured man back to home base for the assassins who
are trying to kill him doesn't strike me as a particularly
efficacious plan."

"What do you mean 'leave my flesh behind'?" I said.
"Sweetheart, I worked too hard and too long to fight my
way back here just to go running off again . . ."

"Perhaps," Kurt conceded, "but I doubt that the top

cardiac clinic in the country would know what to make of our Doman's physiology."

"Oh, and like you do?" was Suki's caustic contribution as she continued to work her cell phone for news of Doctors Mooncloud and Burton.

" . . . besides," I added, lifting a length of the silver cord with my hand, "I'm kind of attached. Any side trips would be severely limited."

Doc One stuck his syringe in my chest near the same point that Michael had jabbed me.

The nurse uncovered her crash cart and selected a pair of instruments that looked like a cross between electronic labelers and water pistols.

"Wait a minute," I said, jiggling the cord in my hand, "I know why these guys look familiar!"

"I demand to know what you are injecting into this patient!" Kurt insisted, taking a menacing step forward. It looked like he was ready to do the whole look-into-my-eyes-and-surrender-your-will-to-mine thing if necessary.

"I gotta second that request," Deirdre piped in.

The Amerind spirit drew a ghostly knife from its ghostly sheath on her ghostly person.

Doc Two leaned into his lapel and murmured something as he brandished his syringe close to my face.

"Either there really is a Charlie Brown and he and his twin brother grew up to practice medicine," I said, "or these boys are related to the mysterious Dr. Pipt!" Twin grandsons, most likely: they had the same round head and striking features as the old guy in my hypnotropic email. The ravages of Pipt's advanced age had blurred the similarities a bit but the likeness was unmistakable.

This was not good.

Before you could say: "Wonder Twins Activate!" it got worse!

The nurse turned and the devices in her hands shot multiple wired darts at Deirdre and Suki. Simultaneously the door opened and another nurse stepped in behind Kurt and Darcy, shooting them both with another set of wired darts.

A little snap, crackle, and pop and they were on the floor, twitching and incapacitated from being tasered.

"Hey!" I said.

And "Hey!" again as I got a good look at the new nurse as she carefully stepped over the paralyzed bodies on the ground around her feet. She looked even more familiar than our pair of docs. There was a pun in there somewhere but I was too distracted by the sight of Theresa Kellerman in surgical scrubs to think it through right now.

And yelling "*Hey!*" a third time as Wendy swung her knife, cutting through the silver cord that connected me to my body. I was disconnected and the remains of the cord evaporated like so much morning mist. "You *bitch*!" I yelled.

"Come, Cséjthe," Wendigo said, "there is nothing that you can do here."

"You let me be the judge of that," I growled as Doc Two peeled back one of my eyelids and stuck the needle of the second syringe between my eyeball and the orbital socket.

Theresa was carrying a zippered valise. She unzipped and pulled out a small transceiver, speaking into it. "Bring the gurney and a body bag. I'll need a couple of extra hands."

"Which one?" the first nurse asked—who, refreshingly, didn't look familiar at all.

"Who would you choose?" Theresa asked conversationally. She unzipped the valise and reached inside.

"A blonde would be more desirable."

"You Aryans . . ." She pulled out a handgun. "You don't like redheads?"

The other nurse shrugged. "The Nipponese would seem the more likely ally."

"More historical, you mean. But I'm not looking to rewrite history and, unlike you, Ilse, lampshades don't float the little man in my boat."

"It is the blood that matters," the nurse said. "It is what drove our master and what drives Josef even now."

"Yeah. Pure blood. That's what gets you all jonesing. But in this case I need the redhead because her blood is tainted." Theresa pointed her gun at Deirdre.

"It doesn't hurt that her bosoms are larger," Doc Two observed as I tried to grab at the weapon.

"There is that," Theresa agreed. And shot Deirdre in the back. With an unwired dart.

I turned on the Indian spook as the eerie quartet set about their preparations to remove the bodies from my room. "Maybe you don't know who you're dealing with, sweetheart," I snarled, dropping into a crouch. I spread my arms and curled my hands into threatening claws. "I'm not just some fangless, half-vampire. I've conquered death many times over! I've defeated vampires, were-wolves, and demons! I command legions of zombies! I've got powers—"

A wind sprang up. Don't ask me how a wind blows so

that a noncorporeal entity such as myself can feel it but I was suddenly caught in the equivalent of an astral wind tunnel. The buckskin dress on the nubile young Amerind girl was quickly whipped into a thousand rotted tatters. The view might have been titillating had not the psychic storm had the same effect on her sweet smooth flesh. In just moments she went from a maid of seventeen summers to a crone of a thousand winters.

A thousand *hard* winters.

And she began to grow even as her feminine ripeness collapsed against harsh outcroppings of bone. Her mouth gaped and her gums turned black as teeth receded in a tangled snarl. Her eyes fell back into deep milky pits in their sockets and began to glow like twin sentry fires in the fog. Her arms and legs grew to inhuman proportions and she towered over me, showing vast expanses of gray-and-brown skin mottled with green and white lichens and fungi.

Cséjtheeee, she rasped, and her breath washed over me like the wind off of the bogs and swamps. She reached down with a spidery, taloned hand and grasped me around my waist as if we were both solid. *Commme.*

She straightened and I was airborne.

Beating my fists against her hand was pointless. My hands passed through her "flesh" as if it wasn't there and yet she held me in a palpable grip like cold iron. She turned and strode from the rooms.

I say "rooms" for we were now one floor higher thanks to her additional height. We passed through walls and floors, both as ghostly as before, but now I was trapped in the intangible grasp of her giant hand.

A squad of paramedics with sidearms passed through us as we ascended upwards to the roof. A Bell/Augusta AB139 helicopter crouched there. It was a bit oversized for the helipad that serviced the "Life Flight" models that made the short hops between the hospital and the outlying accident scenes. Its twin rotors remained in preflight rotation and a black-clad sniper knelt inside the open cargo door, scoped rifle at the ready. Apparently both of us were going for a ride: body and soul.

Wendigo clambered out to the edge of the roof, faced westward, gathered herself and leapt into the evening skies. Too bad Kurt was a couple of floors down and unconscious. I could have quoted some more of that obscure and meaningless poetry about how Wendy "has wings that fly / above the clouds, above the clouds . . ."

Long minutes went by and it became evident that we weren't coming down anytime soon. The creature opened its ogrish mouth and began to howl. It was the sound the wind makes when it comes roaring down off the mountains like an express train, like the gale when the ocean makes war upon the land, like the wail of lost souls in the desolate places of the wilderness when a storm that is not just a storm stalks the land.

Clouds came like obedient beasts to the voice of one who calls them. They bounded and frisked, circling and frolicking until a herd had closed about us and we were borne across the heavens in a stampede that quickly darkened from white to gray to black. Strangely, there was no lightning, no thunder, no rain. Just a new stratum of darkness through which we tunneled like moles through midnight earth. We rode the cyclone like a rodeo cross-country event, the gale ripping an occasional glimpse through the thunderheads to display a scrolling blur of distant landscapes below.

We traveled for what seemed like hours. I couldn't escape Wendigo's implacable grip. At this altitude I wasn't sure that I wanted to. The howl of the wind made it impossible to carry on any kind of a dialogue, civil or otherwise. I just hung in her monstrous grasp and pondered how the cutting of the astral cord would affect my disembodied status now.

And what the future had in store for my flesh and the flesh of my friends and unborn son.

The hurricane scream eventually became a tornado wail, then weakened to a storm-front moan. We finally dropped to earth with a breezy sigh.

We came down on a plateau surrounded by mountains, the corona of the setting sun limning the peaks to the west with pale gold shading to cerulean blue. She released me and began to diminish like a leaf falling down a chasm. In moments the monstrous Wendigo was replaced by the young maiden Wendy. I thought about taking a swing now that she was of a more manageable size but decided there wasn't much point.

For the moment.

"Come," she said, and walked toward a distant grove of trees. The distant grove turned out to be a nearby forest. My perspective was skewed by the size of the trees: twisted, stunted, they resembled a blighted patch of bristlecone pines gone bonsai rather than the tall stately firs one expected to find in the mountainous wilds. It was hard to make out any details in the failing light, though my astral eyes saw some things better in darkness than my physical eyes did in broad daylight.

"Take my hand," said the creature who had returned to looking like the cover girl for Land O'Lakes butter. "See what I see." The hand that had encircled my waist now fell inside my larger grip.

And I saw blight. The trees began to glow a sickly green like radium excited into a cancerous display. Their roots desperately gasped for pure water and found only a choking toxic broth wherever they turned, probed, or plunged. The creatures that burrowed between their roots, scurried over their bark and branches, or nibbled at the newer leaves and tender shoots, either dropped dead or passed on chromosomal damage to their offspring.

We passed through this nursery of death and came to a lake on the other side. Perhaps giants did their laundry here: a whitish gray scum lay over the surface of the water and vast collections of sudsy bubbles had collected into hive structures along the shore on the westward shores. Here and there the water churned with flashes of body parts that were neither identifiable as mammal, fish, nor amphibian.

An eye broke the surface and rose another three or four inches out of the water on a flexible stalk of segmented blue flesh. It cruised about like a submarine periscope for several minutes, contemplating an ancient log where something dark and spiny huddled. A sly tentacle slid out of the water and made a half circle move around the spiky lump. As it touched the log's occupant, the dark shape seemed to explode with an audible snapping sound and scores of quills flew in all directions like a land mine full of nine-inch nails. A bubbling scream sounded under the roiling waters and a shredded tentacle disappeared as a dark and huddled shape waddled off of the log and onto the scorched-looking earth that ringed the dark and scummy waters.

We passed by the lake and turned toward a jumble of rocks where the ground sloped upwards and the mountain continued.

There was a cave.

More like a burrow, actually. Too small for a human to enter without crawling. But we walked in without ducking our heads. Apparently the connection I shared with Wendigo not only gave me extradimensional vision but provided automatic resizing capabilities as well.

Handy.

Especially if I ended up haunting rat holes throughout eternity.

At this point I couldn't rule anything out.

Farther in, a bearlike creature curled in on itself, deep in slumbered hibernation. Its right paw was draped across its chest, its claws blunt and misshapen like the toes that splayed from the central pad: they resembled stubby, infantile human toes more than ursine phalanges, despite the fur and coloring. The other paw, draped above the long-snouted skull, was a bifurcated appendage, more like the "hand" of a two-toed sloth with great curving nails that were the size of small tusks. The creature seemed immersed in uneasy dreams and the twin claws clacked together like restless shears as it shifted and grunted in its sleep.

I remembered back to the visions Wendy had shown me in New York on the night of the reception.

Things in the water with extra eyes, no eyes, feelers, and worse. Things in the forest that gave birth to abominations, things that shouldn't have lived but did. And things that were hungry in obscene ways . . .

Snow was falling when we emerged from the cave. The skies were thick with flakes yet the ground remained bare and dry. The lake steamed and vapors marked the passing of the largest ice crystals which lasted long enough to actually touch the ground.

"Do you see?" she asked. "How the land is poisoned?"

"This isn't my forte," I said.

"Of course not," she said. "This comes from the stronghold of The Mangler."

"I don't mean fort like fortress or stronghold. I mean 'forte' like strong point, specialty, strong suit. Some people mispronounce it and say for-tay like the musical term but that's a misnomer." I considered that I was lecturing an ancient Native American woodland spirit on linguistics and stopped. "Anyway, I'm no biochemist but this looks like something way beyond heavy metal poisoning. And how do you get industrial runoff this high up in the middle of nowhere?"

"I will show you. But first I must show you how to ride so you may withstand Nikidik in the flesh when you finally meet."

"Nikidik . . ."

"Nikidik and The Mangler are one," she elaborated. "And, at the same time, they are many."

"Thanks for clearing that up."

She tilted her head back and howled.

The howling grew in volume and intensity after a moment but no wind sprang up, no breeze stirred.

The howling took on multiple tones and became a threnody, a funereal organ playing night hymns. Then they came. Two, three, five, and finally seven in all. Wolves. A scrawny, half-starved pack.

"You must begin by seeing the *animus*," she explained. "It is not enough to pull the flesh around you. You must pass through the spirit skin and move within the *animus* to ride and to steer. Do you understand?"

"Not really."

"Look," she said, pointing at the largest male. "What do you see?"

"A wolf."

"Do you see his heart's fire?"

I looked. Just a dark lump: at night all wolves are gray. "Nope."

She walked over and stood before me. "I give you the gift of second sight so that you may take on flesh to meet flesh." She poked me in the forehead with her finger.

She poked me *in* the forehead!

Her finger went in about an inch or so above the bridge of my nose and sank into the space that should have been occupied by my cerebral cortex.

"Look again," she commanded.

I glanced at the dark blob. "I don't—"

She twisted her finger a little.

A red-and-yellow rose bloomed in the midst of the dark blob. Threads of orange and purple began to weave a skein on a wolf-shaped loom of silver.

"Holy cow!"

"Is that an expression," she asked, "or must I make further adjustments?"

"I'm—fine," I said, wondering if I truly was.

"Then look above the heart's fire. Look for the thought pool."

It was not so much a pool as a vortex. A chakra revolved over the canine cranium and its blue swirls were a cool contrast to the orange pulse of the heart chakra positioned between the creature's ribs.

"You must enter the thought pool as you would dive into a pond from the cliffs above. Only you must dive sideways and stay under once you have entered." She touched my forehead again. "My thoughts to yours, Morning Star. Your thoughts to mine." She reached down and grasped my hand. "As we jump, we will change our size and shape once more. Pay attention as I lead for you shall have to do this on your own, soon."

I opened my mouth to ask for a point of clarification but she was already leaping.

And I was already shrinking.

The cliff jumping analogy was pretty apt: there seemed to be time to point my feet and adjust my trajectory into the heart of the small, blue whirlpool. Even the resizing process seemed more second nature this time around. We entered the wolf's head and a new disorientation set in.

I was caught up in a psychic ménage à trois—Wendigo, the wolf, and me. She was wrapped around my mind in a lover's embrace while the beast panted and warily circled us like a jealous suitor.

More distracting was the return of physical sensations:

the feel of the artificially warm earth beneath my paws, the cold wind ruffling my fur, the gnawing pit of hunger in my gut, the rasping chuffs of winter air going in and out of my lungs. More chilling than the arctic mountain breeze was the realization that I was already starting to forget the former sensations of the flesh, so strongly had they slammed home again just now.

I crouched as I waited for the overwhelming kaleidoscope of impressions to subside to manageable levels.

The wolf crouched close to the curiously warm earth.

Go ahead, Cséjthe, take the reins. The toddlers of the Ute People learn to ride the village dogs before they sit astride a pony and then the horse.

This ain't no dog.

And it is not a horse that you must learn to master before your work is done on this mountain.

Whatever happened to the art of simple conversation? Why does everyone talk to me in riddles? I reached up and scratched an itch behind my ear and then felt Wendigo laugh as I realized I had just done so with my hind leg.

Very good, Cséjthe! Let the beast's instincts come through without losing hold of the reins.

Yeah? I growled. The wolf growled. *I just hope I don't fall over when I try to pee.*

Actually, it was easier than either of us expected. First of all, I had a Native American spirit working her mojo in the mix, which gave me an advantage over all those Amerind skin-walkers or such who had to figure it out on their own and with their own juice. Even so, making the transition from primate and biped to canine and quadruped would have been a major adjustment except I had already done it on several occasions.

So to speak.

Ever since Dracul-Bassarab had showed me how to travel along the dreampaths—translation: limited translocation—I made the not-quite-instantaneous trip in some sort of mental wolf mode. When I arrived, I was still human. Or what still passed for human these days. The wolf form was actually a totemic mental/spiritual state in-between. But for a momentary head-rush it felt amazingly real.

And then there was the werewolf blood that I had received from Lupé . . .

So, not such a big adjustment for the beast within my own self.

After about twenty minutes of bounding around the plateau and chasing my own tail, Wendy said I had mastered the basics and it was time to go.

Okay, I said, *where are we going?*

Up there.

I tilted my head up in response to the unseen finger pointing inside the wolf's skull.

Thousands of feet above us, near the mountain's summit, was a regularity to the outcroppings and ledges that thumbed its collective nose at the rest of the natural stone of the mountains all around us.

What is that?

It is the reason that the ground is warm in the winter and the water burns all but unnatural flesh. It is where monsters are spawned and the ladder of life is twisted until the ancestors cry out from the deep and ancient places that the world itself is being unmade. It is the fortress of The Mangler, the Nikidik, the undying and forever being reborn. And you must stop him!

Why me? This is a little out of my jurisdiction. In more ways than one. Have you tried the local authorities—both official and not so . . . you know?

Legally? He owns the land. This mountain and the ones which surround it. That which is not done legally is covered by bribes, extortion, and even murder.

Oh sure, since it's too big for the Royal Canadian Mounted Police, send in Cséjthe.

You underestimate yourself. And we are not in Canada, we are in the land your people call Colorado.

Everyone underestimates me. That or believes the phony rep. It's the only reason I've survived so long.

If this is true then perhaps the earth is doomed. Once he adds the secrets of your blood to his many baskets, he will drown the world in darkness!

Jeez, and here everyone's been worried about Hezbollah and Al Qaeda.

Come, Cséjthe, we must go now. Your best chance for entry is while night rules the skies.

And I felt her exit out through the head chakra.

I followed and we rose into the sky like two carnival balloons that had escaped the grasp of cotton-candied fingers.

"You mean *our* entry. Right?"

"What?"

"You said 'your best chance for entry' but you meant to say 'our best chance for entry.' Correct?"

"I have brought you here, Cséjthe, because you can do what no other man can do and you can go where I cannot go."

I looked back down. The wolf we had just exited was staggering around in circles, alternately whining and snapping at the other wolves who ventured too close. Another wolf had separated from the pack and was running away toward the mountain's upward slope on the leeward side of the plateau.

Looking up, I could see the outcroppings of the fortress a little better now. Dark and sinister against the backdrop of the barely waxing moon, its curving walls of stone were parted by a long arc of steel-framed panes of glass that made the great edifice look like a giant, blind predator, smiling over some sardonic secret. As we rose higher and drew nearer, I could see that each window was probably six by ten feet of tempered glass and stacked so that there were actually two rows instead of just one.

"Grandmother," I whispered, "what big teeth you have . . ." I turned to Wendigo. "Is this part of the Native American afterlife? Because I'd like to know if it isn't too late to convert to Islam and get the seventy-two virgins?"

"The Mangler is of your world, Cséjthe, not mine," she answered as we touched down on a broad ledge outfitted with a helipad. "But he corrupts what is mine as well as what is yours. Once he was a man—just as you were once a man." She began walking toward the main building a hundred yards away.

"So now we're both—what?" I asked, following reluctantly. "More . . . ?"

"Now he is much more."

"And me?"

She waggled her hand. "A little more."

"Great. So what's the plan? Any wolves or large dogs inside I can hop into and use to tear out this Nikidik's throat? And what are you going to do in the meantime?"

"Nothing."

"Nothing?"

"I cannot enter."

"Why the hell not?"

"Because The Mangler—the Nikidik—has warded his fortress with the Ttsilolni."

"The what?"

"The Sunwheel. The sign of the Whirling Logs: its power shuts me and all of my tribe out from all paths and all means of seeing. I can go no further."

"The Sunwheel?" That term was vaguely familiar.

"It is a timeless sigil of power, predating the Egyptian ankh. Not just my people but the ancient Hindus, Buddhists, Vikings, Romans, Celts, Anglo-Saxons, Mayans, Aztecs, Persians, Jews, Christians, and Neolithic tribes used it as a totem. In China it was called the Wan, in Japan it was the Manji, while in England the Fylfot. The Greeks called it Tetraskelion and Gammadion, the Germans, Hakenkreuz. The Mangler has taken the Ttsilolni and reversed the turn of the great wheel: it spins in reverse and its powers are turned back upon us!"

I looked up. There was a great stone eagle spreading its wings over the massive double doors leading to the inside of the fortress. Above the eagle's head, wreathed in a circle of leaves, was an irregular icosagon.

"Jesus Christ!"

Wendigo flinched and stopped moving.

I already had. "Well, maybe once upon a time the Germans called that thing a Hakenkreuz but ever since the Salzburg Congress of 1920, the so-called broken cross has been remembered as something entirely different!" I would have grabbed her and shaken her if I could. "It's a swastika, Lady! You don't want me! Maybe if there were vampires or werewolves or zombies on the other side of those double doors I'd be your man. But if you're wanting someone to take on the Third Reich, you should be calling Indiana Jones!"

She shook her head. "As I have said, the Ttsilolni wards my power to see within the walls of the fortress of The Mangler. I do not know what manner of creatures he employs, only what comes and goes without."

I stared at the thing the Wendigo called a Ttsilolni. There was no way around it: the emblem of the eagle and the wreath surrounding the "whirling logs" pretty much removed any doubts about the Adolf connection. "And then there's the inscription just below," I said, nodding at the chiseled lettering that spelled:

Brut Adler

"What does it say?" she asked.

"It's German. 'Adler' means eagle—I'm sure of that much. 'Brut' is tougher; too bad Deirdre isn't here." Too bad on more than one level. "I had a German zoology professor in college. I seem to recall that Brut could be used to denote either a nest or aerie—or progeny . . ."

"Progeny?"

"Yeah, like brood, clutch, covey, fry, spawn . . . off-spring."

"I think 'nest' is probably the logical interpretation given the location and circumstances," she said.

"The Eagle's Nest," I mused. "The Eagle's Aerie . . ." Something rustled in the black trunk of forgotten memories in the basement of my brain.

"You hesitate, Cséjthe. You fear that the Nikidik is served by an army of Nazis within?"

Okay.

That was my reality check.

The only Nazis you could find in this brave new century were skinhead dorks who couldn't organize a bake sale. Hitler and his fellow architects of the super race must roll in their graves every time they see who inherited the mantles of the Aryan Brotherhood. Nope. Judging from the weathering on the stonework, this stronghold had been built a long time ago and whoever the present occupants were, I could do worse than pinheads with delusions of past glories or nonagenarian storm troopers in wheelchairs and walkers.

Besides, I was all ghostly and they couldn't see me, hear me, or touch me. What was I worried about?

And given all that I had been through in the past twenty-four, it was about time I started dishing out for a change.

"Keep your skirt on, Poca-haunt-us," I said, starting toward the doors again. "If there are any brown shirts inside, there'll be more than a few brown pants before I'm through. There's a new furor in town."

"Don't get cocky," she called as I reached the entrance.

"Remember what I taught you about riding within the *animus*: your will must be stronger than the will of that which you occupy. Otherwise you will fail."

"Yes, Mother . . ." I stepped through the door and into Hitler's nightmare.

Chapter Twenty

THE NIGHTMARE STARTED off slow, with a pair of wrought-iron boot scrapers, just inside the door. It was an unassuming beginning—as was the carpet runner of industrial-grade material. The red weave bore the marks of dusty boot prints and stretched the length of a stone-flagged corridor leading to another pair of double doors some forty feet away.

I drifted toward the next set of doors, strangely self-conscious in the brightly lit but unfurnished hallway. I was, after all, invisible to the human eye.

Still, the layout was a bit intimidating. It made sense to have a temperature lock up here in the mountains where even the daytime wind chill could drop below freezing in the summer. But I was also mindful that the arrangement was identical to a *suicide run* in a medieval fortress. Although there were no obvious murder holes or arrow slits, modern technology made hidden panels and trap doors all the more likely. I shook my head: replacing

arrows and molten lead with sensor-guided lasers and jets
of poisonous gas shouldn't make any difference. I was as
transparent to conventional traps and weapons as I was to
walls and doors.

But I couldn't shake a prickling sense of unease. If
something as big and as bad as the Wendigo couldn't get
past the first door, then being all other-dimensiony might
not be any protection from what might lurk around the
next corner.

The next set of doors was more ornate. A second look,
however, indicated that the ornamentation was appliqué.
Heavy blast-doors lay beneath the façade, more functional than the outer doors and tricked out with electronic
locks. Breaking in without the right key code would
require a portable Cray with penultimate hacking software. Or enough high-yield explosives to bring down half
the mountain.

I swam through the doors in a couple of breast strokes.

The other side opened out into a great atrium. Forget
spooky old castle, this was Grand Hotel, done in '30s Art
Deco with heavy Bauhaus influence. There were great
staircases leading up and down, curving about a glass-cage
elevator with gleaming brass fittings. Corridors curved off
to my left and right, suggesting a greater labyrinth beyond.
Assuming the old adage that you "can't go wrong if you go
'right'" I turned in that direction and began following the
great hall as it arced further into the mountain's bowels.

The lighting in the corridor was dim, possibly set for
the circadian rhythms of the occupants to match day and
night outside. The rooms on the other side of the doors
were darker still. I got the impression of maintenance

facilities, meeting areas, offices, recreation facilities, weapons lockers, and numerous storerooms as I made my rounds and dropped down to the next level.

There were people down here. Men sleeping in barracks, women in dormitory chambers, couples in private apartments. And a nursery for children.

A lot of children.

It was hard to get a head count as the rooms were dark and I kept messing up my night vision by moving through the partially lit corridors and then sticking my head into another block of pitch-black darkness.

It suddenly occurred to me that my infravision wasn't kicking in. Had I left it behind with my flesh? It was one of the dark gifts bestowed with the vampiric infection. Was there a dividing line between the baggage of my past life and the carry-on luggage I was still toting around? I instinctively reached for the light switch, checking myself as my fingers passed through the wall plate.

There were too many targets to count by searching for hearts' fires. Maybe I'd have better luck upstairs.

I struggled up the mushy stairs, no longer possessing a silver cord to use as climbing leverage in my ascension. And I noticed something else: I was getting tired.

Maybe ghosts were supposed to take naps during the day. I couldn't remember the last time I'd slept—in the flesh or out of it. And maybe losing my astral connection had taken an additional toll. Whatever the reason, climbing the stairs up to the third level felt more like climbing a mountain. Maybe I should find a nice, dark storeroom and catch a little shuteye—a difficult proposition under any other conditions now that my eyelids were transparent.

No storerooms were immediately evident on the third floor. What was evident was a profusion of laboratories, medical facilities, and operating theaters. Each room, each chamber differed from the others in its equipment, layout, and appointments.

Take the operating rooms. One seemed geared for a broad range of procedures, another for microsurgery, a third specifically set for OB/GYN procedures, and a fourth that—well—looked like a vivisectionist's wet dream: everything up-to-date and state-of-the-art while offering a sense of retro familiarity for adherents of the Spanish Inquisition.

The labs had some commonality—I recognized gene sequencing and splicing equipment in more than one— but the remainder of the setups were alien beyond an electron microscope, some optical models, a number of centrifuges, and a dozen or so microworkstations net-worked to something likely mainframesized in the base-ment somewhere.

And then there was the Worm Farm.

One lab looked like a pet shop given over to aquarists with a couple hundred fish tanks lining the walls and situ-ated on most of the tables, as well. The tanks, however, contained no fish, no snails, no crab, shrimp, or amphib-ian populations. There was variety but it all fell within a single phylum of the animal kingdom: *Platyhelminthes*.

Flatworms.

And on the walls above the softly burbling tanks: a gen-eration of scrawled notes and formulae related to engrams and the theory of biochemical memory.

I stood there in the dim, green glow of the illuminated

aquariums and felt the nonexistent hair on my nonexistent arms prickle and stand away from my nonexistent flesh.

"It's very pretty in here, don't you think?" said a strange voice from behind me. *Which didn't help the prickling the least little bit.* "I come here often, at night, because of the colors."

I turned around slowly.

There was no one there.

"The colors?" I asked, trying not to croak. My voice that is.

"The creatures. The water. The way the light moves through the tanks and out again. It changes, you know."

"What does?" I thought I saw a shadow fall across the jade luminescence of a long, low tank.

"The light. It's made up of many colors, you see. It only looks white most of the time." The shadow darkened. "Did you know that when you look at a red rose, it isn't really red?"

"It isn't?"

"No." The voice was young, almost girlish. Almost but not quite. "The petals absorb all of the colors of the spectrum except crimson, which is reflected back to your sight and registered on the retinas of your eyeballs." There was a hint of bored petulance in his tone and I wondered if puberty would tweak it to surliness or nurture something nastier within the next several years. "So you might say that the rose is every color but red."

"I—I hadn't quite thought of it that way," I said.

"As long as you're going to think about it, consider that all reflected colors are the ones that are essentially reject-ed by the objects that fall within our vision . . ."

"Interesting," I said, trying to figure out just who and— more importantly—*what* I was talking to. "Reflection is one thing," I added, nodding at a spill of turquoise light from the nearest aquarium, "but refraction is quite another. Does the water strip—absorb all the colors save one?"

"I had not considered . . ." the shadow said, taking on substance. "But it stands to reason that the visible color is, once again, the rejected hue from the spectrum. All other wavelengths are absorbed by the transmitting medium." A young boy stepped out of the darkened recesses between two tanks on opposing tables. "Which begs the question . . ."

"The question?" I didn't like the sound of this. I couldn't think of a single question within recent memory that I had ended up liking. And, lately, they had taken a definite turn for the worse. An orange flatworm with green striations oozed up the side of the tank behind the boy. Perhaps I should have thought of the creature as every color but orange with green markings. But I was a little distracted by the fact that I was able to debate the thing's color scheme since it remained visible through the kid's upper torso.

"You and I," the ghostly boy said. "What are we?"

Such stuff as dreams are made of, Prospero had said. A man grown weary of life and looking forward to escaping life's tempests in the restful oblivion of the Big Sleep—so maybe Shakespeare's magician was a tad biased.

"Are we the rejected light?" the kid continued. "A reflected color while the rest of what we were is absorbed into the landscape?"

Like I said: not particularly keen on the questions that were coming my way these days.

"You're new, aren't you?" he asked, switching to another question that I hesitated to answer directly. "I haven't seen you around here before. I'm Beppo." He didn't stick out his hand; what would be the point?

Beppo? Were the ghosts of the Marx Brothers waiting in the wings? What was next? *Smurf Nazis Must Die*? I was definitely past tired and edging over into hallucinatory. "Robert Walton," I said, trying to keep my guard up and simultaneously letting myself go with the flow.

"That name sounds very familiar. Should I know you?"

That depended upon the reading proclivities of twelve-year-old boys. "I shouldn't think so." And dead ones at that.

Of course, given that context perhaps I should have selected a nom de plume from *Rebecca of Sunnybrook Farm*.

"Did you have an accident or are you a part of one of Grandpère's experiments?"

"Beg pardon?"

"Where's your body, Herr Walton? Is it in one of the labs? Down in the morgue? Or did you find your way here on your own from outside?"

"Uh, I don't know," I lied. "I'm kind of confused." That, at least, was pretty truthful. "Where am I?"

"Brut Adler. The Eagle's Aerie. Or, perhaps more accurately, the Eagle's Rookery. Grandpère hatches many fledglings here in this granite nest. Someday soon he will hatch himself and be reborn. Perhaps then he will rename it *der Phönix Scheiterhaufen*—the Pyre of the Phoenix." He said this with a curious mix of pride and wistfulness.

"Really?" I said. "And how is he going to do that? Some kind of breakthrough in blood chemistry?"

"If only it were that simple," answered a new voice. The other nurse from my hospital room back in New York had just entered the lab and she did not seem happy. "He prepares to be reborn by killing the unborn! He butchers babies so that he may live a second life! And a third! And *Gott* knows how many more!"

The boy howled back at her, rage suffusing his features, contorting his face into a nightmare mask of hate and fear and even sorrow. He ran at her, his arms straight out from his sides, his hands balled into impotent fists. "Shut up, Gretchen! Shut up! Shut up! *Shut! Up!*"

He ran into her without slowing—passed completely through her—and continued on, passing through the wall. His wail was audible for a few moments more, fading down the outside corridor.

She sighed as she stared at the wall where he had phased through. "I really shouldn't have been so blunt in front of Beppo."

"Any boy's liable to take it personally when you dis his grandfather."

"Any boy, perhaps," she said absently, "but for Beppo any attack upon his grandpère is the same as an attack upon himself . . ."

The tumblers in my brain spun and finally clicked into place: *the twins, the spitting image of their old man, the reproductions of my unborn wife and daughter . . .*

I turned toward the new apparition. Yep. Semitransparent and wearing a white gown instead of a nurse's uniform, now. But no question about it: she was the spitting image of the nurse who had assisted the Pipt twins and Terry-call-me-T in my hospital room a few hours earlier this evening. Entirely too much spitting in the imagery department.

"Gretchen?"

She had turned to consider the boy's exit but now turned back toward me. "Yes?"

"Your name isn't Ilse?"

Definite frown: "No."

She had the look of one who had grown accustomed to her noncorporeal state. Which meant she hadn't kicked the bucket in the last several hours. "And you don't have a twin sister, do you." I don't think it was really a question at this point.

Her frown became a harsh line slashing across the bottom of her otherwise pretty face. "I have no sisters."

"A daughter, then? More than one daughter?"

"I said that he butchered babies," she finally answered in a tremulous voice. "I didn't say that they all died!"

Gretchen followed me as I stalked out of the lab and began trotting down the corridor in a half march. I set a deliberate pace that enabled me to poke my head through a door and check a new room every forty-five seconds.

"Isn't it rich?" I muttered harshly. "Aren't we a pair?"

"What?" she asked, hurrying after as I checked another lab with refrigerated storage space.

"But where are the clones?" I grumbled, "Quick, send in the clones . . ."

"Then you know."

"Know? No. Not everything. But I should have guessed sooner. The Pipt-Nikidik connection for example."

"The what?"

"If laughing boy was going to be consistent with his little Oz code names then I should have connected Dr. Dick to Dr. Pipt right away. In *The Marvelous Land of Oz* Dr. Nikidik was the original inventor of the Powder of Life and lived in the mountains of the Gillikin Country. Later, in *The Road to Oz*, Dyna reported his fall from a great precipice and he was presumed dead. Interestingly enough, when Dr. Pipt turns up later in *The Patchwork Girl of Oz* AND also has the recipe for the Powder of Life, one has to wonder if maybe Nikidik faked his death and changed his name to avoid persecution for the illegal practice of magic."

"What are you talking about?"

"Serendipity. Synchronicity." I stuck my head into another room. "How many of him are there?"

"How many?"

"Yeah. I make two from the pair of docs—" Oh. *Paradox.* That was the stupid pun that kept rattling around in my subconscious. I grimaced. "—the twins— except they aren't really twins. Any more than Ilse is your sister or your daughter." I moved on to the next door. Surprise: a private gym. "So, how many?"

Her alabaster and transparent flesh was a wash when it came to displaying contrasts; I almost missed the furrowing of her brow.

"What? Can't count that high?"

She shook her head. "It is just that I don't know *how* to

count them. Do you ask how many there have been? Or how many are currently viable?"

"What? 'Viable'? You mean unlike our boy Beppo?"

"The boy's death was an accident. He, at least, survived for more than a decade. Some died while still in the womb. Others . . ."

"Others what?"

"The handivork of *Gott* is not mocked, Mr. . . ."

What name had I just given Beppo? "Um, Krempe."

"Mr. Krempe. The same samples, the same treatments, the same procedures—the same flesh—and the outcomes vary. Some don't survive. Some *shouldn't* survive. *Herr Doktor* has become very particular as the time for his consummation draws near. He tolerates little short of perfection."

I stopped sticking my head through doors and walls and brought my face close to hers. "You're telling me Pipt had other versions of himself destroyed?"

"In some cases it was the humane thing to do. In others . . ." Her voice trailed off.

"Yeah, I'll bet. I've seen *Herr Doktor*'s handiwork."

"That is not to say he destroyed them all. He keeps several alive downstairs to better understand what can go wrong with the processes."

I turned away and began checking doors again, wondering what fresh horrors I might find if I looked in enough of the rooms. "So tell me, Gretchen—alive and viable—how many Pipts has this guy pooped?" The next room contained a small indoor swimming pool.

"There are seventeen living children between six months and twelve years of age. Nine adolescents. Seven adults in their twenties and thirties. Three in their forties. One in his fifties. He is the most dangerous. . . ."

"Oh? And why is that?" A private bathroom and sauna lay behind the next door: I was getting closer to Pipt Prime.

"*Herr Doktor* did not perfect the biochemical transmission of memory engrams until a month or so ago. He experimented with controlled environments, hypnosis, and duplicating key events and experiences during his doppelgangers' development."

"Sort of a *Boys From Brazil* scenario, huh?"

"I do not understand."

The next room was a private office. The furniture and décor more appropriate to a CEO than a midlevel manager. "Read Ira Levin. Most people prefer *Rosemary's Baby*. But I'm more interested in his 'monsters are made, not born' thesis."

"Well, his oldest doppelganger received conditioning that was designed to enhance certain aspects of *Herr Doktor*'s personality beyond the original parameters and this turned out to be a mistake that even he admits to. The man must be watched carefully and constantly.

"In the decades that have passed since his first attempts, he has worked toward perfecting a chemical means of memory transfer. It has taken decades of bloody sacrifice and horrific failure but he now believes he has made a critical breakthrough. Very soon now he will attempt to place his actual memories within an infant version of himself!"

I thought about the lab with the multitude of flatworm species creeping about the aquariums adorning the walls and benches and tables and remembered the Thompson and McConnell "worm-running" experiments from the previous century. "Don't tell me the doc plans on grinding up his brain and feeding it to his clones?" It was something that the Nazis might have experimented with in the death camps of World War Two but no one in their right mind would seriously attempt with another human being—much less themselves. Of course the evidence that Pipt was in his right mind was seriously AWOL at this point. A *Platyhelminthes* with flatworm instincts and impulses was a far cry from the complex organism with higher brain functions that calls itself human.

She shook her head. "Not grind up, no. He extracts fluid from the brain tissue—I do not understand the full process. It is most effective when reinjected into an embryonic host and allowed to wash over fetal brain cells."

"And the doctor, himself, would survive this process?"

"No. Not the original brain tissue, anyway. That is why he has waited to perfect the process with many test subjects . . ."

That was creepy. Even more so if he was using cloned versions of himself as guinea pigs.

The *physical* clones of Pipt wouldn't possess identical psyches: he couldn't mimeograph the original mind and memories without destroying it. The question was how many versions of himself had he lobotomized trying to develop the means to perpetuate his own consciousness in successive copies? They might not possess the same thoughts and memories as his own but he would have a means of discovering how effective the actual transfer of

memory and personality might be if he was willing to sacrifice enough human replicants over an extended number
of years. I shivered. It was a monstrous concept to under-
take with any group of test subjects . . .

To engage in a premeditated pogrom of atrocities upon
the mirror versions of your very own flesh and blood? My
mind just couldn't get a foothold there. Instead it turned
its attention to whether or not Pipt might have finally discovered how much of the human personality template was
"nature versus nurture"—any distraction as a port in the
emotional storm.

But I couldn't afford any distractions now. "Gretchen?
You said that the doctor has finally achieved the breakthrough he's been searching for all these long years?"

She nodded. "Well, actually, he finalized the process
several years ago."

"Then what's he waiting for?" I asked. But I already had
a pretty good idea as to the answer.

"He is afraid. What if something goes wrong? What if
the transference is more like a copy and the destruction of
the original is still death and final oblivion?"

I nodded. "So what's finally changed all that—besides
his time running out?"

"He speaks of another breakthrough these days," she
said. "A new kind of blood infusion that has recently come
to his attention."

"A blood infusion that might enable him to survive the
process," I guessed, "and even permit a different
approach to longevity if not immortality."

"Yes. It is to be delivered tonight."

"And Hitler?"

"I'm sorry, I do not understand."

"You're sure there's no *Fourth* Reich, spooky resurrection, rule-the-world plot afoot?"

She looked at me like I was speaking gibberish.

"Yeah, well, hidden castle in the mountains, Nazis working on secret experiments, the laws of God and Man being broken—or at least severely dented—I can't believe that Hitler's brain or clone or cryogenic carcass isn't behind one of these doors. Or the box that Jay is bringing down the aisle."

She looked around in confusion.

"Never mind." I stuck my head through the next door *and found myself looking at Adolph Hitler in full dress uniform, very much in the prime of his life.*

I jumped a little: the painting was that realistic.

I pushed on through the door and found myself in a spacious library. Not a lot of books but a whole lotta fireplace off to my left. The fireplace I had last seen in Pipt's psychotropic email. The fire was damped for the night and the main lights were off except for a single beam from a track light in the ceiling.

Der Führer was attired in an army greatcoat while the painting's other occupant wore the full-dress uniform of the Waffen SS. He was a captain and the breast of his tunic bore several medals. The so-called mastermind of the so-called master race clasped his hand in a congratulatory manner. There was a brass inscription plate affixed to the bottom part of the frame but, as the subjects were rendered in life size the frame stretched from just inches off the floor to nearly a foot above my head. As I moved closer, I could see that the painting was very detailed, adding to the initial impression of realism. What most drew my eyes, however, was the face of the other man in the portrait. The rounded head, the dark hair and eyes, were becoming more and more familiar with each passing day: a younger version of the mysterious Dr. Pipt, an older version of Beppo, an exact match for the pair of docs who had shanghaied me from the hospital. As I got right up to the canvas my eyes moved to the inscription near the floor and I knelt to make out the finely etched script:

> *1942—The Iron Cross—First Class,*
> *The Black Badge for the Wounded,*
> *The Medal for the Care of the German People—*
> *Awarded to Captain Josef Mengele, M.D.*

The room lurched around me and I fell through the floor.

Mengele!

No one person better embodied the horrors of the Nazi death camps than Dr. Josef Mengele.

The idea of six million human beings rounded up and systematically sent to their deaths is horror enough but the genocide of the Jews is only part of the story.

The forced relocations, separation of family members, cattlelike internments, death by gassing or bullet, mass immolation of human corpses—all seem almost humane and even prosaic by comparison when the stone of history is turned over and the hidden, squirmy atrocities are brought forth from the dark, secret places.

The concentration camps were more than just holding

pens for Germany's undesirables. More than just waiting rooms until the showers and the furnaces were able to play catch-up. Some were special windows into Hell where portions were set aside to serve as horrific research facilities. And staffed by scientists who carried clipboards instead of pitchforks and whose heads sported surgical caps in place of horns.

Here were opportunities to research the effects of extreme cold on the human body. For every hundred Jews or Poles or Gypsies forced to endure frigid temperatures and then treated to painful, often fatal, rewarming experiments—perhaps a German soldier serving on the Russian front might someday benefit.

Perhaps.

Battlefield medicine could be advanced without risking the Fatherland's troops. Prisoners could be shot, burned, have ground glass, sawdust, caustic agents rubbed into their wounds—and then be restrained while gangrene and sepsis taught the doctors what they wanted to know about pain thresholds, morbidity, shock, and the human will to live.

Biological warfare was birthed in the camp clinics as children were injected with infectious agents and progress of each disease was painstakingly documented and mapped.

Gruesome accounts were legion. But Mengele's reputation overshadowed all the others, rendering them into nothing more than mere sideshow thrills outside the dark castle of horrors that was Auschwitz-Birkenau.

He was Hitler's point man on eugenics research.

That was the given excuse.

It was one thing to cleanse the earth of the subhuman races. The Aryans believed they were destined to be the master race, the über ideal. But as superior as the German peoples were supposed to be to the flotsam and jetsam that had infiltrated Europe, they knew that they still fell short, as a whole, to the fuller potential that lay dormant within their own genes. While they were supposedly further up the evolutionary ladder than the rest of mankind, there were rungs yet to climb. There was still a gulf between "man" and "superman" that the Nazis' selective breeding programs had failed to close.

Enter Captain Josef Mengele, M.D. War hero, medical doctor with a background in eugenics, party loyalist, and cold-blooded sociopath. The death camp at Auschwitz, Poland, was the perfect laboratory to explore the full spectrum of cruelties conceivable by the human mind and their effects upon the human body.

He was movie-star handsome, well groomed, and always impeccably attired—dark green tunic neatly pressed, medals prominently on display, death's-head SS cap jauntily tilted to the side revealing a precision part in his dark, wavy hair. Even amidst the dust or the mud of the unloading docks, his black boots were always polished to a mirror shine, his white gloves immaculate—except for those occasions when his temper would flare and he would lay hands on a prisoner in a bloody-minded rage.

He would meet the trains bringing new consignments of human misery to the camp every day. Other doctors involved in the selection process required drugs or alcohol to help them face this repugnant task. Only Mengele seemed to enjoy the process, showing up even on his days off to select his human guinea pigs and consign the rest to the work details, gas chambers and the furnaces.

For the most part he stood apart and above, flicking his riding crop to the left or the right, as he divided the prisoners onto separate paths. To the right, life. The showers that were not showers waited on the path to the left. It was calculated that, one by one, he sent four hundred thousand souls to the gas chambers. Infants, children, parents, grandparents—generations selected for extermination one soul at a time

For many, however, the path to the right was not the kinder choice.

Hitler had passed laws forbidding the vivisection of animals for any purpose, even medical research. No such laws protected the Poles or the Gypsies or the Jews. Mengele's approach to his research was less that of a physician and more like a Torquemada, torturing the flesh to yield up secrets yet unimagined. Twins were a particular obsession for him and he managed to acquire nearly 1500 sets between 1943 and '44. The majority were sent to Cell Block 10, where they were housed with dwarves and other "exotic" specimens to occupy what came to be known as "Mengele's Zoo."

Less than two hundred children survived by the war's end.

The stories that emerged after the war shocked even the battle-hardened veterans of brutal campaigns and vicious hand-to-hand combat.

Mengele, the survivors testified, would take daily blood samples from the children, sometimes in such great and persistent quantities that they bled to death into his syringes. He would exchange the blood between twins of differing blood types just to measure and record the full range and varieties of suffering that resulted. A mother testified that Mengele tried to starve her newborn baby to death to see how long it could survive without food. The experiment was spoiled after six days when she killed her own child to end its suffering. Multiple eyewitnesses told of the dissection of live infants and major surgeries performed without anesthesia, including a stomach operation on one occasion and the removal of a living patient's heart upon another.

Presaging the Crystal Gayle hit by nearly forty years, Mengele injected methylene blue dye into the irises of brown-eyed children. Perhaps he hoped to find a way to bring his own, darker coloring closer to the Aryan ideal. The results were predictable: some died, some went blind, all suffered horribly. One of the walls in his office was studded with the human eyeballs of his failures, pinned like a butterfly collection for everyone to see.

Everyone else, that is.

Twins were forcibly separated and placed in isolation cages, then subjected to a variety of stimuli to see how they would react. Others were surgically joined together to artificially create grotesque "Siamese" twins.

Men were castrated without anesthetics, women endured electrical shocks to their genitals for the "scientific" purpose of measuring their endurance. A group of Polish nuns were hideously burned when Mengele experimented with using an X-ray machine for sterilization techniques.

One eyewitness account, near the war's end, placed

him at a particularly horrific event. The allies were approaching and the furnaces were woefully behind in eradicating the evidence of German war crimes. Everything was in short supply including Zyklon-B, ammunition, and petrol. A pit was excavated. Firewood dropped in. Enough gasoline was added to make a good start but the calculations depended upon the wood and then the fatty tissues to sustain the combustion process.

Mengele arrived with a coterie of SS officers on their motorcycles, laughing and joking, before the trucks, ten in all, were backed up to the edge of the pit. As the human cargo was dumped into the heart of the flames, some children actually survived long enough to clamber over the other bodies and climb, screaming, up the sides of their earthen hell. Some of the officers had to take sticks and push them back in until they were overcome by the flames or the smoke from their own charred flesh.

Shortly thereafter, the future "Doctor Pipt," along with hundreds of guards and medical personnel, slipped away in the night as Soviet troops advanced on Berlin. January 17, 1945.

I fell three full levels before I caught myself. I just managed to reassert the solidity of my surroundings before plummeting into the solid bedrock beneath Brut Adler and, even then, I had to fight an ongoing sense of disorientation.

I'd suspected from the beginning that "Pipt" was merely an alias, a code name designed to obscure any trail back to the "good" doctor. But even after tangling with demons and vampires and necromancers, I suddenly found myself very unnerved by the thought of one feeble old Nazi.

Well, not just one . . .

But they were still human and still fairly limited in number—thanks to Mengele's self-experimentation. *For now.*

The question was how could I throw a monkey wrench in the works while I was having this out-of-my-body experience? I could borrow some flesh and bones, perhaps? And then what? One guy against a fortress full of Nazis? Even if I could find enough plastique in the various weapons lockers, and acquire detonators, and wire everything to go off simultaneously, AND not have anyone else find me or the charges first—I wouldn't know where to place the bombs so that *all* of the Pipts' destruction could be guaranteed. No, my best bet was to find a phone and call the Israelis. *They* wouldn't be fooled again.

They hunted him throughout the years. First the Allies, in their pursuit of war criminals, and finally Wiesenthal and the Jews who understood that monsters must be irrevocably staked and exorcised or they will return again and again to haunt succeeding generations.

Mengele was captured and held as an anonymous POW near Munich but escaped before his true identity could be established. Assuming a false identity, he worked as a farmhand near his native Gunzburg until it became clear that he would never be safe in Europe. With the help of his father's business connections, he obtained Italian residency papers and, from there, escaped to South America in 1949.

Argentina turned out to be the Nazi Riviera of the post-war decades. Juan Perón ruled his country with an iron hand but was popular with his people. The German expatriates understood life under a dictatorship and how to be an asset to those wielding the power. There and elsewhere the postwar Nazi networks provided aid, shelter, intel, and escape routes to those who had worn the death's-heads and the twinned lightning bolts during Germany's fevered nightmare. The Underground established a series of "ratlines" to Argentina, Brazil and Paraguay, funneling refugees and resources. The Angel of Death benefited in both aspects and eluded arrest and capture for thirty more years.

In the end, it was said, he escaped man's justice but not God's. Mengele was relaxing at Beritoga Beach in Brazil in 1979 when he decided to go for a swim in the ocean. Away from the shore, he suffered a stroke and began to drown. No one knows whether it was the cerebral infarction or the aspiration of seawater that did what no human jury was able to accomplish. If it was the Hand of God, it seemed to many that He had been rather indolent in finally getting around to it. The only thing that the witnesses agreed upon was, that by the time the man the locals knew as Wolfgang Gerhard was brought to shore by the other swimmers, he was dead. Dr. Josef Mengele had gone to face a greater Tribunal of Justice than the one at Nuremburg.

So the story goes.

The rumors didn't even leak out until 1985 and not everyone bought into the forensic evidence after the body was exhumed. It wasn't until 1992 that DNA was taken from a bone and compared to Mengele's wife, Irene, and son, Rolf, that the casebooks were finally closed. The body in the Brazilian grave had Josef Mengele's DNA.

Yeah.

Sure.

And so did several dozen other people here in Chez Xerox.

As I began working my way out and up I was shaking my head—as if that simple act would clear it of nightmarish thoughts.

Vampires.

Werewolves.

Zombies.

Perhaps the classic horror stories are meant to distract us from the fact that the worst monsters are the human ones . . .

I ghosted through a maze of pipework that seemed related to the fortress's heating plant and stuck my head through a wall in search of an exit.

The next room had a furnace, an old-fashioned iron-works monster that seemed divorced from the tangle of ductwork in the adjacent spaces. Dim orange slots flickered in its heavily gated maw but the room was overlaid with a ghastly green glow that I could attribute to no single light source. The caged incandescent bulbs that lit the room for human eyes were switched off.

As I looked around I heard the faint whimpers of a child. The next room beyond? As I walked toward the far wall, a baby's wails joined in: two voices. A third began to keen as I pushed my head through the far wall. Nothing.

Blessed silence. I had stuck my noncorporeal skull into solid bedrock.

The sounds increased and multiplied as I did a reverse ostrich and checked the other walls: more bedrock and an outer chamber with something that looked like a cross between a dumbwaiter and a freight elevator. Many voices were in full cry, now, sounding distant yet present, like someone had upset an entire preschool just next door.

Beyond the chamber was a hallway. As I stepped outside the sound receded. I turned and stuck my head back in. The volume grew. I considered the stainless steel tables in the dim blue glow. The shelves along the walls with their profusion of bottles, containers, and cases. Cabinets. Countertops with instruments and tools. A couple of sinks. A display case.

In the display case were three rows of skulls ranging in size from infant to adolescent. Some were distorted in disturbing ways. Most were blackened with soot and charring. All glowed a bright blue in the dimness. As the wailing grew in crescendo, the glass front of the case rattled and vibrated.

I turned and ran.

Chapter Twenty-One

I USED EVERY CURSE word, every phrase of profanity I knew before I got to the top of the mushy stairs and up to the next level. I was working on inventing new words, a whole new profane language, when the guard came around the corner.

Actually he looked more like the night watchman at a Sandals resort than the "new and improved" *Schutzstaffel*, upgrade 2.0. His khaki "uniform" was nothing more than a pair of pleated-front Dockers and casual shirt with faux epaulettes. On one side of a Sam Browne belt he wore a holstered sidearm with a snap-down cover, on the other, a large ring of keys—a surprise as I thought everyone had converted to hi-tech electronic pass cards by now. A small walkie-talkie was jammed in his hip pocket. A heavy, six D-cell, baton flashlight swung loosely in his right hand and he occasionally spun it in an elaborate pattern suggesting that illumination might be its secondary function.

First things first: I wasn't going to accomplish much as long as I was Mister Permeable. I had to get some solidity if I was going to do anything about the Reich-ous Brothers. And since wolves were in short supply and opposable thumbs were a marked improvement over paws, I turned and followed him, trying to figure out just when and where to pimp my ride.

The perfect opportunity came just one floor down and ten minutes later when we ducked into a bathroom. Instead of "number one" or "number two" he did "number three": smoked a cigarette while the vent fan sucked the evidence out of the air. Alone, out of sight, stationary—I had sufficient time to relax and refocus, visualizing the chakras, the energy gates, and preparing for insertion.

I dove, twisting in mid-arc, and the trajectory was perfect.

Until I bounced off instead of in.

Had I missed? I tried again.

Bounced again!

It was like the gate was open and yet still closed. Were humans and wolves that different? I mean, obviously they were but Pauly was evidence that other spooks could hitch a ride inside a man's head. So why couldn't I?

I didn't have the time to figure this out by trial and error. The Wendigo had accelerated my learning curve by poking around in my own not-so-solid skull; maybe another adjustment was in order.

I went ripping back upstairs and shot through a blurred succession of rooms until I was out the front door.

The helipad was empty so either the copter hadn't arrived yet or it had already lifted off again. Which? The landing lights were turned on—they'd been dark when I had arrived. I looked around: no Wendigo—young Indian maiden or giant, rotting crone.

There was, however, a lone gray wolf. It was pacing about, outside the great double doors, on the "porch" as it were.

"Wendy?" I asked.

It trotted up to me and sat back on its skinny haunches.

"Are you in there?"

"The dark spirit that brought you here has moved higher up and around to the other side of the east tower."

I did a good old-fashioned double take. Vampires and demons and zombies do tend to expand one's horizons but they don't really prepare you for a conversation with a wolf. Well, okay, a werewolf fiancée does prepare you somewhat but it is still rather disconcerting to have a canine jaw drop open and have a human voice emerge.

"Really, Father, I am quite concerned about some of the company that you choose to keep," the wolf said.

The voice was disturbingly normal, not the guttural growl that Lupé produced when she tried to speak in wolf form. And I noticed that the jaw remained open: the mouth did not actually form the words; it merely got out of the way of the speech that emanated from somewhere inside.

But how? If a werewolf's vocal chords were hard pressed to approximate human speech then . . .

And that's when the other part of the riddle caught up to me.

"Father?"

The wolf inclined its head. "Do you prefer 'Dad?' Or

should we keep this on a first name basis until I'm actually born?"

"You . . . I'm . . . that is . . ." The questions were rear-ending each other like a fifty-car pileup on the Long Island Expressway. "You have a name?"

"I have many names. As do you. As does nearly every-one: it doesn't begin here, you know. We have a name for every time and every place that we inhabit. And since I am still unborn and you and mother have not yet named me—unless 'Will' . . ."

I waved that idea away. "Forgive me but I haven't really had any time to think about it."

"Of course." The wolf, swear to God, actually sighed! "There is so much to do and so little time to do it in. If I should not be born, then this particular question becomes moot."

"Wait a minute! Lupé! She's okay? The last I knew she was caught between pack politics and a vengeful demon."

"Mother is safe for now. She has acquired a powerful protector. It remains to be seen, however, if she can stay safe while involved with you. It is not just a question of your enemies but, as you say, the politics of the pack. And until the current situations are resolved here and in New York, you are both at extreme risk." His head dropped again. "As am I."

"Is that why you're here? To make sure we all get the right to life?"

"For myself?" I didn't think it was possible for a wolf to shrug but the hunching of his shoulders was very eloquent. "A door closes . . . another opens. Although I would be sorry to not have the opportunity to try this particular portal. "But there are more important destinies at risk beyond my own."

"No kidding," I said. "At least now that you're here and a little more vocal, maybe I can get some answers to some questions."

"Maybe," he said. And growled. And lunged at me!

And through me!

I whirled and watched as the wolf attacked a guard who had just come through the outer doors. The man wasn't expecting a canine attacker and went down primarily due to the element of surprise. His bulky parka made maneuvering difficult so he was staying down for the moment. The wolf's body, however, was suffering from malnutrition and my son seemed rather inept as a four-legged predator.

"Dad!" he panted. "Hurry!"

"Hurry what?" I rushed to help but how could I? "I don't have a physical form!"

"Take his!"

"I can't! I can't do humans! I can't enter their chakra gates!"

"Try another way!"

"What other way?"

"I didn't use any chakra stuff to get inside this wolf. It's like it was my blood birthright."

"Courtesy of your mother's lycanthropy, no doubt."

"I'm sure that your blood had something to do with it."

"There is power in the blood," I said, quoting the old gospel hymn. This really wasn't the time or place to argue that blood or genetics seemed a non sequitur to the subject of soul transference. "The problem is he isn't a wolf and I'm not a lycanthrope."

"The blood! That's where your power lies. Use the blood!" His jaws snapped at the man's face: sharp teeth grazed a cheek and blood began to trickle down his face.

The guard shrieked and threw the wolf off. My furry ally went rolling and before he could regain his feet, the guard was on his knees, getting a grip on his HK semi.

I jumped, aiming for his cheek instead of the swirling blue gateway over his forehead. The world turned crimson and clover, over and over. A rush of physical sensations and the gravel-strewn ground was rushing up toward my face.

My mother had a cruel streak: she didn't believe in letting me sleep in past noon on school vacations. If I didn't set my alarm clock on my own recognizance, she would let King into my bedroom and the big old boxer would give my face a tongue bath until I erupted from a tangle of sheets with cries of disgust and dismay.

This time there were no sheets, no soft mattress, no summer sun casting leafy silhouettes on my bedroom wall. It was cold and the ground was hard with flinty, sharp points of stone that turned any movement into a topography of discomfort. King's woeful bus-smash face was replaced by the elongated muzzle and crafty-eyed visage of my—er—boy-to-be. The tongue, however, seemed pretty much the same.

"Okay, okay! I'm awake!" I sat up and attempted to wipe the bulk of the wolf slobber off of my face. "How did you know that blood would be the gateway?"

"It is your gift and your curse. It is the seat of your power."

"Even so, a hell of a lucky guess. Now, where were we?" I tried to climb to my feet. My newfound flesh wasn't immediately cooperative. "Oh yes, you were refusing to answer my questions. This doesn't bode well: my son isn't even born, yet, and already he's lying to his father."

"I'm not lying! I'm being moderately evasive!"

"Nevertheless, mister, consider yourself grounded."

"Look, I know a lot of things that I'm not allowed to talk about. I'm breaking all kinds of rules just by being here in the first place."

"Which brings me to my next question—"

The wolf put a paw on my chest. "No questions. Think of it like I'm Captain Picard and you're asking me to violate the Prime Directive."

"Well, I take more of a Captain Kirk approach to rules, myself."

"No kiddin'."

I struggled up to my knees. The flesh I wore felt heavy after the incredible lightness of being without. Somewhere down deep in the cellar, beneath my consciousness, the body's original occupant crouched in the darkness and shuddered with his hands over his face. With any luck he'd stay down there until it was time for me to leave. "So this place you came from before you came here, they get all the Trek editions first run? Or just in syndication?"

"Dad . . ."

I was lucky that Whozits was too stunned by the turn of events to resist my taking over his body. It was hard enough just learning how to walk all over again. All aboard the Disorient Express. By the time I got the outer door open I was able to stagger about after a fashion but I had zombies in my backyard that shuffled with more grace and speed on less flesh and bone.

Will—I couldn't keep calling him "wolf"—looked up at me as I pulled the door closed behind us. "What's the plan?"

"What do you mean, what's the plan? You're the one who's omniscient!"

"I never said I was omniscient, I only said that I know some things that I can't get all loose-lipped about. This is your gig; I'm only trying to lend a helping hand."

We both stared down at his paws.

"You'd think I'd get some credit for crossing all sorts of metaphysical barriers, chasing after you all the way to New York, watching out for your innards after you lost your outtards, hitching a ride with Witch Hazel out there all the way to the Rockies, and then pushing this poor old wolf carcass up the mountainside to help you again. Omniscient? If I'd known you were going to give me this much grief I would've stayed home and hung around haunting Mom."

"Sorry," I said. "I'm having a bad day. You've got to admit these aren't the ideal circumstances for meeting your future offspring."

"Not if they're human, anyway," he agreed, scratching at something behind his ear.

"It's not that. It's all this!" I swept the hall with my arm. "Nazis. Secret mountain fortress. Laboratories equipped with advanced genetics technology. They've cloned my dead wife and daughter and are using their fetuses as hostages! Who knows? Maybe they've cloned Adolf Hitler."

Will shook his head. "It's been done."

I stared at him, aghast. "It has?"

"Another story, not here, not your karma." He hesitated. "I don't think . . ." He shook his muzzle. "Not now, not tonight. Try to stay focused, Dad. Plenty of fascist fish to fry later if all goes well tonight."

"Swell. Even if you do learn from history, you're doomed to repeat it." I turned and staggered up the hallway toward the inner door.

"So what is the plan?" he called after me.

"I'm working on it."

I opened the inner door. Another guard met me on his way out. Cigarette-break man.

"Hans? What happened?"

"What?" I hoped my voice didn't sound strange.

He was too busy peering at my face to pay attention to the vocal inflections of a single syllable response. He wasn't one of Mengele's clones. That shouldn't be too surprising as Gretchen had counted eleven surviving adult replicants and I'd already noted at least four times that many in the barracks, alone.

"You look terrible!" the guard exclaimed. "Did you have an accident?"

"Uh," I half-coughed, half-grunted, "yeah. Fell down."

"The transport will be here soon but I think I have enough time to help you down to the infirmary if you need assistance."

Decisions, decisions . . .

"Don't move!" he whispered. His hand went down to his holster and unsnapped the cover.

Uh-oh.

"There's a wolf behind you."

Oh. *Oh!*

I clenched my right hand into a fist. Then I stepped in as he drew his pistol and punched his jaw with a swift uppercut.

He stepped back and looked at me in disbelief as I shook my stinging knuckles. "What did you do that for?"

Apparently Hans was a "lefty." And I had grown overly dependant on the preternatural strength of my former body.

"Uh, Greenpeace?" I said. As Will leapt past me and knocked the man to the ground.

I pointed the Heckler & Koch at man and beast as they rolled over and over but there was no way to get a clear shot. And putting a fortress full of Nazis on red-alert was not part of any potential plan that I was still working on.

Suddenly it was over. The guard got a firm grip on the wolf's head and gave it a wrenching twist. There was an audible cracking sound and the beast went limp.

"Son of a bitch!" I hissed as I swung the automatic weapon up and at the man's head.

He threw up his hands. "Whoa, Dad; best not to invoke family lineage in the house of one's enemies."

"Will?"

The guard wiped some blood from his hand onto the fur of the dead wolf and climbed back to his feet. "In the flesh." He staggered a little. "Bipedal. Going to have to work on this balance thing a little." He felt his face. "And what happened to all of those wonderful smells?"

He staggered toward me a little and I felt tears gather at the edge of my eyes.

"Dad? What's wrong?"

I shook my head and sniffed. "I just saw my baby boy take his first steps."

We killed another ten minutes in the temperature lock before returning to the main "lobby" of Brut Adler. It took that long for Will to get his "land legs" and me to get the pass code to the inner blast doors from the gibbering consciousness that cringed in my current body's hind-brain.

"And you say it takes babies like forever to learn how to do this?" he asked as I placed "my" palm on the scanner beside the double doors and keyed in what I hoped was the correct sequence of numbers. "Man, I'm going to be a prodigy when I'm finally born."

"I wouldn't get too cocky, boy. You'll be working with a carcass that's still evolving from a quadruped to a biped with no muscle tone." There was a click and I pushed the door on the right open. "Besides, I'm betting the rules will still apply to you, as well."

"Rules?"

"Don't be surprised if you come into this world with a hefty case of amnesia, just like the rest of us." I poked my head through the opening and looked around. The lobby was still deserted. "Of course, if your memory is as wiped as the rest of ours is, there will be nothing to be surprised about."

"Seems like poor planning on God's part," Will mused as we moved across the mezzanine.

"Don't get me started on God's grand design," I griped as we paused at the foot of the staircase. "My first question, if we ever meet in the hereafter, is why do two-year-olds have so much energy with nothing to do while grownups—particularly parents—have so much to do and so little energy. Seems like an inequitable distribution of resources to me."

"If you like, I'll ask for you when I go back."

I turned and looked at him. "You've met God?"

"Not exactly, no. But I've met some who say they're on a first-name basis with Him."

"Oh. Well. It's pretty much the same here." I raised a foot to the first step and stopped. As difficult as climbing the stairs was in a noncorporeal body, I had the distinct feeling it was going to be harder wearing flesh other than my own. And Will?

"Can we take the elevator?"

"Okay," I said, turning back to the glassed-in cage at the big room's center, "but just this once for you."

"And lets make a pit stop at the nearest restroom."

"Why? You gotta go already?"

"No." He reached out and touched my bleeding cheek. "You need to wash your Hans."

"I'm beginning to understand why some animals eat their young."

"Plenty of time to give me pre-childhood complexes later, Pop. We still don't have a plan," he pointed out as we waited for the lift to descend. "Are we going to raid the weapons lockers and go all berzerko, running around like the Dirty Dozen?"

"If you're going to use movie analogies you'd more likely end up with Butch and Sundance, *mise-en-scène* freeze-frame and fade to black. And what kind of movie subscriptions are you getting on the Other Side? You're a bloodthirsty little tyke for a heavenly personage."

"Who said I was heavenly? There are more places between Heaven and Earth, Horatio, and you can't make assumptions about everyone's zip code."

"Boy," I sighed, "when this is all over we gotta have ourselves a long talk." The elevator arrived and we got on board. "In the meantime, we've got two bodies to liberate and a mad doctor—or doctors—to put out of business. I figure if we can find some kind of communications center, we can call for help."

"Who you gonna call?"

I gave him The Look. "I was thinking," I said slowly, "of calling for backup from my own demesne. Or from Seattle. And that the Simon Wiesenthal foundation might be interested in learning that the Death Angel of Auschwitz didn't actually die in 1979 after all."

"That might work," he agreed. "If you can convince them that you don't sleep with tin foil over your noggin and you're willing to wait a few days. Your people are hours away. How long would it take them to prepare a strike team? Assuming that they were willing to go to the extra effort and risk instead of cutting their losses and electing a new, purer-blooded Doman? And assuming they were able to find this place once they got here? I mean, it's not exactly on the maps and you're only going to be able to land one helicopter at a time if they do find the needle in a mountain range of haystacks. Face it,

Dad, we're it as far as you and your girlfriend's bodies are concerned."

"Deirdre is not my girlfriend."

"That's not the way Mom sees it."

"Your mother is going through some difficulties right now and has made some mistaken assumptions."

"And I should butt out of the grownups' business, right?"

I leaned in as the elevator slowed to a stop. "We will discuss all of this later, at a more appropriate time. Right now we have a job to do."

"You got it, Pops," he said as the doors slid open. "Just tell me what I'm supposed to do."

"You are supposed to meet the copter and assist them in transporting the cargo to the operating theater," Gretchen answered, standing just beyond the doorway. "Fools! What are you doing back here?" Her tone was as cold, now, as it had been warm in the lab scarcely an hour earlier.

Will held up his hand where, as a wolf, he had nipped "himself" before swapping bodies through the blood bridge. "We were attacked by a rabid wolf!"

"*Mein Gott!*" she exclaimed.

"What is it, Ilsa?" Another Mengele-the-Next-Generation appeared behind her.

I suddenly realized that this "Gretchen" was very solid and no ghost at all.

"These *idiots* are not at their posts *und* now Franz, here, says something about a rabid wolf!"

Mengele Junior frowned. "Perhaps I should roust an additional security team from their bunks. We can't risk the cargo—"

"The wolf is dead," I said. "We killed it."

"Then what are you waiting for?" Her face contorted into something ancient and feral. "Get back out there and pray that nothing goes wrong with the cargo or hydrophobia will be the least of your worries!"

I nodded hurriedly and stabbed at the button that would take us back down to the main level. The doors started to close but she caught the edge of one with her hand and leaned in. Hissing just inches from my face she said: "Do you know why they called me the Red Bitch of Buchenwald?"

I swallowed convulsively but my mouth was suddenly dry. "Yes."

"I am remodeling my apartment very soon, now, *und* I am thinking of replacing my lampshades . . ." She gave us both long, searching looks and then released the door.

As the elevator finally began to descend, Will turned to me. "What was that all about?"

I shivered. I didn't feel so invulnerable ensconced, once again, in the frail nest of flesh and sinew and blood. "Ilse Koch," I said. "She was the wife of Karl Koch, the original commandant of the Buchenwald concentration camp during the early years of World War Two. I don't know if they had children but the Antichrist couldn't ask for a better pedigree."

"War criminals?"

"Oh yes! What makes them somewhat unique is that Ilse and Karl were tried by the SS back in 1943 on a whole list of charges ranging from embezzlement to incitement to murder. Seems Karl got a little too wanton on his own human game reserve, even for the Nazis. The judge found him guilty and ordered his execution. Mrs. Koch, however, was acquitted." The doors opened and we exited. I resisted the impulse to look back up over my shoulder to see if she was watching us from an upper-level balcony.

"Pretty serious, though, if the Nazis were trying their own for war crimes," Will said out of the corner of his mouth.

I nodded. "There was a lot of stuff going on at Buchenwald at the time. Medical staff gave friends and relatives souvenirs . . ."

"Souvenirs?"

"Human remains. Shrunken heads. The story was Ilse made lampshades by tanning the skin of some of the inmates. Supposedly she favored the epidermal areas that sported tattoos."

"I can see that might add a festive touch."

I looked at him. "You really aren't a higher being, are you?"

He shrugged. "The apple doesn't fall far from the tree."

"The problem is, Ilse Koch was tried twice after the war and eventually sentenced to life in prison."

"Looks like she got out."

"Yeah, the hard way. She committed suicide in 1967."

"This is very disturbing."

"What? That a woman who is supposed to be dead is still alive? Or that she's too young to have merely faked her death? Or that she doesn't look anything like the surviving photos of the Red Bitch?"

"That my father knows enough about the Nazis to put out his own special edition of *Trivial Pursuit*."

I didn't have a comeback. I was working out the logistics

of blonde, blue-eyed "Gretchen" being the DNA donor for the Ilse Koch revival. It made a certain kind of sense as the photos I'd seen of the original "Red Bitch" were nothing to cross the street for. Perhaps Mengele had petri-dished Gretchen for her physical attributes while utilizing Koch's memory engrams for a more compatible soul mate.

And since this Koch was addressed as Ilsa while the one in my hospital room was called Ilse, there was apparently more than one.

Another thought suddenly occurred. If Mengele *had* perfected memory transfer across differing genetic hosts, then he could reincarnate himself in a different body with a different identity in the future. He could effectively disappear into humanity's gene pool with scarcely a ripple! The clock was ticking and it was more and more apparent that time was running out on a number of fronts.

We came to the double doors leading to the temperature lock and the outside entrance. "Well, so much for Plan A," I muttered as I opened the door to my left and stepped through.

Will followed and started to giggle as the door closed behind us.

"What?"

"I just realized something."

"What's that?"

"Our names."

"What about our names?" I zipped up my parka as I approached the outer doors.

"She called me 'Franz'."

"Yeah?"

"You're Hans!"

"Uh-huh."

"Hans and Franz!"

"So?"

"So, like," his voice took on a heavy and not too convincing Austrian accent, "ve are Hans und Franz, and ve are here to *blow*—" He clapped his hands together once and pointed. "—you up!" He began cackling like a demented magpie.

Kids.

I pushed the outer door open and went back outside to wait for my body to be delivered.

The wind was bitter and we both had to stomp our feet to keep some semblance of feeling inside of our boots.

"Okay, one more time, let's go over our options."

"Or lack thereof."

"That's my boy. Never too early to learn that pessimism runs in our family."

"Runs? It practically gallops!"

"Two of us, lots of them. Quasi-military structure. Stone fortress, resistant to fire . . ."

"I don't suppose they have a nuclear reactor we could SCRAM to go critical?"

I shook my head. "The only evidence my pipe crawling yielded in the basement was an older, steam-heat system, supplemented by a more modern, forced air flow furnace and duct system. Probably upgraded the facilities a couple of decades back."

"Fuel?"

"I don't know. Probably oil, originally. Maybe natural

gas, now. Or even electricity. But if you're thinking about setting charges and using the reserves to multiply the force of the blast, we'd have to find the explosives, find the fuel storage area, bring the two together, and I get the feeling that Madam Lampshade is going to have us on a very short leash as soon as we set foot back inside."

He nodded. "I could still try to go for reinforcements but physical troops—assuming your people would come—would take too long to physically get here."

"And what about noncorporeal troops?"

He looked at me. "What? An army of ghosts? I don't know any. I'm unborn, not deceased, remember? Besides, a bunch of ghosts are practically worthless when it comes to influencing the realm of the living." He kicked a stone so that it skittered across the stony ground and disappeared over the edge of a drop-off some thirty yards away.

"First of all, the vast majority of them don't care," he elaborated. "They've moved on. They don't want to risk screwing up their karma by sticking their nonexistent noses in where they don't have a personal stake.

"The ones who are scary and violent enough to do you any good are so dangerous that you don't want to have anything to do with even one of them, much less a whole army.

"As for the rest? What good is a bunch of spooks whose bag of tricks is pretty much confined to slamming doors, moving ashtrays, and leaving cryptic stains and marks on the floors, walls, and ceilings?"

"That is why I have gathered an army," answered a harsh, guttural voice above us.

We looked up. Towering over us was a giant crone, an

ancient hag of rotted flesh and scabrous skin. I was suddenly aware of the gathering silhouettes just beyond the reach of the helipad lights. Wendigo leaned down, her death-mask face close to ours, and spoke again. "I have called together The People of The Land and told them of the Evil that poisons the earth and the waters."

As I turned aside from the charnel downdraft of her slaughterhouse breath, Will leaned over and whispered in my ear. "Problem solved, Dad. Wendy's siccing the Indian EPA on our nest of Nazis."

"Long have the white-eyes despoiled the sacred places," Wendigo continued in a voice like a funeral wind, "and each tribe has resisted in their own time and place. But The Mangler threatens all of The Land and in ways that the European invaders could never imagine. I have told the Ancestors that we must unite to destroy him before his numbers grow beyond containment."

"So what have we got?" I asked her. "Better be more than a few dozen bows and arrows because the arsenal inside could hold off the Colorado National Guard for weeks."

Then I noticed that the few "Indians" that I could actually make out at the edge of the light had small horns and antlers sprouting from their foreheads.

"The Manitou do not fight with weapons, traditional or otherwise," the Wendigo said, gesturing in their direction. "Their powers are greater than flint points and wooden shafts."

A platoon of tiny, ugly people crowded to the front of the pack, some of them sprouting hair from their faces like were-midgets turning into unkempt Pomeranians.

"The Nagumwasuck and Mekumwasuck are normally peaceful," she continued, "but can be fierce in defense of their territory. It was no simple matter, however, convincing them that their territory extended as far west as the Rockies. Likewise the Squonk, the Kewahqu, the May-may-gway-shi, and the Albatwitches but not so the Chenoo . . ." Giant, stony forms reared up behind them. " . . . they *like* to fight!"

Fireflies darted in and out of the shadowy forms. "The Elves of Light come from the Algonquin territories for they know what great losses may ensue if the land is not defended from the Defilers. They have come in their twilight time to make a stand with us.

"From the North are come Watchmen, the Hodag, the Pu'gwis, the Inua Yuas, the undead Angiaks, and Kushtaka!" I caught a glimpse of the latter which appeared to be very like human-sized otters.

"From the Northwest and the West I have gathered the Sasquatch, the Bokwus, and the Numuzo'ho. From the South and Southwest: the Kachina, the Cucui, the Chindi, the Surems, the Huacas, the Jimaniños, and Dzoonokwa. The Yunwi Amai'yine'hi, the Nanehi, and the Yunwi Tsundsi from the Southeast.

"From the East: Mothmen and the ancient entity known in latter days as the Jersey Devil."

Enormous forms arrived, dwarfing even the rocklike Chenoo. "For the first time in the living memory of the Ancients, the Giants have come together on the field of battle. Heng of the Huron. Manabozho. Achiyalatopa of the Zuni with his feathers of flint knives. The Pawnee wind-spawn, Hoturu. Tcolawitze, Hopi fire-giant. Ga-oh, wind-giant of the Iroquois. The twins, Enumclaw and Kapoonis. Aktunowihio of the Cheyenne. Hastsezini of the Navajo. Wakinyan of the Dakota. Even the ogress Utlunta Spearfinger of the Cherokee.

"The mountains are the ancestral home of the Gans so they will fight fiercely in their defense. Likewise the Ohdow who dwell underground and have suffered the poisons of the Mangler these past decades. The Tunghat and the Canotili have climbed up from the plains to join them lest The Mangler some day come down from these mountains and unleash his own, dark Anisgina across the plains."

I was suddenly aware of great wing beats above our heads. Dark silhouettes blotted out portions of the stars and fantastic shapes and visages were briefly revealed by flashes of heatlike lightning. "What are those?"

"Oshadagea, giant dew-eagle of the Iroquois. And the Wakinyan, also called Hohoq and Kw-Uhnx-Wa. Your people know them in legend as Thunderbirds."

"All right, then!" I said, rubbing my hands together. "What are we waiting for?" Somewhere down deep in the dwindling recesses of my conscience a tiny voice was asking about the fates of the women and children inside Brut Adler. What wasn't immediately shouted down by the growing cold-blooded nature of the vampiric trans-formation was outlogicked by the greater potential evil of any part of Mengele's project surviving to reproduce itself in another generation or two. "When do we attack?" I asked.

The Wendigo's mouth opened inhumanly, impossibly wide and she began to howl. A thousand other voices, inhuman as well, joined in sounding like a funeral wind from the heart of the glacial North.

I was nearly deafened by the time the noise ceased so I barely heard her say: "We cannot! It is, as I said before, geased and warded by sigils of power!"

I looked back at the bas-relief over the entrance to the citadel. "What? The swastika? Isn't there a back door?"

"We have traversed the stronghold round and round," she said, shrinking back down to human size. Unfortunately, she retained her ancient corpselike visage instead of reverting to the attractive Indian maid getup. "All points of entry are warded with the backwards Ttsilolni. So, I fear, would many of the passages within. All we can do is wait without . . ."

The faint sound of an aircraft engine intruded upon the night wind. I looked up and spotted the distant lights of an approaching helicopter. Theresa and Co., no doubt, delivering their precious cargo to Mengele's operating theaters.

"And," Wendigo cried, starting another growth spurt, "destroy any and all who seek to come here as The Mangler's allies!" The giants and the Chenoo roared, the creatures closer to our own height howled and stomped their feet. Heat lightning flared along the wings of the Wakinyan.

It terms of body counts, it looked like Deirdre and I would be among the first casualties of the siege of Brut Adler.

Chapter Twenty-Two

"NOW HOLD ON there, She-go!" Will went stomping up to stand toe-to-toe with the ghastly Wendigo. Unfortunately she had attained a size that only permitted him to intimidate her knees. "You're talking about destroying the helicopter carrying my father's body—a body that he's going to want to return to when this is all over!"

As he spoke those words I suddenly found myself wondering if that was actually true. I hadn't had much of a chance to consider my new repository but the flesh and bone seemed reasonably fit, not too old, and—most importantly—free of the necrotic virus that was transforming my old digs into something monstrous and inhuman. Did I want to return to that once this was all over? Of course there was always the question as to whether it would ever be over.

And the question of the original occupant, Hans—or Franz—or who or whatever he was . . . what about his rights to his own flesh and bone? Had he abrogated those rights when he chose to join a different demesne of monsters? And even if I could take unto myself the right and role of judge and jury, how could I cast him out of his own body? It was not something easily undertaken by the willing. Was the alternative, keeping him locked down in the cellar of his own mind, even a viable one?

Maybe the damage was already done, the erosion of the soul sufficiently progressed, that I could even consider taking another man's flesh from him.

"And not just his life," my unborn son was saying, "but the life of the woman he loves!"

Huh?

"Um, wait a minute . . ." I said.

"Do you have a better plan?" the twenty-foot-tall Ghast of the Wild challenged back.

"I think you may be confusing love and lust," I said.

"Well," said Will, "you're really wanting inside the fortress, right?"

"And while I do love her," I said, "it's more of a platonic love—a friendship thing. Not that there aren't overtones of attraction . . ."

"Of course! But, as I have said, every door, every window, every point of egress is marked, at some point, by the sigil of the Whirling Logs, turning in reverse, turning us back. The Ttsilolni is a mark of darkest sorceries in the hands of the Ochkih-Haddä!"

" . . . but it's really your mother that I love. Oh, I know that we haven't been getting along, lately . . ."

"So, if we can find a way to get you and the rest of the AIM Irregulars into the Hitler Hilton, here, you would agree to leave the helicopter alone?" Will pressed.

" . . . but relationships are like that. They're like the tides, they ebb and flow. Sometimes they go out and leave you stranded on the beach . . ."

"And how do you propose to do that?" Wendigo asked.

" . . . but if you're patient . . . and don't panic . . . the tide always comes back in."

"I'm working on a plan."

"At least it *almost* always comes back in . . ."

"Will this plan take long?" Wendigo asked, shrinking back down to tête-à-tête size. "I am no general and The People are no coherent army. If they are not given purpose or opportunity soon, they will either depart or wreak havoc on whatever targets are most convenient!"

"Dad!" Will called over his shoulder. "We need to talk!"

"No kidding," I said as we walked toward each other to meet in the middle of a semicircle of Native American Guardian Spirits. "About your mother and me—"

"I know there's a lot that you don't understand, Dad," he said, steering me away from the helipad and over toward the edge of the plateau. "And after this is all over we can sit down and I can try to help you understand some things. But for right now we gotta focus on the task at hand. How do we pull a *This Old House* and do a Bob Vila on all the swastikas inside Nazis-R-Us?"

Right.

I wasn't going to save Deirdre—or Lupé, for that matter— standing around and dithering over where my emotional loyalties lay. I turned my mind over and gave it a little shake and, like a mental Etch A Sketch, it was cleared and ready for action. Even in a new body, freed from the progress of the virus, my emotions were becoming easier to discard.

"We need a way to remove the swastikas from some of the entry points to the fortress," I repeated.

Will nodded. "But not just some entry points. Once inside, there are so many places our, um . . ." he looked back at the profusion of grotesque shapes and forms, " . . . troops would not be able to go without a complete scouring of the fortress' interior."

I nodded. "There could be hundreds."

"Thousands . . ."

I shook my head. "I don't think so. Mengele was—is— a narcissist. I don't think he's all about bringing Hitler back or rebuilding the former glory of the Third Reich. I think it's all about Mengele Without End, Amen. Any trappings of the Nazi Party are about structure and control for the loyalties of his minions." I rolled my eyes. "Jesus! First I'm talking about Nazis and now I'm using the word 'minions.' I've really got to get myself a secret decoder ring sometime soon!"

"Still, hundreds of Nazi stop signs are still a lot of scutwork before General Wendy can give the order to attack."

I stuck my hands in my pockets and stomped my feet. I had forgotten the frailties of untransformed flesh and the numbing cold was taking its toll. "If we start now, we could run a sweeping action ahead of the troops, clearing the obstacles as the fighting moves from room to room."

"Except these bodies are likely to be the first casualties in any confrontations," Will countered.

"What about noncorporeal mine-sweeping?"

"Ala a little poltergeist activity?" He considered. "Unless you're a young, adolescent spirit, in the throes of an emotional rage, you're not going to be able to sustain the ectoplasmic cohesion to deface or ruin enough swastikas to clear a couple of rooms, much less three or more levels."

"So, we'd need an army."

Will nodded. "Preferably an army of adolescent spirits who could muster the psychic rage to tear through this abomination and break the power of every single symbol of Nazi hatred and darkness they could find."

I tried to smile: there was still hope for us here in the cold, howling darkness where one man's evil had outlived generations of mankind's justice. But there was a catch in my throat and my eyes rimmed with frost as I turned to my unborn son and said: "Time to take out the Eurotrash. I know where you can find such an army . . ."

The helicopter was coming in low so there wasn't enough time to diagram a detailed plan. We trotted back to the helipad with more of a sketchy theory and tried to present it to Wendigo as if we totally knew what we were doing.

She glared at us with black-rimmed, fire pit eyes. "You are mad, of course! But then the Human tribes of The People have always recognized that the mad are often god-touched and sacred." She turned to Will. "Where is this place you must go to?"

"Brzezinka."

"Is it far?"

"Halfway around the world," I answered. "So he'd better get going."

"Oh, I thought I'd stick around for a few more minutes and see if I can cut the odds a little. After all, I've got the easy job: single-handedly raising an army." He pulled back the slide on his H&K. "You have to single-handedly hold one off until I get back."

"More like keep 'em confused."

Wendigo snorted. "At last a use for your natural talents."

Despite the downward wash of the descending copter's rotor blades, a wind sprang up, swirling around us and rising upwards. Wendigo shredded into a thousand dark ribbons and disappeared into the night air.

"I think she likes you," he said, punching my shoulder.

"What? No!"

"Aw, c'mon, Dad. The old Cséjthe charm—maybe I'll inherit it someday. Get me some girlie monsters to make goo-goo eyes at me . . ."

"Just remember that after you're born you'll be completely helpless and at my mercy for a number of years to come."

He grinned. "Jeez, you're contemplating child abuse and I'm not even born, yet."

"Think I can be abusive? Maybe I'll get you a baby sister to really make your formative years a living hell!"

His eyes turned sad and deep. "Maybe a baby step-sister . . ."

And the helicopter was drowning out any further conversation as it settled down just forty feet away. The cargo door slid open even before the engines were cut.

It was absolutely the wrong move to make under the circumstances but I instinctively reached for my son to give him a farewell hug. Fortunately he was already moving, ducking his head, and headed toward the chopper to assist with the unloading. I followed, a cold pit of dread starting to open in my borrowed stomach as I anticipated what would come next.

There were two stretchers. Deirdre and I were both securely strapped and buckled down. Although they had discarded their hospital garb it wasn't difficult to pick out the pair of docs since they were sticking close to their patient/cargoes and flanked by Theresa "Scraps" Kellerman and Ilse "The Red Bitch of Buchenwald" Koch wearing Gretchen's cloned flesh.

Some of the other commandos and flight crew might have been clones, as well, but it was hard to tell in this light. I wasn't sure if Mengele would use replicants for grunt work but, if he was willing to make Ilse Koch into multiple Brides of Frankenstein, there might well be other matched sets of Godonlyknewwhat. The best I could do for now was count heads and note positions. My main attention was drawn to their hostages and what Will was about to do next.

He had planned to wait until everyone was off the copter. If it turned out to be part of a getaway plan, we didn't want to do anything that would damage the equipment. The pilot and copilot, however, remained on board to go over their post-flight checklists as the rest of the away-team disembarked and began heading for the main entrance.

I led the way, walking as slowly as I dared to delay the procession, while Will positioned himself to the rear. These guys were probably good but they were tired after a long flight and not expecting an ambush on their home doorstep. Three bursts of automatic weapons fire took down four of them before I could turn around and the rest could react.

Two more fell as the stretchers were dropped and offensive measures were taken by the survivors.

Will was at a devastating disadvantage, now. He couldn't move to the helicopter for cover—we might need it later. He had to choose his targets carefully lest he hit Deirdre or myself—or Hans/me, for that matter. And there was no place to run to with a thousand-foot drop-off just thirty yards behind him.

He fired another burst and caught one of the two Mengele brothers, spinning him around to fall on top of me. The strapped-down-on-the-stretcher me, that is.

"What are you doing, fool?" Ilse screeched at me. "Choot him! Choot him!"

I brought my Heckler & Koch up and fired a burst over Will's head while stepping to the side to give him a clear return shot. He took it and the Red Bitch turned the color of her nickname as she flew backwards and went down.

The great doors behind us began to open, signaling the arrival of reinforcements and now the pilot and copilot were coming, pistols drawn, attempting a flanking action. Will fired one last burst through the opening doors and then turned and ran. He dropped his gun as he reached the precipice, spread his arms, and launched himself into space like Peter Pan taking his leave from Wendy Darling's bedroom window. He must have soared some fifteen feet before both darkness and gravity claimed him.

If he made any sound before hitting the rocks a thousand feet below, it was lost in the sudden roar of an express-train wind. Pushed back toward the entrance, the rest of us turned and fled before an invisible storm, retreating to the madness within the mountain.

The Mengele version who entered the detention facilities looked as though he were pushing fifty, a trim and vigorous fifty. And something else. Something vaguely reptilian lurked about his eyes and mouth. And something of the stalking panther resonated in his gait and movements.

I sat up a little straighter and, for the umpteenth time, tested the handcuffs that locked Hans' left wrist to the chair arm.

Mengele II pulled a chair out, reversed it, and sat astraddle, leaning forward on its back some five feet away. He did not speak but continued to stare at me the way a kid would study a spider caught in a glass jar.

As he studied me, I studied him. If this was the dangerous one—the clone they had attempted to enhance through psychological conditioning—I had to wonder what had they actually done to him. How do you duplicate an intellect capable of murdering four hundred thousand men, women, and children? How could his childhood have been processed to produce a doppelganger of the monster that used hundreds of children like lab rats for sadistic experiments, atrocities that did nothing to further the cause of science or German superiority?

And then ratchet up those traits to higher levels of "efficiency?"

The fading, human scraps and snippets of my soul still shrank from the necessities of killing, even in a righteous cause. But this guy had the look of an infectious disease:

he could probably make the Pope rethink his positions on abortion and gun control given a short audience in a soundproofed room. And now his cold, soulless stare was boring into my own eyes.

"Hey, Joey, take a picture; it lasts longer." I didn't have time to play "made you look away" with Death Angel, Jr.

"What happened out there?" he asked quietly.

"Hell, I don't know. Ole Franz went Rambo. Ask anyone." I raised a mental glass: *Confusion to the enemy* . . .

He shook his head. "I meant before. I did a quick review of the security videos. You were outside and were attacked by a wolf. Then you got up and it followed you inside like a faithful dog. Then Franz reports that the wolf attacks him before it is killed. Both of you have behaved strangely since then."

"You get attacked by a wolf and see how strangely you act right afterward." The answer was borderline rote and pro forma: there was no way I was talking my way out of the handcuffs with this guy.

"Who are you?" he asked. "Really?" He was no dummy.

"Mossad, you Kinderfucker! Israeli Intelligence knows where you are, now, and your hours are numbered!"

He didn't blink. He reached into his pocket and pulled out a large, folding buck knife and unfolded it with careful deliberation.

"Did you hear me? I said 'hours', not 'days!'"

He nodded and said, "Karl . . ."

The security goon who'd been standing behind me suddenly grabbed my free arm by the wrist. It was like being locked in an iron vise.

"I am going to ask you a series of questions," he continued quietly, "and every time I don't like your answer, I am going to shorten a finger by one joint. Understood?"

I had hoped to lure someone in close enough to bloody a nose. Now that was patently impossible. I hadn't signed up for Advanced Pain and Mutilation, either, and I wasn't about to stick around and audit the course. I banged around the interior of my borrowed skull a couple of times and shot back out into the ether. Perhaps, I thought as I exited through the wall, poor Hans would be well out of it, still crouching and whimpering down under the cellar stairs of his hindbrain.

But the screaming started before I was halfway down the hall. And the closed door did little to muffle Hans' bewildered protestations and howls for mercy.

Object lesson for the squeamish and irresolute: mercy begets mercy. But when you swim with the sharks, payback's a bitch.

Something I'd do well to remember if I ever made it back to New York.

It took me close to an hour to find my own body.

I had to search two levels and a half-dozen clinics and ORs before stumbling across the green-tiled theater where they'd stashed my mortal remains. It—*I*—lay on the stainless steel table, secured by two simple straps. The sheet was pulled back to the waist and I contemplated my waxy appearance like a talent scout for Madame Tussaud's. I needed an astringent. A loofah wouldn't hurt . . .

But I was really looking for two things.

First, a hint of the *animus*. Some sign of a Divine Spark to indicate premises weren't totally vacated. But I looked dead. Not peaceful. Not sleeping nor in repose. Not even a hint of nobility or any other indication of character seemed stamped on my slackened visage.

I was gone.

The question was was I gone for good?

This brought me to the other thing. I looked for the heart's fire and saw only ashes upon the hearth. Looked for spinning chakras and found only entropy.

That left only one, sure ingress: blood.

A wound, an injury, an entry point. An IV needle clumsily inserted might have done the trick. But no one had come along, yet, to hook me up. *Hello? A little service here for Mengele's Holy Grail, please!*

Apparently they had something going on. Scanners passed back and forth over me like upended Xerox machines and sensors were affixed to my epidermis like computerized checkpoints for the bank of computers along the wall. A variety of monitors were displaying a variety of readouts and a cursory glance suggested some kind of biotech programming was in progress. I looked back at my body. *Nanobots?* The Wonder Twins had injected something into my heart and my brain back in the hospital room. Were they reprogramming thousands of microscopic machines now awash in my blood and tissues?

Maybe this wasn't the time to zip up in my wetware suit and go lumbering around in a castle full of armed Nazis. But it did seem like a good idea to go find some kind of solidity and get back here before any more alterations were accomplished with my flesh! I considered the two tough-looking guards inside the room with me. Popped into the outer corridor and contemplated the second pair stationed right outside the door. Nope. Gotta thin the ranks a little. Even the odds. Balance the scales. In other words, FUBAR Brut Adler.

And, to do that, I needed blood.

Funny how some issues dog you well into the afterlife and I had a regular *theme* going on here. I hunted the hall, nearly making a complete circuit before opting up the next staircase and trying another level.

I hit pay dirt ten doors later in a sickbay area that was more clinic than surgical facility. Two members of the away-team were perched on the examining table being treated for superficial gunshot wounds, arm and leg respectively. Sizing both up, I opted for the one-armed guy—I needed to move about and too many areas of the complex weren't wheelchair accessible.

A hop, a twist, and a little "Johnny, may I cross your red, red bloodstream" put me inside. No time for niceties: I elbowed the resident psyche out of the way and tried to hop off the table. The good news was they had already administered some kind of morphine so the arm wasn't hurting as bad as it should. The bad news: they had already administered some kind of morphine so the rest of my new body wasn't working as well as it should.

It all worked out for the best, though: the nurse who stepped in to catch me got my elbow in her face and staggered back with a bloody nose.

Sorry, hon, but I may need another getaway vehicle . . .

The weapons were stacked in the corner and, as I made my way toward them I noticed a couple of valves protruding from the wall. I opened the one marked "*Sauerstoff*" and, as pure oxygen began to hiss into the room, I heard the door open behind me. As I scooped up a handgun an all-too-familiar voice asked: "What are you doing?" I looked back over my shoulder. Sure enough, a blood-speckled Mengele II stood on the threshold, a security goon at his side. "Stop!" he commanded. "Drop your weapon!"

This wasn't looking so good all of a sudden. My hastily conceived plan—short on detail, long on improvisation—depended on the elements of surprise and confusion. For them, not for me, unfortunately.

"Sergeant, shoot that man!" he ordered.

I dropped behind the exam table before he could get his rifle up but I was deep in trouble, already. Mengele Junior was no dummy and he was already watching the rest of his men for suspicious behavior. And while I lucked out this time and got a "right-handed" body to match my own orientation, it was the right arm that was all chewed up and practically useless. Furthermore, I was in a box—a box that everyone else was starting to exit—and the call had doubtlessly gone out for more reinforcements. I raised the pistol in my shaky left hand and considered my options. Stick my head up and probably get it blown off? Keep my head down and fire blindly over the tabletop?

I went with option three: I put three bullets into the wall before the fourth hit the opened oxygen nozzle and turned a four-room complex into a phoenix pyre that flipped its own fiery bird at Mengele Redux.

Fire alarms were blaring their klaxon distress calls throughout the complex as I exited the large, charcoal briquette I had spent all of ninety seconds possessing. I drift-ed through the flames and three more walls before reentering the corridor and resuming my search for another host body.

Brut Adler was looking less and less like an eagle's nest and more and more like an anthill someone had kicked over. Personnel swarmed through the hallways, some fleeing the fire, others moving toward it with firefighting gear. Thirty seconds of mind-surfing the human currents and I retreated to another office and resumed my search away from the confusing kaleidoscope of mental chatter.

Office, office, closet, storeroom, lab, storeroom . . . Bingo: another OR! Or, rather, the viewing gallery for an operating theater one floor below.

Theresa Kellerman lay across the operating table, a cross-stitch pattern of bullet wounds marking her own, borrowed flesh from right armpit to left hip. And she was screaming.

Not in pain but in annoyance. "I don't want an anesthetic! I don't *need* an anesthetic! The last time you knocked me out for reattachment, you cross-wired two of my fingers!" Her voice had an unnatural, electronic sound and there appeared to be a modified vocoder taped across her throat. "I need to be awake this time to make sure all of the nerve endings are matched properly! When we're done I'll have a permanent body and no one's going to screw it up on my watch!"

I leaned forward for a better look, pressing my palms to the slanted observation glass. No sign of Deirdre anywhere below. About the time I realized that my "palms" were insubstantial it was already too late to recover. I continued the "lean" into a horizontal skydiver's pose, dropping forward and down into the operating room.

Onto the table.

Into Theresa Kellerman!

Her flesh was like a dry sponge, thirsty for spiritual essence: it sucked me in like that paper towel that bills itself as "the quicker picker-upper." I had a new body if I wanted it.

Well, why not? She was doubtless part of the inner circle. Why not see what kind of havoc I could create wearing her identity? Plus, they couldn't very well go ahead with the head swap while I was hijacking the *donee*. Or would Terry-call-me-T be considered the *donor*? Come on, Cséjthe; focus! Plenty of time to muse after the dust settles. I shook my head and was rewarded with a most peculiar sensation.

In fact there was a whole lotta peculiar sensations. Every new body was a different experience, though I was getting faster and more intuitive at mastering the process with each new "jump." But this latest insertion felt— well—*wrong* in a way I couldn't quite pinpoint.

Movement seemed difficult. I tried to sit up and convulsed more than actually moved. I wrenched myself up with a major effort on the second try and the doctor and two nurses standing across from the table staggered back. A nurse started to scream. The other nurse joined her— no, that was the doctor! He was a better screamer than she was.

Theresa Kellerman was screaming, too. Her high-pitched keening sounded especially eerie through the electronic filter of the vocoder. Time to send her to the mental cellar. I rummaged around in my skull but couldn't find her. Not even down in the dark depths of the hindbrain.

I lowered my feet to the floor and carefully placed a little weight on my right foot. My legs felt sleepy and unresponsive and I had to lurch a little to make the position. Everyone else took a step back. One of the nurses grabbed a scalpel. The other snatched up a metal instrument tray, scattering dozens of implements, and then held it before her like a shield. The doctor threw up a gloved hand to his white-capped brow and shrieked: "It's alive! Alive!"

I took a faltering step. This body had a lower center of gravity, being a woman with the typical hips configuration, and I was having a little more difficulty than usual in finding my balance.

The nurse with the scalpel threw it. Maybe she had "carney knife-thrower" listed somewhere on her resume. In any event, it landed blade-first in my left breast. There was some wetness and I was suddenly three cup sizes smaller on that side. I pulled the scalpel out as the nurse bugged for the door and the doctor fainted. Then I reached over and cupped my remaining breast. Implants. Based on the runoff I'd guess saline rather than silicone.

The other nurse was backing toward the door, still holding the stainless steel tray up like it would protect her.

Protect her from what? I mean, I might be worried if *I* saw Theresa Kellerman coming toward me—we had a "history," after all. But all this abject terror? Maybe it was the expression on "our" face. Was I doing something to appear particularly ferocious? If so, I needed to practice more: I had a whole castle of Nazis to spook into submission.

I took another step. And then another.

The tray moved, trying to stay between me and the whimpering woman who kept shuffling backwards. As I came closer I could catch glimpses of my reflection, a little distorted and wavy, and very brief as the tray trembled and shook in her white-knuckled grasp.

Finally I was close enough to reach out and grab it, myself. At that point she relinquished her hold and ran screaming from the room. I let her go. I was more interested in my reflection. I turned the tray this way and that but the results were the same: no particular expression on my face.

No face.

No head.

I turned and looked back at the operating table I had just vacated. Theresa-call-me-Terry-call-me-T's head was still there, still screaming through her vocoder. I dropped the tray and reached up to feel the space just above my shoulders: nothing was there.

I felt a ghostly smile where my head poked out of Kellerman's corpse of crazy-quilt cadaver parts.

Cool.

Very cool!

Chapter Twenty-Three

DEAD FLESH ISN'T easy to animate and it should have been downright impossible. But then I was getting to the point where words like "impossible" and "unlikely" and maybe even "coincidence" were being eradicated from my vocabulary. Ever since my sojourn among the Loa and subbing for Baron Samedi, the dead seemed to respond to my presence with a preternatural vigor. Maybe this was just more of the same.

Sort of.

Alas, this stitched-together semblance of a body wasn't good for anything much beyond lumbering around and scaring the bejezus out of any rational beings it encountered. Which was plenty good for the next twenty minutes as I cleared the second-floor hallway from one end to the other. But sooner or later it was bound to come down to a fight and this putrefying mass of dissolving muscles, rotting sinews, and decaying bones wasn't up to throwing a real punch, never mind a kung-fu kick or beating a hasty retreat. I needed firearms and opportunities for grander acts of destruction.

I also needed to get back to my own body and get it disconnected from those machines before Mengele completed his Bionic Manikin play.

I staggered on down the corridor, moving a small herd of fortress personnel before me like a cattle drive of the damned as I searched for the nearest staircase back up. Another pair of security goons appeared, pushing their way through the crowd to approach me.

Now I was in trouble.

The first burst of weapons fire went wide. These guys had cojones but you would need bowling balls to face what they were looking at and not have a little tremble in your trigger finger.

The second burst clipped me. The third sent several rounds right to my torso.

Having been in actual combat I've seen machine-gun fire pick a man up off his feet and throw him three or four feet back from the shooter. At the very least it will knock you down.

I kept to my feet. Kellerman's liquefying flesh was an ineffective barrier to the bullets: they passed through me without meeting enough resistance to affect my frame as a whole.

The guards dropped their HKs and ran.

I picked them up, bracing the stock of each against the insides of my cadaverous elbows and forearms, and stalked on down the hall like Sigourney Weaver.

Sigourney Weaver on a coke-fueled *Aliens* pub crawl and missing her head, if you will.

I finally reached the stairs after Ramboing my way through about twenty more of Mengele's staff. I was starting to think this might work and maybe I wouldn't be needing backup after all.

But then I reached the stairs.

Going down might have worked. Going up, however, required some motor skills that were a little more demanding. After a few Pratfalls of the Living Dead, I reluctantly turned and shuffled off in search of the elevator.

Precious time was passing and the word had evidently gone out. I encountered no other personnel on my way to the lift. The elevator, when it arrived, was empty as well. I stepped inside and pressed the button for the third level. The doors closed and it started upward with a slight jerk.

Halfway between floors it stopped with a big jerk.

I punched buttons but nothing happened. It looked like I was the big jerk: someone had cut the power

I turned and looked out through the glass walls at the lobby below. People were coming out to observe the headless corpse in the big specimen jar trapped between the second and third levels.

No point in hanging around: I quit the cold, lifeless flesh that had toted Theresa Kellerman on her last mission and jumped through the wall to land back on the floor I had just left. As a spook I could move more swiftly, now, but the stairs were still going to be a bit of a problem. Behind me and above, the headless corpse fell against one of the glass walls and then slid to the floor of the lift, leaving a greasy orange smear in its wake.

☠ ☠ ☠

I passed by the OR and checked in on T's head before continuing the search for my own. It was gone. Too bad I hadn't taken the time to stash it in the autoclave before leaving.

The stairs were a bitch but at least I wasn't providing anyone with a visible target this time around. Eventually I made it to the top and hurried down the hall like a narcissistic Diogenes in search of self.

The fire had been put out, though it still smoldered here and there. No bodies were in sight. I had to hand it to these guys: even after more than sixty years the Nazis were still an efficient lot.

I moved ahead and noted that, as I approached the area where I had last left myself, new guards had been posted. They were doubled in number and spaced out in pairs so that every man could watch and be watched by the others. The Mengeles were quick studies.

But were they quick enough to stop me from popping into the nearest warm body with a paper cut? And then starting a chain reaction of bloody noses that would have them killing each other off as I kept skipping ahead to new *corpora delicti*?

Before we had a chance to find out, I spooked on ahead and checked the room where I had last found myself.

It was empty.

I moved on, afraid I'd spend another hour before I found it again, afraid I'd be too late, afraid—

I found it a couple of doors down, in the room at the end of the hall.

I'd been moved from a surgical facility to a security

hub. Rows of monitors showed a multiplicity of views throughout the complex, including several perimeter areas on the outside. The overturned anthill analogy was morphing back into an orderly beehive of recovery and reconnoiters. Groups of personnel—some uniformed, most drafted from support staff—were sweeping the various levels for signs of further disturbance or incursion. Treatment of the injured was proceeding apace. Surgeries were being performed in six different theaters.

And I was in here, secured to a padded gurney with enough leather straps to delight a leather queen and restrain Houdini. Like I said, these guys were no dummies. Take one little corpse for a stroll and suddenly they were locking down bodies left and right. And keeping three more guards in the room as well as a doctor wearing a handgun in a belt holster and a scary-looking nurse who looked like she was recruited from the Russian Olympic shot-put team.

The IV needle lodged deep in my arm would probably allow me ingress to my own flesh but unless I could unbuckle a few belts and convince a half-dozen people to look the other way, I wasn't going any further.

Still, I had to do something and I had to do it soon! The needle in my arm was directing my unique blood chemistry through a tube connected to an antique blood transfuser and, from there, down an adjoining tube to another needle in another arm.

Mengele Prime.

His wheelchair was momentarily abandoned and he lay on a small couch that had probably been carried in for this "battlefield" procedure. At least I hoped they had just brought it in. It didn't match the rest of the décor and you don't want people doing highly dangerous direct transfusions if they regularly mix their *art nouveau* with their *art deco*. The original Mengele looked like nothing as much as an ancient mummy being prepared for a fresh round of wrappings and vestments.

Only . . . tock tick: he wasn't getting older, he was starting to get younger!

As I watched, his crinkled, parchment skin began to lose its papery look. Livered age spots were starting to fade even as the pale, pale hue of his epidermis took on a faint hint of color. In just a few minutes he had turned back the clock, moving from a centenarian to a man merely in his nineties. The Death Angel of Auschwitz, The Mangler, the Evil Genie of Eugenics, was being reborn for another generation, perhaps for all time, in this hour, in this place . . .

And by the power of my blood!

He trembled and groaned as his ancient flesh convulsed and the infinitesimal timepieces at the heart of each cell shivered into reverse. The couch was short but still wide enough that there was no danger of his rolling off. And he didn't need restraining straps while the nurse who looked like a cross-dressing truck driver sat beside him. Still, the needle was jostled in his arm and a small cranberry tear wept from the place where he received my unholy communion.

There was no doubting what had to be done and I jumped with only the slightest hesitation.

I should have known better. The previous incursions

involved victims who were caught completely off-guard. My last fleshnapping bypassed a competing psyche altogether.

But, as I said, the Mengeles were quick studies. They learned, adapted, prepared. Counterpunched.

I jumped into the body of a feeble old man. There was nothing, however, feeble about the intellect waiting for me inside.

Ahhhh, Cséjthe! I was wondering when you would return.

As easily as I had knocked over and trampled the previous psyches I had run into, I now found myself put into a psychic half nelson by this current encounter. And as much as I struggled to free myself it was becoming abundantly clear that I was completely and effectively trapped. Maybe Mengele had more experience in wrestling personal demons: I was thoroughly pinned to the mental mat of his consciousness.

You'll never get away with this, Mengele! I grunted impotently.

My dear Mr. Cséjthe, I have always gotten away with "it." Do you know what I used to say to my Juden guinea pigs back in Auschwitz? "The more we do to you, the less you seem to believe we are doing it." It was true then and it continues to be true today. Most of the filth that thinks of itself as "mankind" is merely cattle, fit only to serve the purposes of its Masters. Their herd mentality only leads them to the slaughterhouse that much more quickly.

Oh, yeah? I was a little short on defiant comebacks and it was the best I could come up with for the moment.

Yes. And now you have to decide, Mr. Cséjthe, whether you want to eat the hamburger or be the hamburger.

Meaning?

If I had more time I could construct some sort of electromagnetic device to restrain your noncorporeal essence. As things stand now I have one of three courses of action. One, I could continue to restrain you by the power of my superior will and intellect . . .

But you gotta sleep sometime.

Agreed. So, two, I could strike a deal that would put us on the same side—

Not bloody likely!

A mutually agreeable arrangement, then. I have things that you want; you have something that I want.

What do you have that I want?

Your body, for one.

Yeah, and I suppose you'll just give it back.

In time. If I can successfully clone your preternatural flesh and your unique blood-producing marrow, then you can have your pick of the original or any number of copies.

Sounds like I might be in for a bit of a wait. Unless you have some sci-fi short cut to speeding up the maturation process.

Alas, no. This is reality, Mr. Cséjthe, not some hack writer's fevered dream. But what is twenty to thirty years compared to losing your body forever? Then there is also the matter of your wife and daughter . . .

Jenny and Kirsten are dead. You can't hold them hostage.

I have their DNA. They are already reborn anew.

Big unfucking deal! All you've done is duplicate their genetic material. That's not the same thing as what and who they really are. Did you make backup copies?

You suspect I would create multiple hostages?

I'm pointing out that if you make more than one Jenny, which one is really the woman I married? You've taken the sacred concept of personhood and turned it into a carnival shell game. Spiritual three-card monte. Three Jennies? Which one contains the original soul? Shuffle 'em up and make us guess. And assuming that one clone even ends up with Jenny's soul, what about the other two? Do they get dupes or whatever's next in the queue? Or do they get anything at all? You may be able to clone biological matter but what about the non-material? Is it immaterial?

Does it matter so much to you, Cséjthe, as long as you get your wife and daughter back?

I can see where the question of a person's soul has never been an issue for someone like you, asshole. The problem is I don't know that I'd get my wife and daughter back! What you're doing might be no different than finding a woman and child who resemble my deceased family and performing enough plastic surgery to make them physically identical but no more duplicates in mind and personality than complete strangers. And, at the other end of the spectrum, there's the possibility that you would be doing something much worse.

Worse?

Check your Bible, Igor. Jesus said something interesting in the twelfth chapter of Matthew about what happens when a spirit departs from the body and then tries to come back later. It seems you may get some renters who weren't listed on the original lease. Occupants who are likely to do way more damage than any security deposit can cover!

Then perhaps you should be worried about returning to your own jar of clay.

I've been doing nothing but, Doctor Demento. Let go and I'll do a quick bed check.

I think not. Your body isn't going anywhere for the time being.

So I noticed. The point is you think you're all hot snot when it comes to Xeroxing the human genome but you're just cold boogers when it comes to the metaphysical.

The metaphysical?

Like the question of what rushes in to fill the void once you've set up the housing. You may have hostages, they may look like my wife and daughter right down to their mitochondria, but I'm betting that the hearts and souls of my family are beyond any human reach now. They've gone where science cannot yet reach and may never go.

Then let us speak of something less theoretical and closer at hand: the woman, Deirdre.

Deirdre?

Even now she is in surgery where my promise to the Kellerman woman is being fulfilled. If all goes well my little protégé will finally obtain a body that will not rot out from under her in a matter of days or weeks. As soon as the nerves in her neck are properly fused to the host's central nervous system, the original head will be excised and removed so that a full transfer of conscious and autonomic functions can take place and symmetry can be finalized. I assume that you would prefer that your friend's head not be discarded.

Bastard!

And if, as I suspect, her consciousness should survive in the same manner as the Kellerman woman's, there's a good chance of finding her a host body as well. Possibly cloning her her own over time.

I struggled but still found I was unable to extricate myself from his mental grasp. *Is that all?*

All? What? Would you like for me to offer wealth? Riches? Power? Something else to sweeten the deal?

Oh yeah, that would do it. Move me into a higher tax bracket and I'll happily spit in God's eye, betray the memory of my family, and buddy up with the greatest child molester and murderer of all time. No, shithead, you said three courses of action. I think we've eliminated one and two from the list.

Agreed. The third option is actually my preference, Cséjthe. I have everything I need without your cooperation. Your body continues to function separate from your consciousness. And I don't believe I can trust you to keep any promises that violate your cattle code of ethics. So the third and preferable course of action is to simply snuff out your dislocated mind like a pinched candle flame.

Oh. Kill me. Now there's a surprise.

Really?

No. Only in that you're trying to talk me to death, first.

I needed time. While it is obvious that my will is stronger than yours, holding you is one thing. Destroying you may take a little more of an effort. As your transformative blood drips into my veins, it makes my flesh younger, my body stronger. As the vessel regains youth

*and vitality, the mind is invigorated, as well. Even now my
hold upon your own consciousness grows ever stronger. It
will not be long before I can crush your thoughts as effortlessly as I would crush the hollow, matchstick bones of a
bird or a mouse!*

And the pressure that surrounded my thoughts began
to increase, pressing in upon my consciousness as if my
head were still corporeal and being squeezed within a
heavy steel vise.

I heard a shout and thought it was my own. Then the
pressure lessened a little and I could see through
Mengele's eyes. An alarm had gone off and the room was
filling up with security goons.

Someone was pointing at one of the monitors. A switch
was thrown and the image was duplicated on the large,
master screen above the rest.

The view was of the outside. Specifically the front
doors. Which were wide open. No one was in sight,
though.

Of course the Wendigo and her army of Amerind
guardian spirits probably wouldn't register in the electromagnetic spectrum so they wouldn't be picked up by the
security cameras. But something would have had to have
been done about that big Ttsilolni—the swastika—over
the entrance for them to breach the outer doors.

Someone turned a knob and the outside security camera zoomed in, enlarging the entrance area. There was no
eagle, no wreathed swastika, no "Brut Adler" chiseled
above the entrance, only an amorphous mass that rippled
and writhed over the rough stone.

"What is that?" a guard asked.

The camera zoomed in closer. The mass was predominantly orange, shot through with black.

Orange and black suddenly rose up and obscured our vision completely. Mengele reached up and brushed at his eyes. I tried to pull away, actually getting halfway out of his head before his mind grabbed hold again. His fingers, meanwhile, came away with a captured insect. It was a monarch butterfly; its orange-and-black wings dusting his fingers with a fine powdering of scales.

Another one fluttered by to land on his arm near the needle feeding his vein.

"Where are they coming from?" he wheezed.

He might well ask that in the larger context: monarch migration paths took them from Florida, the coast of Texas, and the mountain forests in Central Mexico to the Canadian borderlands and back again. But while they traveled various routes over the Eastern Plains and along the West Coast, the migratory patterns avoided the Rocky Mountains. And sightings were rare during the summers and never during the winters.

We weren't in a large room so it didn't take that long to answer his question in the smaller context: a dozen more orange-winged invaders were crawling between the metal vanes of the air vent and spilling down from above.

As another wave of monarchs fluttered over, circling Mengele like curious gliders, I made another attempt to pull free. This new distraction was sufficient: I popped out of the old man's carcass like a cork from a champagne bottle. He stopped waving at the insects long enough to make another mental grab for me and he, too, popped out. Mengele's body collapsed and the nurse and doctor were suddenly faced with the double duty of shooing butterflies while checking their patient's vital signs.

Meanwhile I had a very tenacious foe still attempting to put me back in a psychic headlock. Any hope that a sudden shock had killed him disappeared as I noticed the silver cord that snaked back to his physical body. I was facing an astral projection of the Death Angel of Auschwitz, not his ghost. His vague, translucent form resembled the photographs of Mengele in his prime, not the wizened old man sprawled on the couch. Which reminded me: with every minute that ticked by, his body was absorbing more of my blood from the transfusion and growing younger and stronger in the bargain.

He lunged for me and I decided, strategically, that the floor beneath my feet just wasn't that substantial, after all. I dropped like a stone in a well, catching a glimpse of hundreds of butterflies on the floor below flying reconnaissance patterns.

Just in time I decided the basement floor was solid and bounced to a stop before losing myself in the mountain's bedrock beneath. I took a moment to examine my plan and prioritize. I needed to find Deirdre and stop the operation before it was too late. I needed to return and stop the transfusion before it was too late. I probably needed to hook up with Wendigo and her troops to: (a) get their help and (b) keep them from harming either of us on their bloody rampage before it was too late.

And to cover the most ground the fastest, a physical body would be an asset. So, first on the list: head for the upper levels and look for another bloody staff member on the way.

I was five ghostly strides into my revised plan when Mengele bungee-jumped into the basement behind me. Like I said, a quick study.

I ran.

"I'm not letting you escape, again," he called after me. "I'm not safe as long as you are loose!"

"Ditto, Dr. Frankenfurter." I dove through the wall next to the door and found myself in a narrow service corridor. I turned left and ducked around the corner. It was a dead end. Too late to reverse my steps, I waited, hoping he would go the other direction.

He didn't. "Now you're trapped," he said, coming around the corner and blocking the entire width of the passage.

"Boy, you're really new at this, aren't you?" I dodged sideways through another wall. I found myself in a room full of corpses.

The morgue that served Brut Adler was only set up to accommodate up to four cadavers at a time. Current events had forced the staff to stack bodies on the tables and the floor like so much firewood. As I picked my way through the constricted maze of dead flesh, I fancied I could hear vague stirrings from within some of the piles. If I hung around long enough maybe the dead would reanimate like the neighbors back home.

Considering these guys' resumes, that was probably the last thing that I wanted.

There were two doors in this room, one to my left, one straight ahead. I headed for that one as Mengele burst through the wall behind me. His cord was slowing him up a bit; it dragged at him like an ectoplasmic leash made out of garden hose. I pushed through the door without opening it and found myself out in a main corridor.

This part of the downstairs area looked familiar. If memory served, the stairs leading up were another sixty some yards on down, past where the curve of that corridor placed them beyond my line of sight.

I took two long strides and then skidded to a stop as Mengele popped out ahead of me. Damn! His learning curve for astral maneuvering was considerably shorter than mine! Worse, he was anticipating my moves!

"Anywhere you can go, I can follow," he taunted. "What is more—as my physical body grows stronger and younger, this intangible form seems to grow stronger and faster!"

In the meantime, my psychic batteries were running down. There were no ectoplasmic jumper cables connecting me to any kind of an external power source. I was cut off from rendezvousing with Wendigo upstairs and, even if they found their way down here in time, there were no guarantees as to what any of them could see or do while we were in our present state.

A swarm of butterflies came fluttering around the distant curve of the corridor as if responding to my silent question.

Mengele had his back to them but must have noticed something change in my face—this guy didn't miss a thing. He turned and took a step back as they flapped and spiraled toward us. Then he shrugged and turned back to me.

"Insects?" he asked. "You storm my citadel with insects?" He shook his head. "Not that it would have made any real difference but I might have seen the logic in bees or wasps. Maybe spiders . . ."

"Spiders aren't insects," I said.

"I know spiders are not insects! They are arachnids! I am not stupid!" He swung his arm out to gesture behind him. "Butterflies . . . butterflies are stupid!"

I wasn't sure what was going to happen next. Maybe nothing. But I took a step back anyway. "The Aztecs didn't think so."

"What?"

"The Aztecs. Native Americans. Inhabited Mexico from the north to the central region, flourished around the twelfth through the fifteenth centuries."

"Extinct savages!"

"Funny, I would have expected a little more professional courtesy. Even respect. The Aztecs developed a high culture and civilization while your Hohenstaufens were in political freefall and your Habsburgs were kicking and pulling each other's hair over the dynastic toy box. The Aztec high holy days made your *Triumph of the Will* look like *Waiting for Godot*."

Mengele jumped: a butterfly had just fluttered by, grazing his ear.

"Anyway, the Aztecs—who were self-styled experts on the subject of death, by the way—believed that the *Danaus plexippus*—that's the monarch butterflies for the taxonomy challenged"—another flew through his shoulder and he grabbed his upper arm as if stung—"were actually the souls of the dead. More specifically, dead children."

The butterflies were starting to swarm him and he

began to scream as they darted about, dipping in and out of his translucent form.

"That's funny," I said, though there was nothing remotely funny to be found here, "they're butterflies. Even if they were bees or wasps or spiders—who aren't insects but arachnids, by the way—they couldn't hurt a noncorporeal being. Could they?"

"They burn! *Burn!*" he shrieked, swatting at them with his hands. It was worse than ineffective: his hands passed through his orange-winged assailants with no resistance but his palms began to bubble with psychic blisters.

"So, even though this wasn't a part of the plan, I'm betting that you're suffering psychic feedback from the memories of your victims."

"What? *What?*"

"The plan was to get some help in covering up your swastikas. Didn't know they'd show up as butterflies. Or that they'd bring the pain. Think of it as a little Vulcan mind meld—a whole lotta little mind melds—with a whole bunch of your victims."

"Butterflies!" he screeched, staggering down the hall toward me.

I backpedaled and the monarchs stayed with him. "Not just butterflies, Joe; spirits of the dead. A lot of spirits of the dead! We didn't have much time to round up an army who'd be willing to abandon the peace and grace of their eternal rest. Much less get involved with unpleasant earthly matters and distasteful people like yourself. Under the circumstances, there was just one place to go: Oswiecim."

"Oswiecim?"

"Well, more properly the fields of Brzezinka, Birkenau, the largest cemetery in the world. Jews, Poles, Gypsies, Soviet prisoners of war—their ashes form a very deep sub- strate of the soil, there—as you should well know. Your Nazi masters thought to rewrite history and, failing that, to burn and bury the evidence. Well, you know the old saying: 'Kill 'em all and let God sort 'em out?' Well, God sorts, *Herr Doktor*! Sooner or later He gets around to it. No task is left undone on the eternal time clock. All rivers run to the sea. Every dog has his day. All birds come home to roost. The same goes for butterflies."

He staggered about like a man on fire, the orange wings wreathing his wispy form in a semblance of mock flame. "It *hurts*!" he gasped. "Hurts so *bad*!"

"I can't begin to imagine," I said. "But then, I wasn't there. You were, though. I'll bet a trip down memory lane through the mind of one of your victims is as painful as if it actually happened to you. So, I'll bet a dozen trips are unendurable. Or are they? What about a hundred? A thousand?"

With a shriek of mindless agony, he lunged toward me. I stepped back and passed through a wall into another room. A familiar room. I kept moving. Past the stainless steel tables, past the shelves along the walls with their pro- fusion of bottles, containers, and cases. Past the cabinets. Past the countertops with instruments and tools. Past the sinks. I stopped by the display case as Mengele came through the wall after me.

The butterflies did not come with him. Their physical bodies were stopped by the physical wall that was no bar- rier to our ectoplasmic flesh.

It took him a few moments to shake off the effects of the assaults on his mind and memory. Slowly, however, he seemed to gather himself while I wondered if I was smart to be staying and not running. I couldn't run forever so it made sense to make a stand wherever I might find allies. I just hoped my instincts were trustworthy in this case.

"So much for your butterfly brigade," he panted, drawing himself back up to stand erect.

I shook my head. "You think that's it? You can cheat fate with a flimsy wall, a closed door?"

He smiled and gave a ghost of a shrug. "I'm in here. They're out there."

"'Death is here and Death is there, Death is busy everywhere,'" I mocked, "'All around, within, beneath, Above is Death—'"

"'—and we are Death!' Do you think to frighten me by quoting Shelley?"

I shook my head. "You can't stay in here forever."

"I don't intend to. After I deal with you—" He paused and cocked his head. "What was that?"

I knew what it was—or had a pretty good idea—because I had been in this room before. Perhaps he had, too, but not without the protective insulation of flesh and blood and skin and bone.

There was a vague suggestion of haze in the air, like the taint of a recently extinguished cigarette. As the sound of weeping became more audible, the air thickened and took on a blue tinge. Light began to spill forth from the display case where the treble rows of craniums stared down in ghastly judgment. As the light grew in intensity, the illumination from the skulls shaded more toward green than blue, however.

"The dead down here aren't the same as the dead out there, I'm betting."

"What are you talking about?" he demanded, his voice rising to overmatch the increasing volume of the chorus erupting around us. The wails that had sounded like frightened children on my last visit now sounded angry.

"I'm talking about spirits that have had their resting places consecrated and blessed," I said. "Who have had the prayers of millions to tuck them into their long eternity. Who are visited daily by mourners and well-wishers from around the world and new generations with each passing year, assuring them that they are remembered and will never be forgotten.

"But here . . ." My arm swept the autopsy tables and instrument trays with their ghastly collections of flensing knives, bone saws, and tools whose jaws, blades, and teeth were starting to glow with an emerald radiance that hurt my transdimensional vision. " . . . what peace can come to those who perished in pain and horror and, most terribly, anonymity? To be forgotten? To lurk through eternal darkness, forever alone and unknown? No one prays for your soul. No one acknowledges that you lived or that your life had value. Your dust and ashes forever sealed in iron and stone, unable to return to the soil, unable to be reborn in the blades of grass or a flower, to feel the cool baptism of rain or follow the smiling warmth of the sun."

"Bah! Dead is dead!"

"And yet, here we stand, all ghostly, while you cower and cringe from a bunch of butterflies out in the hallway."

He lunged at me and screamed. That scream was echoed a hundredfold and sickly green light burst from the cabinet with such intensity that I was momentarily blinded. I heard the crystalline cacophony of shattered glass and suddenly the chorus of screaming doubled and trebled in volume. I was knocked back and vaguely felt the shadow of another wall pass through me. About the time I realized I was in the furnace room, Mengele was through the door and pressing his astral hands to my own silvery throat. We stumbled backwards and, had we been solid, we would have slammed up against the iron behemoth that served double duty in providing heat for a portion of Brut Adler and disposal for unwanted biological material.

Instead we kept going and found ourselves struggling waist-deep in flames!

Knowing where we were probably gave me a slight psychological advantage: I pried his fingers away from my neck and grinned in his uncertain face. "Welcome to Hell, Doctor! Don't worry about your luggage; you're on express check-in."

He stepped back and looked around like a frightened child. But the effect didn't last for long. How could it? The flames didn't burn us. The iron walls of the great furnace were well illuminated from the inside, showing every weld, every rivet, the venting high above.

He laughed. Bent over and tried to scoop an armful of flames into his embrace. "Do you see, Cséjthe? Do you see why the Master Race has discarded the childish fairy-tales of Heaven and Hell? There is no God! Only gods among men! The gods who have learned to evolve beyond the petty cattle morals of lesser societies!" The flames dropped in intensity. Instead of licking at our waists they barely reached our knees, now. "Poor Cséjthe, trusting in a higher power that isn't there or doesn't care. Do you know what Marx said?"

"Say the secret word and win a hundred Reichmarks?"

"That men are the apes of a cold God," he snarled as I watched a swirl of ashes rise up from the grating behind his feet. "So many of the unwashed masses are no more than beasts. You, at least, come close to thinking like a man. But you are still an animal. You and all the other apes who think they are men and will always be disappointed that, when your God finally does appear, he is someone like me!"

The swirl of ashes had risen above our heads forming a gray canopy that thickened and opened like a swaying, hooded cobra.

"Yeah?" I took two steps back and leaned against the inner wall of the furnace but willed myself to remain inside. "Well, welcome to the Monkey House!"

The flames had died all the way down to our ankles but now their color Doppler-shifted from orange to green as if someone had set fire to a huge spool of copper wire beneath our feet. The flames began to rise, again.

"Ah!" Mengele looked down in shock and surprise. "*What?*"

Tongues of teal licked up his legs, reaching his thighs, and he began to shriek again. He ran for the nearest wall. A thick coating of ash slid up to form an inner coat of gray. He rebounded instead of ghosting through and fell down into the fire. He reappeared almost immediately but his silvery visage was marred with gray and black weals as if his ectoplasmic form was physically burned by the green flames.

"Cséjthe! Help me!" he cried, stretching an arm wreathed in greenish gasses toward me.

"You really must be mad," I said.

He began to scream and curse, then. But not for long. The ashy canopy that had unfolded gray-and-black wings above and over us now swooped down and narrowed like the fine grains of sand falling through an hourglass. Pinching into a tight stream, they spun a seething cable the color of filthy silk and poured into Mengele's open mouth, choking off his profanities. The weight of the ashes forced him back down into the heart of the conflagration.

I am no voyeur when it comes to suffering and death but part of me wanted to stay and watch.

The flames had no effect on me and I remained untouched by a single flake of ash or soot. I knew in my heart of hearts that there was no escape for Mengele this time: he was in the hands of a jury, a jury of very special Threshers who would not release him until every little scrap was shredded, consumed, and obliterated so that his like might never again walk the earth in this form or any other. I could leave and trust them to take this particular threat from this world and, quite possibly, from the next.

Still, it only seemed right that someone bear witness.

That the monster who had done so many terrible things in secret, have someone who could return from these dark, anonymous rooms and testify to his final disposition.

Not for his sake but for all of the victims that the world would never know about.

It would have been fitting.

Perhaps I would have risked my own flesh to spend the extra moments. I dared not risk Deirdre, however. I flew from the Hellish judgment in that great iron furnace and rushed back toward the outer corridor and the stairs leading upwards.

It was over before I got there.

Wendigo had already freed my physical body from the restraints so she had to hold me back once I'd slid back in and got all systems back up and running.

"They are all dead," she told me as the slender Indian maiden helped the guy in the hospital gown totter down the hallway. "We made sure there were no survivors. No one will carry any part of the nightmare forth from this place."

"There were women and children—"

"Everything dies here!" she insisted, her sweet face morphing into skeletal planes and hollows for the briefest of moments. "The dream of this madman will be forgotten! The Ohdow who know the ways of the earth and stone say it is but a small matter to cause the mountain to fall in upon itself. We will bury the evil here and it shall remain hidden from the Race of Man as long as the Spirit Guardians may endure."

"Look on my works, ye Mighty, and despair," I murmured.

"What?"

"Shelley's *Ozymandias*. 'Nothing beside remains.

Round the decay / Of that colossal wreck, boundless and bare / The lone and level sands stretch far away.'" I bowed my head. "What about Deirdre?"

"I am sorry, Cséjthe. I am taking you to where they kept her body but I must warn you that we were too late. It is not a pretty sight . . ."

It felt, in that moment, as though the Ohdow had begun their work prematurely: the world seemed to cave in. I stumbled after her, legs numb, mind numb, heart numb, unable to speak until we reached the bloody operating theater where Theresa Kellerman had hoped to replace Deirdre's head with her own.

The Wendigo had a vast capacity for understatement.

The rescue *had* come too late.

And it wasn't pretty at all.

Chapter Twenty-Four

I WANTED TO sleep for a week. I didn't even get a full day.

The sun was up when Wendigo leapt from the shattered top of Mount Adler so I was wrapped in blankets and carried, papoose fashion, for the return trip to New York. She was loaded down with twice the weight she'd flown out with but I managed to convince her to bring along one large, metal suitcase. If there was Nazi gold stashed in a vault somewhere I hadn't seen it but what was in the valise was far more precious than Rhineland gold or Argentine diamonds or anything convertible to legal tender.

Needless to say, the suffocating but frail shielding of bedclothes and the buffeting of high-altitude flight without the amenities of a pressurized cabin or adjustable seat, made the several hours' journey somewhere between uncomfortable and harrowing. Fortunately I was exhausted, in mind if not in body, and I spent half the journey drowsing between a series of restless catnaps, clutching the metal

valise to my chest. The only REM state I achieved, however, was with my eyes wide open.

We arrived a few hours before sunset and I roused
enough to help Wendy smuggle our additional baggage
past the security checkpoints and down into the heart of
the Gotham demesne under Central Park.

Getting into my quarters might have been a little tricky
as I didn't have my key with me but Wendy went all wind-
walker and zipped through the keyhole like an errant
breeze. A moment later she was opening the door from
the other side and I staggered across the threshold with
my terrible burden. I looked for Suki but the guest bedrooms were empty. Only after I gave up and staggered
into my own quarters did I find her curled up in my own
bed and wrapped around my king-sized pillow in a pose
that was most unvampiric.

Rousing a sleeping vampire before sunset is not supposed to be easy. Maybe Asian vampires are different: she
sat right up as though sleep was an elusive commodity
these days.

Rousing a sleeping vampire is supposed to be dangerous: they tend to attack upon awakening. Suki lunged at
me immediately, wrapping her arms around my neck and
applying enough pressure to crush the vertebrae of someone without my preternatural strength.

Before either of us could say anything, her posture
stiffened: she had just realized that we were not alone.

And then she got a good look at what I had brought
with me.

And screamed.

☠ ☠ ☠

The bat guano had hit the fan in my absence.

According to Suki, Kurt had a pretty good idea that his "niece" was involved with Cairn. He just didn't know that she claimed to "be" Cairn. Asking her any additional questions on the matter was difficult as she had disappeared after the multiple stun-gunning in my hospital room. No one knew whether she had hotfooted it out of town or was lurking around the next corner in disguise. The best he could do for the moment was keep any of the other family or clan leaders from guessing that a Szekely might be allied with their greatest enemy.

While Suki had been close enough to see Darcy point her gun at me and intervene, she hadn't heard her actual confession. When I told her that Spook claimed to be the Vampire Boogeyman who had bedeviled the enclave for the past fifty years, Suki was taken aback.

"But that's impossible!" she said. "Darcy's human. She can't be that old!"

"She's not. It's a multigenerational role. She mentioned her mother and her grandmother before she pulled the trigger," I said. "Aside from the part of Cairn, 'himself,' I'll bet she isn't running this counterinsurgency all by herself. Other humans, maybe even other vampires, are involved. The Cairn persona—never seen, never heard—is a front but not a solitary person. The symbol cloaks a network that probably has moles within the various tribes and families."

"This girl is good," she agreed, "and the potential of additional operatives make her a more formidable opponent than anyone's supposed. But she's not your main problem, right now. The heads of the clans are putting pressure on Kurt to pronounce you lost or dead so a new Doman can be appointed." She looked at me meaningfully.

I sighed. "It's tempting. But I'd have to go back to a life of always looking over my shoulder—"

"You're suggesting that there would be a difference if you stay and rule?" She was trying to regain her impassive mien but some incredulity leaked through.

"The difference is I do things on *my* terms. Before I'm done they'll want me dead worse than if I just walked away." I shrugged. "But I've been given a second chance. Or maybe a third . . ." I shook my head. "Hell, I don't know: I may be on my fourth or fifth life, now. The point is there is more to my life—or even my unlife—than the brief time I spend running around in this carcass of flesh. And while I do still wear the flesh and the blood, I need to find a better use for it than just trying to hold on to it for a little bit longer."

"So, you plan to win stars for your crown by playing high mucky-muck to the biggest, baddest vampire enclave in the Western Hemisphere?"

I hung my head and stared at the bedroom carpet. In spite of repeated scrubbings, residual elements of my bedtime snacks remained in faint, trace amounts here and there. "I don't want the responsibility for a bunch of cold-blooded killing machines," I said, "but I'm stuck no matter what. Walk away and let another Liz Báthory or Vlad Dracula take over and my karma is pretty much up on concrete blocks in the Backyard of Eternity. Stay and take direct accountability, I'll lose what's left of my soul in six months. I could become a bigger monster than either of them ever was."

"I don't believe it."

"Doesn't matter. I do. Which is why I've got to pull the pin on the grenade."

I heard the frown in her voice. "I don't like the sound of that."

"Nobody's going to like it. That's how I can be sure it's the right thing to do."

We sat in silence until Wendy entered the room.

"All tucked in," she said. "Now what?"

I looked over at Suki. "You convince Kurt to call a meeting of all of the leaders—families, clans, tribes, gangs. Tell him to tell them that you have news of my— uh—disposition."

"Your disposition is cranky as usual."

I ignored that. "Try to make the meeting as late as possible. The closer to sunrise, the less recovery time everyone will have for a while." I turned to Wendigo. "We'll be leaving shortly after the meeting. I need for you to arrange transportation."

"To the airport?" she asked.

"No. We'll be driving, or have you forgotten?"

"Oh."

"A large, windowless van would be preferable." I got up and went over to rummage through my drawers. "Tinted windshield and movable seats. Curtain enclosures if possible. And sunblock. I'm going to need lots of sunblock." I handed her a black plastic card. "Charge it."

"I can steal the van. No paper trail."

"I can afford to buy it. I can't afford to *take* it."

Wendy looked at Suki. "It's a metaphysical thing," the vampire said inscrutably. Wendy took the card without a word.

"Now, we need to pack and be ready to leave quickly . . ."

"So this *is* a retreat," Suki argued.

"A strategic withdrawal," I said. "I'm walking away, not running. And I'm still going to be Doman. At least for a while. If I survive."

"It sounds like you actually have a plan for once."

"I do."

She shook her head. "Now I *am* scared!"

I slept, trying to grab whatever additional strength I could find before the night's showdown. Unfortunately my bed proved less restful than the Wendigo's jet stream red-eye. I tossed and turned as a dark and terrible shape drew near in my dreams, a juggernaut of pain and death and fear that seemed close enough to reach out and pull me down into the cold dark depths of Cenote Camazotz now. It had stalked me through my dreams since I'd left Louisiana. I'd been free of its nightmare travails while out of my body but, now that I'd returned, it seemed to have homed in on my location and closed the distance rapidly. I awoke with the feel of its gory footprints tramping across my doorstep.

Was it real or imaginary?

The palpable despair that accompanied each of these sleeping visitations felt too vivid, too painful, to be the product of indigestion or unresolved issues in my subconscious. It felt . . . external. And it kept coming closer.

I sat on the edge of the great empty bed in the dark room and weighed the darkness and emptiness in myself. Did it matter? Nothing was changed except the heaviness of my heart. I had to stay and do what I had to do whether there really was a bat-headed demon with a grudge or not. I could hope to pull everything off and buy myself another six months or a year. That might be enough for the generations of humans who might otherwise die—or worse—if I took any of the easier ways.

But if this thing was real? I knew, instinctively, that I didn't have a chance against something that old and powerful and consumed with rage and death.

"Give me time," I prayed to the darkness and the emptiness. Not "let me live" or "escape." What I needed was to be gone from New York before I met my fate or the plan would collapse like a house of cards.

Just give me enough time to do what's important.

"Time, my lord?" asked a familiar voice.

I looked up. Someone was standing across the room. My tired, aching eyes switched over into the infrared spectrum and contemplated the human-shaped rainbow of yellow, orange and red.

"Deirdre?" I croaked.

"It's Bethany, my lord."

"Bethany?" My mind was fuzzier than my eyes; it took a moment to click. White-blonde hair, Lutheran on the wine list. "Who sent you?"

"No one, Master. I felt your presence. I sensed your thirst."

"My thirst." It suddenly occurred to me that I had taken nothing in food or drink since reacquiring my body. And the last time I'd sat in the driver's seat I'd found the bloodlust to be a constant buzz in the back of my head. Was the silver in my system dissipating and lowering my dependence on fresh infusions of hemoglobin? Was it a

Zen thing, more physical mastery as a byproduct of astral progressions? Had an infusion of Michael's "blood" healed more than a pesky little bullet lodged in my heart?

Or were tens of thousands of microscopic nanobots retuning my tissues to a different pitch, a different state of being? *What were those little buggers doing inside of me, anyway?*

"Are you not thirsty, my lord?"

I didn't feel thirsty. I felt tired. But staring at the human-shaped candle flame in the darkness I realized that I needed more strength if I was to prevail over my opponents this evening. And that Bethany's blood might be just what the doctor ordered.

"I have your teeth, here," she said. And walked toward the bed with her arms out, trying to feel her way through the lightless void.

"Bethany," I said, taking her by the hand, "you once told me that the money was very good for serving in the wine cellar."

"Yes, Master." She pressed the box into my hands as we sat back down together. "Enough to pay all of my debts, college loans, and live very, very well."

"Ah." I set the box aside for the moment and clasped her hands in mine. "So you're a college student. What are you studying?"

"Architecture and design. At—at least, I was."

"You've stopped." It wasn't a question and I could feel her nod in return without actually looking at her. "Well, it obviously wasn't for a lack of funding . . . poor grades, perhaps?"

"Four-oh average." Her voice was proud and yet wistful.

"Sorry, I had a feeling you were honor roll material. The thing is," I squeezed her fingers, "a perfect grade point requires more than intelligence, it requires drive. You were motivated." Again, it wasn't a question but I let it hang in the air between us like one.

"Yes," she said finally. "My lord, I am ready. Slake your thirst with my body."

"In a moment," I said. "I'm just curious. You seem bright, capable. Why waste your talents on something boring and dreary like architecture?"

"But it isn't!" The colors in her head, neck, and chest burned more brightly. "It's the perfect fusion of art and science! The utilization of space and materials, matched to human need in all axes: physical, emotional, psychological . . . spiritual . . ." She lapsed into a ten-minute lecture on the aesthetics of redesigning environments and their impact on the human condition, ranging from the individual to whole societies.

"So," I asked when she finally paused to collect herself, "when did you finally fall out of love with it?"

"I—I—realized there wasn't any point . . ."

"Becoming a bloodsucking creature of the night has derailed many a budding career," I agreed.

"Will I be changed soon, Master?" Her voice had lost its vitality and gone dead, not with dread but with lack of purpose.

I turned and fumbled with the inlaid box in the dark. "We'll see." I slipped the exquisitely crafted fangs over my own dull teeth. "Give me your neck, child."

She tilted her head back and I caught her upper back with my left arm. She was all unwrapped and ready: a dinner

table from head to toe. Her throat arched toward my mouth
but a neck wound always runs a high risk of bleeding out so
I lowered my mouth to her shoulder. She sighed as my faux
fangs pierced the trapezius muscle and, as her rare essence
began to enter my mouth, I entered her mind.

It was different, this time. I wasn't storming in to take
over her flesh. I wasn't pushing her consciousness down
the cellar stairs and locking it in the basement of her
hindbrain. And Bethany and I already shared a psychic
connection from my previous feeding and reward session.

I was, however, doing something far more intimate this
time than diddling her to a physical orgasm. I eased into
the master bedroom of her subconscious and began to dis-
creetly rearrange the furniture.

Friederich Polidori entered the council chamber late.

Not just fashionably late: the other family representatives had pressed Kurt to hear their grievances without
waiting any longer and Christopher Cséjthe's seneschal was
well under siege when the head of the Polidori clan entered
the soundproofed room draped with red satin curtains. It
was the same room where I had received the heads of the
various clans and families just a couple of nights before.
The great throne was symbolically empty. Kurt Szekely sat
in the large chair to its right. Suki was perched on the chair
to its immediate left. The various representatives, number-
ing between fifteen and twenty-five, sat in curving rows of
chairs facing the throne on the raised dais.

Polidori moved up the center aisle and found an empty
chair on the front row but created scarcely a ripple in the
debate with his passing.

"He's dead and that's the long and short of it," Silvanio Malatesta was insisting. "We cannot wait any longer. A new Doman must take his place." Heads nodded and voices murmured agreement around the room.

"He's not dead!" Suki stood up from her seat near Kurt. "I have knowledge of his continued existence and his instructions for the Council!"

"My dear," Carmella Le Fanu cooed, "even if we could trust something as tenuous as a blood-bond in this matter, you've admitted that he neither sired you, nor you, him. Unless you can produce the Doman in the flesh, some purported psychic connection is just not something that we can seriously consider."

"The fact of the matter is that he was all but dead when he was abducted," Malatesta elaborated. "He had no chance for survival in the hands of his friends and he's been two days, now, in the hands of powerful enemies. He is either dead or as good as, for our concerns. A new Doman must arise and arise quickly!"

Kurt stirred from his position deep in the right-hand subthrone. "You seem awfully anxious, Silva. Could it be that you have designs on that role, yourself?"

The Bloodfather of the Bava opened his mouth but Dante Inferno jumped in. "We have good cause to be anxious, Szekely. These unnatural edicts from your half-human puppet need to be rescinded! The Lupin are restless and need to be reminded who holds power."

"It's not just that," Valentine Le Fanu added. "There are rumors that the Doman got a wolfbitch with child."

"What?"

"Abomination!"

"Impossible!"

While the majority of the room's occupants were unanimous in expressing shock and outrage, Valentine moved to the back door and opened it. More Le Fanu clan members entered, flanking a tall, rangy man. A very familiar-looking, tall, rangy man. The shaggy widow's peak, the angular ears, the overall impression of wax-resistant body hair—it was the man from my sewer dream, the one Lupé had called "Grandfather."

Carmella stood as the older man was escorted up to stand next to her and the room quieted. "Why deal in rumor and gossip," she announced, "when we can get a firsthand report?"

It was plain from the expression on his face that Kurt was caught off guard. He started to protest then realized that he wanted to know as much as anyone else. "Is it true, Silas?" he asked the older man. "We've heard stories that the Garou woman is pregnant with our Doman's child. How is such a thing possible?"

Gramps, who looked like he'd been fed a regular diet of prunes and they were affecting him at both ends, shuffled his feet and growled: "I do not know . . ."

"The law . . ." someone hissed.

"We did not break faith!" he barked back. "She did! It was our intent to bring her to you for judgment!"

"Liar!" someone cried.

"Then where is she?" someone else asked.

"Dead," Silas said.

"My, how convenient," Blackstar Sabertooth purred. "Wouldn't you say, Friederich?"

Friederich Polidori made no response beyond a silent

impression of Yuler, after drinking my silver-laced blood.

"So where is the body?" Kurt queried. "You don't expect us to take your story at face value without any evidence."

"We could not—recover—the body." The words came out of his throat, bitter and difficult. "Five of us died. The rest—barely escaped with our lives!"

"It sounds like," the head of the Aluka said after a moment's silence, "she put up a hell of a fight . . ."

His Oneidan counterpart nodded. "If we are to believe your account."

"You know nothing!" the old werewolf roared back, additional fur beginning to carpet his cheeks and jaw line. "It was a demon! A monster from Hell come to punish her for her sins! It was our ill fortune to come between them when it attacked!"

And he launched into a detailed, horrific account of how a bat-headed demon plowed through a pride of were-warriors as if they were mere puppies. How it ripped a two-story house to shreds with its scaly, clawed hands to reach its ordained victim. And finally, after tossing two full-blooded vampires into the river as if they were new-born infants, how it carried Lupé Garou and her unborn child down into the bowels of the earth to meet the fate of those who break with the ancient laws and ways.

When he was done, no one seemed inclined to challenge the depth of horror and shame that radiated off of him throughout the telling. No one believed that it was a lie.

Kurt turned to the assemblage as the old man shuffled

back out with his vampire escort. "It would appear that our problems with the Lupin are in abeyance for now—"

"But there is still the matter of Cairn—what is his part in all of this?" Carmella retorted. She still had not sat back down.

"And one cannot help but wonder where your young hound Darcy has gotten to, Szekely," Valentine drawled on his way back from the closing door. "Are the rumors true? Has she flown the nest? Does she seek to ally herself with the wolves? Or has she been working for this cursed Cairn all along?"

Kurt stiffened in his chair. "How *dare* you!"

"How dare *I*?" Valentine waved a limp hand. "How about how dare *we*? The gossip has gone throughout the five boroughs and beyond."

Silvanio made a stab at playing the statesman. "If it's true that she shot Domo Cséjthe we are hardly prepared to condemn her. Each Doman rises to power by eliminating his or her predecessor. Perhaps she was acting on another's behalf. Yours, Domo Szekely?"

"You presume too much!"

"Do we? Because if she did not attack our Doman on your orders one must ask who she is working for."

"And whether you can adequately serve any Doman," a tall, black man wearing a green suit, added, "if you can develop such a blind spot."

"It is a fact that your brother perished the same night as Domo Cséjthe was taken down, *n'est-ce pas*?" This from a small, dark woman in lavender taffeta.

"Your point?" Kurt grumbled.

"Well," said Valentine, "whoever becomes Doman might be well advised to appoint a better advisor."

"Perhaps it is better for you if the half-blood does not return," Dante mused. "He might blame *you* for the misfortunes that have befallen him."

Blackstar chimed in with: "You've been the obedient lapdog, Szekely, but would you willingly bare your throat for him?"

They were all ganging up to back him into a corner but Kurt showed he had lost neither his political nor street fighter's instincts as he steepled his fingers and said: "Assuming we were to agree that we are, once again, without a Doman . . . how would the families come to an agreement regarding a replacement?"

That did it. Too many clans would lose big in the one-vote-to-a-member model. The squabbling commenced with Kurt watching the various family heads while Suki watched Friederich.

Polidori ended up just staring at the floor.

Eventually there was a lull in the threats and oaths and half-baked plans. Carmella had joined Suki in regarding Polidori's contemplative mood and took the opportunity to address him. "You have been silent, my lord Friederich. What are your thoughts on these matters?"

"I thought," said Kurt, "that we were here to listen to a message from our Doman through his representative here."

"She's not his representative," someone called from the back, "she's Pagelovitch's proxy from Seattle!"

"Nonetheless—" Kurt began.

Suki reached over and touched his arm. "I'll gladly yield the floor to Master Polidori."

Friederich seemed to shake himself from his reverie and slowly rose from his chair.

"My lords and ladies," he began after a moment's meditation, "I have held my tongue while you have discussed these matters of import and now I ask you to cede me the floor for a few brief minutes that I may make my thoughts clear to you. I ask that you listen to what I have to say without interruption so that I may finish quickly and succinctly—then you may discuss my words and decide as you will." He looked around the room. "Are my terms reasonable to the rest of you?"

Heads began to nod but Carmella smirked and said, "You worry me, Polidori. It is not like you to 'ask our leave.'"

"Ah, but it is like *you*, Carmella, to interrupt and so I ask your indulgence just this once."

She disliked that comeback but closed her mouth and nodded.

"Let me begin with a simple statement. Your Doman, Christopher L. Cséjthe, *is* alive and well. And he is anxious to address the heads of the clans and families on several key issues."

No one kept their word: the room erupted into a cacophony of shouted questions and half-muttered oaths. Polidori made no attempt to answer any of them or be heard over the din. Eventually, he sat down and waited. Eventually the room grew quiet as the rest of the representatives realized they would learn nothing as long as their own mouths were open.

"I know the questions you have and those questions will be answered if you will just be patient and listen and—" Polidori's voice became very quiet so that the others had to strain to hear his words, "—pay very close attention.

"As I was saying, your Doman is alive and has several key issues to discuss with you. But first you should know of recent events. He has faced and defeated The Mangler, also known as Doctor Pipt, also known as the Nikidik, better known to history as the infamous Nazi doctor, Joseph Mengele. It was he who sent the cybernetic creatures against our Doman's homes here in New York and back in Louisiana. Cséjthe's victory came at a terrible cost but it has also resulted in enhanced powers and abilities that he did not possess previously. Among the Northern Wilderness Clans, he is now known as Chixu Manitou and is called 'Bloodwalker.' The reason for this shall shortly be obvious."

Cries of "Where is he?" and "Why should we take your word for it?" interrupted and Polidori made as if to sit down again but the room quickly grew quiet.

"You think our demesne is impregnable," Polidori continued, "but it is not. Our security protocols are designed to warn us of even our own comings and goings—they are not foolproof. Your Doman has returned to New York and has walked among you this evening. He walks about even now."

Again the room erupted and Polidori had to sit down this time. It took several minutes of shouted exhortations for everyone else to shut up to accomplish just that.

"Where is he?" Valentine growled as the room fell silent.

"I cannot say it aloud but, if you will come over here," Polidori said, "I will whisper the answer in your ear."

Scowling to show his disdain, nevertheless, Valentine got up and strode impatiently to the head of the Polidori family. Friederich stood and leaned toward Carmella's brother who turned and cocked his head to receive the information. He opened his mouth as if to whisper, then dropped his jaw and struck like a viper, burying his fangs in Valentine's neck.

There was no real struggle. One moment a Polidori was clamped to a Le Fanu neck, the next the former was on the floor while the latter staggered toward his sister.

Carmella was unprepared for the assault on her brother. She was even less prepared for her brother's assault on herself. His teeth were in her throat before she could even cry out. The two nearest clan leaders stepped in to separate them. One ended up with an unconscious Valentine, the other with a bloody-minded Carmella. The attacks unfolded like a chain reaction of fang-to-throat quickies diagrammed by Rube Goldberg and choreographed by Busby Berkeley. Each attack lasted mere seconds and then turned upon another victim as soon as the victim in question was unfanged. In short order nearly sixteen family, gang, and tribe representatives were left bloody and gasping in various states of disarray across aisles, chairs and floor.

Silvanio Malatesta got up, brushed himself off, and walked up to the front of the room. "Go sit with the others," he told Kurt.

The seneschal, as yet untouched and unbloodied, looked up at the undead gangster as if to measure his chances for one-on-one combat. Malatesta shook his head and said, "Please. Your Doman commands it."

Kurt got up slowly and moved to the nearest seat in the front row.

Suki stood as Malatesta turned to her. "Go," he said, "it is time." He leaned in and whispered: "Fifteen minutes. Twenty, tops."

As Suki left the room he turned and sat down in the Doman's chair of judgment.

"As most of you now know, I *am* your Doman. At least the mind of Chris Cséjthe, anyway. For the moment I speak to you from Silvanio Malatesta's body. I entered the room a short while ago in Friederich Polidori's flesh. During our little exercise a few moments ago, I passed though the minds and bodies of most of the full-blooded vampires in this room. While I was visiting, I was in full control of your flesh just as I'm playing puppet master for Malatesta now. Any questions so far?"

Well, of course there were questions but those would be asked later. For now everyone was too stunned to do anything but try to absorb this sudden turn of events.

"I'm not the man I was four days ago. Not just in what I can now do but in how I now feel. The first thing you need to fully understand is *what* I am capable of. I can, if I wish, take your body when I please and you cannot stop me. While I am wearing it, I can use it to torch your nests, drain your children, and then take a little stroll outside on a bright, sunny day. Right after I pop out of your dissolving, carbonized remains I can go and pop inside of the next vampire I take a shine to.

"Are we clear so far?"

There were a few stunned nods.

"Perhaps you did not understand my question. *Do* you

understand that I can show up inside your heads unannounced, wreak bloody havoc, and disappear again without effort or cost to myself?"

Heads were nodding all around now. It looked like a bobble-head convention.

"Good. Because the other change is just as important. As I said, I'm not the same guy I was four days ago. Back then I was essentially the Rodney King of fangdom, just wishing we could all get along. Guess what? You have a new Doman now and the survivors *will* all get along."

I let that word "survivors" hang out there for a moment for them all to contemplate.

"Rule number one," I continued, "anyone who doesn't follow the rules is gone. No 'ifs,' 'ands' or 'buts.'"

"Gone . . ." someone murmured.

I nodded Malatesta's head. "Gone. Not 'banished.' Not 'kicked out.' Not designated 'rogue.' Just . . . 'gone.'"

"How will you know," Blackstar Sabertooth asked, "if one of our gang members doesn't fully sign on?"

I made Malatesta grin what I hoped was a truly unpleasant grin. "Word gets around. One of the other clans or gangs or families produces evidence. Then that group is . . . *gone*."

Eyes goggled.

"Don't you mean that individual?" Dante countered with an uncertain glower.

I shook my head, all pleasantness. "No. It is up to you to see that all of your people are on board. If a member of your gang looks like he or she might betray the cause, it's up to you to make them 'gone' before I find out and make all of The Deads dead and gone. Capeesh?"

Polidori was picking himself up off the floor. He shook his head as if to clear the last vestiges of my intruding consciousness from his skull. "You threatened severe consequences the other night and then allowed Yuler to live after his attempt on your life. Why should we believe you now?"

"Because I hitched a little ride in your head to get into the room, Freddie-boy, so you should know how deadly serious I am, this time. All these past months of you guys sending assassins after me, playing politics once I was here, pushing to see if I would push back—you know what? I *get* it. You guys are predators. You're hard-wired for it. And, as if the bloodlust wasn't enough, all that preternatural power tends to corrupt.

"You should be proud of yourselves: you're a great bunch of teachers and I think I'm ready to graduate and apply what I've learned now. You've convinced me that I really can't do this any other way.

"Now, rule number two: no more killing humans." I expected the room to erupt like Mount Krakatoa but they all just sat there and glowered at me like students trapped in after-school detention. "I'm not forbidding you to hunt or feed. But I *know* that it can be done without killing. So no killing the warms."

"Not even in self-defense?" someone asked from the second row.

"Self-defense is like the insanity defense. You can only invoke it once and then the odds are seriously against your acquittal. So don't get in a 'kill or be killed' situation—you're only postponing your own execution.

"Rule number three: undead birth control. No

more adding to the ranks of the undead without my permission."

"We have to ask your permission to sire?"

Malatesta and I nodded together.

"Won't that get a little complicated?"

We shook our head. "Not really. The answer will be 'no,' ninety-nine times out of a hundred. And that's if I'm feeling generous."

"Anything else?" Valentine asked dourly.

I stopped smiling and the real Malatesta down in the crypt of his hindbrain whimpered. "Yeah. There was supposed to be. Rule number one was supposed to be no one—NO ONE—was to lay a finger on my wife or child . . ."

Carmella's face registered a mixture of distaste and disbelief. "The wolfbitch was your wife?"

I was down off the dais and plowing through the chairs in the blink of an eye. My own arm couldn't have raised Valentine's sister off her feet and held her struggling in midair. Malatesta's could and did. "She *would* have been my wife," I growled, pulling Carmella's face close to the undead mask I wore for the moment. "But someone sent assassins with silver bullets and poisoned more than just my blood. She would have been my wife and I would have been with her instead of leaving her to die alone and unprotected!" I hurled her across the room and turned on the others. "In case you haven't been taking notes, I'm internalizing a great deal of rage right now! If anyone else would like to tap into that, I could use the catharsis!"

No one moved. No one said bupkis.

I turned and started to walk toward the door.

"Is that it?" someone whispered in the back.

I stopped. "No. That is not it. That's just for starters. But lest you think I'm all about punishment, there will also be rewards. For those who are my eyes and ears, those who bring me word or evidence of any that speak rebelliously, that plot in secret, that might be my enemy now or in days to come—I know how to reward, just as I know how to punish."

I turned back toward the exit. "Sunrise is coming and I have other things to do yet tonight, as well as tomorrow. I will meet with you all again in three nights. For now I wish to be alone."

It would all begin here in a few days if not a few hours, I thought. *Chaos, panic, rage, disorder, and the preemptive betrayals: my work here was done.* I took three steps before the door flew open and vomited broken, bloody vampires.

"*Cséjthe!*" an inhuman voice bellowed from beyond. A bat-headed silhouette filled the opening and then some.

Chapter Twenty-Five

IT WAS JUST a moment, a couple of eye blinks really. First the hulking brute was outside in the cramped corridor, peering through the too-small egress at the lot of us.

Then it was in the room with us.

It should have taken out half the wall to do so. I didn't doubt that it could. Aside from the old werewolf's testimony regarding another house investment gone bad, the creature had arms that made the fire department's Jaws of Life look like chopsticks.

But the demon merely stepped through the opening. And, for just the briefest of moments, I thought I saw a small, neatly dressed man take its place.

There was nothing small or neat about the behemoth that crouched past the threshold, however. It was as if some demented genetics lab had blended bat and human DNA in ways that only Bruce Wayne could imagine in his darkest nightmares, and then gene-spliced the growth hormones of an African elephant into the mix. Its head was the size of a wrecking ball—and that did not include the large, tufted ears that erupted from the sides of its skull like inverted jet engine scoops. Its nose was like a flint knife, its teeth like the stalactites of the underworld realms that spawned it. The creature half squatted on legs that were, each, as big around as a human torso. Leathery wings draped beneath furry arms that could tear a man in two without flexing. And over one of those massive shoulders was draped the lower half of a human body.

My human body—if I recognized the clothing I had dressed in just a couple of hours before.

"*Cséjthe!*" It bellowed again, casting about the room like a hound dog hoping to pick up a scent.

I looked at the rest of the vampires in the room.

They looked back at me.

I could order them to defend their Doman.

Yeah, right. They were probably thinking that batboy was the answer to all their prayers. It takes me out; they get to go back to the big blood orgy.

Since taking the demon on, myself, was obviously a no-win situation, that left me with taking the body I currently had and beating a hasty retreat. My original birthday suit could be counted as lost at this point but I could always dump Malatesta's skin and find something more appropriate down the road.

The trouble was I was never very good at walking, much less running, away from no-win situations. More importantly, this bat-headed bastard had killed Lupé and Will.

"Over here, Zotz," I said, and stepped back from the tangle of chairs so that there was open floor between us.

The rest of the vampires scrambled to the back of the room as the monster stomped toward me.

And then past me.

It moved up to the dais and, lifting my limp body from its plateaulike shoulder, placed it upon the throne. I looked nothing so much like I had dozed off during a tedious meeting.

It turned to Malatesta-me then and said, "Will you return to that which is yours?"

Well, hell, why not?

If I was going to die with my boots on, better they were on my feet than somebody else's: a twist, a pop, a glide, and then splish-splash, I was taking a bath all inside my own little husk. My eyes popped open just in time to watch Malatesta keel over and then Batzilla loom over. His very size blotted out most of the light in the room.

Then his face was dropping toward me and all the lights went out.

You can't imagine darkness as a human. You can only experience a certain lessening of light. Until you've gone down into the darkness under the earth, slept under a sky of earth and stone, where no breeze blows, no sound sighs, you do not know the darkness beyond the land of the living.

And that is but the outer darkness.

There is an interior landscape of eternal night that the living may never know. Yet I knew both as profound emptiness swallowed me. I was cast adrift in an interstellar gulf as lifeless and lightless as anything that might be grasped and still sustain cohesive thought. A limitless void made up of dark years stretched in all directions, cold and vast and deep and lonely.

Years passed.

Lifetimes.

Centuries.

Eons.

The darkness began to resolve into dim images like a backward Doppler shift, moving toward that which had been left behind.

Traveling back in time . . .

        space . . .

                memory . . .

                        experience . . .

                                being . . .

Pre-Columbian Mesoamerica. *Desmodus draculae*, the gigantic ancestor of the modern vampire bat, *Desmodus rotundus.*

In the *Popol Vuh* they dwelt in the fearsome Underworld realm of Zotzilaha; in the real world they inhabited the mountain caves, the giant trees of the densest jungles, and the mysterious depths of the greater cenotes. The Zotzil peoples of Mexico still refer to them in legend as Black-man and Neckcutter. In their day the Quiché Maya named them Bloodletter and Camazotz after their god of fire, Zotzilaha Chamalcan.

And they made sacrifices to them.

One thousand.

Ten thousand.

Eventually hundreds of thousands of souls went into the earth and the watery wells of sacrifice. Mass graves to rival the Nazis' Final Solution though the results were accomplished over a much longer time frame.

Something else was accomplished, as well.

Something was awakened.

Not a collection of separate entities as suggested in Mengele's butcher shop but a single, mass mind.

A single mass hunger . . .

That fed on life and blood and glutted itself into an indolent sleep that lasted centuries, then millennia, while the Maya and the Aztecs passed from glory and their cities crumbled and their sacred wells were lost in oblivions of green and brown.

But that sleep did not last.

Blood calls to blood and, though the surviving descendants of the Mesoamericans had ceased their sacrifices, other tribes had taken up the practice. The ceremonies were different, the methods varied, but the pain and the blood and the vast numbers of the dead were much the same. The world was a smorgasbord of terror and death and it could gorge itself from a variety of menus over a succession of generations. There were pogroms in Russia, world wars in Europe, spreading to the Pacific on the second go-round. South American revolutions and African genocides. Then there came a day when It grew tired of the feast. Sin sick and full of the pain and death of billions, it turned back home and, sinking into the dark depths of the bottomless lake beneath the well of souls, where it had been spawned a thousand years before, it once more sought oblivion, a nirvana of blackness.

But the blood festered.

The pain would not subside nor be mastered.

And, having overpowered death so many times, there was now no strength remaining to serve it in a final, personal solution.

I came out of my trance to find the massive creature kneeling at my feet with its huge head cradled against my knees. My trousers were soaked from its tears as it sobbed and sobbed and finally said in a very small voice: "Please . . . help . . . me . . ."

It followed as I stumbled and picked my way through the scattered tumble of chairs. The room looked like the aftermath of a cattle stampede—a stampede of fanged, two-legged, undead cattle who figured their best chance for survival lay in escaping while the demon tore their Doman apart.

Too bad they hadn't stayed around long enough to witness the altar call.

"Get away from me," I mumbled.

"I thought that if any human might understand . . ."

"I don't *want* to understand," I said. "Leave me alone!"

"I cannot."

"What do you want from me?" I staggered, half-blind from the images and sensations still roiling through my brain. "Are you looking for absolution? I'm not a priest."

"You are better than a holy man," the demon answered. "You know the taste of blood, have walked in the pathways of darkness. Yet you strive to do good and prevent others from doing evil."

"Yeah, I'm a regular Boy Scout."

"I am darkness given form and function. I am death given a semblance of life. I am sin that finally chokes upon its own essence. All the lives, the deaths, the years, have made me filthy beyond repugnance. I need the blood."

"Sounds like the blood is the root of your problem, addiction-boy."

"Not mortal blood," it answered. "Your blood. It is said to have healing properties. It gives life to those who would otherwise be dead."

"My blood," I said carefully, "kept a severed head alive to everyone's regret. It caused my lover to leave me and all but killed a vampire who took a little sip. You want to be washed in the blood of Jesus, Zotz, not sampling a little Cséjthe Bordeaux."

"I am not ready to make supplication to another god, yet. My condition is too lowly. I must learn to be human, first. That is why I have sought you out. Your blood calls to me. It tells me that you understand the darkness. That you have known The Hunger and resisted it. That you can teach me how to either make an ending or a new beginning."

"I teach American Lit. Except I'm on sabbatical this semester."

"Please, Master! You are my only hope!"

I stopped and tried not to tremble as I parsed my words carefully. "Listen. I'd be very happy to kill you if I thought I had any chance of being able to do so. Give you the oblivion, here and now, that you think you crave. Except I don't believe it would be possible even with your cooperation."

"Yes," it agreed, "and you must now know what I have known for centuries. Death does not bring oblivion. It grasps us by the neck and rubs our face in our failures, our faults, all the wrongs we seek to flee from. Suicide is not so much a mortal sin as a headlong rush to the seat of our eternal pain."

"Keep talking," I seethed, "you'll inspire me to try even though I know I'm hopelessly outmatched."

"Of course you would want to try. I have no right to ask any human for help when I have fed off of the suffering and misery of the human race for countless gen—"

I whirled and grabbed him by his furry throat. "Look, I don't care diddley about the rest of the human race. We don't need demons to blame for our misery and our own inhumanity to man. You guys kibitz and stir the pot but I've got a pretty good sense that we could blow up the world on our own, thank you." He made no move to escape my grasp. "You ever read *Frankenstein* by Mary Wollstonecraft Shelly? It's an analogy, Batzilla: God is Doctor Frankenstein and humanity is His monster—a mass of mismatched parts stumbling around in search of its creator and committing more atrocities every step of the way." I tightened my grip though it felt like I was making no impression on that column of muscle. "But let's not talk about the millions of faceless, nameless strangers that died in wars and concentration camps and political game preserves providing you with some kind of psychosexual runoff to feed on. Let's talk about you coming to my house and killing the mother of my unborn son!"

"Oh really, Chris," Lupé nagged, "don't be stupid!"

I shook my head. It was just like her memory to nag me as I confronted the monster that had murdered her.

"Why would he hurt me if he was coming to you for help?" her voice continued. *It was as if she were still alive and with me.*

Camazotz nodded, making it difficult to hold on to his throat. "My only thought was to protect her." He turned his head and looked past me. "I thought I told you to wait in the truck."

"It's getting close to sunrise," her voice argued. "I only agreed to wait outside if you got in and back out again in a hurry."

"The sun, while unpleasant, doesn't harm either of us—"

"But Chris might not have his sunblock with him and he may have allies that wish to leave with him. Honestly, do I have to do *all* of the thinking around here?"

I turned then and stared at the apparition standing in the doorway. Lupé looked very real, very solid, and more than a little annoyed.

Another familiar face popped up behind her. Boo, wearing a jacket with a turned-up collar, a muffler, and a Peterbilt cap pulled down low over his eyes. "C'mon, Hoss, I've got an eighteen-wheeler double-parked topside and we're not gonna be low profile much longer!"

I opened my mouth. "What—?" was about all I could get out.

"What did we bring an eighteen-wheeler fer?" the old zombie asked for me. That might even have been one of my questions. "It was her idea. More room for more people. No windows."

"Come on, come on," Lupé urged. "Grandfather showed me the secret ways in and out of this place when I was young, but that was years ago and I wasn't on the wanted list back then. Unless you've got valuables stashed somewhere, I suggest you follow me right now."

I shook my head. "I've got valuables but they're packed and waiting upstairs in a windowless van."

"There's more room in the truck."

I nodded. My brain finally engaged. "We'll split up here and meet on the Seventy-ninth Street Transverse, in front of Belvedere Castle."

Camazotz growled at the zombie: "Get her back in the truck!"

"You get Chris out of here safely," she growled back. Then she turned and sprinted back down the hall. Boo shambled after her as speedily as his rotting limbs would take him.

"Come on," the bat-demon said, taking my arm in his taloned grasp, "you don't want to make that lady mad."

"Tell me about it."

We didn't exactly run but we passed through the corridors, then into the service passageways and up into the sewers before emerging near the Dakota Building on Central Park West. Anywhere we encountered vampires or staff, one look at the Mesoamerican demon and our pathway was suddenly vacant. We met no resistance whatsoever.

As we were climbing up the ladder to the street level he reconfigured his anatomy, compacting down to a smallish black man. By now I had grown accustomed to seeing Lupé transform so it wasn't completely novel. Unlike my beloved and the other Weres, however, he seemed to be able to manufacture clothing out of his residual mass.

Our conversation, however, wasn't focused on matters of sartorial sorcery. Instead he proceeded to explain how among all of the dreams and all of the nightmares of bloodshed and war and murder most foul, a face had appeared. My face. And something had suggested that I might know enough about monstrous hungers and remember enough of the human condition to serve as a guide . . .

"Guide?" I grunted, shouldering the manhole cover up and out of the way. "What kind of a guide? Guide for what?"

"My way out of the blood-drenched darkness that has been my existence for uncountable human lifetimes. My journey back to humanity."

I climbed up and saw that Suki was directing the sparse, early morning traffic around us with a flashlight. I reached down to give Zotz a hand up. "Um, not to discourage you on the whole self-improvement gig, but you were never human to begin with."

"I contain the spiritual detritus of a hundred thousand drowned souls within my own essence," he said, popping up and brushing off his suit. Dirt didn't appear to stick to him the way it did to me. "I think I have more 'human' antecedents than you do in that sense."

"If 'sense' is an applicable word here," I muttered.

Suki came over. "Sunrise in thirty minutes. Who's he?"

"My intern." I kicked the manhole cover back into place. "By the way, there's been a change in plans."

We made the rendezvous and offloaded the van into the truck with minutes to spare. By the time that the rising sun was turning the Manhattan skyline into a shadowbox diorama, we were well along and stuck in morning traffic, Boo and his buddies up in the cab and the rest of us back in the day-shelter of the trailer.

There was a little bit of grumbling on Boo's part about being stuck up front with Preacher. Cam was sitting between them but, as I've pointed out before, he's a limited conversationalist and it was going to be a long road trip. I thought about swapping Cameron out for the demon as both Zotz and Jerome could probably have some spirited discussions on the topics of theology and the afterlife. But that wouldn't necessarily mollify Boo and no one wanted to share closed quarters in the back with a rotting corpse. As it was there were about fifteen automobile air fresheners hanging from the ceiling of the truck cab's interior.

Lupé, Zotz, and the cemetery crew had outfitted the back of the semi with cots and coffins and a sofa from the living room for the return trip.

"I knew you would need rescuing," Lupé said, "you always do."

"Mother's intuition?" I asked.

Her left eyebrow went up but she didn't answer.

"Actually, I was doing rather well on my own," I continued, ignoring the stifled hiccup sound from Suki. "I'd made my points, the plan was unfolding on schedule, and I'd be another thirty miles down the road, by now, if you hadn't interrupted with your 'rescue.' Not that I mind, of course." I gave Zotz a sideways glance as I leaned over and kissed her on the cheek.

"Ow!" She jerked away and rubbed her face as if stung. "Just scoot over there, a little farther away, please! And keep your hands to yourself."

I slid back over to the far end of the sofa where the light from the Coleman lantern wouldn't betray my own face quite so readily.

"What's in the big suitcase?" she asked after a moment. "Nazi gold?"

I looked over at the large metal suitcase that contained frozen embryos of Jenny and Kirsten. "Personal effects." I didn't feel like discussing that topic right now.

"Do you really think they'll agree to put up with your rules and restrictions?" Suki asked, running conversational interference.

"Yes," Lupé chimed in, "it sounds like you gave a convincing display of dominance but how long can that carry you?"

"I'm not a fool," I said, feeling somewhat the fool for different reasons. "You cannot domesticate vampires." *Or werewolves . . .*

"Then what was the point?" Zotz asked, moving to sit on the cushions between us.

"Oh, it's obvious, Cammy," she answered before I could open my mouth. *Cammy?* "Chris couldn't bear to preside over a demesne that allowed the hunting and killing and turning of humans. He's just one man and even a full-blooded vampire couldn't go up against an entire enclave and survive. So, he's turned them against each other."

Suki nudged my foot with hers. "You've read Sun Tzu, haven't you?"

"It won't last," I said. "I knew that when I set it up." *Cammy?*

"You buy whatever time you can, using what you're given," Lupé said. "The thing is, by the time they've thinned their own ranks to eliminate competition and curry favor they'll realize that they need a new Doman to coordinate the survivors in bringing you down."

"Which will bring about another round of assassinations and bloody infighting," Suki summed up. "In the meantime, your precious humans are given a reprieve and you have a chance to stop and catch your breath."

Theresa Kellerman cleared her throat. "Speaking of stopping . . ."

We all turned to look.

We'd all been trying very hard not to since climbing aboard and heading out but staring was inevitable.

The stitches that held her head and neck on Deirdre's body were already superfluous due to the accelerated healing factors combined in her flesh and my blood.

"Oh, please!" Deirdre scolded, rolling her eyes. "Did I not tell you to be sure and go before we left?"

Her head was tilted a bit to the left to make room for Theresa's, which tilted to the right.

The Wendigo and her troops had arrived too late to stop the operation from getting underway. Mengele's surgeons had gotten as far as attaching Kellerman's central nervous and circulatory systems before the OR was stormed. Another five minutes and Deirdre's head would have been excised like a five-pound tumor.

So, "too late" and yet . . .

"I tried," Theresa sniffed, "but it's hard. I'm not used to going when somebody else is in the room."

"And you'd better *not* get used to it, either," the redhead snapped. "As soon as we get back to Louisiana, Doctors Mooncloud and Burton are going to perform a *lunk*ectomy!"

"That's not fair," the brunette wailed, "you've had this

body all along! It's my turn to have a body!" She began to sob hysterically. "Not fair! Not fair! Not fair!"

"Not my body, you twit! Now stop it; you're getting hysterical." Deirdre reached over and gave her a little slap with her left hand.

Theresa stopped crying but failed to calm down. "You *hit* me!" She reached over with her right and yanked a handful of auburn tresses.

"Uh-oh," sighed Suki, "here we go again."

"Ow! Psycho!" *Slap!*

"Bitch!" *Yank!*

"Freakazoid!" *Smack!*

"Whore!" *Pull!*

"Nutjob!" *Whack!*

"Bitch!" *Tug!*

"You're repeating yourself, dear."

"Bite me!"

Deirdre obliged by craning her neck and sinking her teeth into Theresa's nose.

"Ow, ow, ow, ow, ow, ow, ow!"

As soon as her nose was released, the brunette reciprocated by doing a Tyson on the redhead's ear.

Things really started to rock and roll at that point. Although they shared a single body from the shoulders down and were (was?) deeply ensconced in a beanbag chair so that they didn't move all that much, heads and arms were quite active for the next several minutes as a full-fledged catfight developed and then subsided with both sides crying "Uncle!" Like their previous "disagreements" since our departure from Brut Adler, what it lacked in range and athletics it had more than made up for in pitch and volume.

I picked up the transceiver and punched the send button. "Breaker, breaker, this is Bat-daddy callin' Big Bubba, you got your ears on, good buddy?"

The response was immediate. A crackle of static and Boo's voice came back over the tinny speaker. "This here's Big Bubba, come on back, Bat-daddy."

"Boo, we're going to need to find a restroom or rest stop or something pretty soon."

"What? Come on, Hoss; you gotta be kiddin' me!"

"'Fraid not, big guy. And one other thing."

"Sure, Long Pall Trucking, we aim to please."

"Be on the lookout for a veterinary clinic or animal hospital or pet supply store. We may need to pick up a couple of those large, plastic head cones."

"Head cones?"

"You know those lampshade-looking collars they put on pets to keep them from chewing on themselves . . . ?"

Theresa and Deirdre turned their heads to look at me. I had their attention now but I knew from recent experience that it wouldn't last.

It was going to be a long drive home.

Vamp It Up with Wm. Mark Simmons

Christopher Csejthe doesn't believe in vampires. Not until he becomes one. He doesn't believe in witches or werewolves, either. Except one of each has just shown up to rescue him and make him an offer he dare not refuse. . . .

"Mark Simmons, who never met a wisecrack, pun, or pop culture reference he didn't like, explores different degrees of deadness in his latest. . . . Poor Chris . . . if he's not being made unwilling ruler of the vampires, he's discorporated and floating through walls. . . . [an] event-packed romp through a vivid world that leaps into existence every time we open a Simmons book."

—Charlaine Harris

One Foot in the Grave
0-671-87721-6 • $6.99

Dead on My Feet
1-4165-0910-0 • $7.99

Habeas Corpses
1-4165-0913-5 • $22.00 • HC

Wen Spencer's Tinker:
A Heck of a Gal In a Whole Lot of Trouble

TINKER
0-7434-9871-2 • $6.99

Move over, Buffy! Tinker not only kicks supernatural elven butt—she's a techie genius, too! Armed with an intelligence the size of a planet, steel-toed boots, and a junkyard dog attitude, Tinker is ready for anything—except her first kiss. "Wit and intelligence inform this off-beat, tongue-in-cheek fantasy . . . Furious action . . . good characterization . . . Buffy fans should find a lot to like in the book's resourceful heroine."—*Publishers Weekly*

WOLF WHO RULES
1-4165-2055-4 • $25.00 • HC

Tinker and her noble elven lover, Wolf Who Rules, find themselves stranded in the land of the elves—and half of human Pittsburgh with them. Wolf struggles to keep the peace between humans, oni dragons, the tengu trying to escape oni enslavement, and a horde of others, including his own elven brethren. For her part, Tinker strives to solve the mystery of the growing discontinuity that could unstabilize everybody's world—all the while trying to figure out just what being married means to an elven lord with a past hundreds of years long. . . .

Epic Urban Adventure by a New Star of Fantasy

DRAW ONE IN THE DARK

by Sarah A. Hoyt

Every one of us has a beast inside. But for Kyrie Smith, the beast is no metaphor. Thrust into an ever-changing world of shifters, where shape-shifting dragons, giant cats and other beasts wage a secret war behind humanity's back, Kyrie tries to control her inner animal and remain human as best she can....

"Analytically, it's a tour de force: logical, built from assumptions, with no contradictions, which is astonishing given the subject matter. It's also gripping enough that I finished it in one day."

—Jerry Pournelle

1-4165-2092-9 • $25.00